Praise for the Novels of
E. E. KNIGHT

THE AGE OF FIRE NOVELS

Dragon Rule
BOOK FIVE OF THE AGE OF FIRE

"Exciting." —The Best Reviews

Dragon Strike
BOOK FOUR OF THE AGE OF FIRE

"Entertaining. . . . Knight turns the familiar features of an epic fantasy upside down in this unique world of medieval politics and ancient magic seen through the eyes of dragons." —*Publishers Weekly*

"Book four of the Age of Fire brings this glorious fantasy to a rousing finish with the three sibling stars of the previous novels finally coming together. . . . E. E. Knight makes his world of dragons soar as the audience roots for them to succeed." —*Midwest Book Review*

"An original tale told from the viewpoint of the dragons. . . . The tale picks up speed on the wings of dragons as they venture aloft, and it carries you with each courageous wingbeat toward the forging of a grand alliance and an exciting new world." —*RT Book Reviews*

Dragon Outcast
BOOK THREE OF THE AGE OF FIRE

"Presents [dragons] in a way that makes them seem almost human . . . interesting." —Fresh Fiction

"Spans decades of time, miles of territory, and a host of philosophical precepts. . . . I must say that I'm really looking forward to the fourth book in the series." —SFRevu

continued . . .

Dragon Avenger
Book Two of the Age of Fire

"Knight breathes new life into old conventions. His characters are complex and compellingly drawn, and scene after scene is haunting and memorable. . . . Knight, a master plotter and world builder, alternately surprises and delights, keeping us on the edge of our seats. Had I a working crystal ball, I'd guess that Knight has written a classic here, a kind of *Watership Down* with dragons—a book that will be cherished for generations to come. It is, simply, a grand tale, full of the mystery and wonder fantasy readers long to discover and too often find absent in modern fiction."
— *Black Gate*

"[A] gritty coming-of-age story. . . . Knight makes the story complex enough to entertain readers of all ages."
—*Publishers Weekly*

"Knight offers a thoroughly crafted fantasy world. . . . For a lushly unique fantasy read, look into *Dragon Avenger*, as well as its predecessor, *Dragon Champion*. You'll never look at dragons the same way again."
—Wantz Upon a Time Book Reviews

Dragon Champion
Book One of the Age of Fire

"Knight, best known for his Vampire Earth mass market series, makes an auspicious trade paper debut with this smoothly written fantasy told from the point of view of its dragon hero . . . a bloody, unsentimental fairy tale."
—*Publishers Weekly*

"This is a heartwarming story full of adventure, where good deeds and friendship always succeed. The characters are wonderfully endearing and the adventures that AuRon experiences as he grows into an adult dragon are exciting and entertaining."
—The Eternal Night

"A refreshingly new protagonist who views the world from a draconic, rather than a human, perspective. A fine addition to most fantasy collections."
—*Library Journal* (starred review)

"Knight did a great job of hooking me into the story. . . . This concern and attention to the details illustrates how strong the overall feel of the book is— Knight clearly is building something more in this world and the amount of backstory to the characters and creatures is very impressive. . . . Very entertaining, the characters were genuine and the world full of depth."
—SFFWorld

BOOKS BY E. E. KNIGHT

The Age of Fire Series
Dragon Champion

Dragon Avenger

Dragon Outcast

Dragon Strike

Dragon Rule

The Vampire Earth Series
Way of the Wolf

Choice of the Cat

Tale of the Thunderbolt

Valentine's Rising

Valentine's Exile

Valentine's Resolve

Fall with Honor

Winter Duty

March in Country

Dragon Fate

BOOK SIX OF THE AGE OF FIRE

E. E. KNIGHT

A ROC BOOK

ROC
Published by New American Library, a division of
Penguin Group (USA) Inc., 375 Hudson Street,
New York, New York 10014, USA
Penguin Group (Canada), 90 Eglinton Avenue East, Suite 700, Toronto,
Ontario M4P 2Y3, Canada (a division of Pearson Penguin Canada Inc.)
Penguin Books Ltd., 80 Strand, London WC2R 0RL, England
Penguin Ireland, 25 St. Stephen's Green, Dublin 2,
Ireland (a division of Penguin Books Ltd.)
Penguin Group (Australia), 250 Camberwell Road, Camberwell, Victoria 3124,
Australia (a division of Pearson Australia Group Pty. Ltd.)
Penguin Books India Pvt. Ltd., 11 Community Centre, Panchsheel Park,
New Delhi - 110 017, India
Penguin Group (NZ), 67 Apollo Drive, Rosedale, Auckland 0632,
New Zealand (a division of Pearson New Zealand Ltd.)
Penguin Books (South Africa) (Pty.) Ltd., 24 Sturdee Avenue,
Rosebank, Johannesburg 2196, South Africa

Penguin Books Ltd., Registered Offices:
80 Strand, London WC2R 0RL, England

First published by Roc, an imprint of New American Library,
a division of Penguin Group (USA) Inc.

First Printing, December 2011
10 9 8 7 6 5 4 3

Copyright © Eric Frisch, 2011
All rights reserved

Map by Thomas Manning and Eric Frisch

ROC REGISTERED TRADEMARK—MARCA REGISTRADA

Library of Congress Cataloging-in-Publication Data:

Knight, E. E.
    Dragon fate/E. E. Knight.
      p. cm.—(Age of fire; bk. 6)
    ISBN 978-0-451-46356-2
    1. Dragons—Fiction. I. Title.
    PS3611.N564D734 2011
    813'.6—dc23   2011031882

Set in Granjon
Designed by Alissa Amell

Printed in the United States of America

PUBLISHER'S NOTE
This is a work of fiction. Names, characters, places, and incidents either are the product of the author's imagination or are used fictitiously, and any resemblance to actual persons, living or dead, business establishments, events, or locales is entirely coincidental.

The publisher does not have any control over and does not assume any responsibility for author or third-party Web sites or their content.

The scanning, uploading, and distribution of this book via the Internet or via any other means without the permission of the publisher is illegal and punishable by law. Please purchase only authorized electronic editions, and do not participate in or encourage electronic piracy of copyrighted materials. Your support of the author's rights is appreciated.

For Mary, Jack, and all the others in the groups. We're crossing a finish line together.

Contents

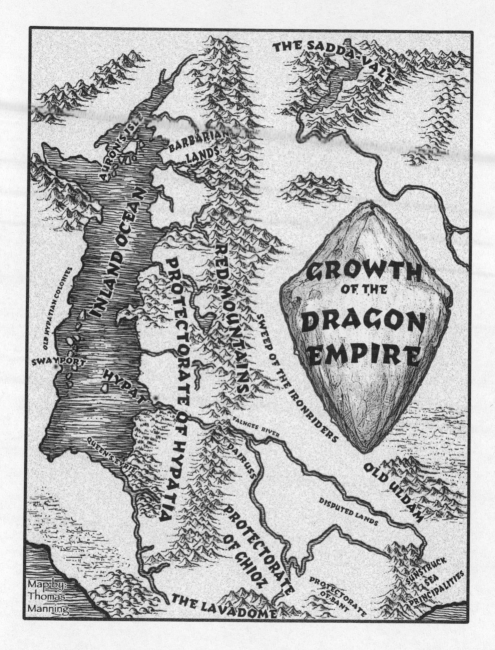

BOOK ONE

Will

"THERE'S NO WORSE ENEMY IN THE
EARTH THAN A FALLEN DRAGON."

—*Dwarfish proverb*

Chapter 1

Wistala, feeling like a newly mated dragon-dame, might have been living an idle, romantic dream, save that she was eyesore from searching mountainside crevices and frostbitten about the nostrils.

She rode chill mountain air, hunting trolls with her secret mate, DharSii, among the peaks of the Sadda-Vale. They'd been up before the sun, hoping to catch the walking boulder of muscle and appetite on its return from pasture country.

There were things she'd rather be doing with her mate, of course. Swimming in the steaming pools at the north end of the Sadda-Vale, for a start, rather than fighting winds that threatened to freeze her blood. The remote fastness of the Sadda-Vale, resting like a twisted skeleton on the vast plains east of the Red Mountains, had a pleasant microclimate in the snake-track vale between two short mountain chains, a gift of the mild volcanic activity in the area—along with an occasional earthquake.

Ancient ruins filled with highly stylized artwork, much of it featuring dragons, their prey, and cowering hominids, still waited to be uncovered and explored. There were secrets to be discovered in abandoned old tunnels and subchambers, icons to be discerned in high corners, relics of lost dragon history.

DharSii, a powerful yet thoughtful dragon whose scale color reminded her of the tigers she'd seen in jungles to the south, had some interesting theories about the old structures of the Sadda-Vale, and she wanted to hear them again, this time while looking at the art and iconography that had inspired such ideas. Wistala had developed her taste for pedantry while doing what her fellow librarians called "outwork," living with a tribe of blighters half a world to the south. She'd seen hints here and there of an ancient golden age of dragons, and DharSii shared her interest in that epoch.

When conversation became too dull among their fellow dragons of the Sadda-Vale, they liked to escape mentally to other times and places. Those were her favorite hours, as they broke down the last few bones of dinner and swallowed after-feast ores laboriously cracked out of the slate-fields. Sometimes the conversations went on until the dawn arrived like a surprise guest. They'd revive themselves by taking a swim in the steamy waters of the pools beneath Vesshall and then snooze on the sunny mountainside rocks above the lake mist.

But life with DharSii in the Sadda-Vale carried responsibilities. Left unchecked, the trolls would devour the flocks and herds and coops and pens that sustained the dragons and their blighter servants. So this particular morning they flew parallel to the western spine of mountains sheltering the vale, hungry and chilled and alert. The mountains, like old, worn-down teeth, were full of crags, holes, and pockets, and trolls could fold themselves into cracks that would hardly allow a dragon's snout. The peaks and ridges caught the wind and sang mournful tunes to unheeding clouds and fog. Above them, bitter winds blew hard and cold enough to freeze one's eyes open in the winter. On the other side of the clouds, she knew, the stars at night were brilliantly clear, with spectacular fireworks of shimmering, flame-colored lights dancing on the horizon like maddened rainbows—if you could brave the chill. But in their shelter, the heated waters of the Sadda-Vale created pools of warmth and the omnipresent clouds and fogs.

DharSii dipped lower, seeing something on the slope.

Just a shadow. He led her higher again, so their hunt might be concealed by the clouds.

Her brother AuRon should be with them. He was a skilled stalker. His scaleless skin, though vulnerable in battle and badly scarred because of it, shifted from color to color according to where he stood, even to the point of imitating shadows and striations in the rock face. But as soon as winter had broken above the Sadda-Vale and flight over the plains of the Iron-riders became possible without fighting blizzards, he'd gone aloft to travel south, risking his life in order to visit his mate. Natasatch, mother of AuRon's hatchlings now serving a new Tyr of the Dragon Empire, acted as "protector" for one of the Empire's provinces. Which really meant humans fed, housed, and offered coin to AuRon's mate.

AuRon, once when he had incautiously drunk too much of Scabia's brandy-wine, had slurred something about "political necessities" separating him from his mate.

Wistala's scaleless brother had to be careful on these visits and use every camouflage of wit and skin. As an exile, he was in danger of death every moment he was with his mate. To manage his brief visits, he made good use of his ability to become invisible at will and also of his many friends in the Protectorate of Dairuss, where he knew the king and queen from old.

But every time Wistala saw him leave, she feared that it would be a permanent parting.

She returned her wandering mind to the hunt.

The air this morning had a hopeful, alive smell. Fresh winds blew from the south, bringing the scents of the coming spring.

She noticed a herd of goats, tight together rather than grazing, the dominant males alert and watchful, all looking in the same direction and sniffing the breeze. Had they clustered at the sight of her and DharSii? It seemed unlikely—goats rarely searched the clouds unless a shadow passed over them, and there were thick, steely clouds today. Hardly a day went by that did not bring mists and drizzle, as warm, wet, rising air met the cooler streams above.

Good for the grasses the herbivores loved, but the patches of fog and wandering walls of drizzle also gave concealment for prowling trolls. You had to get lucky to see one in the open; at the sound of a dragon's leathery wings, they could squeeze themselves into crevices that seemed hardly thicker than a tail tip.

No, the goats were alarmed by something else. Had they caught the scent of a troll? And, if so, would the pair of them be enough to kill it? They really should have brought another dragon so that there'd be a firebladder full of burning fats and sulfur in reserve.

Her other brother, the copper-colored RuGaard, formerly Tyr of the Dragon Empire and Worlds Upper and Lower, wouldn't be of much use on a hunt. Thin and listless, hardly eating, drinking, or caring for his scales, he lived a lightless existence at Scabia's hall, hearing without really listening to her old tales of the great dragon civilization of Silverhigh from ages ago. The only time he showed any sort of animation these days was when AuRon brought news of his own mate, Nilrasha, a virtual prisoner in a tower of rock, thanks to the stumps she had instead of wings and a guard of watchful *griffaran*. She lived on as a hostage to the former Tyr's good behavior.

Or when Scabia told some old tale of desperate vengeance. Scabia loved fiery tales where three generations of men were born and dead before a dragon took his blood-toll upon a hominid nation. Then he grew attentive and his *griff* twitched as he stared at Scabia through lidded eyes.

RuGaard frightened her at such times. She could feel the violence in his thoughts like the muffled pounding of distant hooves.

Thank the spirits she had the comforting presence of Dhar-Sii beside her. Caught between the quiet, reserved AuRon, creepy in his ability to disappear into the scenery and his own thoughts, and RuGaard's gloomy brooding, she needed a companion to provide mental, and a bit of exhilarating physical, escape.

There were flowers just above the ground in green meadows at the colder altitudes below the tree line. Spring had come at last.

Spring. Her hatchlings would be aboveground this spring and breathing their first fire.

Wait not her hatchlings. They counted Aethleethia as their mother, even if they could barely comprehend a mind-picture from the lazy ninny.

The offering of her hatchlings had been Scabia's price for giving the exiles from the Dragon Empire refuge at Vesshall in the Sadda-Vale. Scabia's daughter, Aethleethia, was unable to have eggs of her own, and both were eager for hatchlings in their hall. The other dragons thought the father of the hatchlings was Aethleethia's mate, NaStirath, a foolish but handsomely formed dragon of proud lineage.

She, DharSii, and NaStirath had conspired to hide the truth that DharSii was the true sire. Though one of the males did bear stripes as dark as DharSii's, the suspicious Scabia had been placated when Wistala pointed out that her brother Au-Ron was also a striped dragon.

No matter who they counted as mother, the three males and two females would be ravenous, and if they were to have anything besides the bony fish or carapace-creatures and snails of the lake to eat, she and DharSii would have to find and kill the trolls that had been raiding sheep, goats, and caribou from the mountain slopes and patches of forest in the valleys.

DharSii and Wistala had discovered the remains of troll-eaten game on one of their flights to get some privacy from the other dragons of the Sadda-Vale. A troll could easily eat as much as a dragon and according to DharSii, if the food supply was truly superlative, it would breed.

Scabia's blighter servants had been frantically breeding cattle, sheep, and goats and releasing them into pasture ever since Wistala and her exiled companions arrived. There was ample game for a whole family of trolls, though the solitary trolls didn't form anything that might be recognized as family.

So now they were on the hunt for the most dangerous vermin in the world.

Wistala liked a hunt. She liked it doubly well with a dragon she loved and admired. She'd long since learned she could admire something without loving it or love someone without admiring him; the combination of love and admiration went to her head like wine. DharSii—"Quick-Claw" in the dragon-vernacular—when on the hunt spoke and acted quickly and efficiently, with none of the stupid roaring and stomping that a typical male dragon—NaStirath, say—indulged in upon spotting the prey.

"Troll tracks," DharSii said, waggling his wings.

She followed him down to a felled tree on a steep slope. She had to dig her claws into the earth deep to keep from sliding.

A long, muddy skid mark stood on the lower side of the fallen tree, the mosses and mushrooms devouring it were smashed and smeared where the troll had placed a foot, and it had slipped on the soggy mud beneath, sliding a short way on the slope. They could see broken branches on another tree a short distance downslope where it had arrested its slide.

Wistala sniffed.

"Scat, too," she said. She followed the bad air to a mound of troll droppings, though the less said about it the better for all concerned. For all their strength of torso and limb, trolls had rather haphazard digestive systems, sometimes expelling food that was barely absorbed. This particular mass of skin, bones, and hair was disgustingly fresh and hardly touched by insects yet, though a beetle or two crawled about on the waste, waving antennae as though celebrating their good fortune.

"Looks like it's making northeast, toward our herds," DharSii said, counting the widely spaced tracks heading down the slope. "This is fresh enough that I'll hazard it's still climbing that ridge."

Almost a long mountain in itself, the ridge DharSii spoke of was cut by deep ledges, like colossal steps running at an angle down toward the central lake of the Sadda-Vale, where its bulk forced one of the lake's many bends. On the other side of the ridge were herds of winter-thinned cattle, hungrily exploring meadows springing up in the path of snow retreating to higher altitudes, along with the usual sheep and goats.

"I'll try to follow the tracks, stalking or flying low," DharSii said. "You get up into the cloud cover, so you can just see the surface. If it knows it's being followed, it will make a dash for shelter, and we may be able to corner it. I know that ridge well; there aren't many caves, but there are fissures it will use."

If DharSii had a fault, it was arrogance. If there was a risk to be run, he assumed he would be the better at facing it. Gallant, but vexing for a dragon-dame who enjoyed a challenging hunt.

"Why shouldn't I follow the trail? Green scale will give me an advantage in low flight, if the troll's climbed the ridge already and looking behind and below."

"I know this troll. This track is familiar. Long-fingers, I call him. I've tried for him several times, and he's tried for me almost as many. I know his tricks, you don't, and he's nearly had me even so. One of us must put an end to the other sooner or later. He'll be expecting me to be hunting alone, and he may take a risk that will draw him into the open. Then you may strike."

"As you wish, you old tiger," Wistala said.

"I'm scarcely above two hundred. Hardly old," DharSii said. "Mature and distinguished."

"Just don't distinguish yourself any further with more scars," Wistala said. "Scabia's blighters sew skin closed like drunken spiders, and we've no gold or silver coin to replace lost scale. I'll be above."

"*Ha-hem*. I'll return hearts and scale to you intact," DharSii said.

Wistala snorted and opened her wings. She flapped hard to gain altitude and the concealment of the cloud cover.

She flew out over the choppy water of the lake, then circled around to the other side of the ridge. After hearing that this troll and DharSii were old enemies, she would feel terrible if she got lucky and spotted Long-fingers out in the open and vulnerable to a dive. But given the chance, she would end the hunt quickly. DharSii was prickly about his honor, but he'd understand. Trolls were too wily to let one live when you had an opportunity for a kill.

She hung in the sky, drifting, surveying the terrain below, feeling as though she'd been in this air before, hunting. Once upon a dream, perhaps. Or some old memory handed down from her parents and their parents.

She scanned the ridge, and the more gentle lands beneath, green hills rolling like waves coming up against a seaside cliff. More goats. Some sheep feeding on the north side. Perhaps if the hunt was successful they could celebrate with fresh mutton.

A few more beats to put herself back in the mists. Wisps of moisture interfered with her vision, but still, she couldn't see DharSii. For a deep-orange dragon marked by black stripes, he could be difficult to see when he chose to move in forested shadow. Was he on foot or on wing?

Wing would be safer, but easier to see from a distance, and Long-fingers might hide. On foot DharSii had a better chance of following the trail, so he might spot the troll before it saw him—if that cluster of sensory organs that trolls dangled about had eyes as she knew them, that is—

DharSii would probably be on foot, accepting the contest of wits with a troll.

She headed south, in the approximate direction of the troll's track. It knew the ground as well as DharSii did, and was crossing the ridge in a jumble of boulders and flats that offered concealment—and a possible easy meal of bird or goat.

Still no sign of DharSii, or the troll. She doubted it had

made the meadows; the sheep and goats there showed no sign of being alarmed or disturbed.

She sought and searched shadows, crevices, high bare trails, and thorny hillside tangles. Her mate and the troll had disappeared.

To the winds with the plan!

She narrowed her wings and descended toward the jagged shadows of the ridge.

Wistala flew, more anxious with each wingbeat. She should have met DharSii by now. Visions of her mate lying broken and half-devoured by the troll set her imagination running wild to years of loneliness without him. No chance at more hatchlings to raise as their own, no more long conversations, no more uncomfortable throat-clearings when she scored a point . . .

Dust gave them away. Dust and a noise like glacier ice cracking.

She followed the telltale feathers of kicked-up dust to a boulder-littered hummock in the ridge. Here the ridge broke into wind-cut columns of rock like ships' sails, with brush growing wherever soil could find purchase out of the wind.

The dust flung into the air came from DharSii's wings, beating frantically at a monstrous figure riding his back. His whipping tail struck limestone as he turned, sending more flakes and dust into the air.

The troll squatted astride DharSii, intent on his destruction. Its great arm-legs gripped DharSii's crest at the horns, pulling him in ever-tightening circles.

She felt her hearts skip a beat in shock.

DharSii—oh, his neck is sure to be broken! The troll is too strong!

Her firebladder pulsed, eager to empty its contents.

Trolls were put together as though by some act of madness by the spirits, to Wistala's mind. Their skin was purplish and veined, like the inner side of a fresh cut rabbit-skin. Their great arms functioned as legs, while tiny legs hung from the triangular torso more to steady the body and to convey items to the orifice that served as both mouth and vent. Great plates covered lungs on the outside, working like bellows to force air across the back, and the joints bent in odd and disturbing directions. Worst of all, they had no face to speak of, just a soggy mass of sense organs on a gruesome orb alternately extended and retracted from the torso like a shy snake darting in and out of a hole.

This troll used its thick, powerful leg-arms grasping the horns of DharSii's crest to wrench her mate's head back and down. Wistala braced herself for the inevitable terrible snap that must come.

Wistala had killed a troll once before by breathing fire onto its delicate lung tissue. But dragon-flame, a special sulfurous fat collected and strained in the firebladder and then ignited when vomited by a saliva spat from the roof of the mouth, could hurt DharSii just as much as the troll. Dragon-scale offered some protection, but DharSii's leathery wing tissue could be burned, or he could inhale the fire, or it might pool and run under his scale.

If she couldn't use her fire, she could still fight with her weight.

She folded her wings and turned into a tight dive, not as neatly as a falcon but with infinitely more power.

This "Long-fingers" was perhaps as experienced against dragons as she was against trolls. It had DharSii by a dragon's weakest point, its long neck.

She swooped around jagged prominences, risking skin of neck, tail, and wing. Heedless of the danger to her wing—a hard enough strike might leave her forever broken and unable to reach the sky again—she flew to DharSii's rescue. This was no longer a simple hunt to exterminate vermin but a death-struggle between dragon and monster.

Pick it up—drop it from a height. Stomp and smash! Warring instincts raged.

Teeth would be next to useless on a creature of that size. Her neck just didn't have the power to do much more than score its hide. Better to strike with her tail, or there might be two dragons with broken necks. She altered her dive as though trying to reverse directions, so that the force of her swinging tail might send the troll flying right out of the Sadda-Vale.

The troll, showing the uncanny sense of its kind, threw itself sideways just as she struck, rolling DharSii along with its bulk.

"I'm here, my love!" Wistala called.

Wistala missed the troll, lashed DharSii with her tail. It struck, a whip-crack against horseflesh but a thousand times louder. She saw scale fly and scatter like startled birds.

Wistala roared, half in rage, half in despair.

The troll, in avoiding Wistala's blow, put itself in a position so DharSii could anchor his head by hooking horn on rock.

The great black-striped dragon twisted his body and struck with his *saa*.

This time, instead of dust being kicked into the air, droplets of dark liquid flew. DharSii's claws came away sticky.

Vaaaaaaa! DharSii roared as the wounded troll pulled him around in a circle as though trying to yank his head off by pure effort.

DharSii suddenly lunged into the troll's pull, digging his horns into the fleshy torso. Now it was the dragon's turn to plant his feet and pull.

The troll used its mighty limbs to push itself off the dragon's crest, tearing skin and ripping open its own veins. DharSii's horns and snout looked as though they'd been dipped in ink.

Wistala banked and by the time she swung around, the troll was covering ground in an uneven run, leaving a trail of blue-black blood.

She vomited fire and the troll pulled itself in a new direction with one of its arm-legs. As she passed overhead, claws out and wings high and out of reach, the troll lashed up. Tail and leg-arm struck with a sound like tree limbs breaking.

An orange flash, and this time DharSii was atop the troll. He severed the sense-organ stalk with a sweep of his *sii* and the troll tumbled, righted itself, and ran blindly into a limestone cut.

The troll bounced back and fell, a buzzing beetle-wing noise coming from its lung-plates as the bellows forced air across the vulnerable flesh.

Still, the troll fought, lashing out with leg-arms and arm-legs, but blinded and deafened against two dragons the contest was hopeless.

She and DharSii stood far enough apart that they just might touch wingtips, making a perfectly equal triangle with the wildly swinging troll. They raised their heads in unison, lowered their fanlike *griff* to protect delicate tissue of ear and neck-hearts, and spat, eyes as slits with water-membranes down and nostrils tightly clenched.

The thin streams of oily-smelling flame made a hot, low roar of their own as they met at the troll, painting it in bright hues of blue, red, orange, and yellow. Black smoke added a delicate spiderweb framing to the inferno of sizzling flesh and sputtering flame.

They had the troll engulfed in fire before it could pick itself up from the stony slope. It still writhed about horribly as the heat consumed muscle.

Big-footed rabbits fled in panic from the heat, which set puddles of water asizzle and cracked rock. Birds shot out of the patches of yellow-and-white-flowered meadow about the mountainside.

The dragons ignored them, leaning against each other and crossing necks as they caught their breath. The spreading dark smoke seemed to stain the iron-colored clouds above like blood dark against a sword's edge.

The stench of burning troll was as bad as Wistala remembered. Unpleasant business, but it had to be done if the Sadda-Vale's hatchlings, and dragons, were to eat the herds they and their blighter servants tended.

"You arrived just in time, my gem," DharSii said. "Long-fingers had one more trick behind his ears for me."

"Next time, let me follow the troll-tracks while you watch from the skies."

"Trolls interest me," DharSii said. "Look at them, my jewel. In form and function they're like nothing else in the world."

"Couldn't the same be said of dragons?" Wistala asked.

"Well, there are great birds, as you know —the Rocs, for instance. I've seen art in bestiaries of two-limbed dragons—wyverns, though they appear to be incapable of breathing fire, but the record is vague on that matter and there's no way to settle it, as they appear to be extinguished from our world."

"I wish the same could be said for trolls."

DharSii panted. Wistala let him breathe, suppressing her need to reassure herself that he'd come through the ordeal safe of body and sound of mind. DharSii had had a scare, and soon covered it with analysis. "The interesting thing about trolls is the ancient hominid books have no record of them. There's plenty on dragons, Rocs, even fanciful creatures like winged lions. Anything that carries off livestock and a hunter here and there is bound to be the subject of some interest. Yet the best dwarf compilers of arcana are mute on trolls, which have huge appetites and are very difficult to corner and kill."

"I know. Mossbell was plagued by one when I was a drakka."

She'd grown up on a gentle elf's lands. The elf Rainfall had been like a father to her after she'd lost her own to war with the Wheel of Fire dwarfs.

"Odd that they have no relatives. Think of all the varieties of fish in the sea—they're broadly similar in form. Reptiles, cats big and little. The insects that live in and above the earth, the variety of four-legged herbivores, rodents, two-legged hominids—all come in a range of forms. Where are the smaller troll cousins, the heavier ones, the ones adapted to living in the surf, as seals and sea lions have?"

Wistala found the question interesting but the need for discussing it curious. DharSii was a dragon of strange obsessions. Perhaps this was the reason he'd never quite fit in anywhere— the Lavadome, here in the Sadda-Vale, or while serving hominids as a mercenary warrior. She found it charming. In all her travels among the beasts, hominids, and dragons of the earth, she'd never found anyone quite like him. Powerful but open and friendly, intelligent but not pompous—well, rarely pompous— well traveled and experienced but still full of a young drake's wonder.

"Odd, too, that they don't appear to communicate, socialize. I'm not even sure how they mate, or if they do."

"They plant a young in a corpse, something big and meaty. I saw a young one once, in a piece of a whale," Wistala said. She'd cleaned out the troll's cave after disposing of the troll. Bad business, killing young, but she'd regretted the necessity, not the result. Without the troll, the lands around Mossbell were prospering.

"What's in its hands?" DharSii sniffed. "My jewel, you didn't tell me you were wounded."

"I wasn't. A bruise or—"

"This is dragon-scale in its claws. Look, there's another at that mouth-vent orifice. Green."

"Green? The only other female here is Aethleethia. You don't suppose—"

"Aethleethia hunt trolls? Not even if our hatchlings were starving. Oh, I'm sorry—"

They had an agreement not to speak of the hatchlings as theirs. Too much pain in that. Better to pretend, like the rest of the Sadda-Vale, that Aethleethia had laid the eggs.

Not that there weren't still issues with their upbringing.

DharSii and AuRon had almost come to blows about having the hatchlings fight. Male hatchlings instinctively turned on one another as soon as they came out of the egg in a struggle for dominance of the clutch. AuRon and RuGaard had killed their red sibling together before turning on each other. AuRon won that contest. RuGaard survived despite crippling injuries. The rivalry echoed to this day. DharSii believed the tradition, being based on instinct, was part of a dragon's natural heritage and should be respected.

Finally her brother RuGaard, crippled in his front *sii* since the hatchling duel with AuRon, pleaded with Aethleethia and her mate, NaStirath. NaStirath was a silly dragon who treated everything as a joke and had no opinion, though Wistala would always be grateful to Aethleethia, who'd been taking counsel from DharSii all her life, for defying him on this issue.

"The more hatchlings, the better for us," she'd said.

Giving up her eggs to Aethleethia rankled. Wistala would have liked nothing better than to care for her own hatchlings, but her position, and her brothers' as refugees from the Dragon Empire in the Sadda-Vale, demanded that she accept the bitter bargain.

Scabia, with some eggs around her in the great round emptiness at Vesshall at last, could not care less how Wistala spent her time once the eggs came. She could spend all the time she liked with DharSii, even though publicly she was NaStirath's mate.

She even suspected that she and DharSii could appear openly as mates, but the suspicion wasn't strong enough for her to engage in what a human might call "rocking the boat." Too much depended on Scabia's goodwill toward her and her brothers.

"So if it didn't come from you, who does this scale belong to?"

"Let's find out," Wistala said. "We followed the troll-tracks in one direction, I think we may go in the other equally easily."

"Happily. The sooner we leave this smell behind, the sooner my neck will recover."

"Poor little drake. Good thing you're so taut. Being stiff-necked about everything was good training."

"*Ha-hem,*" DharSii grunted.

The trail gave out halfway up the mountain.

"Now what?" Wistala asked.

DharSii answered her by inflating his lungs and bellowing. His bellow was loud enough that she tracked echoes even from the other side of the lake.

"That may even bring RuGaard running," Wistala said.

A faint cry answered.

They found the troll-cave, a little quarter-moon cut in the rock. DharSii made it through easily enough, but Wistala had to twist to fit. She had always been a muscular dragon-dame, stronger than either of her brothers.

They found the source of the green scale. She was a dragon familiar to Wistala, her own sister removed by mating through RuGaard. Incredibly, it was Yefkoa of the Lavadome, one of the fastest dragonelles Wistala had ever known. She'd pledged herself hearts-and-spirit to the Firemaids and fought in battle after battle.

Wistala couldn't imagine what kind of catastrophe would take Yefkoa from her sworn sisters. Now she knew: Yefkoa lay pinned by a great boulder across her neck, trapping her on her side in the cave.

Wistala put her spine under the rock, ready to carefully shift it off her former commander in the Firemaids, when DharSii grunted and pointed with his tail.

A horrible sort of leech clung to Yefkoa's torn-away skin. It was a newborn troll, or at least that's what Wistala guessed it was. It resembled a full-grown troll about as much as a tadpole resembled a frog. It looked to be in the process of burrowing under her skin.

"What do we do?" Wistala asked.

"Get it out, please," Yefkoa said. "I think the troll put it there, I thought it was eating me at first. I can feel it moving."

"Grip it with your teeth, Wistala," DharSii said.

She did so. Yefkoa screamed in pain.

"It's tearing into me. Biting!"

"This is going to hurt. Prepare yourself," DharSii said, extending his sharpest and most delicate *sii*.

Wistala had to close the eye facing him. She heard more cries from Yefkoa and the splatter of dragon-blood striking the floor of the cavern.

"If I die, there's a message—" Yefkoa said.

"Go' eh," DharSii said through locked teeth. *Go ahead.*

She heard him spit something out and opened the eye facing him. The troll-tadpole lay on the floor, giving a residual twitch now and then.

"And I thought the smell was bad! I shall never get this out of my mouth," DharSii said, spitting *torfs* of flame in an effort to burn out the taste. "They taste like no other flesh."

"Better in your mouth than my hide," Yefkoa managed.

"I'd rather eat poison ants," DharSii said. He kept extending and retracting his tongue. The flapping tongue reminded Wistala of a dirty rug being shaken out by a blighter.

Wistala shifted the rock.

"Thank you," Yefkoa groaned, able to raise her head.

"Wistala, find some dwarfsbeard for this," DharSii said. "I believe I saw some on the downed tree where we first saw the troll-tracks. Who knows what kind of filth this thing left in the wound."

"In a moment. What do you need to tell us, Yefkoa? Why did you come here? What's happened to the Firemaids?"

"Lavadome. Tearing itself . . . apart. Firemaids . . . broken up. Ayafeeia begs your help . . . and attendance," Yefkoa managed to say.

Had she gone mad from the pain?

"We can talk later," DharSii said. "Let's see to the wound."

Wistala squeezed herself out of the troll-cave and flew downslope.

She, who as Queen-Consort had once directed the defense of the Lavadome against an invasion, who had held the Red Mountain pass with a handful of Firemaids against the Iron-rider hordes, now waged campaigns against trolls and hurried to find dwarfsbeard to patch a painful but minor wound.

The terrible methodology of war, the chaos and life-and-death decision making, the ceremonies over the dead and the praise to the heroic living . . .

She didn't miss any of it one bit.

She would so much rather be trading philosophy with DharSii after a good dinner, or watching birds go about their clockwork routines, or trying her voice at poetry.

Alighting at the fallen tree, she searched for the ropy mass of dwarfsbeard. Yes, there it was, a thick tangle of hair run wild on an ancient dwarf. When broken and pulled apart, the thick white glue, like a thicker and stickier dandelion milk, acted on wounds, both cleaning them and speeding healing.

Unlike on her long-ago errands with her father to gather dwarfsbeard, now she simply broke off the rooted end of the trunk, thick with water that was pooling and rotting out the wood, and flew back, holding the piece of tree tight under her chest. They could pluck it off the stump at leisure.

She returned and found Yefkoa unconscious.

"Just as well," DharSii said. "With that skin missing and torn, it must be painful. She won't have an easy recovery."

"I doubt she'll be able to move," Wistala said. "We'll have

to fly some blighters up here to tend to her wounds and sew her up again."

"She endangered her life to bring us this news," DharSii said. "A brave dragonelle. Yefkoa. She's an important dragonelle, I believe."

"A member of the Firemaids. Ayafeeia's personal messenger, I believe."

"Strange of her to ask for you, then, if there's war building," DharSii said. "She's breaking the Tyr's law. That could be used against her."

"No, she's too popular. Ayafeeia has an irreproachable reputation for fairness. The new Tyr and his Queen would be fools to go against her."

"Oooh, glad that's over," a new, high-pitched voice squeaked.

DharSii and Wistala turned and sniffed.

A huge leathery bat emerged from behind Yefkoa's ear like a groundhog coming out of its hole.

"Beggin' your pardon, your worship. M'name's Larb, one of Tyr RuGaard's faithful servants. Oooh, I'm chilled. No bat was ever meant to fly so high. I'm frozen from ear-tip to fantail. I'm not askin' too much by supposin' you could—"

"Don't listen to him," the exhausted dragonelle said, opening a bloodshot eye. "He's one of your brother's dragon-blooded bats."

"Then he can leave off begging us and go to work on your wound," Wistala said. "No opening up a fresh vein while you're in there, either, you little flying rat, or I'll toast you with some mushrooms."

"No need for threats, now," Larb said, scuttling behind Yefkoa's crest for cover. "I'll lick the wound clean, I will. It's just that I'm so stiff and sore from the cold of the airs."

The bat scooted across Yefkoa's flank and buried its nose in the wound, licking and snipping ragged flesh with sharp little snaggleteeth.

Bat saliva, Wistala had learned, brought a pleasant numbness to minor wounds.

"We'll need to close that up as soon as possible, dwarfsbeard or no," DharSii said. "Perhaps, Yefkoa, you can make it out into the light. Fresh air and what passes for sunlight around here will help keep it clean until we can get you stitched up. I know instinct is to retreat to a cave to lick your wounds, but in the interests of hygiene—"

"My love," Wistala interrupted. "Your turn to run for help. Go back to the hall and get some blighters who can stitch wounds, won't you?"

"Of course," DharSii said. "I shall return with help before the sun peaks."

He exited and Wistala listened to the fading beats of his wings before returning to Yefkoa. She nosed more dwarfsbeard into the trail left by the cleaning bat.

Yefkoa winced as the bat incautiously planted a wing on raw muscle beneath torn-away skin. The bat's tongue quickened, dabbing up blood and bits of ragged flesh.

"What brought you such a distance, through cold and winter storm and danger?" Wistala asked, both curious and eager to divert her relative-by-mating from the bat's not-so-tender ministrations.

Yefkoa managed to raise her head. "Another civil war's begun. Struggle for power between NiVom and Imfamnia against the twins. Skotl kills wyrr. Assassin hominids kill Protectors in their resorts. It will be the death of all of us."

It all sounded dreadfully familiar.

More war, more deaths, more pain. RuGaard would be in agony of the fate of poor Nilrasha. And AuRon, on his way to one of his secret meetings with Natasatch—what was he flying into?

All that could wait. Once more, she had duty to attend. It wouldn't do to have Yefkoa fly all this way just to die on their doorstep.

Chapter 2

The Copper dragon, formerly Tyr of Two Worlds Upper and Lower, Protector of the Three Lines of Dragonhood, Grand Commander of the Aerial Host, Patron and Solace to the Firemaids, Lord of the Imperial Rock, and Guardian of Clutch, Hatchling, and Youth, probed a loose tooth with his tongue.

The bad tooth had occupied him of late. If it weren't for the annoying, dull ache, he would have welcomed its irritation.

The proper course to take with a rotting tooth was to rip it out. A sudden, sharp pain and the task was done. If Miki were still alive he could have done it in a moment with his viselike beak. You'd taste blood for a day or so and then wait for a new tooth to grow in. Plenty more in the mouth, after all. Hardly miss it. But the Copper, deep in his funk, preferred to take his time with the pain.

The ache of the tooth ate up other, older aches. His loneliness for his mate, Nilrasha, held hostage against his continued good behavior, for example. Or the nagging doubts about his decisions the last few weeks when he'd occupied Imperial Rock in the Lavadome. That, too, nagged at him, before the sore tooth's preoccupative power revealed itself.

Miki's absence bothered him more than he let on. The old bird had been his last reminder of the formalities and honors of being Tyr. Now that what he'd always thought of as traditional nonsense was gone, he found himself missing it more than he would have believed possible, sitting upon his throne in the Lavadome.

Poor old bird. He wished he'd saved the feathers, instead of giving them to the hatchlings as playthings and decor. He'd burned the body for fear that the blighter thralls—servants, as they were known in the Sadda-Vale, of vast appetite—would dig it up and eat it, stringy flesh and all.

He reclined on the floor in the wettest corner of the Great Rotunda, a vast round room, the heart of Vesshall Palace, filled with elegantly-shaped dragon perches protruding from the walls like exploring claws. A circular portal to the sky admitted light, fresh air, and, of course, water.

A drainage channel ran to a discreet grate in the wall and he idly cleaned it with the tip of his tail. The blighters who lived in the Sadda-Vale and acted as servants to the dragons in exchange for protection of their flocks and families swept dirt and refuse from the meals into the channel, where it was carried away to an underground pig wallow. Faint swinish sounds echoed up from the chute behind the grate.

In this, his chosen spot, the drips drowned out the chatter

of hatchlings and the inanities being exchanged between Scabia the White, the ancient dragon-dame who'd given them refuge in the Sadda-Vale, and her daughter Aethleethia. Aethleethia was a well-bred female, perhaps a little on the slight side, especially when compared with his muscular sister, but something of a drip. Perhaps, having been badgered and nudged by the domineering Scabia her entire life, she never had a chance to develop much of a personality.

The other dragon of the Sadda-Vale, Aethleethia's mate, NaStirath, would have been much admired back in the Lavadome, where the Copper had grown up and eventually ruled. NaStirath had golden scale and a sense of humor that was alternately biting and clownish. Even the tiniest court needed a jester, the Copper supposed.

He could climb up onto one of the comfortable, dragon-contoured perches and get out of the wet, but that seemed such a bother. Besides, anytime he reclined on one of them, he started thinking how comfortable the design and how a few such perches scattered around Imperial Rock would add to everyone's enjoyment of the gardens and view, and then he remembered that the gardens, and the view, now belonged to another Tyr.

The hatchlings started chasing around the center of the Grand Court, pouncing and rolling, and he decided to go deeper before one of them scurried behind his flank for protection and they started teasing him about his scale again or asking him when the wheels on his wing would be repaired so they could watch the artificial joint in action.

He ambled down to the blighter alley, still poking at the troublesome tooth with his tongue.

Everyone in the Sadda-Vale recognized his step. He had a hopping, three-legged gait, thanks to an old injury in his hatching-duel that left him with the right *sii* crippled. The *saa* just behind it was somewhat overmuscled to compensate, adding to his corkscrew balance. His mate, Nilrasha, had used healing arts she'd learned in her youth as a Firemaid to massage and stretch it back to some sort of utility, but without her constant attention it had lapsed into near-uselessness again, and he kept it close to his breast.

Once he'd directed armies of three races. Now he had to content himself with the duties of a few dozen lazy blighters.

The other dragons didn't bother with blighter alley, but the Copper had taken it up as a project to occupy his mind when he and his siblings arrived a few years back. Once, he suspected, it had been a winery or apothecary or some other sort of workspace that required a good deal of sorting and cubbyholing.

The blighters had taken up the long, tall-spot in the deep tunnel and put wooden walls, platforms, and ceilings into the honeycomblike walls. It suited blighters to live on top of and across from each other. They were always shouting across the tunnel to their neighbors opposite or swinging up and down the ladders to visit.

Even so deep in the earth, blighter alley was warm and comfortable. Three pipes the thickness of his forearm ran, spaced out, from floor to ceiling, placed in such a manner that they weren't too difficult to keep clear of when passing down the alley. That stiff-necked striped dragon DharSii kept the lines in repair. They led from natural hot springs beneath up to the kitchens, where they fed out into great copper sheets and pans for the dragons' food preparation. Scabia was fond of her meats grill-cooked and dripping with juicy sauces and gravies.

Condensation running from the pipes and leaking steam emptied, rather cleverly, he had to admit, into cisterns, so the blighters always had access to clean, warmed water. There was therefore no excuse for the scraps and ventings and waste heaped in the gutters.

"Squawker," the Copper bellowed. As he inflated his long lungs to yell again, a rather scabby old blighter scrambled out of the biggest cubbyhole, a terraced multiroom wooden pile with some decorative carvings.

The Copper didn't know his real name; he'd called him Squawker from the first.

Long arms smoothed down the blighter's sparse fur. "RuGaard-Lord! I attending!" He practically danced in front of the Copper, bobbing.

"Trash and muck everywhere," the Copper said. "Get it cleaned up at once."

"Make proper! Make proper!" Squawker bellowed in Drakine, pointing to wheelbarrow, trash-cart, and scrub-broom. Blighters popped in and out of their habitats like startled rats in a trash-heap. The Copper's one remaining purpose in life was being the prowling cat in the alley.

Most of the blighters could speak a few words of Drakine: *yes, beg, at once, very sorry.* Squawker was practically an Ankelene scholar, being able to carry on a conversation.

Squawker watched the action. "All fix up proper, many busy hands lighten tasking, for noble dragons orders being mine dragons obey always at once," he blatted out, with a sweeping gesture at the cleanup action. A female blighter hurled a week's worth of charcoal dust off her balcony and the Copper watched it descend like snowflakes. A current of air caused by the Copper's breathing pulled the floating ash toward him and Squawker beat at it in the air like he was fighting off gnats.

"That was quite a speech. Where did you learn your Drakine, Squawker?"

Squawker explored a crevice thankfully out of the Copper's line of sight. "Father learn in dragon tower. Father teach Squawker growing up."

"What's the 'dragon tower'?"

"Far off in sunset place, on water, high," he said, sniffing the results of his probe on caked fingertips and scowling. "Father feeder and scale cleaner, travel many flight dragons, but fall off this side mountains, loose dragons, loose circle man. All find here settle."

"I want you and only you to prepare the Vesshall dragon dinner tonight, Squawker. No other hands are to touch it. Were there many dragons in this dragon tower?"

"Lord, yes, mine many more thans here. Good big dragons. For need stitching and cleaning and feeding. Fighting dragons, mates, ittle-ittle hatchlings. Lord RuGaard want scale cleaned? White soft very bad, Lord, scrape off grow new."

Insolent cur. "It's my scale! I'll attend to it," the Copper growled.

He tried to get a bit more about the dragon tower out of Squawker, but it was of little use. Confused tales from his father that may have been mostly brag anyway. Blighters always

33

talked up their situation in life. Basking in the reflected power of their betters brought them status, and the better the betters, the better the blighter. Still, it gave him something new to think about.

He probed the rotting tooth, pushed hard—

It came away in a painful ecstasy of relief. The Copper had a foul, bloody, rotting taste in his mouth and spat. He took a mouthful of freshly condensed water from one of the cisterns and spat in the gutter again. Looking in the cistern, he saw the tooth, yellowed at the tip, then brown, then black at the rotted spot at the root.

His mouth already felt better. He'd have Wistala find some herb or other to soothe the pain and clean the hole. Like her dragon tower companion DharSii, she was clever about many things, but had an especially good nose for medicinal herbs.

He picked the tooth up with his lips and tossed it to Squawker.

"Treasures, my lord! Thank you, thank you, thousand thankings. May your claws breed inside many enemies throats. All proper not a moment too much!"

"You're welcome, Squawker. I enjoy our little conversations. They're so refreshingly deranged."

"Always best deranged for you, Lord RuGaard," Squawker said, bowing deeply.

The Copper prowled the tunnels of the Sadda-Vale. If he'd cared about art and stonemasonry, he would have found interest in every arch and decorative tile. Artistic flourishes might intrigue DharSii and Wistala and engage them in one of their interminable discussions. To the Copper, the facades were so much dirty old junk, with a potential to shelter bugs or vermin. Beauty was found in usefulness, like the perches in the great hall or that hole in the top of the stone ceiling that allowed you to fly in and out of the hall at need. As for these tile-decorated passages, they should burn it all thoroughly, just to kill off the scale nits and eggs and ear-diggers no doubt lurking in the moister crevices.

So there were other dragons, here in the north. His impression, from the experiences of his brother and sister, was that the only dragons not part of the Dragon Empire were a few back-to-nature oddballs and this vestige of the first age of draconic greatness in the Sadda-Vale. He'd heard of some mercenary dragons—his former bodyguard Shadowcatch had been one—who were the remnants of some mad wizard's army. He should have questioned Shadowcatch more closely; it never occurred to him that the dragons were established and breeding.

Scabia would no more think of risking her dragons' lives in the world outside the Sadda-Vale than she'd scrape out her nostrils during one of the interminable feasts she'd throw to celebrate some long-dead ancestor. She'd seen too many relatives die, sticking their snouts into the affairs of hominids and trying to change the flow of history. "One might as well beat back the tide with your wings," she liked to say.

The Copper ate his evening meal alone, as usual. What wasn't usual was the reason. Instead of making himself miserable through loneliness, this time he wanted to think.

How would a band of dragons support itself, if not as part

of the Dragon Empire? Were they mercenaries who fought for food and gold, or independents banding together for protection, or some vestige of the Circle of Man who'd employed the Dragonblade, the fierce man who'd briefly helped the idiot Tyr who preceded him control the Lavadome? Perhaps men who wished no part of domination from the Empire—or their pet Hypatians—paid the dragons to protect them.

If there was bad blood between this dragon tower and the Empire, all the better.

One danger, though.

The Copper stretched muscles chilled by the blood diverted to digestion. He looked over his scale. It was thin and shabby. The metals available in the Sadda-Vale were the next thing to inedible. One ate "gravel" made out of shales that had bits of heavy metals in it. It cleared the digestive tract and kept the scale growing—just. But there was no pleasure in eating it. Gold and silver, that brought the thick saliva to the mouth and, once consumed, left one tingling and pleasantly heavy. There'd never been much coin or plate or scrap when he arrived, begging for shelter and succor in the Sadda-Vale. A few blighter traders brought in metals, mostly copper and tin, to exchange for dragon-scale and claw-sheaths, but the Ironriders had grown desperate and robbed even those poor pack-merchants. The trickle had dried completely, leaving them with nothing but unpalatable ore.

Worse than the flimsy condition of the scale, he had the telltale white edging, a rot forcing itself toward the scale root.

Of course, it was all pointless. He suddenly remembered he couldn't fly. The pulley contraption that served as his wing joint—he'd been crippled as a hatchling before they even emerged—had broken down and was in poor repair. He probably wasn't in condition to fly far even if it were working.

He'd have to beg DharSii to take a look at it and see if he could engineer a solution.

Well, never too early to improve one's health. Walking with more purpose than he had in years—his walk would never be graceful, with his withered *sii*—he passed out into the vast courtyard before Scabia's hall and wandered down to the steaming lake. There was a good moon for hunting.

Long ago, there'd been some kind of human settlement on the shores of the lake. They'd died off or fled, or possibly been eaten, and the blighters had occupied the few buildings with intact roofs. This morning it smelled like last night's boiled fish and blighter feet. The humans had made game pools, perhaps for crab or freshwater mollusks. They were near a warm spring and conveniently dragon-sized for bathing.

The Copper couldn't fly, but he could swim. He dove in the steaming water and nosed around in the wreckage of old docks and boats. Not being able to see in the underwater gloom was to his advantage—he was forced to rely on his probing tongue and claws. He smashed an overturned boat—something about the nature of the minerals in the water of the Sadda-Vale prevented metal from disintegrating. From the hull he rooted out a few nails others had missed or hadn't bothered about, then, miraculously, found a pair of oarlocks and an old sword blade buried in the muck.

He came up to the surface, then noticed that some fish—big-mouthed hunters—had come to investigate and eat creatures stirred up by the disturbance. He was quick enough to catch two in his jaws before they could swim away. He let the lake water run out between his locked teeth and swallowed the wriggling fish.

The oils in cold-water fish flesh were good for the fire-bladder.

The Copper bent the sword-point and swallowed it. The nails and then the oarlock followed the weapon down into his gullet. Gold or silver would be better than steel and iron, but health was health.

The water cooled fast once the chill winds of the Sadda-Vale could play over it. The metal in his stomach shifted as the weight pulled it into the gizzard that would digest and distribute it.

Feeling better than he had in years, he gave his tail a final shake, vented loudly, and decided to turn in. Sleep would speed the nutrients to the scale-root, or so he'd been told in his days in the Drakwatch.

He saw a dragon flying north toward the great hall. It reminded him of something his old instructor had said in the Drakwatch: Think of either good deed or crime, and the opportunity to pursue either course will present itself forthwith. He recognized DharSii and spat out a glob of fire—his wounds prevented him from doing more.

DharSii adjusted his wings, circled, and descended.

"How goes the hunting?" the Copper said. He spoke to other dragons in a sidelong manner, hiding his bad, half-closed eye by pretending to gaze out into the distance across the steaming lake. DharSii was too polite a dragon to mock a disfigured comrade, but old habits remained like scars. He'd been told, innumerable times, that his eye gave him a half-witted expression.

He thought about inquiring after his sister's health and success in the hunt, but did not want to provoke DharSii. The atmosphere under Scabia had lightened a great deal since Wistala's hatchlings arrived and went under her and her daughter's care, but there was no particular need to be direct about their quasi mating.

DharSii's *griff*, the fanlike shields protecting his throat and neck-hearts, rattled and his scale smoothed.

"RuGaard. You're out late," he said. He settled his wings. "Yes, the hunting's been good. We managed to take a troll, so the sheep in the west-side pastures should thrive this summer. It was an unusually canny troll that I've been after for years. Your sister was beyond helpful. I'd attest that she's the best hunter in the Sadda-Vale, particularly when it comes to those monstrosities."

"You smell like blood. Was either of you injured?"

"Your sister is fine. We were both knocked about a little." DharSii exhibited some cracked and torn scale. "As I said, he was a canny fellow. You smell a little of blood, too, when you speak."

"Lost a rotten tooth, and good riddance to it."

DharSii's wings rippled, and the Copper felt that the great Red was getting set to end the interview. He had something on his mind, obviously, and he might give a quick agreement just to return to whichever intellectual obscurity was working on his thoughts this week.

"I need a favor, DharSii. When you have the time, I was wondering if you'd take a look at this wing joint of mine. A band or something has come loose."

"Thinking about flying again? Excellent. A dragon needs exercise. I'll see what I can do. There's a decent blacksmith among the blighters who will assist."

"More than exercise. A change of scenery, now and then. I was thinking of going west. Sort of an extended hunt. I'm famished for wild game and some decent metals."

DharSii looked closely at him. "Not breaking the terms of your exile, I hope. I wouldn't want the Aerial Host to get an excuse to appear over the Sadda-Vale."

"Nothing like that. Though I do hope they've forgotten about us. I feel like I've gone venerable here, it's been so long."

DharSii's tail lashed. The Copper suspected he hated Vesshall, the Sadda-Vale, and his relatives here, but he felt bound to them. "It's the fogs and mists. It feels like one endless season, or being underground."

DharSii was an exile, too, the Copper decided—an internal exile, forbidden from indulging his own preferences.

"You have powerful enemies," DharSii said. "They'll kill you if they can."

"AuRon slips into the Empire now and then to see his mate. I don't intend to fly anywhere south."

"AuRon was never anyone of consequence in the Lavadome. You were the Tyr, and as it stands now, you're the only former Tyr who has survived the office since my grandsire's egg was laid."

"About my wing?"

"I'll get some blighter toolmakers and have a look tomorrow. Good enough? I'm off to Scabia's wine-cellar. I think there's a brandy mix that would do your sister and me some good at the end of this hunt. It's been an arduous one."

"Why didn't she return with you?"

DharSii made that throat-clearing rattle he liked to do when making up his mind or stifling the truth. He was an excellent dragon, but he couldn't lie convincingly to save his life. "Ahem. She's exploring a cave to make sure the troll didn't leave another generation behind."

"Grim business. I don't envy her the job," the Copper said.

"Grim business indeed," DharSii agreed, and this time the Copper was sure he meant the words.

DharSii was good to his word. He and a few skilled blighters bearing tools and materials showed up after breakfast.

The Copper smelled a good deal of wine and brandy on him the next day, and his eyes were exhausted and red. It wasn't like DharSii to overindulge in anything save boring conversation. He ate lightly and politely, was often the first dragon up and about in the morning and set an example in enthusiasm as he "chewed his gravel," as Scabia liked to put it to the hatchlings.

They worked on the broken pulley, with DharSii trying different qualities of rope, wire, tendon, and banding DharSii kept applying some sort of blue goop to the wood of the pulleys to see where the pressure was falling hardest. The Copper's wing began to hurt from the constant strain of extending it without the assistance of the artificial joint.

Finally, he was able to take a short flight, keeping low to the ground. Sure enough, the joint gave way, and he came to a clumsy, tail-dragging skid of a landing.

"Were there only a dwarf about," DharSii said. Written on his face, clear as dwarf letters, was pity with his relative's state. With most dragons, pity and contempt were one and the same, and the Copper suspected this was so of DharSii. "We don't have the right kind of material."

"I remember Rayg speaking of 'gut-core,'" the Copper said.

"Not familiar with that," DharSii said, pulling leather tighter with his teeth.

DharSii took the afternoon off and flew south to see Wistala again, bearing two bags across his chest. The Copper wondered if they hadn't found a comfortable cave and were setting up digs where they could be free of Scabia six days out of seven. They were suited for each other. DharSii's scale hardly twitched when Wistala's name was mentioned, but that was just his self-possessed nature. His sister, however, practically dropped scale with the intensity of her *prrum* when they spoke of DharSii.

"What is that you're doing there with my nephew?" Scabia herself said, as the blighters reattached the joint on his wing. It might not work right for flying, but it was comfortable and provided support when it was folded, so the relief was palpable.

"We're trying to fix this wing of mine," the Copper said.

"In better days a dragon would use crippling injuries to improve himself in philosophy and mind the next generation, Tyr RuGaard. You hardly spend any time with the hatchlings.

They might benefit from a better male example than Na-Stirath."

Scabia never said so directly, but she treated the Copper as an equal and gave him grudging respect. She was a great one for titles, and the fact that he'd been Tyr of Two Worlds, etc., etc., meant more to her than it did to the Copper. To the exile, it was just a stream of words his court majordomo used to recite to save himself having to come up with anything pertinent to the matter at hand.

"You're scratching the floors!" she bellowed at the blighter workmen, picking up their tools and placing them back in wooden trays with long handles. One of the blighters loosed his urine in fear, poor devil.

"Am I the only one who cares for this last vestige of Silverhigh?" Scabia asked the ceiling, which was as close as she came to reprimanding the Copper.

"I should have been watching them, Scabia," the Copper said. "We are poor guests, I'm afraid. Your hospitality should make us grow more grateful over time rather than careless of it."

He'd learned a diplomatic tongue in the Lavadome, dealing with the egos of powerful dragons and dragonelles. With his tail, he both sheltered the blighters and nudged them toward one of the servant-cracks leading down to their quarters. He'd smelled fire on Scabia's breath and was afraid she would burn them, scorched floors or no.

"Nonsense," Scabia said. "It's good to have some dragons about. My nephew is always coming and going, which leaves me nothing for conversation but Aethleethia and NaStirath.

My daughter, though I've raised her to be a respectable dragon-dame, is in possession of more appetite than wit, and I don't care for NaStirath's jokes."

Mentioning that he was considering a journey was out, at least after that speech. When Scabia got an emotional updraft under her, she could peck and scratch at all around her until the sun disappeared and the stars turned circles.

"How are the hatchlings?" he asked.

"So quick! They have excellent memories and are serious even in play. Not at all what I'd expect from that ninny."

Scabia was still under the impression that NaStirath, Aeth-leethia's mate, had sired the clutch.

"They say hatchlings often resemble the sire's sires," the Copper said.

"Perhaps, Tyr RuGaard," she said. Then she switched to mindspeech. He hardly understood one word in three, but it was something about Wistala being of better quality than first impressions allowed.

For Scabia to use mindspeech with him, even unsuccessfully, was a high compliment. It was possible only between dragons of natural affinity who'd long grown accustomed to each other's minds or between mother dragons and their hatch-lings.

The Copper warmed at the compliment, even from Scabia. He'd known so few others in life who genuinely liked him. Most dragons, even unusually bright ones like DharSii, saw only his injuries and deformities. There was something deep and dark in most dragons that hated weakness, clumsiness, deformity of any kind. It had served him to advantage in the snakepit of the Lavadome, where the contempt of the other ruling dragons kept him safe from suspicion as he grew up and made him an agreeable choice for Tyr—such a wreck of a dragon would never grow popular or powerful.

The warmth turned to bile. He'd won the intimacy of a vainglorious old recluse. Some achievement. He made a few excuses about wanting to soak his sore wing in the hot springs and left her as soon as he decently could.

DharSii spent another day away and returned at night. Again he assured the Copper of Wistala's health and safety. The hunting was just exceptionally good on the south slopes of the Sadda-Vale; as proof he brought in a big, wide-horned, hairy creature called a yilak. Wistala had stayed behind to keep an eye on the herd. It was a wild descendant of a beast of burden that the blighters had used in their days of power and glory, large enough for each dragon to have a satisfying haunch, plenty of flank-meat for the hatchlings, and the organs could go to the blighters, who had dozens of recipes for what they considered to be the delicacies of yilak brain, heart, and digestive organs.

Wistala thought it likely that if the dragons watched over the herd, killed or drove off the predators, they might take up residence in the south passes and see a good deal of natural increase. They were tough creatures, able to withstand a winter on the slopes. It would add some variety to their diet and if they could capture a few, the blighters could put them to work.

The Copper enjoyed his haunch, so much so that he followed it up with a double helping of gravel. Already, new scale was beginning to bud up under the worst patches of the white-rot stuff, and the diseased scale was beginning to drop off in twos and threes. The blighters didn't even bother to collect scale with white-rot to trade, though he'd been told they ground up the healthy bits and put it into weapons and tools to strengthen the metals.

But that was for the future to reveal. After the yilak feast, DharSii ordered up more wine and drew the Copper aside.

"I've given it some thought and I think I have a solution that will allow you to fly." He said no more until his blighters could be called, and they went to work.

"Solution" wasn't the word the Copper would have chosen; it was more of a second-least-worst outcome, the worst being not able to fly at all. DharSii put in a locking mechanism so his wing could be either open or shut, and taught the Copper how to alter the configuration by means of a heavy pin and a pair of metal bands with hooks.

When the wing was locked open, he could fly, but the joint didn't work, and it was fatiguing to make the adjustments with this wing that the natural joint, and Rayg's flexible arrangement, allowed. But it did stay open and support his weight in the air. When closed, the wing didn't settle quite right against his side. It looked like he was trying to shade his limbs on that side with his wing or keep a wound exposed to air, but it was not particularily fatiguing to do so. The Copper did discover, though, that his shoulder was unusually sore after the test flight. He was terribly out of condition, and asking his muscles to fly in a different manner than they'd done his whole life.

But the feel of air under his belly and his neck and tail

making the hundreds of adjustments of muscle and scale they did while in the air on his brief flight made him feel that the soreness had been purchased in a fair transaction.

He decided to trust Wistala's incognito mate. "I need a change of conversation, DharSii."

"I am sympathetic to the inclination," DharSii said.

At dinner that night the Copper decided to make his move.

"I'm terribly out of condition," he said. "I was swimming the other day."

"I thought your odor had improved," NaStirath said.

"I could hardly climb out of the water."

"The heat," Aethleethia said, tossing her hatchlings another shred of meat. They promptly fell on it and the big one, CuDasthene, ripped it away from the others so they were left with only a mouthful. "It relaxes one so. I must nap through the afternoon if I spend the morning bathing."

"I would have liked to see this hall full of dragons," the Copper said.

Scabia sighed. "Full? Not even I have ever seen it full, but once, when I was not much older than these fireless squirmers here, there were enough dragons so that they seemed one continuous wall of scale about me. Safe—I can't remember when I felt so safe."

"Perhaps we should invite some other dragons here," the Copper said.

"What, for a party?" NaStirath asked.

"No, to stay with us."

Scabia picked a bone from her teeth, snapped it, and used the sharp end to clean her teeth. "There are no others. None worth having."

"You have said that many times before," DharSii said. "Since then, Wistala joined us, with her two brothers. They're worth having."

NaStirath chuckled low in his throat. "Well, I think we can both agree she is, anyway."

"NaStirath, you really are tiresome," his mate said.

"I've heard of some dragons at a tower on the Inland Ocean."

"I know them," DharSii said. "You can hardly call them dragons anymore. They've been serving men for three generations now. The first were allies. Their children were paid subservients. This generation—you can hardly call them servants. The next generation will be slaves. Well-fed, carefully groomed and cleaned slaves, but still slaves."

"All the more reason—," the Copper began.

"Crusades! Tyr RuGaard, do you know why this hall is so empty? Dragons with fancy ideas about altering the world. The world is what it is, we are what we are, and the less we try to alter the course of the world, the better we'll do."

"I was only thinking out loud," the Copper said. "Please forgive me if I've brought back painful memories." He hated playing the supplicant. But then, wasn't that his rightful place? He was living on charity in another's home.

"You are used to the company of dozens, or hundreds," Aethleethia said. "With us, it is always the same three or four faces. Why shouldn't you go visit some new dragons?"

"Be prepared for disappointment," DharSii said.

"I would like the exercise—and the challenge," the Copper said.

"If you go, I fear you will never return," Scabia said. "Something in my hearts' beating tells me this."

"Perhaps I should remain," the Copper said. "Your wisdom seems worth listening to. The idea of a long flight was an idle fancy, perhaps."

"My fantasies are a good deal more idle," NaStirath said.

Scabia nodded, tossed away the bone toothpick. A blighter rushed to retrieve it.

Had he overplayed the gambit?

"I am old and cautious, Tyr RuGaard," Scabia said. "Perhaps a challenge would do you good. You've been gloomy for years. The prospect of action seems to be bringing you out of it."

Perhaps not.

"You do know, RuGaard, that some of the dragons—I think I heard you called them hag-riders—who took over the Lavadome in your predecessor's reign, were trained there? It is an old outpost of the Wizard of the Isle of Ice. It's the last stronghold of the Dragonriders."

"If it's the last, they may welcome another dragon about the place. Are there any other objections?" the Copper asked.

The dragons were all silent. "Then I think I will visit this dragon tower."

He spent a week in practice flights. First, he stayed over the water. The rising heat from the lake helped him with air currents. After two days of that, and heartier eating each night, he felt well enough to circle the interior of the Sadda-Vale.

He kept his eyes scanning for Wistala. He thought he smelled her at the southern end on the air, but the trail led nowhere.

Once, at night, he tried following DharSii, but the striped dragon flew hard and well, faster than he could fly with his patched-together and mostly frozen joint. DharSii flew into the thick night mists and disappeared.

There was some mystery here. DharSii would never harm Wistala—of that he was certain—nor would he betray the other dragons of the Sadda-Vale. So it wasn't treachery.

The Copper, with his years in the Lavadome, was used to considering any phenomenon as a threat. Were they keeping some secret from Scabia? Perhaps Wistala was ready for another clutch of eggs and they were hiding her from Scabia. But why wouldn't she welcome more hatchlings? Now that her daughter had her eggs . . . No, it could not be that. Though Wistala was a dragonelle of strange ideas. Perhaps she'd want her hatchlings to be free of Scabia's ideas.

What were they hiding, and from whom?

He felt his body waking to the activity and his mind—he was feeling again. Even the pain of his exile, from the knowledge that he'd sworn to be permanently separated from the one of his kind who'd always loved him without reserve, could be felt and reckoned with. Pain taught. Pain strengthened.

It was during one of his training flights—he fought his way to the highest altitude he could stand, where it was much easier to ride the wind—that he at last marked Wistala returning to Scabia's hall.

He dipped his wings and descended side-to-side in a series of sweeping motions. He didn't have the flexibility or the trust in the wing joint to do a true dive.

On his last swoop he passed just above and behind Wistala. His shadow flicked across her back. She turned and dove, closing her vulnerable wings and lashed up with her tail. It caught him across the neck, and he saw some of his loose scale fall glittering in the sun.

Then, evidently recognizing him, she opened her wings again and circled around behind. With three powerful beats—Wistala was one of the strongest females he'd ever known—she was beside him.

"Brother," she called. "I'm so sorry!"

"Let's land, by the bathing rocks there." He gestured with his good *sii*.

They alighted and Wistala brought her head close to his.

"Just a little weak scale is all. You're hardly bleeding."

"Your tail felt like a thunderbolt. I'm glad my neck isn't broken."

"I said I was sorry. I'm not used to you flying. DharSii told me he'd worked on your joint."

"Impolite of me to come down on you from behind. I should have called, but my wind isn't what it was. I'm out of condition."

"An aerial chase is a good way to get yourself back in training, I suppose. You should just warn the chasee. I thought I was in for a fight and I reacted by instinct."

"If it were an aerial combat, I wouldn't last long," the Copper said. "My fire isn't reliable, I can only make wide turns and can't dive at all, and I'm slow."

"All the more reason to remain safely here. Your scale is dreadful, you know. You should improve your diet and wait a season."

"If it is so safe here, why did you startle so?"

She shifted her *saa* back and forth and her tail tucked down. Like DharSii, Wistala wasn't much of a liar, and when she fought down the truth it showed in her feet. "Old habits only slumber. They do not die, brother."

"I make for the dragon tower. DharSii said you'd been there."

"Briefly, while searching for others of our kind, before I arrived here. It is not a place to inspire much hope for the future of our race. The dragons there are saddle-bred."

"So DharSii says."

"I can't imagine what you intend to accomplish."

"A change of scenery and some fresh conversation, at the very least. I just hope the dragons there have not joined the Empire. I would hate to break the terms of my exile."

"You are now of the Sadda-Vale, and therefore my responsibility," Scabia said. "I shall give you something you may find useful in your journey."

She extended a wing toward the blighter runs and four

came forward, each bearing an ornate silver object about the size of a dragon-egg on a carrying-canvas held between them.

DharSii and the others craned their necks to see what Scabia's servants had produced. Her daughter let out an appreciative breath. "So lovely!"

The Copper couldn't make out what it was, other than some kind of decor. He'd been expecting, perhaps, a harness or similar bearing-frame such as the fliers of the Aerial Host put across their backs for carrying dried meats and honeycomb.

Wistala figured out what it was for first. "May I put it on?"

"I did not send for these just so you could admire them," Scabia said.

She lowered her head and the blighters set it over her eyes.

Ah, a headdress. The Copper wondered if it was some ancient standard of Scabia's family. He bowed his head in Scabia's direction as well. The old dragon-dame purred in pleasure. She enjoyed ceremony so, whether it was a call to dinner, a hatchling viewing, or a leave-taking.

"It tingles," Wistala said.

Indeed it did, when first put upon him. The Copper had the uncomfortable sensation of a static charge passing through his head somewhere behind his eyes.

"These are relics of Silverhigh. There are more—sadly there are more relics of Silverhigh these days than dragons— but do take care of them. I will accept breakage only if they save those thick skulls of yours from a splitting by an axe."

Scabia spoke of Silverhigh so often that the Copper sometimes wondered if she didn't live half her existence within the confines of her imagination, longing for that perfect past. He was no philosopher like Wistala, nor a cynic like AuRon, nor even a dragon always hewing close to the possible and practical like DharSii, and, while he enjoyed the stories of the lost glories of Silverhigh, he doubted it had been quite so perfect an age. The contentious nature of dragons—even with peace and plenty—forbade it.

"It'll take more of a disguise than this," Wistala mindspoke. Her words and feelings came across so strongly that the Copper jumped as if she'd stuck her snout in his ear. He'd never heard mindspeech of this intensity.

Scabia's eyelid flicked. "I see they still work. Those are mindspeech amplifiers. The dragons of Silverhigh, provided they were capable of it to each other, could communicate over great distances. I myself have never had such an affinity of mind with another dragon that they worked for me, even with my dear old mate, earth harbor his bones. But I thought you might find them useful in your journeys."

"Do they work?" DharSii asked, looking at Wistala. "I thought their magic was long dead. I never enjoyed so much as an intuition over one."

"You are like me, DharSii," Scabia said. "A dragon of singular mind." She turned back to the Copper and Wistala. "In any case, if you are going to venture out into the world, Tyr RuGaard, it may be useful to have this connection."

The Copper had tried to discourage Scabia from using his former title, and succeeded in everyday conversation, but his leave-taking had brought the habit back. He'd been Tyr long enough to know that gifts rarely came without the expectation of something in return.

"Your kindness, in great matters and small, cannot ever be repaid. Perhaps I can return with some trifle unobtainable in the Sadda-Vale, to return this favor?"

"I learned long ago to reconcile my wants with my needs. For myself, nothing. But I won't live forever. I would like more hatchlings around this place. There may be other dragons who, for honest and admirable reasons, would rather not live in the new world those down south are building. If you find any young and vigorous mated pairs, they are welcome here. Feel free to bring home a mate yourself, Tyr RuGaard."

"My present mate still lives."

"Don't throw your life away trying to get her back. I may not be wearing the work of ancient Silverhigh, but I know what is on your mind. You are lonely, but she is hostage to your exile. Were you, by some miracle, to retrieve her, it would bring war to the Sadda-Vale."

So that was it. The gift wasn't so he could communicate with Wistala; it was so she could spy on him in his activities. He wondered how many of his thoughts Wistala could read.

"Why this hostility, RuGaard?" Wistala communicated. *"Are you worried I'll give away your plans?"*

Fine. She couldn't perceive his thoughts, precisely, but she could sense his mind. He sensed some conflict in her as well. Wistala was building toward a decision of some kind.

"As I said, I need change and exercise," the Copper said. "I will get both without starting a war."

He exchanged bows with each of the dragons of the Sadda-Vale. With Scabia he was careful to bow lower than her, with his sister they touched noses at the bottom of the bow, with

DharSii the pair kept their snouts carefully in alignment, each conceding nothing to the other. NaStirath did an elaborate sweep with his neck and bade the winds and weather to be his servants, and Aethleethia wished him a fair journey and a quick return and didn't mean a word of it as she nudged her hatchlings forward. They were shaping up as likely young drakes, but apart from endless lessons on how to interact with the blighter servants, they were spoiled rotten. Each could use a few years in the Drakwatch or the Firemaids under stern guidance, the Copper thought.

The blighters swept him with fresh-cut birch branches and leaves as he exited the palatial expanse of Vesshall. With skin tingling and scales clean, he left the Sadda-Vale with no intention of returning.

Chapter 3

AuRon the Gray clung to the shadowed side of Eagle Nest Mountain, hanging over the dragon-city like a watchful spider.

His skin matched the granite, cold against his belly, to perfection, right down to the white veins crisscrossing through the stone. It wasn't a trick he willed; his skin just shifted and rearranged its tiny faceted leaves and the play of light did the rest.

AuRon sometimes wished he'd been born a scaled dragon rather than an oddity. His father once told him that fewer than one in a hundred dragons were born this way. Certainly, his color-shifting skin came in handy when he didn't wish to be noticed; from a distance or in any kind of cover he was the next thing to invisible. It was also quieter, since there was no sound of metallic scales clinking against each other or whatever surfaces he passed around. In the air he wasn't weighed down with half again his bodyweight of armor, making him faster in the air than the fleetest scaled dragon—though still hardly a match for the great birds, the Rocs and *griffaran*, he'd at times been forced to fight.

And that was the sore spot. In a fight, without the tough covering, he'd suffered from arrows and blades and lost his tail to enemies. Twice. It had regrown, of course, but you could still see the slight indent where he'd lost it a second time. When breathing heavily, he still felt a twinge where an arrow had pierced his lung when he was a hatchling.

So he'd learned to avoid fighting if at all possible. He waited and listened his way out of trouble. He'd trailed his mate, Natasatch, here without so much as a snap of his jaws.

Once, this had been the capital of the Red Queen's Empire of the Ghioz, the stonemasons who'd learned their craft—and their proud obstinacy—by copying dwarfs. Before her, he'd been told, it had belonged, alternately and in what order he couldn't remember, to elves, dwarfs, and blighters. One might say the city was like a fought-over throne, occupied by which-ever great power now ruled the lands beyond the mountains east of the Inland Ocean.

In this epoch, the Imperial City was that of the dragons. More specific, the dragons whom his outcast brother once ruled, with some help from Wistala now and then. A score of years ago he'd wandered into their giant, crystalline cavern, the Lavadome, and been reunited with his siblings. Since then, the affairs of his brother's Dragon Empire with its wars and po-litical plots had stalked him like a hunter.

As for the name of the mountain above the city, he had no idea what the dwarfs or humans or dragons called it. To an accommodatingly garrulous raven, it was the Eagle Nest, thanks to a vast snow-filled hanging valley that reminded condors and other high-flying avians of an eagle's creche full of fluff. He'd suspected the raven of being a spy, but as it refrained from asking him a single question and instead prattled on about the lateness of the spring—"surely a sign of a hot summer"—and the doings of insects—"the dragon reek has banished the whole sunrise side of the mountain of bluebottles"—AuRon decided he was just an odd bird who enjoyed the glamour of talking to dragons. That or he hoped for exclusive rights to the head of his next bighorn kill.

AuRon didn't care for the raven's world and its troubles. He'd learned over the years that there were very few friends one could trust, and those who he could trust either died or drew him into their affairs thanks to bonds of friendship and honor. Every dragon had a weak spot, his father used to say, and AuRon admitted he had several, starting with his skin, but it was this accursed habit of sticking his nose into the affairs of hominids in support of old friends that had brought him within a tail-flick of death more than once.

This time, however, he was snout-deep for purely selfish reasons. He wanted to feel his mate next to him, listen to her breathing, smell her old familiar, welcoming—to a male dragon—scent. While the Sadda-Vale had its points, the conversation had grown stale, and even his sister's intelligent companionship was no replacement for the dragon who'd curled around their eggs for long winter months.

The shadows rolled across the city of Ghioz as the sun turned the mountains bloodred. AuRon didn't believe in omens, but he still had to suppress atavistic, fearful thoughts brought up by the dusk-washed granite.

May as well chance it.

He glided down the mountainside. Most probably he wouldn't be noticed. The whole city was thick with dragons, and masses of slaves—"thralls," to use the euphemism of the Lavadome—there to do the work of feeding and washing them.

Tracking her was not as difficult as one might have thought. Natasatch still occupied the modest cave they'd shared as Protector of the poor province of Dairuss. He'd found an old servant who remembered them—one of King Naf's veterans, a peg-legged man who thought the smell of dragons tolerable, and certainly better than the carrion-strewn battlefields of the Ghioz wars, and he was discreet about the occasional visit of the great king's old friend. He'd told AuRon about the enormous feast planned in Ghioz to commemorate the victory over the Ghioz that had established dragons in the Upper World. AuRon, who'd played a role in that victory, settling his own score with the Red Queen, suspected they'd chosen the date on the basis of likely pleasant weather for gathering rather than on that of history.

AuRon wondered how the Ghioz felt about a mass of dragons descending on them, to eat their cattle, pigs, and sheep and leave nothing but hooves and other offal to be cleaned up.

In any case, he learned where Natasatch had temporarily established herself—the old hippodrome, now called the Dragonhalls. She'd gone early to aid her friend Queen Imfamnia—remarkably now on her second turn as mate to the ruler of the

Dragon Empire after serving her own exile—in preparing for the party.

The hippodrome/Dragonhalls were easy to find from the air. Two small horse tracks flanked the building, which was then enclosed by a much larger horse track for long races. The outer track had multiple fences, and dogs between the fences, and guards posted behind the dogs, to keep out beggars and scale-filchers.

There was an interior ring as well, covered against weather save for a small hole in the peak. Remarkable construction, yet typical of the Ghioz. The seats had been converted to dragon-sized benches; evidently meetings of some sort were held here, though the place smelled a little of blood, which set his *griff* to twitching. There was a wide corridor behind the seating for bringing horses to and from their stables. The stables had been enlarged to make sort of small apartments, though the ones near the roof looked more spacious and had a view out of the city, judging from the light bleeding in.

He heard snoring dragons, saw piles of wine casks, still wet at the bungs. From one apartment above he heard the tussling, flapping sound of mating.

AuRon shook his head. Dragons mating indoors, in secret. He followed his nose until he found Natasatch's scent. It was in one of the bigger spaces at the top, what used to be an old promenade where viewers could look down on the horses or into one of the rings. There was a nice sort of arching gallery giving her a view of the city. He found an empty apartment, passed through to the balconies, and slipped into Natasatch's temporary residence from behind thick draperies.

He heard voices, human and dragon. Natasatch was saying something about scale-polish to a human with a head shaved and tattooed with a design that reminded him of interlaced dragon-scale. When she finished, he used DharSii's quiet throat-clearing sound to draw her attention.

Natasatch let out a frightened squeak and raised her neck, ready to spit fire.

He met her gaze, let one *griff* twitch. "Sorry to startle you, my dear."

"Au— FuThazar, whatever are you doing in my chambers?" Natasatch said. "I commissioned you to find a cache of old Hypatian coin to give as a gift to Imfamnia, not to intrude on my chambers."

"I will withdraw, but first I must speak to you, Protector," AuRon said.

"Ah, well, as long as you're here," Natasatch said. "Begone, you," she told her servants. "Not a word to the Sunlight Queen of her gift. I want it to be a surprise, and if it gets spoiled you'll hang upside down on my balcony from dawn to dusk."

The servants scuttled off.

AuRon felt a stab at her casual mention of punishing her human slaves. He'd seen a good deal of cruelty in his life, and rather than becoming hardened to it, he'd grown more sensitive over the years. Not that any dragon dared admit a missing patch of scale for any of the two-legged races.

Worse, his mate looked as if she'd been living in the wild, and not living well at that. "You look thin," he said. "Are you eating?"

"Very well. I get the best calves-livers in Dairuss," she said.

"It's not doing you much good. Have you been ill?"

"I expect it's Blood for the Empire."

"What in the air is 'Blood for the Empire'?" AuRon repeated the phrase to make sure he'd not misheard.

She cocked her head, as if he'd asked her why her scales were green. "I forget how long you've been away. Blood for the Empire. We're bled regularly. There's good coin in dragon-blood, especially from the rich Hypatians, and in extracts sold on the other side of the Sweep of the Ironriders."

Fine. His mate was looking sickly and aged so some shriveled old Hypatian galleon-master could frolic with his fifteenth wife until he impregnated her.

"So, they have an Empire that spans two-thirds of the world, and they have to bleed you to acquire gold to eat?"

"It's so much more than that, my—old friend," she said. "Excavation projects need dwarfs. Roads must have surveyors and shorers. Armies to maintain order. They're rebuilding the old Sailing Market so it can circle in the Inland Ocean once more, as in Hypatia's glory."

"I thought the point of the Empire was safety for dragons. You look like you're about to topple, and you're young and healthy. What happens with older dragons?"

"Less is expected of them, of course," she said. "NiVom is brilliant. He thinks of everything."

"I wish my brother were still Tyr. He had less brilliance and more sense. I don't remember seeing any starved-looking dragons in his—"

"Hush! Are you flapping mad? Don't speak of him! Every important dragon from the Sun Empire, and a few from the

Dark, is here. The place is thick with *griffaran* and the Queen's spies."

"The birds are stuffing themselves with fruit and nuts, as far as I can tell," AuRon said. "As for spies, half of the dragons here seem to be slipping on and off one another's balconies or meeting in hillside glades. They're going to keep busy reporting who is engaging in a quick tryst with whom. What sort of dragons are these? They've got the morals of mead-addled blighters at a spring mating festival."

"Would you like a look around my sleeping chamber? I assure you, it's cold and empty."

"No colder than mine," AuRon said.

"We could change that."

"Were we to join, I'd prefer it to be up in the sun and clouds, as proudly mated dragons. I'm not about to join in some dreadful scuffle like a furtive blighter."

"You know very well that's impossible, my lord." Sometimes she used the traditional honorific to poke fun at him when he grew pretentious. "Were I to take someone up, it would be remarkable. Every gossip would try to figure out who it was. Unlike some dragonelles of my acquaintance. It's more strange if they aren't cavorting over the city during a celebration, with Imfamnia setting the social tone."

"Pity," AuRon said.

"Will you remain long? Perhaps you could return to Dairuss. You could hide in the high pass."

AuRon looked at the astonishing layout of tools for dragonelle preparation. There were knives and files and hooked cutters for scale, paints and dusts and glues and brushes and rags and mysterious pointed sticks for decorating scale, and vast quantities of a reddish clay.

"What's all the clay for?"

Some of Natasatch's good humor returned. "You really are out of date. It's a wing-skin soother and tightener. A folded wing should look smooth and supple. It's hard work, standing there with your wings stretched until it hardens. Then you do it again with them folded. Takes the better part of a day."

Hard to think of his fiercely practical mate transformed into a vanity-ridden frivol. "I don't suppose I can interest you in forgoing the clay treatment and instead eating a brace of ducks."

"And spoil my appetite for the party?"

"Is there any way I might attend?" AuRon asked.

"It will look strange if I arrive at the Grand Feast with any but a Firemaid from my uphold. But there are so many dragons invited—I'm sure you can lose yourself in all the comings and goings."

"I've no wish to speak to anyone but you there. But I am famished. I've been flying hard these past ten days."

"Perhaps—perhaps we could find some time together. Again, with all the pairs of dragons at this feast. Stay about the fringes, and for the Four Gifts' sake, don't come near me when Imfamnia's about. I think she suspects you and I communicate in secret."

She quieted, and switched over to mindspeech. *I'm unsettled, AuRon. Imfamnia and NiVom are up to something with this feast.*

But what? Whatever would they try, with so many of the leading dragons of their Empire in attendance?

I may not show it, but I'm so glad you're here. I feel safer with you about.

AuRon warmed at that. He felt the pulse of emotion returned across their mind-link. *Very well. I'll keep to the fringe of the crowd.*

"You'll need to blend in," she mused aloud, half to him and half to herself.

Now it was his turn to cock his head in astonishment. "That's my specialty."

"No, with the Empire throng. Paint and such."

"You are the expert," he said, wondering if she had thralls just to run tools back to the worktables while her cosmeticians worked on scale.

She gestured with her tail at a bowl set high up, out of reach for a hominid but accessible to a dragon-neck. "You'll need some coin. I keep some silver around for guests who want a polite mouthful. Take some of that."

"Where does it come from?" AuRon asked.

"What does that matter?"

"You know how I feel about this whole Dragon Empire. Organized robbery."

Natasatch stiffened. "There were some bandits in the mountain pass—you know, the high road above the capital. I found their camp, burned out the bandits, and recovered a good deal of livestock and bundles of fabrics. The Merchants' League gave me half the worth of the recovered goods in exchange. This was two years ago, and a good deal of it is left. As Protectors go, I don't live high. Our cave is still much as you remember it."

AuRon felt ashamed, both by the explanation and by her use of "our cave." To him, their cave was back on the Isle of Ice, the shelf where their eggs had been hatched. Her use of the phrase suggested that her most happy days had been spent with him in the Protectorate.

Humans, elves, and even dwarfs, he supposed, had elaborate notions of love. They all had elaborate rituals for courting and aligning with prospective mates, oftentimes with extensive involvement of both families. Blighters looked on wife-gathering much as a herdsman tries to increase his herd—it meant more wealth and power. He'd heard stories from the ancient black dragon NooMoahk, his mentor after the loss of his family, of dragons in the distant past tending more toward the blighter view than the human. With several females surviving hatching to each male, powerful males sometimes accumulated what NooMoahk called a "harem."

Dragons used the word "love," and it meant something that was oddly more practical, yet deeper than the human notion. A male dragon did not obsess over the object of his affection or write odes to her various perfections, but he usually admired the one he wanted for his mate for specific, practical reasons. Once mated, it was his duty to provide and, if necessary, to lose limb or life defending her refuge.

With Natasatch he admired her courage in adversity. He would have given in to despair had he spent most of his youthful years chained in the dark, as she had. He liked her wit and her open-mindedness to his ideas that dragons could—*must!*—do better, lest their kind fall into twilight and then vanish from the world.

Her expression of concern, desire for him to be there, troubled him. She was a dragon who was hypersensitive to trouble, the way you could feel a thunderstorm before the dark clouds appeared. Perhaps it was all those years in the dark hatching cavern on the Isle of Ice.

He scooped up a mouthful of coin.

"I'm grateful," he said, meaning so much more than the money.

Even in the predawn, dragons were already preparing themselves for the feast. AuRon saw a mass of torches in a mountain pasture, and assumed food preparation was under way. He glided down to investigate, wondering if they would accept a trade of manual labor in hauling whatever sides they were smoking in exchange for a hearty meal.

It turned out that the flames weren't from pits for charring and smoking flesh, but banks of light for thralls already at work decorating.

He scanned the waiting crowd of dragons for familiar faces—their own hatchlings all served the Empire in one capacity or another, and they would quickly recognize him from his twice-stumped tail. Not recognizing anyone, he landed and settled his wings so that they tented and changed his outline as much as possible. All eyes were on the workers, mostly men and blighters, shaping and prepping scale.

Some of the cosmeticians were creating outlandish, colorful designs on their dragons, working paint and shaping scale into swirls or spikes or what looked like vines or jagged bolts.

He recognized some iconography from the Lavadome. He knew enough to recognize a toothy Skotl sigil from the pen-quill-like flourish of the Ankelenes.

At the other end of the spectrum were dragons just giving scale, teeth, ears, and wings a good cleaning and oiling.

AuRon opted for something in the middle. He joined a line for an artisan who was deepening faded greens on older females and pulling misshapen scale from male dragons' faces, making them look neater, sleeker, and wind-friendly.

"I'm Jussfin, your honor," the human said when AuRon's turn came, in decent Drakine. He had the squat body and heavy shoulders of a Ghioz stonelayer. "Some skin-painting, sir?"

"Make me look a little heavier and more imposing, if you can," AuRon said.

"Of course, sir." He gestured to some colors and a blighter assistant started to pour paint into a pan.

"So, where will you be seated, your honor?" Jussfin asked.

"Near the roasting hogs, I hope," AuRon countered.

They fell into chitchat. AuRon decided to try his story, that he was a small-time trader who flew into the Far East selling "medicinals." He'd been east a lifetime ago with the Chartered Company in its traveling towers and could describe the markets of the East from memory.

"Ah, so you're an aboveground most of the time," Jussfin said.

"I've always been a traveler," AuRon said.

AuRon tried to imagine what a dragon of the Empire might possibly talk about with someone painting his body, and finally asked if he knew what color the Queen would be wearing.

"Black, I hear," Jussfin said.

"No," the dragon next to AuRon countered. "I'm sure it will be red, to commemorate the battle. Yellow highlights."

AuRon deployed DharSii's famously noncommittal throat-clearing, lest he fall into a conversation with this dragon.

"You're done," Jussfin said, coming to his rescue. "No scale makes for light work. I appreciate the rest. I feel up to pulling misshapen scale from the most elderly dowager now."

He surveyed the results. Jussfin had taken his natural dark stripes and enlarged them, adding a bone-colored outline around them to make them more pronounced. He'd dusted his wings with something that made the skin redder and a little reflective.

They settled on a price. AuRon argued only a little; Jussfin had named an amount lesser than any other he'd seen pass up and down the ranks of dragons. He ended up giving over two golden coins and telling the artist to never mind about the change.

"Many thanks, your honor," Jussfin said. "I think you'll find the roast pork at its most succulent to the north, by the overhang and the waterfall, your honor. Keep well above and behind the Queen's dinner-path."

AuRon made a special effort to rise early the day of the feast. He wanted to find a few hiding spots, should there be guards checking names or who knew what sort of introductory rituals. Still, he was not the first dragon aloft—there were messengers and a few dragons of the Aerial Host up and around, and more than a few males and females returning in the predawn gloom from assignations. Keeping to the shadows, he explored the monument to draconic vanity looking down on the city of Ghioz from the Red Queen's old palace.

He'd been here before and had nothing but unhappy memories of the place. He'd been told that the side of the mountain had been reshaped several times; it had first been carved into the likeness of some kingly dwarf or other, for the foundations of Ghioz were as a dwarfen trading post at an important river junction. As the city changed hands and empires came and went, the face on the mountain changed races as well. When AuRon first laid eyes upon it, it was the classic, sharp-jawed visage of the Red Queen looking down upon Ghioz.

Now, with a good deal more carving and the addition of a great bronze snout and copper scale gone green with age, it was a dragon's face, snout tucked toward breast and watchful eyes looking southwest, somewhat in the direction of the Lava-dome, he supposed.

Vanity. Monuments to power. If any of the Empires had given thought to the temporary nature of the mountain's appearance, they showed no sign of it.

AuRon wondered if deep in his hearts, his Copper brother didn't miss the feeling of being atop the pinnacle of power represented by that carving. He frequently said that NiVom, the most intelligent dragon he'd ever met, would make a better Tyr in any case, but AuRon wondered. It seemed NiVom maintained his hold only by the exercises of Imfamnia, whom no one dared call the "Jade Queen" these days.

They were still at work on the mountainside, it seemed.

Scaffolding and signs of digging ran from the eye like a twisting wooden tear. There were no construction noises this morning, however; all the thralls were hard at work preparing for
the feast.

AuRon explored the works and found his answer among
the ironmongery and picks. The builders were at work on the
chamber behind the eyes, fixing two great lenses and fire-
braziers in the manner of navigation lights he'd seen on the
shores of the Inland Ocean. His own Isle of Ice had had such a
fixture, though much smaller, on the cliff above the docks. Au-
Ron guessed that when the great braziers were filled with hot
coals, the light would be refracted by the lenses and intensified
so that it might be seen a horizon away.

Still, among all the clutter he could watch events below.
There were several hiding places amid the lumber and tunneling and sheets for keeping the dust down, and he could wriggle
out and escape around the lenses if the other access points were
blocked. Yes, it was quiet and safe. Warm even, out of the
weather. He'd been afraid that he would have to cling to some
windswept outcropping again.

For that matter, Wistala sometimes questioned DharSii
about his former expectations when he'd been part of the Lavadome's elite in his youth. Did Wistala wonder how her face
would look, glaring out over Ghioz?

The feast would take place in the gardens beneath the
carved mountainside and palace, above the city of the Ghioz
yet below the palace of this NiVom who called himself the Sun
King.

The garden was pleasantly arranged, designed to rest at a

midpoint between nature and artifice. Watercourses had been routed, waterfalls conveniently placed for refreshment, stones shaped to provide comfort, and a circular track laid out with fresh wood chips that the thralls would follow bearing their platters, sometimes two or four at a time, up from the cooking pits.

AuRon had taken his blighters to war with less planning and organization. Though for all the beautiful surroundings and the glittering dragons, the whole spectacle disgusted him more than it impressed.

AuRon, with a fine view of the feast from his spot between the eyes of the dragon-face, had never seen such waste. Entire bullocks were slaughtered, with just the blood, loins, and liver extracted to be turned into delicacies, leaving hundreds of pounds of meat and marrow for who knew what purpose. The myriad thralls wouldn't be able to eat a tenth of a tenth of it. His old blighter tribe, with their great herds of cattle, wouldn't have done that with the stringiest old billygoat, down to little but skin and horn.

Once the feast was in full swing and the sweating wine-runners dropping and replaced with fresh legs, he ventured down to get a better look at NiVom and Imfamnia.

Jussfin was right—she was in red with yellow highlights. She had blackened her wings as well and jewels and peacock feathers ran along the edge of her spinal fringe. He had to admit, she looked splendidly wealthy, though perhaps not healthy. Thin and bony and nervous. A few of the females in her coterie had aped her coloring, though perhaps in less vivid red or shining black.

NiVom had done little to his white but give it a clear polish so it caught, alternately, sunlight and gold from the great damask rug he lay upon for the feast. A pair of *griffaran* stood at firm attention on high perches to either side of him, wings outstretched as though signaling. AuRon thought their pose looked imposing but uncomfortable; they must have done a good deal of exercising to keep the pose hour after hour. Still, they were relieved by other *griffaran* who adopted the exact same outflung-wing stance.

Imfamnia was much more the socialite, roaming around from group to group, exchanging brief words and issuing constant orders to her staff of thralls for more.

Natasatch had been seated a little behind Imfamnia, up toward where Jussfin had claimed the best pork would be. AuRon saw only some overweight dragons there, some with imposing battle-scars. Jussfin may have had the Queen's coloring correct, but he was wrong about the pork.

A distinctive curve and a thickening of the blade at the outer edge caught his eye. He'd seen that shape before—the fireblades! The distinctive curved swords with their heavy, chopping rise near the point, an arc that imitated a dragon-tooth.

Yet the white turbans bobbing were those of the warriors of the Sunstruck Sea. AuRon's one great act of generalship while serving as the protecting dragon of the blighters of Old Uldam had been to turn back an invasion by these selfsame white-turbaned warriors. He knew, by blood and bone and kidney, that they'd been human. Yet only a fool would fail to recognize blighters under the white turbans.

Well, perhaps not a fool. Perhaps it was only meant to fool someone who was ignorant of the difference.

They formed a great crescent and waded fearlessly into the dragons. From AuRon's vantage, they looked like a stream filled with cherry-blossoms washing into rocks. Some fetched up against the rocks and clustered there, stuck, while others flowed around until they fetched up against more stones downstream.

Dragons fell with astonishing speed. The turbaned men may just as well have been slaughtering cattle in a pen for the speed of dragons falling.

The men yelled as they charged, a high wail. Some beat gongs and cymbals to add to the clatter and confusion. Clever. Dragons have good hearing, and a cacophony of sound confused their senses more than rain or darkness would have.

Rather than rallying, forming a line, and fighting, the dragons scattered. The old and fat ran, the younger dragons took to the air—and just as often fell, struck with bolts fired by deadly-looking crossbows held by pairs of missile-men.

NiVom turned the slaughter around, and for that AuRon admired him. As the wave washed toward him, tightening into a spearpoint as it neared, he threw that thick damask bedding around his neck and over his back and charged, calling to the scarred dragons behind. Crossbow bolt after crossbow bolt sank into the material. AuRon assumed the thick weave slowed the bolts enough that they couldn't pierce his armor.

NiVom belched out fire, high over the swinging, screaming swordsmen. It fell like burning rain on those behind with the crossbows, and their fire slackened.

Bright *griffaran* swooped in from all corners, plucking heads from the swordsmen like children gathering dandelions.

AuRon found Natasatch in the crowd, back by the waterfall with Imfamnia and some of the scarred veteran dragons, who'd formed a ring around the Queen and a few friends. The dragons beat their wings hard, kicking up a whirlwind of dust, fierce enough to slow the crossbow bolts.

Now NiVom and his dragons slithered down like snakes, protecting their tender bellies and neck-hearts. The turbaned men fell back from the line of snapping jaws, and from falling back it was easier then to turn and run for their lives. The slaughter ebbed as quickly as it flowed, some of the soldiers actually running down their fellows in their haste to escape the draconic fury.

A few bands of warriors put their backs to decorative rocks and tried to sell their lives dearly. But the raging dragons uprooted trees and boulders and sent them bouncing into the men. The shattered few who managed to dodge the projectiles were pounced upon and torn to bloody pieces.

AuRon, transfixed on his perch, had never seen dragons die like this. This day would no longer be a triumphant celebration of the destruction of the Red Queen and Ghioz. It had become a day of mourning for a tenth part of dragonkind.

That night he sought Natasatch in her quarters. She was attending to the travel expenses of a thrall or two and seeing that her dyes, paints, and dusts were properly sealed for transport.

"Thank the Gifts you're alive," AuRon said.

"That was a . . . distressing scene. I'm glad none else of our family were there."

Silence took over, as though it sat down between them. A clatter of sandaled footsteps along the passage outside broke through.

"Your honor! Your honor!" A gray-clad thrall burst in, panting. "The Queen comes!"

AuRon glanced outside, saw one of the *griffaran* guards swooping along the promenade-balcony.

Next room! It's empty. Up and over the divider! she thought to him.

He slipped up and over the divider and landed lightly. He pressed tight against the wall, so that anyone glancing in would see an empty apartment. He heard the distinctive tinging of decorative coins clinking against scale.

"Ah, Natasatch, I'm so glad you're still here," Imfamnia said. "I'd like to speak to you."

"I thought my Queen might need me," she replied. "It is a black day."

AuRon heard a frustrated sigh echo over the partition. "NiVom says we'll have to come up with a new word to describe such losses. He thinks we've lost one dragon in ten, so he's calling it the 'Decimation.' Most of the losses were among the Lavadome dragons, fortunately. No one of importance lost. Oh, the male twin, that pseudo SiHazathant, Regalia's brother. He was killed. She's become quite imbalanced, as they were very close. I don't expect she'll be able to rule the Lower World without him."

"With dragons so established on the surface, I wonder why even keep the Lavadome, save as a curiosity," Natasatch said.

"You don't understand. You've always been a surface dragon. It means more to us than any egg."

"Will there be some ceremony for the dead?" Natasatch asked.

"If only your mate were here, Natasatch." Imfamnia sighed. "He's a sensible dragon and hates the Lavadome almost as much as I do. He'd get to the bottom of this killing."

The walls were decorated with copper plates, AuRon noticed. He could just make out reflections from Natastach's lodgings.

"He also keeps his side of bargains. He's staying in exile, with his brother, the former Tyr," Natasatch said.

"Does he indeed?" Imfamnia turned away and made a great show of inspecting a woven hanging. "Never slips in for a quick, discreet visit?"

AuRon held his breath.

"He has no wish to become entangled in politics. I suspect he's unhappy. I am, too, truth be known. I get lonely."

"Do you now? You know, Natasatch, I could hear your claim of abandonment—I promise you the Sun King will act in your favor—and find you a suitable mate. True, you run a very small province, but it's an important one. Half our slaves come from the lands of the Ironriders. With the new tunnel to the Lower World that those miserable dwarfs overcharged us for, you're second only to Ghioz as the most important entry point west of the mountains."

"I've been . . . disappointed—with mating once. I've no wish to take a second."

Imfamnia touched her snout to Natasatch's. "Taking a second mate is the best decision I ever made. The great NiVom is such a fine dragon. So many good qualities. So quick-witted. Who would have imagined him using a decorative throw to stop poisoned crossbow bolts?"

AuRon heard Natasatch shift her hind legs about. *Don't squirm, dear, you always squirm when you're trying to come up with a half-truth.*

"I don't understand half his conversation," Natasatch finally said. "He's such an intelligent dragon. I wish . . . I wish he'd make allowances for dragons who do not have the benefit of education."

Infamnia laughed. It was an unnatural sound for a dragon to make at normal times and the racket sent nervous chills up AuRon's spine—a dragonelle choking or having a fit might make that yakking sound. Typically dragons kept amusement to themselves with a private *prrum,* what a human might call a *chuckle.* Only dragons who'd been much among humans imitated their laughs. Imfamnia's sounded like a dying hominid caught in her throat. "Oh, I just sing songs to myself when he gets going. I caught him rolling various sorts of balls and plates off the Gold Palace roof once. He was breaking some relics dating back to the blighter charioteers, or so the Red Queen's elvish historian claimed. Said he was experimenting with shapes that might allow riders to travel dragon-back with easier passage of wind. Speaking of wind-passage, NoSohoth said that if you lacked a vigorous young escort, he'd be happy to sit next to you at dinner. The old lecher. I always thought Tighlia had him snipped."

"Me?" Wistala said. "Why would he be interested in me? He's rich enough to buy and sell my province ten times over."

"That's just what I was wondering. If he reveals the answer, I'll be most grateful if you'll tell me before you tell anyone else. . . . I would like to enjoy your confidence. Have you ever wondered why I've visited you so often, my dear?" Imfamnia asked.

"The duties of a Queen are constant. Don't you go around to all the upholds?"

"Duties?" That dreadful laugh came again, only briefer this time. "I'd much rather be looking at what the artisans in Hypat have developed this year in fringe extensions, or enjoying some sun-dried saltwater fish. I have attendants for duties. No, you're an important connection for me, Natasatch. That family of your mate's—they're a strange bunch, certainly, but the fates seem to have picked out certain dragons to survive anything."

"I wish the fates had selected more dragons today."

"I agree. Still, it is a historic day. So much for the bloodline of Tyr Fehazathant," Imfamnia said. "NiVom, curse him, wants the bodies removed by barge. Something about the Ghioz stealing trophies to turn into icons to their old Red Queen. Such loyalty is touching. I wonder if anyone will ever fashion a fetish dedicated to me."

"Why would NiVom need the bodies?"

"You know these scientific types. Ever pickling brains and grinding teeth into suspensions. Dragon-blood is mixed with preservative and bottled in beeswax. Among the humans of the Aerial Host, it's said it can bring a man frozen and with altitude sickness back to life. I expect he'll dump them, probably in the Star Tunnel. No Ghioz-man would dare go down there to pry out a few dragon-teeth."

"What is the Star Tunnel?"

"Oh, you missed that part of the wars, didn't you? Before your time. Wistala was muchly involved in it. I don't know much of it, either, save that it was the last refuge of the independent demen. The Firemaids finally drove them from the place. I believe it's some vast underground garden, not as great as the Lavadome, of course, but important enough in its own way. The chasm is located in those disputed grounds between Ghioz and your daughter's blighter uphold in Old Uldam."

Natasatch was never overly interested in geography, but AuRon, on the other side of his barrier, wondered why the bodies had to take such a journey. Didn't the Lavadome dragons have ceremonies for honoring their dead?

Too much had gone wrong today for it all to be bad luck. How could such a mass of men from the Sunstruck Sea travel such a distance without being detected? It seemed that the Ghioz cosmetician had warned him that some plot was in the offing, yet he must have been the only dragon who listened, for there was only the smallest of guards around the feast-grounds. But why would NiVom and Infamnia want to kill enemies, especially in so unsure a fashion? The men might not kill enough, or might poison far too many with their wretched blades.

He owed the dead an answer.

Chapter 4

The morning clouds in the Sadda-Vale hung low, meeting the mists rising from the lake like ghostly dancers.

Wistala forced herself to have an appetite. She stomped dark teardrops of shelled creatures drawn from the lake by the blighter servants and picked up the mucousy flesh with her tongue. The blighters sank wooden beams by the garbage pool, and every few months drew up the creatures who'd anchored themselves to the accommodating timber.

She surveyed her reflection. The diet of the Sadda-Vale and infrequent sunshine had lightened the coloring of her scale progressively. She looked like young straw, so yellow the green had almost disappeared. She was wider of hip and longer of tail since her first clutch, and her fringe had grown out to a luxurious length. From the neck down there was no question that she was a different dragon, physically.

With a little paint, her face could be changed. According

to Yefkoa, hardly a female in the Empire went about without scale painted. The richer ones decorated further with gemstones, the more daring added bits of feather, silks, or netting.

She'd fought, again, with DharSii last night about answering the Firemaids' call. Neither of them had slept well in the vast old perch room, though each pretended to slumber to avoid further words. Wistala kept the eye DharSii couldn't see on the weather through the circle in the roof that admitted light, air, and the usual condensation. Sometime in the early dawn she decided to leave with Yefkoa, who was testing her wings in the warm currents of the lake in the more wholesome waters nearer the springs.

Wistala lifted a crab-pot with her tail, found it only partially full, chewed it with an effort, and took another to keep it company. In her mood, the frantic pinches of the crabs and the effort to pop a few rivets and bend tin were welcome. It wouldn't hurt to have some metals in her diet, just in case. Scale tended to drop on a long flight and the old habits of scrounging metals from her hatchling days. Scabia would be aggravated—crabs in *garlocque*-vinegar were her delight—and the blighter blacksmiths would need to make new cages.

"Scabia will be displeased," DharSii's voice said from behind, echoing her thoughts.

She startled despite herself. For a mature male dragon, he could be eerily silent when he wished, almost as quiet as her scaleless brother.

"Worried about being turned out of the Vale?" she asked.

"I'm not worried; annoyance is good for her. Expressing

displeasure is her only regular exercise." DharSii flicked a dropped rotten potato into the pool where it belonged.

Wistala didn't like Scabia, and Scabia's grudging kindness in allowing her exiled family safe harbor in the Sadda-Vale heightened the dislike.

DharSii's color was up around his neck-hearts. She knew him well enough now to know that was the chink in his invincible aplomb. Eyes, wings, tail, claws, *griff*, and teeth would never betray his mood, but his capillaries let him down.

"Are you still determined to carry out this foolishness, bouncing off south like a broken chariot wheel?"

"I told you last night, the only way you'll stop me is to break my wings. Care to try?"

"Sticking your nose into Lavadome politics might mean they gets lopped off, high up, where your fringe meets your head. I couldn't bear that."

Curse him! She would have covered twoscore horizons just on nervous friction.

"Ha-hem," he harrumphed, falling into his old habit of clearing his throat as he made up his mind what to say, or to cover for keeping his tongue still. "I've met exactly one sensible, cultured, and lively dragonelle in my whole life. Can't the world sort itself out for once? Who knows how many crises have passed in our score of years here, yet the sun still rises and the snows still come and go. We've had so many meetings and good-byes, I've resolved never to have another."

"Ha-hem," she harrumphed back at him, which was her only option other than twining her neck as tightly around his

as she could. But if she began the embrace, she and Yefkoa would probably remain in the Sadda-Vale until their joint-scales grew brittle and dropped with age.

"Take this advice," DharSii said. "Ask permission of someone to enter the Empire. It's a thin bit of scale, but it may serve to confuse the issue enough for you to. I'm an old hand at exile."

"Yet you yourself returned."

"My sympathy for the Lavadome had not quite run out. But with the dragons gorging themselves on the world like Silverhigh of old, I'm content to leave them to their fate."

Sometimes he could be as cold-blooded as a lizard. The dragons of the Empire might not be worth a blighter's cuss, but what of the generation still dreaming in their eggs? What gorging had they done?

"I'm not," Wistala said. "We owe something to the generations not yet born, even if their grandsires are fools."

"A fair point. Would it be unfair for me to mention the new generation here? They may need you someday."

"Having you with me will better my chances of returning to them," Wistala said. "Will you not come with me?"

"I have my own phantoms to chase. While you are away, I'll indulge myself in a little exploration."

"More history of the Lavadome?" she asked.

"There are some missing pieces to the Lavadome's story I'd like to find. I've indulged myself too long here. For the first time in my life, I've enjoyed the companionship at the Sadda-Vale. I mean you, of course. And your brothers. They're each stimulating. So alike in their resourcefulness despite their disadvantages. Still, I can't bear the thought of listening to Scabia without you others around."

"I wish you luck, then. I will—miss you."

"One last warning. There have always been powers who want to use dragons, alive or dead, for the strange substances that course through our blood. Our magic, if you'll forgive the word. Long ago, Anklemere was attempting something with dragons—what, I do not know—and I fear his plans; perhaps even his mind, if you want to look at it that way, lives on. The Dragon Empire may think they rule sky, ground, and tunnel, but my vitals tell me they are being used like puppets. Who or what has the other end of the strings I cannot say."

Yefkoa had behaved oddly at the Sadda-Vale once she was well enough to meet the other dragons. She bowed low before Scabia, as Wistala had coached her to do, and complimented her on everything from the taste of the sturgeon pulled from the lake to the intricate carvings in the passages.

"You just don't see workmanship like this except in Imperial Rock in the Lavadome," Yefkoa said. "Who made it? Dwarfs?"

"There are some dwarfish makers'-marks, but also blighter and human," Scabia said, dropping out of her usual formal speech in an unusual condescension. "You can tell the difference in the details. The dwarfs will make a support look like rope, or piping, whereas the blighters will be more organic and men imitate leaves and vines of nature, as most of their artisans were probably trained by elves in the days of Silverhigh."

Most strange of all was Yefkoa's praise of the Copper. Wistala had forgotten over the years in exile how her brother had been loved by some of those he used to rule. Yefkoa spoke of him in tones of gratitude and awe, and was deeply disappointed that he was away. Wistala knew in a vague sort of way that he'd done some favor or other for her in her youth—had he given her a place in the Firemaids despite her slight frame and thin scale? Well, in any case, here was another dragon who loved her brother deeply. Wistala, when she looked at him, saw only a collection of injuries and an expression that verged on half-witted thanks to the eye injury she'd given him after their parents were murdered. She'd ceased to hate him long ago, but still wondered at the respect such a limping, undersized wretch seemed to inspire in others.

The bat Larb outdid Yefkoa in his praise of Scabia. He declared he'd never imagined such a Queen of snows—she was simply the most breathtaking female dragon in the world. He waxed on about the vastness of the Vesshall, his echolocation quite inadequate. This went on for a full shift of moonlight. Scabia reacted to the bat's obsequious patter in a way Wistala had never imagined. She let loose with a *prrum* and invited the bat to eat his fill, complimenting him on his Drakine.

After dinner, when Scabia was amusing herself by telling stories to the youths, Wistala and Yefkoa looked over an old map of the Red Mountains.

"Where shall we reenter the Empire?" Wistala asked.

"East of the mountains would be best," Yefkoa opined. "The climate is harsher and fewer dragons choose to settle there. Wallander is a possibility. It is on the Falnges."

"Just above the old works of the dwarfs," Wistala said. "I know it."

"The Chartered Company, yes. It used to belong to them. Now it's just another poor province. An entry there would attract little notice; there may not even be a dragon there to supervise. Probably some Hypatian hireling. It makes Dairuss seem like the Lavadome—a little riverbank squat with a few docks doing some trade with the Ironriders."

They said their farewells and thanks to Scabia the next day. Larb the bat had been invited to stay as Scabia's messenger, in the hope that Tyr RuGaard would return and he could go back into "the family service," as he styled it.

Wistala said she would accompany Yefkoa to the borders of the Empire. Which was perfectly true. She would also accompany Yefkoa all the way to the Lavadome, if need be. She owed her life to Ayafeeia.

She added that she was grateful for the old dragonhelms of Silverhigh. She'd check on RuGaard on the way back.

With a wish of fair spring weather from Scabia, they departed together.

Two more contrasting females in flight could scarcely be imagined. Wistala, heavy and muscular, with an enormous wingspan, set off in a steady series of lifting beats and glides. Yefkoa, slight and narrower of wing, flapped as steadily as a duck migrating.

The frosted plains of the north, visited only by migratory herds and the men and beasts that hunted them, gave way to the low, rolling hills of the Ironrider lands.

Spring had advanced so many horizons to the south and

the Ironrider lands were at their most beautiful. Sunflowers were opening and the fields were filled with wildflowers. The ground-birds were already out with this year's offspring, lines of pheasants and quail poked around the tough bushes clinging to the highlands, and in the lower, damper parts ducks abounded.

Had Wistala been traveling for pleasure, rather than with dispatch, she would have gone south along the coastline of the Inland Ocean. She had friends in the Hypatian north, and it would be nice to see how the descendants of Yari-tab were getting along at the Green Dragon Inn in the old village where she'd grown up under the protection of Rainfall, the old elf gentleman who kept the great bridge and highway in repair. Perhaps she would find time to visit one of the Hypatian Libraries and meet students seeking to become sages and experts—she still held the title of "Librarian" for collecting some of the works of NooMoahk the Black in her hunt for AuRon.

But Yefkoa was on a mission and could not afford to lose days in that manner.

The plains held their own interest for her. She'd never traveled this route south before, though she had taken shorter flights out of the Sadda-Vale to keep herself in training, hunt, and take a break from Scabia's conversation.

Wistala had explored the lands of the nomadic Ironriders decades ago in her hunt for AuRon and she wondered if the changes she marked now were some seasonal variation or a sign of plague or catastrophe. Before, she'd observed masses of the Ironriders in movement, flowing on their horses like a brown stain across the landscape, with shaggy and woolly herds surrounding the mass of riding and trudging mankind.

This time, the herds were reduced to a few poor animals closely watched by children just outside tents and huts set up out of the wind in some hard-to-find notch in the earth.

The shining armor, the bright, proud pennants, the songs from the tall riders in their woolly, tower-shaped hats—all gone, apparently. Once these warriors had grown such long and cultivated mustaches coated in shining, perfumed fats that they could be seen from the air; now the men were shaggy and unkempt.

Wistala tipped her wings and banked, closing up on Yefkoa, who fell in behind the vastly larger Wistala, riding the air off her wing.

"Aren't these the lands of the Ironriders?" Wistala asked.

"You would know better than I," Yefkoa said. "I believe so."

"Are they off fighting somewhere?"

"The Ironriders? No. The Hypatians took—oh, you don't know about the great raids."

"No."

"It was mostly the Aerial Host with Hypatian troops. They hunted down the Ironrider bands, fought the warriors and made thralls of the rest. They're mostly gone, but some dwarfish slavers still hunt the area. They bring the thralls to Wallander and sell them to us."

That struck Wistala as nasty work. She could understand making slaves of a vanquished army—part of the chance one took in setting out on war—but to hunt hominids like wild animals solely to enslave them . . . that led to what? An empty land reverting to wildness. No trade, no camps full of song and the shrieks of children at play.

"How far until Wallander, Yefkoa? These steppes are depressing me."

"We should reach it tomorrow, I think. The ground is more broken now as we approach the river. I understand your dislike for this country. It makes me feel like the only presence in the world, too. Or that someone is watching me."

Wistala had no love for the Ironriders—she'd won some distinction among the Firemaids and the Tyr's dragons fighting them, as a matter of fact. But she couldn't help feeling that some continent-spanning wrong had been committed and that sooner or later the crime would demand atonement.

The crickets in Wallander were happy in the balmy spring evening. Yefkoa and Wistala had their wings partly spread out, carefully massaging hot muscles, cleaning wing skin, and flexing and contracting tender tendons to distinguish injury from exhaustion.

It felt good to be with a female close to her own mind. Scabia was so busy playing elder dragon-dame and head of household that one could never feel friendship, only condescension, and Aethleethia's mind ran on a very few well-worn tracks.

"Why this hunger for slaves?" she asked Yefkoa.

"We go through thralls like chickens these days," Yefkoa said. "Remember when there were herds and flocks in the Lavadome? Now the pens are filled with thralls, waiting and being examined for work, or breeding stock, or even training to support the Aerial Host. The old and sick are simply eaten, and most of the rest are worked until they drop, then slaughtered for food."

"Life is cheap in the Empire these days. NiVom's doing, or the twins?"

"NiVom has plans to enlarge the living space and passages in the Lower World. He has an army of demen now and he plans to have them move below the earth at speed, so they can appear in any city of the Empire without warning. In the end, I think he means Lower to rule Upper. So we're all eating more worn-out thralls than we ever have."

"Seems inefficient. Pigs put on flesh more quickly and easily," Wistala said.

"Pigs can't tunnel. There are vast works in process, under Hypatia and the other Protectorates. Any dragon who wishes to be thought a Someone needs a resort, above- and below-ground."

"What do they do in these resorts?"

"Stuff themselves and hold parties for each other and try to attract some rich hero of the Aerial Host. Even the Hypatians, who've benefited from the Empire's extension the most, now are grudging about feeding. Hardly a drakka goes into the Firemaids anymore; they want a position in one of the Protectorates where they can sunbathe and send thralls out into the markets for paint and dye. Most of the young males fight to get into the Aerial Host, for the glory and the plunder. The Drakwatch is also withering down to little more than a cadre of impoverished or outcast families, supervising thralls in their work."

Yefkoa was an unusually attractive dragon, if you liked the slim-framed type. "Why haven't you found a place in the Empire? Taken a mate from the Aerial Host and joined the painted set?"

"No mates for me. I was once betrothed to a fat old gasper who already had more mates than he knew what to do with. After my parents agreed to my mating him he took me to survey his hill and almost as soon as we were out of sight he pinned me, wanting to mate then and there, out in the rocks like a couple of herdthralls. He was too fat to fly and too lazy to swim for mating, I imagine." She shuddered at the memory. "Tyr RuGaard took pity on me and put me into the Firemaids."

"Anyway, no mates for me. I'm oathed into the Firemaids and meant every word of the Third Oath. Nowadays there are Second-Oathers who speak the words as though they mean to say, *Sundering myself from mated life for the protection of all (until a likely dragon starts a-courting, that is)*.

Wistala chuckled. She'd been oathed into the Firemaids as well, but political troubles and DharSii had come along before she'd spent enough years among them for the most solemn Third Oath vows.

Wallander was still a dumpy little collection of hovels on the riverbank. All it had to recommend it was a lake of slack water in the Falnges River and a wide beach for landing trade-craft. The only difference Wistala could mark was that the wall had fallen into even greater disrepair, and there were slave-pens everywhere, inside and outside the walls.

Wistala watched the wretches in the pens. Poor things. The dwarfs would chuck them into one of the barges, and from there they'd be taken to a tunnel portal. How many would never see the sun again, sicken, and die after a few years of hard work underground?

She'd never given much thought to thralls before, but the ones she'd known were the descendants of warriors who'd fought the dragons and were warm and clothed and fed decently. If the occasional gravely injured or sick thrall had been given quick death to ease their passing before being devoured, she shrugged it off as part of the long, unfortunate history between hominids and dragonkind. Ninety-nine times out of a hundred, a dragon of any age caught by men or elves or dwarfs would be pierced with spears and end up with its bones adorning some thane's trophy room or great hall. Gentlebeings like Rainfall were the rare exception in a hard world.

Remembering Rainfall's kindness, his hatred of cruelty and injustice shamed her. What was her excuse for coarsening over the years? Rainfall had been cast away and forgotten by the Hypatian Order, its chivalry he'd preserved and kept until his dying breath.

"They aren't part of the Empire yet, are they?" Wistala asked, pointing with her tail tip to the pens.

"They're still outside the walls. The dwarfs are probably negotiating the sale," Yefkoa said.

"There's a problem with taking a long time bargaining. You may be shocked to find out your wares suddenly aren't worth so much."

The men and dwarfs of Wallander barely looked at the

pair of winged females idling beside the river. When they'd washed the dust of travel—an amazing amount of spiderweb and bug-grit would get caught in one's scales during flight and the ability of insects to reach every claw's-breadth of the world continually impressed Wistala—from their bodies, they sunned themselves and cocked their heads to get a better view of the headhunter dwarfs and their captives.

Old animosities burned like embers deep in Wistala's hearts. Slavers had come for her family, once, killing her mother and sister. She tussled with herself. The first job was to pass through and into the Dragon Empire.

Yefkoa introduced her to the Protector of Wallander.

He was a young silver dragon with black tips on his scales, with wings so fresh they were practically still wet. Wistala could see the faint scars of the emergence of his wings, where scale had not quite overgrown the crocodile-smile wounds running along his back.

"I am Yefkoa, and we are of the Firemaids. We are on our way back to the Lavadome and seek permission to reenter the Empire." Yefkoa had chosen her words better than Wistala could have hoped.

In one of the wood-beamed lodges behind, Wistala heard shouts. Human and dwarfish voices were trying to win one another over in a debate of noise rather than ideas, as Rainfall might have put it.

"I am OuThroth, page to NoSohoth, exchequer of Wallander and knight-esquire of the Empire." Wistala thought he'd collected an interesting assortment of titles for such a young dragon. "You are welcome, Firemaids. Enjoy the poor hospitality of Wallander before continuing your journey. There are some nice fish running in the river, if that's to your taste."

"Is this your own Protectorate, or do you serve as steward for another?" Yefkoa asked, carefully keeping her head below the young dragon's and setting and resetting her wings, as a flirtatious young dragonelle might.

"I speak for NoSohoth. My father used to run the uphold trade in *oliban*." Wistala remembered the strong-smelling resin burned in the Lavadome to subdue dragon odor. Male dragons became fierce and argumentative when crowded among the smells of too many of their sex. "Wallander is one of the smaller provinces NoSohoth oversees and they sent me here to gain experience."

The Empire had changed, Wistala thought. Stewards now, for Protectors who had amassed more lands than they could manage. No surprise that NoSohoth would have a collection of provinces; he always was a rapacious dragon.

"Have you gained any, young dragon?" Wistala asked.

He blinked, perhaps unused to questioning from Firemaids. "I've learned how to survive with no polite society. If you've been out in Ironrider lands, you've been long without wine. Would you like some of mine?"

"Please," Yefkoa said. They followed him from the gate. The contest of voices faded.

"What was that ruckus with the thrall-gatherers?" Wistala asked.

"The dwarfs are exhibiting their usual arrogance in pricing their captives. It's more than the Hypatians are willing to pay, yet I'm still expected to fill a tally of thralls or NiVom and

NoSohoth will have me supervising diggers, with one day in the sun out of thirty. I've never been able to figure out where all this pride comes from in dwarfs. Unless being dirty and uncouth is something to be proud of."

"What will you do?" Wistala asked.

"If I must, I'll make the difference out of my own funds, limited as they are. Thralls must be found."

OuThroth's hall was a work-in-progress. A good stone foundation had been laid—Wistala saw a dwarf working figures on a piece of paper next to a small fire with an infusion kettle atop it—but the roof timbers were still half-done, gaps covered by a mix of canvas and cordage.

A vast amount of lumber was piled near the riverbank, but it was poorly situated. The bottom trunks were wet and rotting and she could see mosses and mushrooms the size of chest-scale growing out of wet cracks in the bark. If OuThroth wasn't careful, half of his purchase wouldn't be fit for bedding-chips, let alone roofing. A shame, since they were fine big boles. Some venerable stands of timber had been cut, only for this heedless youth to leave it to rot along a riverbank where it had been dumped by a barge.

Waste. Her old guardian Rainfall would have been outraged to see such ancient trees cut but then left to rot.

Inside, OuThroth's hall was sparse but comfortable. His bed-platform was set up in the coziest corner, if the winds today were the prevailing. A mass of copper tubing ran beneath it, giving a hiss now and then.

"It's the latest thing, a bed-warmer. Steam flows through it and returns to a sort of big chamber as water, where it is turned to steam again. There's all sorts of dwarfish inventions like valves and cooling chambers involved, I don't know the half of it, but it will be a fine perch for my hall. The dwarf has arranged a summer-bed as well, a clever thing like a great thick fishnet."

"Aren't you afraid, with all that space beneath where you sleep?" Wistala asked. "Assassins could get in under there and be next to your breast without waking you."

"Oh, the hominids are beaten and they know it. I have a few Hypatian lancers and whip-hands here to keep order among the thralls. They make sure no one is hiding weapons or secretly making shields in the smithy. As for the Ironriders—well, you've just come from there. Did they give you any trouble?"

"We could hardly have found trouble had we looked for it," Yefkoa said.

"Yes, I used to bring in a dozen or more gold coins a month in purchasing commissions," OuThroth said. "Now it's a few pieces of silver here and there. That's why the hall is taking so long to complete—the thrall trade's drying up or moving to other provinces. Most of them are coming from the north in the hill country of the upper Inland Ocean these days. If only I'd been posted there! Wallander buys wild horses and feed-stock rounded up from the plains by the Hypatians, but that's nothing compared to thrall-trade. There's talk of war with the southern princedoms. I'm hoping that since now I've become experienced I can win a position there. The massacre threw the whole Empire into a tumult and there are titles up for the swallowing like summer bats."

"The massacre?" Wistala asked. She felt a little sorry for

OuThroth; he seemed starved for other dragons to talk to. Callow, yes, and perhaps a little lazy. If this was an example of the generations being raised by the Dragon Empire, it was no wonder war and revolution were in the offing.

"Oh, you wouldn't have heard if you've been in the wild. A vast number of assassins from the Sunstruck Sea infiltrated the Queen's feast, posing as thralls. They used terrible poisons, first in the wine to addle their heads, then on their blades. Seventeen dragons dead, including the male Twin, and the Sun King and Queen only just escaped. Infamy!"

"Who else was lost?" Yefkoa said. "Any Firemaids?"

"Mostly Lower World dragons. Ayafeeia was the only Firemaid I'd heard was killed. I'm thankful NoSohoth declined his invitation to attend, as he was engaged in important negotiations with the northern provinces in Hypatia, or I might have lost a most important ally and any chance of soon gaining another title."

Shallow, callow youth! was all Wistala could think. Even in the great war with the Red Queen and her Ironrider allies, they'd never lost so many dragons in any one battle. Rainfall would be sure to retreat into short, polite phrases so as not to give his mind away.

"May you get what your work here deserves," Wistala said.

They fed and restored themselves from the fast flight over the barren steppes and camped under some vast riverbank willows. When Yefkoa was slumbering soundly, Wistala left her and slipped through the gate to the outer pens.

She walked up to the trio of dwarfs watching over their stock. They sat in a ring, smoking and exchanging quiet words over a beer-cask with Hypatian letters on it.

"Come to view the merchandise again?" one of the dwarfs asked. "No sickness. Plenty of kids, even one mother-to-be. We're not counting the not-yet-born, of course. Bonus for you."

"Yes, I would like a closer look," Wistala said. She reared up, and came down with all of her weight on the dwarfs, trapping them in her *sii*. She stomped furiously.

When the dwarfs were reduced to muddy stains, she turned on the occupants in the pens. The dark-haired Ironriders shrank away from her.

Some were chained together. It was the work of only a few moments to break the links. They set up a wailing.

"All of you! Run!" Wistala managed.

They didn't understand her, so she flapped at them, just missing with her wingtips, until the whole mass was running for the low hills of the southern steppelands. They left only one behind, an old fellow who looked like he'd died from exposure. She extracted his tongue before burning him.

Once she was sure of their departure, she loosed her flame into the pen and on the dead dwarfs.

When she told Yefkoa what had happened the next morning, she expected complaints. Yefkoa stood silent for a moment, then said, "Good. Only fair way to take thralls is battle; this burning villages and hauling them in from the bushes bothers me. It means trouble, though, and things were going well with OuThroth."

"Like you, I was almost enslaved when I was young. It was dwarfs then, too. I can't right the wrong done to my family, but I can save another."

While they ate, OuThroth hurried over.

"I must ask you about one matter. There were some dwarfs camped outside the walls yesterday. We were in negotiations about the purchase of thralls. The negotiations were taking overlong, as being dwarfs, they pressed their advantage to the limit and asked for a price above the very clouds. My watchmen heard signs of fighting last night, and this morning both dwarfs and thralls seem to be gone."

"They are, after a fashion," Wistala said. "Believe me, you wouldn't have wanted those thralls. I've been among the Ironriders for some time, seeking old bones."

"Disgusting custom," Yefkoa said. "Some Ironriders dare to wear dragon-scale, or have the skulls of those killed in fighting as clan totems."

"That's not an answer," OuThroth said. He was capable of pressing a point when a potential profit was involved.

"Your thrall-gatherers were trying to cheat you," Wistala said. "Fully a third of the thralls they were trying to sell you were diseased. It's not an easy illness to spot—they go pale and listless and bloodshot about the eyes, and while not immediately fatal, it does leave the victims vulnerable to other, more quick-killing diseases."

"What did you do with the bodies?"

"We ate them. We were famished."

"You ate diseased flesh?"

"Only after a good roasting," Yefkoa said.

"Don't worry—it does not spread to dragons," Wistala said.

"I understand there is already a great loss of thralls underground," Wistala said. "Had a more experienced person spotted the disease, they would have been traced back to you. Or worse, the signs might have been missed altogether and a vast die-off of thralls could happen underground."

Getting rid of the thralls was an audacious move, but Wistala had her reasons. The way she saw it, OuThroth had two options. He could report to NoSohoth that a pair of dragonelles that he admitted devoured a couple of slave pens full of thralls, or he could feign ignorance of the entire matter.

No matter what he did with the first option, it would reek of mismanagement of his Protectorate. Letting a pair of unknown dragonelles eat stock . . .

No, he would tell the Hypatians to shut up if they valued their slave-trading concession, pass along the disease story, and if worse came to worst claim that killing the dwarfs was rough borderland justice for their attempt to cheat the Dragon Empire.

"It would set the works back years," Yefkoa said, breaking in on Wistala's thoughts.

OuThroth bowed. "You've done me a great service, Yefkoa and errr . . ."

"My oath-sister, Tala," Yefkoa supplied.

"That is a handsome headdress you wear, Tala. It is elegantly shaped. Elven-make?"

"A family heirloom. All I know with certainty is that it is old."

"Tala is from one of the noblest families in the land—but she dislikes when I name names," Yefkoa said, and Wistala grew afraid that Yefkoa would play the game too sharply and arouse the youngster's suspicions.

"If you have any younger relatives, I'd welcome their society here—if they have a yen to travel." OuThroth said, bowing. "I'm still unmated," he added, unnecessarily.

"A dragon under the tutelage of NoSohoth is on his way up," Yefkoa said, simpering.

They bowed out their farewells, thanked him for his hospitality, and took off across the river, heading for Dairuss, the Protectorate of AuRon's mate.

"He's still a bit wet about the wings for a border post, I think," Wistala said.

"Titles are bought and sold these days," Yefkoa said. "Nowadays your title doesn't matter so much as the sheer number of them behind your name. It takes much of a sunrise to list NoSohoth's. He's always willing to sell a few. You see the quality of dragon it gets us."

Chapter 5

ven from an altitude, the tower stood out. Its position when viewed from the east, framed against the sea, presented an unmistakable landmark. And if that wasn't enough, a light burned atop it. The Copper judged it an ordinary fire reflected and magnified with polished metal, set as a beacon for night-travelers, or perhaps a warning for ships about the dangerous break in the coast.

The last time he'd been here he'd been half out of his mind with regret and recrimination. AuRon had known something of the dragons here—he'd had communications with them in his time on the Isle of Ice, and they'd used the landmark to take their bearings. All he remembered was the vague loom of the tower and the cold, misty coast.

On the flight he'd toyed with the dragonhelm Scabia had given him. If it did in fact amplify mindspeech, it didn't work very well on him and Wistala. Perhaps there wasn't enough of an affinity between them. Or she wasn't wearing it. All he received was vague impressions, like a remembered dream, and most of those were of DharSii or Scabia speaking. He'd had enough of both to last a lifetime.

The lands he'd flown over looked cold and unfriendly. Hostile, too. The barbarian villages had piles of lumber and were putting old fences back into repair and constructing new ones around unprotected clusters of buildings. His passage overhead seemed to cause some consternation, the barbarians shuffling their livestock and children about like disturbed ants.

The only philosophy that makes sense is to treat all as your friends, or none. I think all's more pleasant, don't you, lads? Tyr Fehazathant used to say when visiting the wingless drakes in the Drakwatch. The Copper had done well treating all as friends—though perhaps he'd have lasted longer on the throne and kept his mate besides if he'd adopted the latter mind-set.

He circled above the tower three times before starting his descent. Closing the wing today would be extra painful.

The mistress of the tower was an old crone who walked with the aid of a cane. She was supervising the unloading of a dwarf-driven, mule-drawn wagon. The mules didn't care for his presence and brayed an alarm as he landed. She still had bright eyes and a kind of beauty about her, the way a wind-bent tree clinging to a cliff's edge over the sea was picturesque in its twisted tenacity.

"I've seen you somewhere or other before, Copper," she said, in intelligible but flat dragonspeech. "You fly in a very distinctive manner. What's your name?"

"RuGaard," the Copper said, fiddling with his wing and pulling it shut with a pained wince.

"The old Tyr? I have seen you before, years since. Passing eastward, you were."

"Thank you for the compliment of your memory."

"The day I start forgetting dragons is the day I'll be fit for my last trip beyond the surf aboard a flaming raft. But I'm not ready for my last ride yet, if you think you'll be taking over in the name of the Empire—"

"Nothing like that. I've given up all claim to any title or position. It's been years since I've had any part of the Empire. I'm a wandering exile, lonely for the smell of my kind."

"Smell we have, all you want, free as air. You take anything else, I expect you to work for it. Everyone earns their keep in the tower, man or dragon."

"What is the price of a decent meal?"

"A ride to the top of the tower. Don't worry about a saddle, I know how to hook on to scale for short trips. I need to check the fire-wardens up there. I found some drips of whale oil at the bottom of the tower, which means they're getting sloppy again, and I don't want my tower burned to the ground. Ain't like whale oil is cheap, neither."

She introduced herself as Gettel and clung to him using her knees and ankles. The Copper sighed and extended the wing again. He double-checked the condition of the locking-peg. It would be just his luck for it to give way at the top and have him kill the mistress of the tower by accident.

The Copper wasn't used to bearing a person. He'd last

done it in his youth and he didn't like the sensation. His neck was a vulnerable spot for a blade.

"So, sick of old Scabia at the Sadda-Vale, m'dragon?"

"I'm lonely," the Copper said, honestly enough. "I've spent too much of my life in decisive thought and action. A life of contemplation of the day's fish haul and techniques of de-boning and filet preparation isn't for me."

"If it's activity ye seek, I can use you. There's coin in it for you to eat—I know there's precious little of that where you come from. Not just messenger-flying, either, but real fighting. Feel up to taking on some dwarfs? I've a rich commission from the Hypatians."

"I've no enemies among dwarfs. All mine are farther south."

"Your Empire. They tried to get me to join, but I don't care to call another my master. Between them to the south and the barbarian chiefs to the north, Juutfod is in a bad way. Both would like to claim this tower and my dragons."

"I don't care to call anyone my master, either," the Copper said.

"RuGaard, you won't. Partnership is what I'm thinking. I know your reputation. I've heard you praised by tongues that don't find words of praise easily. To be honest, I could use a dragon with some leadership experience in the tower. I can put it on paper if that's your preference. Got a copy of the old Chartered Company articles around here somewhere that I copy from, if your tastes run to laying everything out on a bit of thin rag."

"I'm as rusty as this wing joint. To tell you the truth, being Tyr was mostly a figurehead position. People listened to me because I was up on a golden perch with bodyguards all around."

"We could give it a try for a while. You might find you like it here. I know there's dissatisfaction down south. We might get another recruit or two, and I could sure use 'em, if this tower's to keep free to do our business the way we like."

This was close enough to perfect that the Copper wondered if it was some kind of trap. Was old Gettel holding some kind of bounty offer from the Empire for his death or capture? Would she take him below, just to have an axe-wielding blighter strike his neck from the shadows?

"I'd like to know more about this tower and what it does," the Copper said.

She escorted him to a wooden platform large and heavy-timbered enough to support a curled dragon. It could be raised or lowered from a quadruple brace by means of chains and heavy woven cables.

"Counterweight at the other end," she explained. "This is the fifth version of the lifter. Just six men working a capstan can lift our heaviest dragon to the top. Try to keep to the center—less wear and tear if it's balanced."

She reached up and rang a brass bell three times by its pull. There was a pause and then the Copper felt the wood shift beneath his feet. The platform ascended as though by magic. Guide-cables kept it stable.

In the light-filled upper chambers, dragons reclined with viewing slits to the world outside and wide balconies to the central shaft. The Copper guessed she had eight full-grown dragons. There were two drakes and six drakka, a typical ratio. One female, probably ready to lay eggs, had a splendid retreat near the ground floor, with a heavy timbered egg shelf with huge iron-bound beams forming a lattice that protected her yet gave her light, air, and a good look at the activity of the tower.

The wealth and knowledge that went into the construction of the tower astonished him. When he'd seen it years ago, he'd assumed it was some relic still standing from a lost high civilization, but on closer inspection of the walls and timbers it looked as though it had been built in his lifetime. The Copper had had no idea any humans outside Hypatia could achieve something like this, save under the whips of slave-gang organizers such as the Ghioz.

So there was inspiration and mind in the north, as well. Perhaps the barbarians would one day rise to greatness. "How would you like to be known here? You're welcome to leave your name behind, if you like."

"I've plenty of identifying marks. Still, we might as well confuse the issue."

"Some of the dragons take names in the local tongue. 'Broadwing' and all that. It's more friendly to human mouths."

"I don't know the local language."

"You'll pick it up, if you speak some Parl. How about 'Brighteye'?"

"I like it," the Copper said. "What does it mean?"

She explained that she was referring to the good one, not the milky and half-shut bad eye, and he accepted the name. So he became 'Brighteye' in Juutfod tower. He met Loic Varlson, the chief dragon-handler, and a few stout bodies who knew how to ride or care for dragons. Many of them were descendants of "wizard men" from the Isle of Ice. One of them didn't like the look of Scabia's dragonhelm; he said it "looked elvish." There were a few blighters around to aid in the cleaning and working the capstans, but no dwarfs or elves in the tower.

She set him up with a perch—sort of a section of floor, open to the central shaft of the tower, where the lift ran. It was cavelike, though perhaps a little noisier than he would have liked, for the dragons of the tower—it seemed about six were living there at any one time—enjoyed calling across and between levels to each other.

The dragons of the tower were happy with their lot and their mistress. The tower's most stable source of income was from the merchant shippers, who pooled together every quarter-year to buy flights out into the Inland Ocean to bring back word of approaching storms. Dragons have keen eyes for weather, and at the sight of towering thundercaps they could soon estimate how severe the storm and how quickly it was coming. They'd hurry for the eastern shore of the Inland Ocean and warn the coastal traffic to seek shelter.

Just saving a ship or two this way more than paid for their bounty. Gettel saw it as good exercise for her dragons.

He tried to find out exactly how old Gettel was; she was ancient-looking yet seemed spry and sharp. The dragons said she collected loose dragon teeth, ground them up, baked the powder into her daily bread, and mixed it in her oat porridge. One of her older dragons quoted her as saying *keeps me feisty*.

The Copper believed it. She was quick to reprimand dragons who claimed illness, ate too much, or didn't keep their sleeping-shelves tidy. Any one of them could break her like a twig without a thought, but still she wasn't afraid to rap a dragon across the nose with her cane for not picking up a dropped scale and putting it in the ration bucket. She also quieted the men—twoscore or so lived in the tower, with twice that making the climb every morning from the town below—when they started in on elves or dwarfs as weavers of a conspiracy against men.

"Only conspiracy against men I ever found to be true was their indolence and stupidity working together to keep 'em from getting any work done," Gettel said, putting them to work changing the lift's guide-cables.

Of course there were brushes with the dragons from the south, but at the moment the forces of the Dragon Empire were concerned with other horizons. He heard news of the fliers meeting pleasant fishing expeditions out from Hypatia, or young couples heading out to the wilder western "colonial coast" for their long mating flights.

The Copper explored the foundation of the tower, curious as to where the dragon-waste and other garbage went. There were tunnels beneath the tower leading down the cliff, and natural chutes for dumping waste into the surf. There were always fishing boats in the water around the tower, taking their share of the fish and crustaceans thriving on dragon-waste and scraps.

There were rats in the tower as well. It had a double wall facing the exterior for better insulation, and the rats had passages up and down running the whole height of it. They grew brave at night and came out in search of dropped food.

The Copper had learned that if you really want to know about a place, you should talk to the vermin. Their survival depended on always looking and listening.

"Here's a boon, mates!" a rat said. Their speech wasn't all that different from that of the bats he'd known.

"Maybe he's trying to sucker us out for an extermination," one high-pitched voice squeaked.

The Copper shrank away from the remains of his dinner. "Don't worry—some of my best friends have been vermin."

Some came out and ate; others, suspecting a trap, picked up pieces and scurried away. They disappeared into crevices the Copper wouldn't have believed would fit a big cockroach.

He let them finish his dinner. Like most lower animals, the pecking order was enforced brutally.

"How would you like a share of my food every night?" the Copper asked.

"This much?" a rat with reddish ears asked.

"Sometimes more. Less, if I'm famished."

"Rolling in it," another said. "Yes, yes!"

"I count thirty-one of you," the Copper said.

"If you say. We just call it the mob," the rat with red ears said.

"Well, if any more than this number come, I'll eat the stragglers. Now, in return for your food you have to do a little work. Seems like you all know every nook and cranny in this tower. I'd like to know more about the dragons here, and the humans who work with them. Who fights with whom, who mated with which dragonelle."

"Just dodge dragons, don't listen to their gossip," Red Ears said.

"Start. That is, if you want a choice selection of my dinner."

The rats, in their greedy way, brought back memories of the bats he'd traveled with through the Lower World with Fernadad and his family. But he'd learned his lesson and didn't become close to any of the individuals.

Each day he counted the number rushing to his food, and brought his tail down hard to scare away the extras bringing up the rear. The rats were ninnies who couldn't count—their numbering ascended "one, pair, mob." Therefore anyone who wasn't first or second to the food feared being eaten himself, so they all rushed out of the walls like a living carpet when he called them to dinner.

After they stripped the meat, they gnawed bones and told him of the doings in the tower. Much of it was garbled—"wide wings fighting lopside, luck in for fooding"—and he had to repeat questions to put together a sensible answer. But it diverted his mind from nerving himself for the future.

Most of the gossip they brought was useless. The rats paid very close attention to the biological cycles of the dragons of the tower, for solid dragon-waste was almost as good as a filched meal. According to the disgusting stories of the rodents, dragon-droppings made for a fine meal, being a perfect mélange of the odds and ends the dragons ate, with hides and cartilage conveniently digested.

Though it was useful knowing which dragon was constipated, and therefore irritable and to be avoided if you didn't like an angry bash of a territorial tail as you climbed up to take in some sun and air.

He took a short flight with a dragon named Skystreak, a thin-framed male whose usual employment was sending messages from Hypatia to its reclaimed colonies across the Inland Ocean. The Copper thought it strange that there were no dragons of the Empire willing to take that duty. Perhaps NoSohoth didn't like the idea of another dragon of the Empire handling his mail. NoSohoth always had at least three coinmaking schemes behind his back at any one moment of his life.

Or it was a convenient way for this Skystreak to serve as an agent, reporting on the activities of the Dragon Tower of Juutfod.

Skystreak didn't seem like the sort of dragon NoSohoth would choose as a spy. He was fidgety and inattentive when not flying and kept up a steady stream of chatter that would do the most gossipy old dragon-dame credit.

"All the barbarian tribes right up against Juutfod are the weaklings, little clans that lost out in some war or other. They know the Northerns—as the men of Juutfod like to call themselves, not Hypatians but not barbarians, either—will take alarm at the approach of a war-bent tribe and fight. The best of them serve in the tower, thinking it's glamorous. They usually quit within a year when they see that most of the coin goes down dragon gullets and the workers spend most of their time moving food in and dragoncast out. South of here it's actually less densely populated, even though it's Hypatian territory, because of barbarian raids. Good country for herding, if you can keep the wolves down and the Red Mountain dwarfs from bagging your lambs. There's a scattering of Ironriders who have settled in the woods and are doing well; a few of them even found their way to Juutfod and married. Good to get some fresh blood in the man-strains, don't you think? Juutfod used to be a good trade port, but the local thane—yes, they adopted the Hypatian title—he started leveling dockage or demurrage or some man-word so the merchant houses pulled up stakes. Fishing and lobstering's good here, Gettel says it's all the dragoncast dumped in the bay. The fishermen do their smoking and potting out on the barrier islands to keep the thane's hands out of their pockets. Fishermen think it's good luck to toss a fish to a dragon and they pull up some big blue-tops with red meat, very tasty. If you like mutton you're better off getting it straight from the herdsmen . . ."

On and on it went. The Copper simply enjoyed the salty smell of the Inland Ocean and the strong, steady wind that made flying easier with a fixed-open joint. He re-promised himself that he'd settle with Natasatch within smelling distance of the ocean, if he ever saw their reunion come to fruition.

After his first week, the rats finally brought him an interesting tidbit.

"Down-belows extra-extra fooding," this rat said. The Copper found him harder to understand than Red Ears, mostly because he spoke through a mouthful of boiled potato.

"Who are the down-belows?"

"Cave dragons. No wallspace. Eat rat-folk."

"I'm sorry to hear that. Are you saying there are dragons in a cave beneath the tower?"

"Maybe so not like you. Swim dragons, crawl dragons."

The Copper gave up and decided to investigate.

It took him a while to find the correct cave down. He ended up following a set of rails for a wheeled cart, such as the dwarfs used in their mines, adopted by the dragons and other underground races. A food cart made the trip down every other day.

He spoke to the men who drove the cart. It turned out there was no great secret about the other dragons. They just weren't housed in the tower because they didn't fly. The men called the underground dragons the "pensioners"—most of them were dragons who, because of wounds and injury, could no longer fly.

It was gloomy in the underground. There were a few attempts to grow cave-moss, but it hardly glowed enough to reveal itself. Maybe salt air wasn't good for it. He followed the food cart into a larger chamber, bow-shaped so that dripping water pooled at the center. Dragon perches, some natural and some cut, punctuated each side of the chamber like the holes of a human flute.

The cart-men halted their load and rang a bell. Gettel was fond of bells.

As the ringing faded, he heard a familiar sound in the darkness. Grinding teeth, followed by a yawn from the first alcove on the right.

"Shadowcatch, can that be you?" he asked.

Two eyes popped open wide. "My Tyr!" the black dragon said.

He'd met the enormous Shadowcatch in battle on the other side of the Inland Ocean. Eventually the black had become his bodyguard. He was the only dragon to remain overtly loyal to him after he had resigned the title of Tyr.

"That's all done with, don't you remember?" the Copper asked, regretting the choke that found its way into his voice.

Shadowcatch emerged. He was as huge as ever, but one wing hung crooked. "For me, sir, it's the rest that's done. Truth be told, you're my Tyr, the Tyr, until my last breath escapes."

"What brought you here? Surely not the comforts of a home-cave."

He looked at the dank walls. "Not the best of accommodations, are they? Truth be told, there's not a dragon down here that doesn't deserve better, but we're charity cases these days. We're the tower guard, and that's about all we're good for. Or tunnel-fighting. Our flying days are over, and it's this or starve in the forest and have the wolves scatter our bones."

"Who are these dragons?"

"All veterans of the Wizard at the Isle of Ice, sir. We did a bit of mercenary work with the barbarian chieftains since, but that's the only action I've seen since washing up here."

Back in the Lavadome, a flightless dragon could still do tunnel-duty. But of course this peninsula was far removed from the strange underground byways he knew.

The Copper sniffed the gristle and fish guts the barrow-men were laying out for the dragons to eat. "I hope that's not all you get, Shadowcatch."

"It's expensive to feed us, even on fish meal. We're ravenous for cattle or swine, but that's saved for the fliers, and none of them feel much like passing a quarter down for charity. Flying dragons get the best of everything here."

There had to be a better use for healthy but flightless dragons than sitting in a dark hole.

"Will you introduce me?"

Shadowcatch inflated his long lungs. "Hey, you kindling lighters, this is my old Tyr. His name's RuGaard. Don't mind the scars—he's sharp and quick still. He and I came north together, a dozen years or so back."

The dragons, who'd devoured their meager mouthfuls, raised their heads.

"Here's Red Lightning, a fast, tough dragon in the sky. He can still do a dragon-dash like a first-fire hatchling. He's in charge of the groundeds. Over there we have old Thunderwing. He broke the bowline and capsized three ships in the big fight with the elven ocean city, back in the days of the great sacks. Fourfoes—we call him the Blind Ripper these days—lost his eyesight to a dwarf, but there's no one who knows the smell of them better, and he can hear an arrow coming out of the dark before it hits. Corpsecount, Horseflinger, Wardog . . ."

The list went on, earthy, human-tongue names with deadly deeds. There were sixteen dragons including Shadowcatch.

The Copper wondered at the names. They were all mature dragons; if you added them all up there must have been a thousand or more years of life among them. AuRon had once told a tale of the Wizard of the Isle of Ice and the dragons he'd collected and bred. Most of them had been given such names with meaning in the human tongue.

They looked healthy enough. They must not spend all their days in this chamber, or they'd have thin and chalk-edged scale. "You all look fit enough. What do you do for exercise?"

"Swim. There's a decent-sized tunnel for sluicing out the waste. Dragons produce a powerful lot of it, sometimes more than the tide can handle. We help push it out into the Inland Ocean and have a swim and some sun on the Outer Rocks. Good crabbing round the sluice, too. The carapaces are good for the digestion."

If only they could fly! This number was half the size of the old Aerial Host, and Shadowcatch the Black was a proven fighter. If he said they were good, the Copper could trust his old bodyguard's esteem. They'd have Nilrasha out of her refuge in no time.

"I'm sorry, Shadowcatch. I really should have come looking for you before this."

"What, and risk death? If you don't mind me asking, sir, what are you doing out and breaking your exile?"

"I believe NiVom broke it first when he tried to kill me on the Isle of Ice, so I don't feel bound by it. But to answer your question, I'm trying to puzzle out a way to retrieve my mate. I'm determined to get her back or die trying. Life is too lonely without her."

"Find another mate," Horseflinger said. "A piece of green back's not so hard to come by."

"We're not talking to you," Shadowcatch said. "And when he does, show a little respect, or I'll tie your ears together to remind you to keep a civil tone. Tyr RuGaard once commanded hundreds of dragons."

The Copper put himself between the two of them and accidentally knocked over the feeding cart. Smelly fish juice rose from the mess, hopefully dampening the males' smell to one another and cooling their heads. "Your wing never healed, Shadowcatch? I'm sorry."

Shadowcatch lifted the crippled member and looked at it curiously as if it were a cat suddenly perched on his shoulder. "Oh, I'm not the first grounded dragon and I won't be the last."

"My own mate can no longer fly, as you recall."

That caused a stir among the flightless dragons. Some pricked up their ears and began to pay attention. The Copper saw a glimmer of hope. This might be the core of the force he needed . . .

"Fine lady and a fine Queen nonetheless," Shadowcatch said.

"What ever happened on the Isle of Ice?"

"Had a merry game with that beast Ouistrela, my Tyr. She saw the island as hers more than the Empire's, and when she wasn't hunting me to pull out my throat, she was shooting fire at our—or rather at the dragons of the Empire. Hypatians thought about establishing a fishing village for cod-drying and whale oil and whatnot, but they lost boats in the fogs—or at least that's how it seemed to them. What was really happening was Ouistrela was swimming up under them and knocking holes in them or tearing off rudders. Clever old stump."

"How do you know she's the one who was sinking them?"

"Bit of a long story, my Tyr."

"Let's have it." The Copper had little else to do and it was so pleasant to see old Shadowcatch, he would be happy to hear fishing stories from the fat old black.

"Well, we came to sort of a stalemate, see. Most of the wolves, they knew I was friends with that brother-gray of yours, so they took my side of things, you might say. They kept me abreast of where she was and what she was doing. She had the blighters on her side and if they spotted me they sent her a report. We usually each knew what part of the island the other was on, and kept away from each other. It's a big island—wasn't that hard to do.

"I had information that she was hunting around a glacier-pool way off from the blighters, so I snuck up the glacier and dug into some loose soil the glacier had pushed down the mountainside. When she was snuffling around, following some goat tracks, I jumped out of the loam and had her, or so I thought.

"We took a bit of a tumble down the mountainside and ended up in the glacier pool. Next thing I knew, we were—mated, I guess you call it. I'm not sure when the fighting died down and the mating began, but it seemed well along before I noticed."

The Copper snorted. He'd heard many bawdy jokes in his days in the Drakwatch, about a young winged member fighting so hard in an exercise against a Firemaid that she ended up fertilized. He always assumed such stories had some basis in truth, but this was the first time he'd heard it proven out.

"You're not still on the island, I note."

"Soon as the mating was over, so was the mating, if you understand me, my Tyr. I heard from the wolves she did have a clutch, a small one. One of the blighters sent me a message saying that if I wanted to see my offspring well fed and thriving, I should quit devouring so many sheep and goats and go live on one of the outer islands. Too windy and cold for me, so

I swam here. I used to fly mercenary for Red Hair—that's what I was doing when we met, at that battle."

"The hardest fight of my life, Shadowcatch."

"Aye, I'm not often bested. Red Hair's gray now, but she found me a place with the groundeds. You know, she calls us the 'tower guard,' but we don't earn our keep. I think she just keeps us around because she's carrying a soft spot in her heart for dragons."

"Better a soft spot in the heart than in the head, I suppose. I've sometimes wondered if that's my problem."

He happened upon Gettel as she left a meal with her human staff and mentioned that he'd visited the pensioners.

"Ahh, flying dragons don't go down there much."

"Why not?"

"Same reason as they don't bring new recruits to the lodge for crippled soldiers in the Hypatian legions, I suppose. No one likes being reminded of what might befall them."

The Copper found himself joining with the "groundeds," as Shadowcatch styled them, rather than idling in the tower, learning names and assignments as the aerial dragons came and went.

He had to admire Gettel's setup, but he wondered if it would die with her. All business of the tower flowed through her hands, yet she was childless and only had a rather brittle-looking old elf to assist her. He asked Shadowcatch what he thought would happen when she was sent on a raft out into the Inland Ocean, or whatever the Juutfod custom for disposal of their honored dead was.

"We're in better shape than most days. There's going to be a fight with some dwarfs. There's an old grudge between them and the barbarian chieftains, and the dwarfs are up to their usual cattle-stealing tricks. We've got an upriver swim ahead of us, as soon as the melt's full up. Plenty of salmon to eat on the way. We'll need the oily fish, too; that cursed river is cold."

The Copper tried to learn who had commissioned the raid on the dwarfs, but was stymied. He even took it to Gettel, but she offered only that the dwarfs had made old enemies and that while they were hungry and short on everything but determination, they had a great deal of wealth at their disposal. They'd come to the surface to steal, but not to trade.

The Copper smelled a rat, and it wasn't one of his nightly dinner companions. As Tyr, he'd raked up reasons for enough campaigns to recognize the throat-clearing that came before the battle cry.

They exercised together a good deal. The Copper even suggested a few training games he'd learned in the Lavadome's Drakwatch.

Had they only been able to fly he would have put them up against even the best of the Aerial Host. There wasn't any of the jealousy, the pride that caused difficulties between the dragons of the Host. These dragons, perhaps because they no longer flew, were beyond jostling for place. They relied on and supported each other, as when the Blind Ripper had difficulty finding his way in an unfamiliar patch of open ground and

Thunderwing kept up a steady rustle of his good wing for the sightless dragon to align on.

He taught them a few tricks for tunnel-fighting, like using the walls or ceiling to bounce one's fire around an angle, or how to wedge a dead dragon in a tunnel so he's most difficult to remove from the far side.

The Copper never learned why they left that particular day. Perhaps some shepherd spotted the dwarfs as they used the entrance to their tunnel. Perhaps payment for eliminating the bandits arrived. Perhaps Gettel finally decided she could trust him in a fight.

They stalked out in a file on a fine summer day, each dragon's nose a tongue-flick behind the tail tip of the dragon ahead. About half the expedition was made up of the flightless dragons, led by Shadowcatch.

Dragons are speedy on the march. The Copper had learned that fact to advantage when moving against an enemy who expected him to come from the air. Their long stride and muscles conditioned to the steady exertion of flying meant they could cover ground as quickly as human cavalry and could climb mountainsides that horses could never attempt.

So they shot toward the spine of the Red Mountains at a steady three horizons a day. The winged dragons flew in food and some barrels of water flavored with wine and sweet spirits, for Gettel knew dragons had a taste for wine and liked to keep their spirits up on the march.

It was the Copper's first experience with real evergreen

woods. He'd known a few pines in the mountains in the south, particularly when he served as Upholder in Anaea. There they clung to rock crevices, lonely and twisted in the wind.

These pines were thick as the bristling hairs on a wild boar's back and straight as Hypatian pillars, with branches sticking out in circles like wagon-wheel spokes. And the aroma! It made him feel vital and alive again. Clean and innocent as when he'd first hatched from his egg. If he could ever free Nilrasha, he'd take her to pine-woods and let her clean her nostrils with the faint turpentine smell.

As they traveled into the Red Mountains, the Copper thought he might be descending rather than ascending the foothills, for as the mountains loomed larger, their track remained level on one shoulder. A team of hominid guides led them, including a pair of humans, an elf—and female at that—and a dwarf. They were a grizzled and haggard lot, just the type to float between barbarian lands and the Empire.

For all their speed, dragons don't take to marching, as the Copper had learned in his first year in the Drakwatch. Flying, yes. Short sprints—the surprisingly explosive dragon-dash—certainly. But plodding on hour after hour is oxen work, not dragon. They became irritable and quarrelsome.

The Copper, to divert their minds, had each one describe his favorite food. Most described the tender fats on certain quarters of beef. But not Thunderwing. Thunderwing had a strange scale color pattern, a watery blue covered in tiny white flecks like windblown snow. He claimed his favorite food was corn.

"For its indestructibility?" Shadowcatch said. "It passes out the other end much as it entered." The others expressed similar flavors of disbelief: *perhaps ground and used for breading, it makes fine stuffing, as it absorbs juices like good cotton paper.*

"Ha!" Thunderwing said. "It's my favorite because so much other game grows fat on it. Deer, pheasants, elk, oh, and the pigs. There is nothing like a corn-fed pig." He smacked his lips.

"Well done, Thunderwing," the Copper said. "Thunder-wing, philosopher-king."

The others found so much humor in that, it occupied them until the next meal-break on the march. They looked for excuses to point something out to their "philosopher-king."

They idled for a day while their scouts selected an approach to the dwarf-exit.

"We have a lot riding on this," Shadowcatch said. "These dwarfs have been an irritant to the barbarians in the north with their thefts of livestock. They must have made powerful enemies in Hypatia, or even among the Empire's dragons, for they're paying for this job."

"How do you know that?" the Copper asked. Gettel had continued to be cagey about revealing their employers in this job until the last, though according to the other dragons, that had never been the case before.

"Strict orders! No eating of any kind of valuables. It's stolen property. It all goes to the scouts, to be returned to the commissioners."

To the Copper, it smacked of assassination. All the orders

about returning stolen property might be a vomited-up smoke-screen.

The dwarf-exit was well concealed inside a rotted-out cottonwood tree. Here the campaign met its first difficulty, as the hole was sized for a hominid, not a dragon. The guide-dwarf, the loser in a feud with these others, apparently, went down the hole and returned to say that it widened out just a short drop down, and appeared to widen farther into a cave that smelled of bats.

So the dragons set to work moving earth and pulling boulders up by using the bole of the dead and now uprooted cottonwood.

"With all this racket we're making, they'll have a good head start on us if they choose to flee," the Copper said.

"They're deep, if I know dwarfs," Red Lightning said. "I just hope our trackers don't fail us."

"We want the dwarfs as much as you do," Ghastmath, the human scout-leader replied, testing the edge of his oiled blade. He was gray-haired and coughed a great deal in the morning when he woke, but still hearty-looking. He had the wild and weathered look of a barbarian.

"Do you trust these two-legs, my Tyr?" Shadowcatch asked under his breath.

"I don't trust any humans," the Copper said.

"How about elves?" Halfmoon, the female elf, asked. She had the caramel skin of the south, such as he'd seen in Bant. Her hair had acorns in it, though whether they were wound into it or growing out of it he couldn't say. A raven sat on her shoulder with eyes shut, as though napping.

"I've known only one, as a hatchling. She was kindly, but

not so kindly that she saved me from a crippling," the Copper said.

The dwarf approached. "I think we can fit a dragon in now," he said, as he shook dirt and bits of root from his beard.

The cave smelled a bit like skunk, but that might be a dwarf-trick to keep bears out. In any case, they were soon past the skunk smell and into a cave whose floor was slick with guano. They waded through a bowed water-catch, then climbed down a short chute and reached the tunnel proper. This was dug, not natural formation. There were fewer crevices for bats to occupy, so the droppings thinned out.

The Copper was excited to be in action again. The tension that comes from a mix of fear and anticipation of a fight made him feel alive in a way that he hadn't experienced since well before his exile.

"Let's get past the bats," Red Lightning said. "Once we're out of the stink, we can send our scouts ahead again."

Their scouts examined some obscure marks at a corner. The elf picked up a piece of nail, which she identified as belonging to a boot.

"We're in a bit of the old Dwarf-Kingdoms, unless I'm mistaken," the dwarf said.

The Copper smelled dwarf more than guano now. They were close.

"Why do we still need the scouts?" he asked.

"I don't mind their help, sir. They're the ones who are paying, seems like they're eager to come to grips with the dwarfs. Since spoils are to be shared, they're probably along to make sure no coin gets eaten before it can be counted."

The grizzled ex-barbarian and the elf consulted the dwarf at the next turn of the tunnel. A smaller branch tunnel led down. It had a half-finished look and was small enough that even a dwarf would have to stoop.

"Leave it," the elf finally said, making a mark with a piece of chalk at the intersection.

The scouts found a hidden door in what looked like a piece of tunnel collapse. A pile of heavy and sharp-edged stones balanced precariously at the top made the cave-in look lethal to investigate.

"Something smells. I don't mean the bats," the Copper said.

Shadowcatch sniffed in the direction of the probing hominids, as though he could detect a betrayal by smell. "Right. Well then, if fighting starts, sir, keep an eye on them. Let me and Red Lightning and the Blind Ripper worry about the dwarfs. We're used to handling the front. It's my flanks I want watching."

The Copper didn't have a chance to respond. With a crash that must have been heard in the Lavadome, one of the boulders fell into the hole, revealing the entrance to a larger cave.

The scouts consulted with each other, and a human who was missing his right hand—the Copper remembered he was named Fyrebin; he'd stood out during the introductions because of the lost hand—defied the others and refused to enter first.

"I thought I heard a voice," the old barbarian said.

Shadowcatch pushed up to the entrance to the cave and the Copper followed. He sensed a vast open space on the other side of the phony fall. "Me and the Blind Ripper will go forward. Tunnelbreakers. It's tough duty, but someone has to do it."

"I'll come along," the Copper said to Shadowcatch. "I'll take your place. You manage things with the rest. You know them. They've never fought with me."

Shadowcatch ground his teeth in thought. "I never questioned you before, but now I must, my Tyr. What do you have in mind?"

"I know the sounds and smells of dwarfs. I'm also a good deal smaller than you. If the Blind Ripper starts thrashing about, I can get out of his way. If things go disastrously for us, you can jam your body in this tunnel and delay until the rest find some defensive ground—I'd suggest the other side of the water-wash."

"What do you think?" Shadowcatch asked, tapping the Blind Ripper.

The blinded dragon just shrugged. His dry sockets were disturbing. He tended to draw his lips back from his teeth and then cover them again in a nervous habit, or perhaps it was due to the injury that had robbed him of his eyes.

A grinding noise behind. This time it wasn't Shadowcatch's teeth.

It was a stone, as big as a roof and thick as winter ice on a shallow pond. It began to roll down a smoothed track. His gaze anticipated its track—it would strike the end of its track just beyond the opening to the tunnel, fitting into its position as neatly as a dragon's *griff* behind the jawline.

It pressed down as if the mountain above added to its bulk. He could only slow it, not stop it.

He found the strength for a moment.

"Dwarfs all around," the Blind Ripper said, backing up.

"Out, back to the tunnel," he grunted, slapping at the gap with his tail so the Blind Ripper could find it.

"Out! Out! *Out!*" he called to the Blind Ripper.

He saw the blind dragon's tail vanish. Shadowcatch stuck his head in, saw the rolling stone with the Copper pressing the length of his body against it, scrabbling with his arms.

"Run for your lives. I'm done for," the Copper called.

He'd taken one too many chances. Sooner or later, the luck ran out, or fate settled on you. Exhausted, he let the stone slip at last into the socket.

He turned around, his back to the gigantic wheel of a door.

A mass of dwarfs, fifty or more, stood with axes held before them. The closest was the height and width of a baby troll.

"What'll we do, sir? Eat him raw or smoke him over his own flame?" one of them asked the frontmost dwarf.

Chapter 6

It was easy enough for AuRon to sneak into the great cave of Old Uldam. He'd lived there throughout much of his adolescence and early adulthood as sort of a tribal mascot for the blighters, who thrived thickly on the more hospitable south slopes of the mountains.

He knew each ruin in the old cave, once the principal city of the blighters during their glory days of dominance. Those ancient blighter kings had carved a city out of living rock, taking advantage of an arresting geographic feature, a sort of overhang in the mountain that created a great cave-mouth beneath. Through years of patient excavation, they'd enlarged the cave, keeping it supported by wide columns like teeth in a vast mouth, fangs bared to their enemies on the coasts of the Sunstruck Sea.

Wistala had lived here as well. Then his daughter became the Protector, saving it from a war of conquest from the Dragon Empire. His family's fate seemed bound to the place.

It had been a long, frustrating journey to his old home. He'd probably delayed longer than he should have, but he wanted to make sure that the dragon bodies hadn't been quietly burned in some thick patch of woods or dragged into a swamp and covered with vines. So he investigated every trail, every burned patch of lightning-struck wood, and plunged into more than one marshy dogleg off the river to feel around for dragon bones.

He met the barges at last, making their careful way back down the river, loaded with thick trunks of wood from the ever-shifting logging camps. The barges were making poor progress, with the river falling as summer wore on; sometimes they had to dam the river to put enough water under their flat-bottoms to float. He recognized them by their low timbers—they were probably chosen as the easiest vessels from which to roll a dead body over the side.

He found two sets of promising signs. One was a number of trails and drag-marks leading to Old Uldam, the other a well-trod trail to the logging camp that showed signs of heavy burdens being moved through the brush.

The logging camp trail could be explained by timber. The other one, headed east to the mountains of Old Uldam, disappeared at the first ridge. Perhaps some blighter cattle had been driven down to the riverside, tribute to the Empire.

He paused at that ridge and looked at the familiar spine of the mountains of Old Uldam. Birds, frightened into silence by his arrival, started their chirping again as he pondered.

Why this mad concern about dragon bodies? The dragons had been killed because they were political enemies of NiVom and Imfamnia, or simply useless mouths. Their deaths would bring on the fury needed to take a war to the princedoms of the Sunstruck Sea.

But if that was the case, why go to all the bother with the bodies? No, there must be something deeper going on. If the deaths were simply to inflame their relatives, a fierce oration by NiVom as the heap of bodies burned behind him would serve him better. Flames and memorial words could put fire in hearts weary of battle. There must be some other reason. Was something about the wounds revealing? So many dragons killed, so quickly. The only thing he'd ever seen slay dragons like that was the poison from a venomer.

His brother had told him that venomers were considered so deadly, the Lavadome once put them to death. In later years, they underwent a delicate operation to the roof of their mouth that rendered them harmless, though each clan was thought to hide one or two in reserve for emergencies, in case another civil war broke out.

With what little he knew of Imfamnia, anything was possible. His brother said she was a silly, simple dragon. He had his doubts after hearing her speak to Wistala. But then, being a clever conversationalist to extract a little gossip and executing a murder for profit were hatchlings and venerables away from each other. But then, she may have just sold the bodies for a few extra gems to embed in her fringe. That would explain much. If so, and he could get the evidence of it, he could bring down NiVom and his Jade Queen both.

Whenever he wondered how deeply Natasatch was involved in Imfamnia's plots, he pushed the thoughts from his mind.

Another thought rose, unbidden. If NiVom and Imfamnia fell, Natasatch might fall with them. Clearly she was thought to be in Imfamnia's close coterie and the behavior of the other dragons at the feast proved it. She'd been protected during the bloodbath by her closeness to Imfamnia. Outraged families and clans hungry for vengeance might not be willing to listen to the finer points of knowledge and action in determining guilt.

No, if he did learn anything, he would have to put Natasatch quietly in hiding before acting.

The woods on the east bank of the river proved empty of everything save game and a few blighter hunting camps. He stopped at each and asked if they'd seen any dragons, living or dead, and after they got over their startle at being addressed in their own tongue they told him that the only dragons they knew of were the pair in the ruin, their Mountain King and the Recluse.

Istach wouldn't be called Mountain King by even the most ignorant blighter, so his daughter must be the Recluse.

Istach had always been an odd dragonelle. Natasatch had once believed that she was a nest-clinger, a dragon who would stick close to home and never venture into the wide world. His mate had been partly right—she'd planted herself in Old Uldam.

After a careful examination of the southern slopes of the Bissonian Scarpes, the blighter-filled mountains that were once the heart of their empire at its height, he entered the great cave of Old Uldam. He sought out his daughter in his old refuge, NooMoahk's cave.

He found her in the library. It was smaller than he remembered it, though whether this was due to his being used to the grandeur of Scabia's delvings in the Sadda-Vale, his having grown, or the library being emptied he couldn't decide.

Istach seemed all at once pleased, relieved, and concerned to see him, making her look like a dragonelle with ants digging under her scales.

"I'm not the Protector anymore, Father," she said, fidgeting. "NiVom and his mate didn't think I was managing. So they sent out FuPozat—the blighters call him Fusspot. He's a copper-colored dragon with an off-balance horn on his crest. Fusspot made a mess of things by dividing each herd in two, half for the Empire, the other half for the tribe, and pretty soon the blighters' herds started suffering from mysterious maladies, with a good half of them dropping dead. Actually they were hiding them in the jungle, where they couldn't be easily observed from the air. I did my best to smooth things over, and the region's productive again, but only just. There's been some raiding. Fusspot's in a state of constant panic that more blighters will turn outlaw and Old Uldam will revolt and give NiVom an excuse to reduce it to ashes."

AuRon thought this curious. His brother claimed NiVom was one of the most intelligent dragons he'd ever met. Of course, intelligence and sense weren't always allies. "NiVom would rather have no cattle than a few?"

"I was never a satisfactory Protector," she said. "I let the blighters be. Tyr NiVom wishes tribute—cattle, metals, grains, thralls. . . . We can offer some cattle and sheep. These mountains have copper and silver, though it would take dwarfs for Old Uldam to be truly rich in them. As for grains, the blighters are not great farmers. They 'sow wild' so their herds may graze and they can gather in a pinch. Thralls? Blighters will happily headhunt, but all the tribes of these mountains are only too happy to ally under the dragon banner. The men of the princedoms to the south are on the other side of a trackless jungle, and the nomads to the north in the lands of the Ironriders have a desert lying between, the waste of Anklemere. Only to the west do they have neighbors, and that's the Empire. So no thralls from Old Uldam, except for a few criminals and troublemakers the chieftains wish to be rid of. Fusspot's happy to oblige."

"Do you get along with him?"

"No, not at all. He seems to think that just because we're male and female, out here in the middle of what he calls nowhere, we should mate. I don't mean hatchlings and all that, just mating for the voluptuousness of it. 'Informal mating,' he calls it. Even if I had never heard one word out of his mouth, I wouldn't find him particularly attractive, but now that I know what little there is of his mind, I keep as far away as I can. Not that he doesn't come sniffing about down here every few weeks despite me snapping at his snout."

"Why would they send such a dragon out here as Protector?"

"Maybe NiVom owes him a favor. Still, he's a terrible dragon for a Protector of a border province. He's prickly and he overreacts to everything. He burned a trade caravan in the desert, thinking it was an invading force, and he has his blighters kill the white-jacket men of the Sunstruck Sea when they catch them in the southern jungle, even if they're just taking wood and bamboo."

NiVom seemed determined to start a war with the princedoms. Maybe this prickly FuPozat would put the flame of his personality to the tinder of chafing between the blighters and the men of the princedoms.

Istach had vast wooden racks where she salted, herbed, and dried various fruits, vegetables, and meats. She also had a wall full of brining barrels. Evidently she didn't like leaving the library, and was unwilling to depend on the blighters for her food. They reclined to a meal of her smoked pork-skins and dragon-flame-braised beef tongue, accompanied by dried apple slices.

"The fate of dragons and the fate of the Empire are tangled. Hard to say whether this is a death grip or an embrace."

"I know which way my brother would argue."

"We could just flee, you know."

"Become wild dragons? I'm told that's been happening more lately. Dragons just disappear, usually mated pairs ready for their eggs. That's when the instinct is strongest.

"I've been following a barge—several barges. Loaded with the corpses of dragons. I believe they were headed here."

"I don't know anything about that, Father. But then, I rarely hear anything down here. Even the blighters don't bother to visit the cave much, with their idol gone."

"Where did it go?"

"I'm not sure. All I know is that these stones, their flicker faded as the days passed."

AuRon looked into the stones. He'd examined them, at leisure, when he lived in the cave. Sometimes he'd seen flashes of himself looking at the stone—not as a mirror would show but from another angle.

He thought he saw swirling colors now. Imagination?

He stared deeper. A figure moved in the stone—two-legged, a hominid, not draconic. It played in the stone like a shadow caught on the surface of a rippling pool. The figure faded and he saw a swirl of orange and red light, like slow-moving flame.

The Lavadome.

Were these crystals still drawing some kind of power from the old statue they'd so long accompanied? He wished he'd listened more to Wistala and DharSii. They were both interested in the crystal the Red Queen had given him when he served as her messenger to the Lavadome. They questioned him closely and he answered honestly, and afterward asked them what they were looking for.

The Lavadome, the eyepiece, the statue—they're all connected, DharSii had said. *If we could assemble all the pieces, I wouldn't wonder that we'd experience a revelation.*

Interesting, but he had to return to the matter at hand.

The dragon bodies weren't just dumped in the river. The question nagged—why would they transport them so far? There was nothing between here and the Empire save a good deal of rough terrain. Perhaps on the journey they stripped off the flesh, tanned the hides, and boiled the bones. He'd heard that hominid sorcerers and priests considered dragon bones powerful, as either ingredients or icons. Perhaps he was on a fool's errand after all.

No, it wasn't like sailors to do anything but move cargo. Their vessels were chronically short of hands, and disassembling a dragon would be an enormous task. Would anyone even trust them with the work? He'd been on ships and barges before. They must have simply delivered their cargo to some station or other. There were logging camps, a defunct mine. . . .

They could hide dragon bodies in a mine, he supposed. Salt might even preserve the bodies, retaining the value of the flesh, though he knew of no salt mine. When he'd lived here the blighters had just wrung salt from a clay pit where the mountainside met the jungle.

"There is a mine about somewhere," AuRon said. "I remember Wistala mentioning it."

"Yes, I think it was an old prospecting camp of the Ghioz, though the blighters maintained they were just working the mine so near the blighter mountains in the hope of provoking a war. It's this side of the river, not far off it."

He knew the ridgeline with the mine Istach spoke of once she described the topography in detail. He'd often hunted in those hills and woods when feeding NooMoahk and after he "inherited" NooMoahk's old cave.

So with a half-full belly—it didn't do to explore on too full a stomach, since digestion slowed the blood—he thanked his daughter and set out. He kept to the ground when he left the cave, taking dusty paths through the old ruins where once he'd played hide-and-seek with Hieba, just in case the new Protector was out and up early. According to Istach he ate hearty meals during the night and slept through the mornings, but AuRon had a lifetime of cautious habits spent guarding his thin skin.

The summer sun was hot. AuRon had forgotten how fierce it was in these mountains after the solstice. He gained altitude and found some cool air.

Ah, there was the lake, and the ridge. The mine must be between—

Movement behind caught his eye. A copper dragon was coming fast on his tailline. For a moment, AuRon thought it was his brother—they were of similar size and color.

AuRon executed a rising half loop to gain altitude on the Protector and face him.

"I'm neither assassin nor thief," AuRon called. "I intend no harm to you or what's yours."

"Think you'll take my title away, do you?" the copper dragon, who could only be FuPozat, bellowed. "I paid good coin, my whole inheritance, and no interloper, however beloved of the blighters, is going to take it away." This speech left him panting and he banked to come at AuRon from the side.

The fool had missed his chance. If he'd been careful, he could have followed AuRon on a line between him and the sun and dove out of the light. Evidently he was a dragon not much used to hunting or fighting.

"What makes you think I'm claiming your title?"

"Word came in the predawn. Their old totem-dragon had

returned to claim his own. Stooped and gray old blighters tell stories from their childhood of your days here, how you ate of their cattle only at festivals, and say that peace and plenty are returning with you! They're feasting in their huts in your name!"

Foolish blighters. Well, it was Fusspot's own fault. If he was mismanaging the mountains so much that the blighters were slaughtering fat calves in hope of AuRon's return, perhaps Fusspot should levy a few less head in the name of the Empire.

In any case, rage had driven the Protector out of his senses. He was coming at AuRon like a crazed woodpecker, swinging in from whichever angle with no thought to altitude, wind, or AuRon's suppleness of wing and body.

If he hadn't been called to more important duties, he might have enjoyed toying with the enraged dragon. It was like playing dodge with a tortoise.

Each time Fusspot came at him, AuRon flapped hard and ascended. No scaled dragon could match him in a climb; thanks to the lightness of his frame, he was faster and could rise at a steeper angle.

"I'm no more of a threat to you than you are to me."

"Is that a challenge? I eat challenge and pass victory," Fusspot bellowed. AuRon decided that he wasn't necessarily stupid, just young and inexperienced. The Protector had finally figured out that in a fight you could use the prevailing wind to help you pick up altitude.

AuRon supposed that if he let himself laugh at such speeches, he might lose his wind. Good thing he was in training; had he had to do these steep climbs back in the Sadda-Vale, he might have grown winded.

He wondered at such a character winning a Protectorate. Perhaps the Dragon Empire was already cracking with decay. Such was the way of things. What dragons of ability and skill built, their legacies took for granted and mismanaged. It happened with hominids as well, even disciplined and tradition-bound dwarfs.

Just to vary the contest, AuRon closed his wings and fell. Fusspot turned hard and moved to intercept. AuRon worked his wingtips and adjusted his glide path to stay out of reach.

Fusspot saw his chance, sped up to match AuRon's fall, and spat the contents of his firebladder.

The fool! What dragon didn't know that you vented fire only when flying slow and level or in backing into a climb?

The droplets of burning liquid spread in the air and the dragon plunged headlong into his own flame.

He emerged from the cloud of black and orange with fire coating his face. His bellow of anger turned into a shriek of pain.

Fusspot rolled over, *griff* extended and wings beating at the flame on his face, and plunged toward the earth. For one bad moment AuRon thought he would meet his death impaled on the trees, but he must have sensed the ground approaching somehow, for he turned legs-down at the last second.

Still, he hit hard.

AuRon alighted near him, and saw Fusspot rubbing his face in the dirt. He was a sooty black to the shoulders.

"I'm blinded, I'm blinded!" Fusspot screamed.

AuRon threw his weight on the burned dragon's neck and craned around to check his face. He'd caught it worst around the lips and nose and his eyes were screwed shut against the pain. He would learn a good lesson from the pain, but AuRon didn't envy him it.

Fusspot forced one eye open with his claw and threw his weight around, trying to lash back with his tail, but AuRon kept him pinned at the neck.

"Your eyes are just a little scorched about the lids. You'll heal in a day or two, once the water-lids relax and retract."

AuRon ended up fetching Istach, after a panic attack from Fusspot that AuRon was going to abandon him to starve in the wilderness. By the time they returned, the copper dragon was squinting his way about the woods where he'd crashed.

For some reason, Fusspot made AuRon feel better about his brother than he had in years. Maybe it was meeting a similar-looking dragon, stupid and prickly. Suddenly it seemed that his brother had more good qualities than bad—provided one could forget the family history.

AuRon left Istach unhappily nursing the dragon Protector of Old Uldam and returned to the mine he'd spotted before being attacked.

It was decrepit and hadn't been disturbed in some time, judging from the brush on the ground and the fallen leaves. AuRon was about to resign himself to further searching the river when he noticed that the brush and leaves about the old mine opening weren't from the hillside. Nothing like them grew here, only in the lowlands off the ridges.

Someone had been scattering gathered vegetation to hide a

trail and hadn't noticed the change in plant life as they moved up the ridge to the mine. With eager fanning of his wings, AuRon blew aside the scattered detritus and found unmistakable signs of drag-marks. He sniffed about—death, certainly—and there was a green scale. Ants were stripping it of the fresh meat at its root.

AuRon felt a moment of pity for the poor dragonelle it had belonged to. The scale was cut and ground and given a dusting of silver; some female had dressed expensively for the party, perhaps to please her mate or to impress a new one. But she'd ended up as dead as a fallen sparrow, for a dusting of silver didn't help scale keep out blades, and the reason it grew long and jagged at the edge was to better link with the scale around it and wound jaws trying to rip out flesh.

There had been a time when he envied scale, but no amount of armor protected one from foolishness.

Steeling himself against carelessness and with every sense alive to shadow, smell, and echo, AuRon descended into the mine.

Chapter 7

If NiVom and Imfamnia expected the news of the massacre at the Grand Feast to arouse the dragons of the Lower World, they were greatly mistaken.

Instead, as near as Wistala could determine it, a sense of doom settled over the Lavadome, as though this bloodshed was just the first patter of rain in what would soon be a torrent. Of course, every dragon in the Lavadome was listless and dispirited, with the steady succession of "bleedings" so that the duty could be paid.

There was some halfhearted talk at Imperial Rock, she was told, especially among the Skotl, that it was time to settle accounts with the "pirates" infesting the jungles around the Sunstruck Sea. For pirates, the men of the princedoms of the Sunstruck Sea had a substantial kingdom, with so many inhabitants that even their rulers couldn't count them. The dealers in thralls flicked their tongues and *griff* at the thought of the slave trade, should the princedoms be humbled.

Perhaps the subdued reaction had more to do with the change in the dragons of the Lavadome. It had been vastly altered since she'd last been there.

When she'd last seen it, there were still seven contentious hills of dragons, the largest being Imperial Rock, with the Tyr's relations, a clan that went back to the end of the civil wars when Tyr Fehazathant and Queen Tighlia took over. There were parties of hatchlings engaged in play hunts and combats, feasts, bathing parties at the river ring just outside the Lavadome, young mated couples flying about, plus the herds of livestock, the clay pits filled with kern, and the thrall quarters. Everything felt a bit more spacious, the dragons said, now that so many were in the Upper World engaged in duties in one Protectorate or another.

Now the Lavadome seemed so empty it echoed. There were still vestiges of the three clans occupying their family hills. Most of the Skotl were in the Aerial Host or acting as palace guards in the Protectorate, the Wyrr were, and many Ankelenes had established themselves in the libraries and museums of Hypatia.

Of course many had died at the feast, but most of them were dragons of the Upper World. According to the Firemaids, the feast day celebrating the victory in Ghioz was an event that dragons who remembered the Tyrship of Wistala's brother used to celebrate his memory. Factions against NiVom and Imfamnia met on that day and used the meal as an excuse to organize and increase their numbers.

So it seemed the slaughter had served its purpose after all. It eliminated a good many dragons of an opposing faction and served as a warning to others.

Everyone looked tired and underfed. Wistala and Yefkoa, entering the Lower World, had seen vast pens of livestock waiting to be driven into the Lower World. They'd passed over a "drain drop" near Ghioz, where hundreds of pigs waited to be driven onto a cart floating in a rocky pool like a vast well. Yefkoa had explained that the water came by canal from the river. Then when the canal was shut, the draining water would gently lower the raft to a main artery in the Lower World, where the swine could be put on a barge. Meanwhile the canal filled another reservoir that would be opened to raise the raft again. It was an extraordinarily clever device dating back to the dwarfish kingdom that had once ruled in Ghioz.

She'd seen chests of salt, barrels of biscuits and root vegetables, brined this and dried that and smoked the other all passing into the Lower World, and very little of it seemed to find its way to the Lavadome. Either someone was getting monstrously rich diverting the flow, like the water-elevator developer, or there was a large population of dragons in the Lower World somewhere other than at the Lavadome.

"The tunneling thralls eat a lot. I know that," Yefkoa had said. "Whole nations have been enslaved and driven underground. They always need to be replaced. They sicken and die after a few years, even if they get fresh fruits and vegetables, as the Ankelenes demand."

As for the listlessness of the dragons she'd seen, Yefkoa had an answer for that as well. Each dragon had a "duty," in either coin or blood, that was collected at every change in seasons, as gauged by the sun. The Tyr's Demen Legion carried out the collections, filling cask after cask with dragon-blood—a Fire-maid told her it was mixed with wine to preserve it—and sending them off to one trade-port or another.

The demen had changed, too. They were taller now, lon-ger, with thicker skin and plate grown lumpy and craggy, like certain kinds of crustaceans. They had fishy, lifeless eyes shaded under heavy head-plates and they smelled like a plugged drain. Some of the more traveled dragons called them "the lobsters" because most of them were bright red about the carapace, with leading ranks adding gold paint to their plates to distinguish them from their soldiery.

They'd taken over many of the Firemaid duties in posts where thralls had to be worked. Dragon overseers could be begged and pleaded with, but demen were as merciless as ants.

That was the subject of her meetings with what remained of the Firemaids, at the old egg-refuge that dated back to the height of the civil war. Even NiVom and Imfamnia's dreaded messenger-gargoyles didn't dare enter it, for the Firemaids killed anyone but their own here. With Ayafeeia dead in Ghioz, much of her original purpose in coming to the Lavadome was lost. Ayafeeia had requested her presence, but had died before she could reveal her purpose. Ayafeeia, who'd grown up among the plots and plans of the Imperial Family, made a habit of not revealing her mind until the very last moment, and even then to only a trusted circle.

Wistala suspected it had to do with the dwindling and physical deterioration of the dragons in the Lavadome.

"We know she kept a few notes in her ears," Yefkoa said. "I've seen her slip bone-cases for scrolls in there. That would be a clue."

"Or compromising evidence," another Firemaid said.

DharSii had once told Wistala a story of a dwarf philosopher who said that a frog plunged into hot water would leap out, but if you heated the water slowly, he would happily sit until boiled alive. Tallwillow, the famous elvish recipe collector and food historian, said that was balderdash, but it's a sound philosophical point. If change comes slowly enough, even change for the worse, it meets less resistance than if it comes as a sudden shift.

She'd arrived in the Lavadome on the settled day of mourning for the dead. It was easy for her to disguise herself—she merely put on a good deal of face paint and hung black fabric from head and wings. DharSii himself wouldn't recognize her unless they touched noses and he saw her eyes through the mourning wrap.

She'd been expecting a long procession of murdered bodies, each followed by the family mourners and thralls. Nothing of the sort happened, just small memorial fires of burning scented oils or braziers where family members could lay something that reminded them of the one they were mourning—say, a favorite preparation of fish or a piece of fabric the color of the dead dragon's scale—and quietly watch it burn away.

Only one body had passed through the Lavadome, perhaps as effigy for the rest. SiHazathant, the male twin, had been borne in state to Imperial Rock at the center of the Lavadome.

For the rest, some curious relatives had come to sniff, and perhaps remove valuable earrings and scale decor.

Wistala pulled aside a shaven-headed Imperial Family thrall who trailed in the wake of the procession. He had a heavy canvas sack slung over his shoulder and his job was to pick up any of SiHazathant's scale that accidentally fell off.

"I thought there were dozens killed," she said to him. "Where are the other bodies?"

"They were put in a big tunnel closer to Ghioz," a human thrall said. "Only place that would let them lay out properly."

Wistala believed him. Or she believed that he thought what he told her was the truth. Somehow the thralls passed word around before even dragons could fly with the news, it seemed.

Wistala thought it important enough to find out where the bodies had gone that she bade her sisters in the Firemaids farewell.

"I go in search of the bodies from the feast massacre. Ayafeeia's, of course, is my main interest, but I am curious if the bodies bear some mark that would illuminate the true culprits."

"You'll have a job getting in," a Third-Oath said.

"Why all this digging?" a younger dragonelle with an anxiously flicking tongue asked. "The old demen hold at the Star Tunnel has space equal to what's been planned, and more. But it's off-limits."

"Off-limits?" Wistala asked. "What, to dragons?"

"Even the Firemaids."

"That's curious. What are the demen up to there, I wonder?"

"They migrated nearer to us. The demen live beyond the river ring, guarding the borders to the Lavadome. If you can call those brutes 'demen' anymore. The only one who goes there is Rayg, sometimes with NiVom and Imfamnia."

Wistala wanted to speak with Rayg. If anyone could give her an honest opinion about the cracks appearing in the Dragon Empire, it was their "First Thrall."

Flying to the top of Imperial Rock was still forbidden, so she went in the entrance for dragon-petitioners. It was crowded with dragons lining up to express their sorrow at the death of SiHazathant, so it was easy for her to disappear into the crowd. When a young drake page came in to announce five more names of those who'd won an audience with SiHazathant's sister, she nipped out down the low thrall passage that led to the kitchens.

She knew Imperial Rock well. Once in the kitchens, she grabbed a couple of tonguefuls of meat-broth and a stew joint—odds and ends the cooking thralls wouldn't report her for stealing, but it explained the presence of a dragonelle—then headed for one of the older passages up. Skulls of vanquished opponents still grinned down at her from the tunnels.

Up she climbed. Imperial Rock was empty enough to echo. She heard some noise down at the end where the training wing of the Aerial Host still resided, dragons and dragonelles freshly winged were encouraged to at least do a year in the Host so they could say that they'd faced death, as was expected of any dragon who wished for position and title.

For a human, Rayg had done extraordinarily well on both. He'd never quite won his freedom, for one reason or another, but there were many dragons with less wealth and influence than this particular thrall.

Rayg had built himself a niche that made him virtually irreplaceable. He possessed a rare mind, able to synthesize different facts under the sciences of different disciplines. He was part inventor, part sorcerer, part repairman. He'd designed the original wing joint that kept her brother functional, one way or another, across years of use. According to the Firemaids, he had a long backlog of projects, from better saddles for the dragon-riding men of the Aerial Host to a new mill for grinding grains and corns into better stock feed. The twins had surrendered much of the top of Imperial Rock to his workshops, laboratories, and libraries, and he seldom descended from an observatory he'd built at one end of the rock, sticking out and up from the narrow, arrowhead end of Imperial Rock like a broken mast on a ship.

"Don't stand under it," a thrall carrying water for the gardens warned. "He likes to drop stuff out his window to test new weapons for the Aerial Host. If you hear a whistle, you have about three seconds before a loud bang. Hug ground."

Two demen of the Tyr's Legion stood outside his timber-and-iron door, warmed by their dwarf-beard cloaks trimmed with luxurious silken human yellow-hair scalp. They held long pole-arms crossed before it.

A door. How very human.

"Old friend, here to see the First Thrall."

One of the demen stepped aside to give her access to a pulley. She pulled and a faint jangling sounded from within.

A scraggly-haired head appeared, leaned out over a balcony above, and then a hand made an intricate wave.

The demen parted their pole-arms and she heard something that sounded like a steel ball rolled across planking. The door opened of its own volition; no door-thrall worked it.

He called her up stairs wide enough for a dragon to an open room above. It took up the whole of the tower. She saw level after level above that with circular balconies overlooking the floor where she stood, sniffing the smells of dusty paper and hot lamps. She couldn't see much of the very top of the tower, but she thought she saw a star chart with astrological symbols, rather like the one she'd slept under in the old dwarf fortress of the Wheel of Fire.

Rayg descended a stair. He was a little slow in his movements, but otherwise looked vigorous enough. His countenance was a strange mix of old and young: bright eyes and teeth in a deeply lined, careworn face.

There was a good deal of seating in this room, and a pair of big woven mats, slightly chewed up by scale, that would serve to keep a reclining dragon from losing body heat through the stone floor.

Rayg went over to a pair of matching leather-topped desks—built and paneled in the dwarf-style with many drawers and bins and such for storage—and sat on the cleaner of the two.

"Ahh, Wistala, my dear mother's old friend. How is the old girl?"

"A venerable low churchwoman, when last I heard," Wistala said. "I've been cut off from Hypatia for some years. I'm surprised you haven't asked me about R— Well, my poor old brother."

"Oh, yes, you did go away with him," Rayg said. "He's missed. This arrangement—with Nivom above and the twins below . . . Ahh, it's best not to talk about it."

"I won't say anything. I'd like to hear your opinion," Wistala said.

"Just idle talk," Rayg said. "In return, your breaking of your exile is safe with me, of course. You've taken quite a risk coming all the way down here. Audacious of you."

"I'm trying to figure out what really happened at that feast. The deaths."

"Curious," Rayg said, returning to his papers. "Did you lose someone close?"

"Ayafeeia, the leader of the Firemaids. I could use your insight."

"I don't think I've ever properly thanked you for hunting me down as a child and getting me away from the barbarians. I know you acted on behalf of my great-grandfather, not me, but it's weighed on me that you might die without my making some gesture of gratitude. So here's this: I'll give you a pass to go into the Star Tunnel. According to the pass, you're gathering a specimen I need. No one will dare question that. Were I to complain to NiVom that my work was impeded by some functionary— well, let's just say NiVom has great hopes for my work."

He fiddled about on a mass of shelving behind his desks.

"May I ask, Rayg, why two desks?"

"A man can work for pleasure, and a man can work for reward. Ideally, you'd like both. But anything for our glorious Sun King and Tyr goes on this desk"—he indicated the tidier of the two—"and my own pleasures and interests are piled on this one."

"Thank you, Rayg. You've done well here. I hope NiVom releases you from service so you have a few quiet years with the second desk."

"I've long since come to terms with that. Who knows? I may outlive NiVom. I may have to. There's so much to do."

AuRon, in one of his storytelling moods, had said that the Red Queen talked that way—too much to do to die.

Her pass took her all the way to the Star Tunnel without question. There was a heavy guard of those oversized demen at the old rising narrows to the Star Tunnel, and several different versions of spiny officer looked at her pass from Rayg before letting her through.

While passing along the chain of command, she marked one of the blood barrels resting on a piece of conveniently shelved stone. It had been tapped and had the wide copper bowls that fit a demen's broad face scattered all about. The demen had been swilling dragon-blood like harvest wine.

When she descended again into the passage leading to the Star Tunnel, the demen clacked their mandibles at her as she passed, but Wistala didn't see the humor in it.

Perhaps you had to smell the humor. She picked up a dreadful reek on the flowing air, almost as bad as trolls.

The Star Tunnel was different from the wondrous Lava-dome in that it was a work of nature expanded by dwarfs and demen rather than a miraculous mystery. Much of it was shaped like a triangle, with a wide bottom and sides narrowing to the top. It was scored horizontally, like sedimentary rock. Daylight could be seen here and there at the apex of the triangle, and at night stars could sometimes be distinguished if the air was clear up short tunnels rising like chimneys from the vaster cavern.

The floor was smoothed in most places, save where they'd left a decorative stand of rock or stalagmite.

Wistala had first met Ayafeeia and the rest of the Fire-maids here, when they fought off a last, desperate assault of starving demen. Her brother wanted space between the de-men and the important underground rivers—when talking of his reign, he'd told her that from the first he'd had ideas about expanding the Dragon Empire belowground before re-turning to the surface—and by taking the Star Tunnel he deprived them of some of their best mushroom-soil and worm-beds.

She caught a distant glimpse of scale reflected from light shining down from above, near the huge crack where she'd first seen the Firemaids in action.

Tempted to hurry toward it, instead she slowed, suspi-cious. This air was foul with rotting bodies, certainly, but there was something else in the air. Had trolls ever come down and hunted the Lower World? The smell certainly seemed evocative of them, but muted by more comfortable dragon odors.

She saw a pile of rock with what looked like some human and demen bones, dirt, and what was hopefully just detritus that had fallen through the shafts from the Upper World shoved against the wall of the Star Tunnel. She heard faint banging sounds coming from a downward-leading passage next to it—there must still be mining going on. But the slag-heap made a convenient perch, and she ascended it very carefully to avoid dislodging loose material.

She was never sure which she spotted first, the broken bodies, obviously dumped on top of each other from a height, or the trolls picking over, climbing, shifting, and rending the mass of scaly carrion, most of the color lost to a rusty coating of dried blood.

Gross and misshapen, elephant-sized, scale-covered, and dripping with secretions from orifices of unguessable purpose, they were easily the most loathsome creatures Wistala had ever seen.

Trolls. They had to be. She knew the shape too well, the dangerous power in those heavy-forward, light-rear limbs, and the odd sensory globes extending to examine the picked-over carcasses.

She knew that men fed a little dragon-blood now and then felt energized, in their prime. The Copper, when he was Tyr, kept bats and fed them from his own veins, so it was said, and they grew into great waddling winged things, like dogs. The Tyr's Demen Legion had evidently taken the blood-drinking process a step further and were morphing into soldiers that could grow their own armor, see in the dark, and break down walls with their bare hands.

These trolls had been feasting on dragon flesh, and blood—with the demen skimming a little, it looked like, for who knew how many years?

These had developed not scale as such, but growths that reminded her of the corals of the Inland Ocean she'd seen shaped into art in Hypatia. They even had wings of various sizes, some just vestigial, others dragging behind from their joints like capes, and a few of the biggest ones looked capable of gliding or perhaps flight.

One troll was dangerous to an unwary dragon. Two might just be handleable, if they were caught in the open by an experienced dragon with a full firebladder.

She counted nineteen rummaging around the pile of bodies. Who knew how many more lurked in the recesses of the Star Tunnel, once the home-cave of the demen, who'd spent lifetimes adding to the living and gardening space?

Further writhing, pulsing horrors supped and extended inside the bodies. They had to be troll progeny. They resembled eggs only in their overall mass; the shape was more like some fantastic hairy starfish, extending bits of itself into the dead flesh and twitching as it absorbed rent flesh.

Her stomach pulsed and she didn't know if she would erupt in flame or half-digested ration-meats and joints. She heaved, an involuntary act, and her legs extended as though to brace herself.

She sent a skittering of dried bones and dropped troll-scale down from her perch.

Dozens of troll sensory organs shot upright, turned, and centered on her.

*　　*　　*

She released her flame in a panicked scatter. The trolls leaped over and through it, making excited glubbing sounds out of their rubbery mouths.

They fell on her like an avalanche.

Trolls fight in silence. There's only a sort of smacking gulp as they take in air, a sound like that produced by extracting a limb from deep mud. These had a kind of carapace that lifted and resettled, adding a heavy clapping sound like two milled pieces of construction timber brought together: *Craalp! Craalp!*

She supposed their numbers worked against them. Each hulking, scaled troll pulled at those ahead and pushed back those behind in their eagerness to get at her. Driven by hunger or hate—trolls had no face as most vertebrates know it and were therefore impossible to read—they fought each other so that the cave became a swirling mass of scaly motion.

It was the stench that struck hardest. Trolls smelled terrible, but there was a dragonly smell to them now that made it worse, thanks to the familiarity of that scent.

To steady her mind, to drive the stench away, perhaps to buy herself time, she roared, a fearful sound that made her blood run hot. No wonder male dragons made such a noise when they set to fighting.

The trolls paused in confusion, just for a moment, as the sound bounced, batted between the sloping walls of the Star Tunnel. Perhaps, just for that moment, they believed themselves surrounded by hostile dragons.

If only.

But it did buy her the time to spread her wings and gather herself for a jump into the air. She had no idea whether she might escape through one of the shafts leading to the surface, but it was worth a try.

Luckily the size of the Star Tunnel worked against them. She flapped into the air, spitting fire all around to drive back the plucking and rending arms seeking to pull her down to messy destruction.

One, beating its wings and flying as wildly and irregularly as a bumblebee, rose after her. She turned a tight circle and struck it with her tail, powered by both her muscles and the force of her turn. Her tail caught it across the chest and sent it spinning into one of the sloping walls of the Star Tunnel. It crashed to the floor of the chamber, dead or insensible.

Other trolls climbed the walls, their half-wings buzzing angrily. Trolls are terrific climbers and leapers, and if they couldn't catch her on the ground, they'd jump and hang on— the weight of a single troll was liable to bring her down. That would be the end of her, with that dragon-flesh-hungry mob.

The blow across her back surprised her. Two powerful limbs gripped her wings and she found herself unable to beat them. She plunged, the world whirling, toward the floor of the Star Tunnel.

This is the end of Wistala, the curiously detached part of her mind thought. *What legacy have I left?*

At the last moment, using every iota of her strength, she lurched and flipped onto her back so the troll riding her struck first with her atop it.

The others rushed in to finish her. She dug her claws into

the ones battling her and prepared to sell her life at a terrible and bloody auction.

A rain of liquid fire fell around her like a protective storm.

Wistala! called a voice. It too bounced off the walls of the Star Tunnel. She knew that slightly high-pitched but clear carrying voice, and loved it more than any save one.

AuRon!

Was she dead? Was she lying in pieces on the cavern floor already, and this was some comforting, dying fantasy of her oxygen-starved brain? Was he dead, too, unbeknownst to her, and calling her to join him in this stormy afterlife?

No, it couldn't be a fantastic death-dream. Her brain would have DharSii fly to her rescue, not her moody, mercurial brother.

She stomped the broken and bleeding troll hard and came away with a *sii* full of semi-scale and skin.

AuRon's stumpy tail tip lashed her across the face. "Wistala!" he said again, flapping hard over her head as he shot another gout of fire. This one was thinner than the previous rain. Perhaps he had one more in him. He swooped under a troll diving after him, executing an infinitely more fluid maneuver than the troll could manage. It smacked into the cave floor with a sound like a dropped melon splitting.

"I'm coming, brother," she said, leaping into the air. She tasted blood on her lips.

"Just follow me."

She flapped after him. It turned into a strange escape, half flight and half climb. Soon they were in a rougher tunnel. He pulled her up over the lip of a hole when she swooned.

Cold. The stone of the cave floor was so cold. Had they been transported, somehow, to the permafrost in the far north?

"Wistala, are you hurt?" AuRon asked. It seemed a ridiculous question, with her leaving a trail of blood behind like a snail's track.

Her brother. He tended to babble inanities under stress. He was a most sensible dragon before a fight and turned into a cornered dwarf, for all his lack of scale, once at grips with the enemy. But right after, he turned strange and hysterical until he recomposed himself.

She glanced down at herself, at the patches of rent and missing scale where the troll-blows had struck like boulders of a landslide, the great bite clean through her haunch that she expected would mean a limp for the rest of her life, the loose skin of one wing flapping like old Widow Lessup's hanging linens on laundry day.

"Yes, I believe I am. May we rest for a moment?"

"Of course," AuRon said. He returned to the hole, took a deep draught of air rising from it and cocked an ear so he might listen.

"You need water, or wine and brandy, to help the shock. Dwarfsbeard, if I can find the damn stuff in this thick forest."

As AuRon babbled, she licked the worst of her wounds—the one in her haunch—and almost immediately languished into sleep, tucking her nose under her wing. In fitful consciousness, she assured herself she was still breathing and that her heartbeats could be heard. Then she passed into fair dreams involving DharSii and a matched set of hatchlings, four males and four females. They were residing in a cave painted gold—no, wait, that was just the sunset shining down the cave's throat. White flowers bloomed all around the exit and she heard the distant cries of birds below.

"Eight the rare way," DharSii said in the dream, *griff* out but closed tight in pride at her achievement. "Not one in a thousand dragonelles produce such a clutch," he said.

BOOK TWO

Ability

"EGGS HATCH BEST IN SILENCE."

—*Dragon proverb*

Chapter 8

The dwarfs ringed him like wolves around a hobbled horse. But they hadn't eaten him yet. Maybe they were new to butchering dragons and were trying to determine where the best cuts of meat resided in him.

The fact that they were taking their time about finishing him increased his sense of doom. Dwarfs in doubt about the matter would rush in and start hacking.

Perhaps these weren't dwarfs after all. He'd never seen dwarfs, who took as much pride in a well-groomed beard as a well-balanced axe or a well-filled purse, in rags and bodily filth like this. Such a combination of pallidness with grime would indicate madness in any other hominid, but dwarfs were as resistant to failings of the brain as they were to hunger, disease, or loneliness.

They'd dragged him into a circular chamber and made sure of the bracing on the circular stone that had rolled along a gutter into a sort of natural stone socket. The rolling, wheel-like closing stone reminded the Copper of the support for a wheelbarrow; it even had a giant handle attached so the dwarfs could drag it back and forth by means of a pulley chain. The stone, bound with iron, would not easily give way, supported as it was by the ironmongery and the stone socket. With all the twists and turns in the passage, even a troll or a dragon couldn't force it or wield a battering ram that would crack it. Stout miners with picks would take days to break through.

Help would not come from without, at least not before the dwarfs could make stews and pies of his last leftovers. He had to find it within.

Alcoves ringed the circular chamber, with tiny hearths, some vented by metal housings for the air, others burning next to cracks in the walls, with smoke being drawn up into the cracks as though directed. It offered the cave a homey, smoke-less warmth, and the burning fuel did much to mask the muscat odor of unwashed dwarfs. Knowing the cleverness of the bearded race, he supposed the smoke probably vented into the outer passage. To poison besiegers, they needed only to build up their fires or burn some sort of poisonous chemical in the fire. Perhaps even now, deadly fumes were dropping that elf's dozing raven and the rest were fleeing even farther up-tunnel to escape.

He looked about. How many dragons get a chance to examine the site of their own death in detail?

There was a great deal of writing on the wall, both carved into it and written with chalk. A big stretch of marking looked to be a calendar, but there were other testimonials, some in multiple languages such as:

Fust died here with his comrades
He killed 3 5 6 9 11 enemies before falling.

Jospir regrets never having a son.

Old Kuk the blacksmith swears the best ale he ever enjoyed was brewed by Daza Yellow in the House of Yril.

Dwarfs usually had black or red beards, thick and often glowing, thanks to a curious luminescent fungus they cultivated in the thick mats of their beards. These had faded, and their beards were reduced to patchy hair the color of cold ash. Their arms and armor were rusted and bent, with no two suits matching. Those that had shields had tied them on with bits of twine, and there was not a boot to be seen, though some wore sandals of metal and chain or slippers that looked to be fashioned out of dried mushroom. Their ragged pants gaped, especially at the back where he caught glimpses of their frightfully dirty and hairy backsides.

Still, a few had enough care for their appearance that they'd knotted their mustaches and beards, or washed the filth from some jeweled brooch or an ancient family helm. Dwarfs took a good deal of wear and tear without bending their necks—even the Empire at its height had never managed to make thralls out of them, though a few served for pay and grudgingly fulfilled bargains they made to save their lives. The Copper had heard legends of dwarf prisoners surviving on nothing but licked moisture from a cave wall, until they eventually returned to the rock from which they'd sprung—if you believed old tales. Which he didn't.

A dwarf peeked at him from a slit in a huge oval shield. A blade waggled just below the slit like a taunting tongue. "No wonder they had this one up front. He's half blind and a cripple to boot."

The Copper acknowledged his fear. Doing so allowed you to control it. Sometimes it even came to your aid in a critical moment. He'd escaped death many times; if it came here, he'd still done better than any dragon tossed into the world with his injuries could expect. At least a throng of famished dwarfs wouldn't rejoice and snicker that he'd finally passed up and into the night sky, as they would if the news reached the throne room in the Imperial Rock. He could stand anything, but he particularly disliked being the subject of laughter. It might be better to fall here, unknown and unnamed.

Dwarfs with chains and grappling hooks stood by, ready to throw and snare and drag him over and expose his belly.

"May I ask, Master Dwarf, who finally humbled me?" he asked in Parl. "I am curious to know who it is that finally sends me into the mystery beyond the final veil."

A dwarf with double-rings on each of his index fingers, matching gems of red and blue, emerald and diamond, waved the others to stillness. "First-rank Seeg, dragon, of the Deep Alliance," he answered, using the trade-tongue with more facility than the Copper could ever manage. "My fathers were of the Wheel of Fire in its glory, though we've dwarfs and dwarf-wives of all four craft-marks in our number. We're the last survivors of a punitive expedition sent into barbarian lands by the Wheel of Fire. Abandoned by our king and brothers, we counted ourselves clanless and established a new dwarfhold. Others have since joined, those who can't stand the arrogant Hypatians and their dragon backers, that is. We're the last of the Free Northern Dwarfs."

Enemies of my enemies, eh, Master Dwarf? Perhaps they should know his name.

For all the jewels Seeg wore on his finger, the most impressive was a plate-sized white gem ringed with gold joining his thick girdle. The Copper had to stop himself from gazing into it. Though he hadn't thought about Rayg for years, for some reason the crystal in Seeg's belt made him think of his old assistant.

"I'm called RuGaard in the Lavadome, though now I'm an exile and at enmity with the new Tyr. If you call yourselves 'free,' does that mean others of your kind are slaves?"

"He asks strange questions for one about to be bled and butchered into cuts and roasts," a dwarf observed.

The Copper tried to answer well. "I entered first in the hope of preventing bloodshed. If it causes all of my own to be spilled, that will make an ironic story for the afterlife. I'm curious about you and how you've made enemies willing to hire dragons to destroy you. No ordinary hate burns hot enough to melt that much gold."

"We're the holdouts," said Seeg. "We're the only ones who

don't tithe headtax to your damn dragons and their blood-drinking demen."

"Why did you take me alive?"

"We've got plenty of sick down here. We heard from some blighter runaways from your Empire—before we decided to distribute their heads and bodies to different caves—that dragon-blood was good for ailing folk. Most of our folk are ailing these days, what with the wet roads and dry passages blocked by the cursed demen."

"Let's bleed him a little now—I'm thirsty!" one of the dwarfs with the chain and sharpened, harpoonlike grapnel said.

"Perhaps I can help with other kinds of thirst. Thirst for sunlight, or fresh air, or even revenge."

"We tried an alliance with a dragon once. It ended in our ruin," Seeg said. "Though I do find you unusually coolheaded for a cornered dragon. Usually they spit fire and oaths, and leap."

Another dwarf argued, "If you mean that she-dragon, it was we did her wrong. She came through the barbarians and brought wounded out. How many dwarfs would have died without their last messages, were it not for her?"

"I was Chartered Company. Dragons were a boon for us, until the Empire came. Let's hear him out."

"Let's look at it from your point of view, then," the Copper said. "Bleed me, and you get a few barrels of blood. Maybe not even that, if I struggle and thrash. There's bound to be spillage. As testament to my word, I've done bargains with dwarfs before. Look at this wing joint."

"It's in poor repair, dragon. A blighter could do better."

"A blighter tried. But the design is dwarf work." That wasn't precisely true. Rayg had designed the wing joint, but he'd been trained by dwarfs in his youth.

"A dragon in shackles is worth two—"

"At best, I'm a temporary solution to a permanent problem," the Copper said. "Perhaps I can help you find a permanent solution. I imagine you're sick because you're living off stored food."

"If only! Stone soup, more like, with a few old bones thrown in for flavor. Bootheels and belts ran out a year ago."

"I've only known a few dwarfs, but those of my past acquaintance enjoyed roasts, beer, and a sort of boiled bread with lots of salt on it. Sweets, too, especially honey. I remember giving a good deal of butter, marmalade, and honey to those dwarfs who'd worked with us long underground, and they were most appreciative."

The dwarfs smacked their lips. Saliva ran in disgusting froth into their dimly glowing beards.

"Honey, oh honey!" a dwarf said.

"Beer! What I wouldn't give for a mug . . ." another mused.

"You'll give your life if you keep listening to this dragon," the one with the grapnel warned. "Don't go chasing the chance of a big profit when a purse of coin drops in your lap, however modest. Take the surety, Seeg!"

"Perhaps we could organize a truce," the Copper said, thinking it would be best to ignore the dwarf with the grapnel. Though if he threw at all and a fight started, the Copper would try to reduce him to a creamy holiday pudding before the others killed him. "I'll stay down here as your hostage, and a party can go back to the surface and bargain for a few fresh fruits and vegetables. Yes, we get fruit up from the south coming on the coastal trade, oranges and pomegranates and pineapples. . . . If you've no money to spend, I'm sure doing a few odd jobs would endear you to my mistress in the tower. We have a winch much in need of repair."

"What, fix the hovel of those who do battle with us?" Seeg said. "You've gone mad, that's what's happened." The insult made the Copper believe a sliver of opportunity had appeared, now he just had to widen it enough to wriggle through.

"Who started the war?" the Copper asked.

A scattering of dwarfs chorused: "The barbarians, of course!"

"What was the reason."

Some murmurs broke out as the dwarfs consulted.

"We're sure it was their fault. You know humans. Whatever bargains their fathers strike are forgotten by the sons."

The Copper nodded. "Well, perhaps it was their fault. I certainly wasn't around for it. I do have certain resources, perhaps I can pay, oh, what do you people in the north call it—weregild, is it?"

"Forked-tongue dragon!"

"It's split, perhaps, but that just is so a dragon's most sensitive taste buds may close up so they are protected from his flame. I'd hardly call it a fork."

"How much is certainly important," Seeg said. "But more important still is whether we can find a place safe from our enemies."

"I once had all the wealth of dragonkind at my command," the Copper said. "While I don't expect to get that back, I did have some personal possessions, tributes and presents and such, that I intend to reclaim."

"Ha! Hot air. Just what you'd expect from a dragon," the grapnel dwarf said.

The Copper drew himself up to his full height and extended his wings as far as they'd go without the bad one drooping. "My name is RuGaard, former Tyr of the Dragon Empire and Worlds Upper and Lower, and I don't make idle boasts. I will regain what is mine, or you may sell me to the dragons who usurped my throne. Either way, you will profit."

"You are RuGaard?" Seeg said.

"I heard he was a Copper dragon," a dwarf said in Seeg's ear. "And blind in one eye."

"Crippled, too. By the Golden Tree, it is him."

"*Ha-hem,*" said Seeg. "You may have just won yourself a little more life, dragon. You seem to understand dwarfs well enough that I suspect we could become partners. Certainly not friends, probably not allies, but partners—yes, we may just be able to get that to work."

He gave the instructions for a single dwarf to send a flag of truce to Shadowcatch.

Once negotiations were under way, the atmosphere in the dwarf-den lightened.

"We're not part of the Dragon Empire, either, and we'd

like to keep it that way. What are your standards for joining this 'Northern Alliance'?"

"We never thought of it as standards so much, just each dwarf that joins swears never to betray another of the alliance."

"Might I join?"

"You don't shy away from putting yourself forward, do you? What's your game?"

"I've been a lonely exile these past twelve years. The Empire tried to kill me more than once after I'd agreed to go. In the end, they'll either kill me or I'll get Tyr NiVom. Sad, we were once friends."

"Politics does that. There was no more loyal dwarf to Fangbreaker than myself, yet I curse his name now for the death of my comrades. All for his vanity."

The Copper sent a message to Shadowcatch requesting food and drink, as he was close to starving. True enough, the dwarfs themselves were on rations that hardly qualified as food—tree bark, straw from bedding, and cave lichens went into their soup.

Shadowcatch, reading between the lines, it seemed, or just out of his own oversized sense of what counted as a meal, sent down quarters of beef and mutton, a cask of sweet fortified wine, and onions and potatoes for "ballast." It was carried in by the "scouts." The dwarfs weren't quite ready to trust a second dragon by the Copper.

The dwarfs fell on the foodstuffs like the Copper's rats, barely toasting the meat on sticks before devouring it. It occurred to the Copper that Shadowcatch could have poisoned the food and gotten rid of the lot of them—dragon stomachs were cast from the same material that went into their scale, it seemed, and alkaloids that would kill a hominid found their way into the firebladder.

"I prefer honest beer. This stuff sticks to the tongue, rather than cleaning it."

"Well, dragon, I believe you have a deal," Seeg said.

The alliance almost shattered the first night of the joint dwarf-dragon hike to the tower.

The oddball band of scouts waylaid Seeg and his servant as they bathed in a stream downslope from camp. While they weren't murderers, they were thieves and brigands, for they struck both Seeg and his servant with stones, knocking them senseless. When they awoke, Seeg's rings and crystalline belt were gone.

The thieves fled south to Hypatian lands. Shadowcatch sent two of his grounded dragons after them, though he didn't have hopes of catching the scoundrels.

"That elf's raven will mark the dragons from miles off and the trail will disappear into a stream or swamp," he reported.

Seeg thought the items a small loss. They were most useful underground, where they generated a small amount of light in otherwise pitch-black conditions. Thanks to the poor condition of the lichens in the dwarfs' beards, the crystals were sometimes necessary.

"Why would they strike now?" the Copper asked. "If the dwarfs are to be killed, wouldn't it be better from their employer's perspective to follow them and see where they settle?"

"Perhaps they weren't seeking death after all. When they could take what they were really after, they left."

"But his rings and that belt aren't one-twentieth of his wealth, never mind the rest of the dwarfs. If you're going to steal and run, why not make off with gold and diamonds, not decor?"

Chapter 9

AuRon and Wistala wasted weeks tracing Nissa across the borders of the Sunstruck Sea.

They had both seen the fringes of the princedoms of the Sunstruck Sea. This was the first time either had gone beyond the villages in the jungles bordering Old Uldam.

They found an incredibly rich land. Lush fields bordered by good roads and irrigation ditches, rivers filled with sail, oared, and drawn-barge traffic, and cities teeming with white-clad men.

Everything grew huge in the sun. The heat poured out of the sky and splashed across the ground, boiling up from anything dark. Big-eared, wide-horned cattle, nearly as tall as a man at the shoulder, wandered the fields, long tails swishing at equally enormous flies. They saw wild Rocs above the jungle, riding currents on motionless, outspread wings. The only time AuRon saw wings flap was when a pair flew close enough to them to decide they weren't prey size and went back to circling.

It was a pleasant enough land, too hot to be idyllic as far as the dragons were concerned, but a place pleasing to the senses. For the eyes there were intense greens and blues in the water that matched the sky above. The locals preferred to build in white masonry, though most buildings had colorful awnings.

The people of those countless city-states, each a walled island of civilization surrounded by jungle, riverside, mountain, coastline, or some valuable combination of all the above, fled at the sight of dragons. Wistala's prediction proved true again and again. Archers and spearmen would occupy walls, towers, and high domed steeples. The steeples in the wealthier towns curved and twisted in snail-shell shapes and those in the poorer towns were simple constructs of steam-bent wood and metal hoops.

Even when a few brave souls emerged from a sally-port in the walls to speak to the dragons, there were language difficulties. AuRon and Wistala, between them, knew the trade-tongue of the outskirts of Hypat and some human tongues, but none of them had any effect on the men. Desperate, AuRon even tried mindspeech, but all it produced was a broad smile and nods from the interlocutors.

At night, settling beside each other head to tail as they had when they were hatchlings, they chatted, sometimes in the rain that seemed to strike every afternoon. They switched between mindspeech and words without much paying attention to which they were using, as humans having an animated discussion will use their voices, expressions, and hands.

The talk turned to the origins of trolls.

"DharSii told me a legend once," Wistala said. "He said he heard it from a dwarf. According to this dwarf, trolls have only recently joined the world. They arrived on a piece of stone that fell from the sky. The stone was so heavy and so hard that when it struck the earth, the very land puddled and formed into waves like a lake when a heavy stone is tossed. A hurricane washed over that part of earth, uprooting entire trees and flinging them, scorched, a whole horizon away. When the cataclysm was over, the trolls appeared out of the choking dust and fiery sky."

AuRon said, "One of the blighter sweepers at the Sadda-Vale told me his legend. He'd just lost a brother to that troll that raided our flocks and came right down to the fishing pools two years ago—remember? He was mourning his brother through a cask of beer Scabia allowed him—odd that the blighters brew beer for their own use, but they must get permission from Scabia to drink it—and he said something along the lines of wishing Anklemere had never called them down from the sky."

"DharSii believes trolls are connected to Anklemere, too." Wistala stared off into the northern sky, where Susiron, and presumably DharSii, stayed in place while the world turned.

AuRon, were he to confess his secrets, was a little jealous of his sister's devotion to DharSii. He was an impressive dragon, but he'd treated his sister poorly. Allowing the phony mating with Aethleethia, keeping her twisting like a bauble on a string while he attended to other matters . . . *Cruel* was the only word for it. A dragon should have the courage to name his mate and fight for her.

"I can't see that Natasatch has treated you any better," Wistala said.

Cursed female! Dragonelles and dragon-dames had such highly tuned abilities with mindspeech they could read private thoughts if you weren't guarded in them!

So they followed the coast, zigzagging to visit the interior cities.

It was a patchwork land. Always there was a palace or two, occasionally a fortress, and a city built around the mysterious conical minarets of the priests. Wistala, better read than he, explained that theirs was a fetish that believed in a single vast god encompassing all, but this god's will was so inscrutable he either sent emissaries down or elevated men to demigod status to speak for him. Each of these temples was watched over and named for one of these gods or demigods. The priest caste wasn't as involved in day-to-day life as the Hypatian "low clergy" that Wistala was familiar with—quite the opposite, in fact. They renounced the world and lived lives of simplicity. They sat in the temples, heard the prayers of the locals, and meditated long on them, in the hope that this universal God would nudge the universe in the proper direction.

AuRon preferred the straightforward cults of Old Uldam. You took a deer from the forest and you thanked both your personal god and the deer-god, and you always left a vital at the kill as an apology to the leopard whose game you poached.

It just seemed to him that the blighters got all their business done right away, dealing directly with the gods. Priests and such made him wonder just how much of the offerings to the gods ever made it beyond the priest's purse.

The princedoms of the Sunstruck Sea were a frustrating lot to deal with. They had negotiating intermediaries who came out and spoke to AuRon and Wistala.

AuRon felt like the poor supplicants seeking intervention from the all-powerful. They never managed to speak to any of the princes, just the intermediaries. They did what they could to warn them that the Dragon Empire was readying for war.

They tried to find out about Nissa, inquiring about a princess from the north, or an old arranged marriage from the Ghioz, and mostly received shrugs in return, or blank looks, or some old legend that either illustrated the maxim that it was best to get a good look at the bride before the ceremony of an arranged marriage or a sad story about a heartbroken bride who drowned herself on her wedding eve for she'd been pledged to a rich man rather than her true love.

The princedoms were full of such stories—not really histories, not really legends, but something in between.

"The librarians should really catalog them. There must be hundreds of these little tales."

"I fear we'll hear all of them before we find Nissa, or anyone with real authority to do something."

Outside a city that was fragrant with peppers and more

exotic spices and flowers, so much so it was almost dragonlike, they finally received news of her.

"Ah, yes, the Hidden Widow," said a spice-trader with a good knowledge of Parl who'd been sent out to talk to them. "She was once of the Ghioz court. She resides in the country at the Peacock Palace."

He supplied them with directions, though they'd spotted the building from the air.

The Peacock Palace had a ragged beauty to it. The jungle had encroached across the old walls that ringed the great house, filling fields with vines and grasses. The white—what else?—house stood besieged by green, three floors of balconies, verandas, and shaded walkways so that the air might run free while the sun and rain were kept out. It smelled to AuRon of chrysanthemum, which was growing in profusion in old pools.

He heard a plate fall and break from somewhere within the house as they approached, landing outside the gates and climbing carefully into the grounds.

A dark woman with two neat pleats of gray appeared on a balcony just above the main door. She wore a simple sleeveless dress with a black fabric belt wrapped and knotted about her waist. She reminded AuRon of both Naf—with her height and grave bearing—and Hieba—with her large eyes, elegant chin, and thick hair—so that it pained him to look at her. Just a little.

Wistala called greetings in Parl, but the woman just smiled and spread her hands as though helpless.

"Were you once known as Nissa?" AuRon asked, in the language of the Dairuss. He'd learned a little of it from Naf and more when he'd served in Dairuss.

She looked shocked and answered similarly: "That is the name my father and mother gave me, yes. I have not heard it spoken in a long time, dragon."

"Your flowers are beautiful," Wistala said in the same tongue, though with difficulty.

"They keep the bugs away."

You know the tongue of the Dairuss? he thought to her.

It is similar enough to Hypatian that I can get by, she returned.

"Are you also the person they call the Hidden Widow in the city?" he asked.

"I am a widow. I keep within my home," she replied. "There are rumors I am much wealthier than our own Prince Samikan and the rumors attract thieves like flies coming to spoiled meat."

"I'm sorry to hear you are widowed. I will carry the message back to your mother, if you like. Your father has died. He was a good friend of mine."

"He told me many stories of a gray dragon. I take it you are AuRon," she said.

"This is my sister, Wistala."

"I, too, am sorry you lost your husband," Wistala said.

Nissa clasped her hands in front of her. "No need for regret. It was a marriage of political power. The Red Queen got her mated pairs of Rocs, a trainer, and his apprentice, and in this poor province an impoverished family gained a connection with the high of Ghioz and a dowry large enough to restore the family fortunes."

"We came all this way to find someone in the princedoms

of importance who would listen to us. The Dragon Empire is preparing for war with your people."

"Once I might have been deemed important," Nissa said. "In the days when the Red Queen ruled in Ghioz and the princedoms were eager for her good regard. Since Ghioz fell, I'm little more than a foreign oddity. I tutor students in the Hypatian tongue these days. I've almost forgotten my own, but they are similar enough—"

She stopped, then started again. "I would invite you in, but I don't believe you'd even fit in the entrance hall. I hope you don't mind if I ask you to remain outside. I don't know what food I have that would satisfy a dragon appetite. We do have some cooking lard. My father said you needed animal fats for your fire."

"We will manage," AuRon said.

They ended up eating together in Nissa's back garden. There were stones planted and mortared together between the trees, and the jungle had not yet succeeded in breaking the stones up. Her servants never left the house, so she had to bring them a meager meal of fat and soup-bones herself. Every now and then AuRon caught a glimpse of a face watching them. She sketched out her life as a young girl, part hostage and part student, in the Queen's palace. Though Ghioz had fallen, she wasn't sure that the Red Queen had fallen with it. When pressed, she told this story as the day birds quieted—a pair of peacocks retreated up a tree—and the night birds began to speak:

"The Red Queen told me a story once. She was an enchantress of the Ironriders and lived in a hut woven out of living trees, elves who'd returned to tree-hood and been enslaved to her will. It walked about their lands. She said wherever it went the weather turned bad, so it was almost impossible to find.

"The Ironriders feared her, but the very desperate and the very reckless would go to her. Seeking aid. The wretched, she would dismiss or dispose of. If they had wealth or power, she would promise to double it, which she did, but once they had their crowns and gold, she used her aid in their rise against them and they became her slaves, crowns bowing to her and gold washing into her treasury.

"When the Ghioz rose, they fought a war against the Ironriders in Dairuss. The Ghioz had their own wizards, disciples of Anklemere of old, and the Ghioz managed to burn her walking, living hut of woven trees, and the Ghioz believed the old witch dead.

"She had a new version of herself born in Ghioz, though, and this time her rise was even faster—doing services for the rich and powerful and in turn taking what they gained and more.

"I'll tell you something else. I remember little of my early life, my being brought here, and my marriage. I lived as though in a waking dream—I don't know if dragons dream, but you often move about as though someone else is controlling your actions.

"Then one day I woke up. My husband had died on a trip and I found myself in a palace, with servants and wealth and a parade of people coming to seek my advice and assistance each morning. I didn't begin to know how to get this merchant's wife to love him again, or that young prince a ship that could weather any storm."

"You believe the Red Queen was acting through you?" AuRon asked.

"I was presented to her when I was very young. She questioned me closely and had me play with a crystal ball. I remember how bright it was. Nothing changed after that. It wasn't until my betrothal to Prince Dalparta that I began to have stranger and stranger dreams and then one day the dream didn't end. I felt no fear—I felt nothing, to tell the truth. It just seemed a very long, very vivid dream. For some reason she gave up on me."

"When was this?"

"While I was still young. I had not seen my eighteenth year then. Arranged marriages happen young in this land. It must have been twenty years ago or more."

"About the time Ghioz fell," AuRon said.

"So," Wistala said, "the Red Queen was repeating her trick in the princedoms, it seems, but events in Ghioz intervened and she was destroyed."

"You said you found a tree growing versions of herself?" Nissa asked.

"Yes, but not the way an apple tree produces apples, where they all grow at once. There were 'fruits' all at different stages of development, if you follow. I burned it and the creatures it was producing."

Nissa took a deep breath. "My late husband had a younger brother who became a high minister of the Lion Order. They're an old caste of warriors who call up their own militias and horse-levies when war requires. I could send him a message, but the last news I had of him, he was already involved in a war with the dragons over some islands farther south. They and their men are burning all the ships they can find."

"Men flying with them?" Wistala asked.

"He said nothing of their tactics, only that there'd been losses of ships."

"That would be NiVom's Aerial Host, I expect," AuRon said.

"I take it no dragons who could be convinced to fight on your side live here," Wistala said.

"I've heard of none. There is a story of a dragon who lives with the blighters in the mountains to the north. He was so huge and furious, he destroyed an entire army underneath his impenetrable skin."

AuRon snorted. His skin had been penetrated several times in that fight. But legends tend to treat facts as seeds—what eventually grows is what counts.

"We could make them think some dragons are fighting on your side."

"It might slow them down. Give the princedoms time to organize."

"They'll need that. It takes forever to get them to agree on anything, from what I'm told by my brother-in-law."

They bade farewell that night, lest they eat the poor widow out of house and home by noon the next day. AuRon promised to give Hieba news and Nissa promised to use what remained of her funds to visit Dairuss, if the Dragon Empire ever ceased its rampage.

*　　*　　*

They hurried south along the coast and soon found signs of war. Wrecked and burned ships could be seen in the surf or pulled up on the shore. They also found a dead, half-eaten whale rolling in the surf, with unmistakable arrow-shaped dragon-bites taken out of its fatty skin.

"The Aerial Host seeks to refill their firebladders with whale-fat," AuRon said, as they bobbed in the warm salt water beside the body.

AuRon and Wistala marked a pair of ridden dragons wheeling high together and AuRon and Wistala landed.

"My guess is that's a patrol over their camp."

"Do you suppose they're there? Sleeping?"

"It's midday, but anything's possible," AuRon said.

"Keep hidden. I'll go in fast and draw off the guards. If there aren't any other dragons, I'll attack. If there are, I'll fly north as fast as I can. Stay down if I'm pursued and meet me later at Nissa's palace."

They took water and walked forward toward the camp, resting their wings for the coming exertion and keeping hidden under tall palms. The dragons on guard continued to wheel above.

AuRon tore across the sky. The guards flew down to intercept. He executed a neat cornering swoop, loosing his flame on the boats pulled up onto the sand. It spread widely, thanks to the force of his turn. The salt-dried wood roared into flame at once.

Lightened by the contents of his firebladder, AuRon

climbed to meet the diving guards. Wistala saw projectiles launched by the riders flash across the sky. Her brother dodged them like a writhing snake, flipping on his back and changing directions again in a tighter turn than the heavier guards could match.

One managed to lash out and just tear a mouthful of trailing wing.

AuRon straightened, loose skin on the right wing flapping, and put on speed in his fastest climb. His pursuers followed.

Wistala launched herself into the air, but kept low, just touching the tops of the palm trees with her wingtips. The dragons and their riders either failed to see her or kept their attention on AuRon, chasing him south.

The camp of the Aerial Host was on a wide coastal island, separated from the land by an inlet, save for a narrow, bare neck attaching it to the mainland and curving like a claw around the lagoon. A ridge of slightly higher ground thick with palms ran up the center of the island. There were stone rings here and there, old foundations for huts, Wistala imagined.

AuRon had taken care of the boats, but there were still nets. The fishermen responsible for feeding the Aerial Host were venturing out to throw seawater on their burning ships when Wistala roared out of the jungle and onto the beach, setting their draped nets alight upon their supports.

Then she turned on the supplies drawn high onto the dunes out of the tide's reach.

She smashed barrels and casks, tore open grain bags and set them alight, and hurled anything iron she could find out into the surf. Canvas and cordage, saddle-leather and spare bowstrings, she swept it all into a great pile and set it alight.

She felt a sharp pinch in her flank and looked down to see two crossbow bolts wedged in her *saa*, and a third piercing the slack skin at her shoulder above the wing joint. She heard a pop and saw a hole appear in her fringe as a bolt passed through.

The warriors were brave to shoot at her, but not brave enough to shorten the distance sufficiently so their bolts could get through her scale.

"If you're going to shoot at a dragon, kill it with the first volley," she shouted to them, hugging the ground as she scuttled forward through the patchy grass of the dunes. "All you've done is rouse my ire."

Wistala didn't care for roaring out threats. Male dragons usually were noisy while they fought, but females went about their bloody business quickly and quietly. If she could destroy these men, though, the others of the camp might decide that it would be better to scuttle away and live another day than to die without their usual dragon allies.

She dragon-dashed forward, and the crossbow men decided to race each other in the hope that the slowest would delay her as she devoured him. Wistala spat a few *torfs* of flame after them, all that was left in her firebladder, then left the wreckage and began a low, palm-top-hugging flight back north.

AuRon suddenly appeared above.

"I outlasted them," he called. "The Aerial Host shouldn't leave their camp guarded by two old dragons forced to spend their day in the air, circling. They flagged at once and turned back east."

"Or they went for reinforcements," Wistala said.

They flew first northwest and then north, changing direction by an eighth of a turn every hour or so to confuse any observers on the ground, until they fell, exhausted, into a patch of thick, high grass and bamboo adjacent to a swamp. The wet marsh beneath felt like batting-stuffed cushions to their weary muscles and aching joints.

They were too tired to eat much, save for a few lizards, beetles, snails, and leeches tongued up from the marshy water.

"I smell pig," Wistala said. "Let's sleep for an hour, then try driving them."

"I'm too tired to sleep," AuRon said, exhausted. A dragon-fly with a wingspan like a sparrow hawk swooped by, gobbling up a cloud of insects and alternately exploring and being driven away by acidic dragon-scent, and AuRon lazily snapped it down.

"Then you can keep watch, if you like."

"We've declared ourselves open enemies of the Empire," AuRon said, panting. "A gray dragon with a twice-snipped tail won't be hard to identify, or a long, broad green."

"Worried that Natasatch or your offspring will suffer?"

"Imfamnia likes Natasatch, for some reason. The two in the Aerial Host will be fine. It's my daughter in Uldam I fear for."

"She's clever and unconventional," Wistala said, fading. "I shouldn't worry."

She fell into a deep, rasping sleep and AuRon laid his neck and tail across her. His color-shifting skin ran with thin stripes and green streamers like the bamboo all around. He slowly relaxed, keeping one eye on the sky until night fell.

They both woke slowly and stretched aching bodies. They hunted under a moisture-furred moon. AuRon managed to drive the pigs Wistala had smelled toward her and she brought a big male down with a pounce. Its skin was a disgusting mass of ticks and leeches, but the flesh was tasty.

"Quite a feast for setting out to war," AuRon said.

"I like honesty," Wistala said. "They would have killed us quietly, if they could. Now they'll have to be noisy about it. Questions might be asked. Why we, after the massacre at the Ghioz feast, suddenly oppose NiVom. Odd, though. We're both now set against something we love. You with your mate, me with poor old Hypatia."

"Poor old Hypatia is corrupt, thanks to the dragons," AuRon said.

"We can't fight them here."

"Obviously. We're only two."

"Then back to the Sadda-Vale? It's advantageous ground. Those fogs would work to our advantage."

"Even if we could get Scabia and the rest in the air, it wouldn't be enough."

"Our brother is up to something. While I slept, I wore my dragonhelm. He's in a deep plot—I'm sure of it."

"That's a little like being sure the sun is moving. When is our brother not up to something?"

"I have a sense that's he's in difficulty and there are dragons involved. A tall tower on a jagged peninsula overlooking water."

"Dragons and a tall tower, eh? He's in Juutfod."

"Do you know it?"

"A little. It's the last remnant of our family's old enemy, the Circle of Man and the wizard who needed hatchlings so bad he hired the Dragonblade and the Wheel of Fire to hunt for them."

"I thought that story was long since ended. You took care of the wizard, I avenged our family name upon the dwarfs, and our brother killed the Dragonblade."

"The story continues as long as we live," AuRon said.

Wistala stretched her wings. "I can manage more flying now, I think. Let's continue the tale."

Chapter 10

Scabia the White had more than the usual Sadda-Vale burdens on her mind. The Outside World, which she'd done her best to avoid and ignore, had intruded on her precious hall.

She welcomed her troubles in a way. In the long years of just her daughter and her insipid but well-formed mate eating a long march of similar meals, over conversation as unvarying as the drips through the hole in the great rotunda of Vesshall, they might as well have been three statues frozen in time and space with a group of blighters polishing them and keeping vermin from moving into cracks and crevices.

The arrival of the Exiles, as she styled them, had forced the statues to move. There were hatchlings now—she still thought of them as hatchlings, half in wonder at the word, despite their breathing their first fire and showing thin skin where their wings were coming in. Her senses, exposed to new smells of dragonkind, new voices entering her ears, woke up as if from a dream. Colors struck her as brighter and the smells of the blighters roasting sheep made her as hungry as a dragonelle after her first flight. The Sadda-Vale seemed to be blossoming.

She was even starting to like DharSii again. Before Wistala visited, briefly, all those years ago, she grudged him his trips into the world outside the Sadda-Vale. Now she realized he was just trying to avoid becoming another dusty statue, issuing the same words to the world as though they were engraved beneath their claws like aphorisms. Had he not become intrigued by her—an odd object for affection, she was so muscular as to be ungainly, and her wings never managed to fold up in the neat, tight, attractive manner of a high-blooded female—they never would have had the hatchlings.

Even the idea of setting her home against the power of RuGaard's former dragons excited her. She'd exercised unlimited (well, limited by good manners and tradition) power in the fogs of the Sadda-Vale for too long. Having an outside power to defy and subvert added spice to her life.

Ultimately, the dragons in this Empire would come around to her way of thinking. The lessons of Silverhigh had been forgotten everywhere but in the Sadda-Vale. If she could only speak with one of the better-bred dragons. They could sit down and talk over fish and fowl. Perhaps a sturgeon, suitably fried with breading and a brace of Vale hares. Even the most arrogant or silly dragon came around to her thinking with sufficient discourse—look at NaStirath and DharSii. Dragons must retreat to the most inaccessible corners of the earth and live with as little disturbance to the outside world as possible. If the hominids come, let them come exhausted by long marches in bad weather across bleak lands, hungry and covered in boils and bug-bites. Then let them taste fire and go back to remind future generations of the pain that crossing dragons brings.

This NiVom and Imfamnia might think they were atop a pyramid of domination, controlling the Hypatians, who drew enmity and discontent away from their dragons the way vinegar and soaping fats drew flies away from your feast, but all they were doing was going soft and offering their bellies to those below. The dragons of Silverhigh thought themselves clever beyond hominid ken, too, but they still woke too late to the throat-cutting party gathering about their beds.

No one but stupid NaStirath knew of the emissary who'd come from Tyr NiVom within a few months of the Exiles' arrival, all those years ago. Before Wistala's hatchlings, before the death of that stolid yet beautiful avian bodyguard of the former Tyr.

She and the Empire dragon met on a rocky outcropping overlooking the crossed pylons outside the Vesshall. She arranged it so he squatted facing both her ancient hall and the sun, though the Sadda-Vale's usual overcast interfered with that element of her tactics. The emissary had blustered and threatened that they turn the Exiles out to starve in the far north, or face the wrath of all of dragonkind . . .

All dragonkind. Were all dragonkind gathered, they could probably learn most of each other's names and histories in a few days.

Scabia had the blighters carry off the welcoming food, drink, and ore she'd offered to the emissary. *Orders given to me under my own roof mean that you must be on your way back to your Tyr. My contempt for these demands I'll have you to carry back shouldn't prove too heavy a burden. I decide who enjoys hospitality in my own home.*

As long as it is your home, the emissary had replied.

I heard this dialogue in one of the dwarfish epics, didn't I? Now I'm supposed to ask 'Is that a threat?' and you reply that you were stating a fact or making a promise or some other coolly superior remark. I am most displeased. I am famous for not seeking trouble in the world beyond this mountain ring. But if trouble comes storming in, know this: The Sadda-Vale is the last fragment of the glory that was Silverhigh. Break a glass vase and you will learn. The beauty is gone, but the fragments are more dangerous than they look. You will not be harmed if you leave now and do not alight again until you are beyond the mountains. This audience is at an end.

The memory of the conversation still thrilled her. Too bad her mate was dead—after seeing the emissary snort and turn wing, she felt so invigorated she would have given the old eleven-horn several turns in the clouds.

It did a dragon good to get the blood up now and again. No wonder that Wistala was fertile. Perhaps she'd coddled Aethleethia too much over the years. Well, that was fish heads down the kitchen chute.

In any case, if that silly messenger was a sample of the leadership style of this new empire, there's no wonder that it's already falling apart. Perhaps more Exiles would show up. Perhaps even brooding females. There were caves all over the eastern slopes facing the lake—you had to watch out for trolls, but they could be hunted out of the mountains.

She wondered how she'd manage to pass the word south that there was room for a few more in the Vesshall. Of course, they had to be the right sort. If this NiVom and Imfamnia were clever, they might send a few trusty infiltrators. She would have to question closely and watch closer still.

It had been so long since anyone challenged her for dominance of the Sadda-Vale that she hardly knew how to take it— whether to be insulted that all her efforts here could just be cast aside because of a political feud or complimented that they thought her a potential rival rather than a half-forgotten curiosity.

True, the Sadda-Vale would never support the number of dragons that the Empire to the south could. There were only so many fish even in so long and deep a lake, sheep reproduced only so fast, and it wouldn't do to starve the blighters on millet and dried dragon-waste ground into chicken-feed. Worse, the only metals were the poor ores that DharSii blasted out of the scraggy rocks. The Sadda-Vale was meant to be a pleasant resort for a few months in summer, really, not a breeding ground for dragons.

Scabia, in her younger days, had made a habit of going for either a flight or a swim every morning before eating. The combination of hunger and exercise clarified her thoughts. As she aged, the flights and swims became now-and-again endeavors, though sometimes she had bursts of energy and restarted the habit for a season. Lately, if she was feeling particularly well, she'd rouse herself enough to float around in one of the warmer corners of the spring-fed lake.

This morning, some weeks after Wistala had departed and with DharSii off cracking rock and gathering ore for the week, she roused herself early—even before the hatchlings were clamoring for food—and eased herself down to the lake. Her joints didn't care for the sudden activity so soon after waking and she heard a scale or two clatter to the stone floor as she left her sleeping perch. The sun rose early in the northern summer and the sky was already a brilliant daylight blue.

She plunged into the warm swirls and drank steam through her nostrils as she paddled about. She even snapped at a fish who was hungrily exploring the lake-bottom mud she'd churned up.

Exercise done, she shivered as she climbed back to the decorated entrance with its old dwarfish designs.

Once she was back in the shadows of the entrance hall, Larb appeared, fluttering just above her head.

"You've been exercising, am I right, yer ladyship? You're looking fit and trim, that's a fact. Me, I think I'm coming down with something." He let loose a trio of tiny but significant coughs. "A dab of dragon-blood is just what I need to get my head hanging the right way down."

"You are a ghastly-looking little thing, Larb. Were you accidentally boiled in your youth or does all your kind look that way?"

"It's jes' me benighted upbringing, too long underground with no fresh insects or cattle. Oh, the hunger I knew then! The hunger I know now!"

Disgusting. Presumptuous. Yet there was something disarming about a creature that she might swallow whole and send fluttering down her gullet asking to draw blood for a meal.

"What sort of diseases are you carrying in that snaggle-toothed mouth of yours, I wonder?" she asked. Everyone knew bats transmitted deadly illnesses, though opinions on just how they did it—curses, spellcraft, a poison that worked on the balance of spiritual elements in a dragon, some sort of infinitesimal parasite that leaped from bat to dragon—varied depending on the expert consulted.

"Diseases. Oh, no no no, yer ladyship. Look, do I fly in circles. Am I off balance? Do I pant, or stare? It's only sleeping in the cold that does me any harm."

"Oh, I suppose so. Take it from the base of my ear. Don't bother licking first to numb it—I find that more unpleasant than the nip."

Scabia tried not to twitch at the nip. *Self-control is everything. Control your self, control your world.*

Still, she twitched.

Larb suckled and lapped, then loosed a burp so minuscule she found it cute. Her twisted and bent old fringe rippled. A *prrum* forced its way up her throat in response. What was happening to her of late? She was turning into a simpering dragonelle. *Cute!* Her mind must be going. That was it. Perhaps she'd go noisily mad. That would be a lot more fun for all concerned than waiting for the gray curtain of senility to fall. She wondered if she'd just fly off into the north, raving.

"You will pop like a tick if you keep that up," she said.

The bat glanced up. "Ohh, yer ladyship. If only you knew what a service—" His ears twitched around wildly, then pointed straight ahead, following his nose up. "Mmmph? Oook, yer ladyship. I hears awful wings—beware! Beware!"

Three ugly collections of feather and beak fell out of the shadows above, wings spreading as taloned claws slashed down. Had Larb not seen them, too, she would have thought her mind truly had gone—these fliers were nightmares described and manifested into living flesh. Thick-skinned and covered in a mix of feathers and sharp quills with a massive black beak hanging down almost to their pockmarked chests, they were more like a mix of creatures than any avian she'd ever seen.

Larb shot off into the darkness with a high-pitched squeak.

Being nipped was the luckiest thing to happen to her since the Exiles arrived. The pain had set her on edge, just enough so that her *griff* descended at Larb's shout.

Talons raked off her *griff*. She felt agony across her back as one of the creatures ripped its way down her spine, leaving a trail of torn loose scale and blood. It clamped just below her ribs and began to dig.

She smothered it with her wing and flipped onto her back, rolling and crushing. The creature gave one desperate heave as its hollow bones snapped.

The third, wheeling above while the other two drew her attention, saw its chance. It dropped like a missile and hit her in midthroat. She felt a sense of strong pressure but no pain, and when it rose again, dripping blood and scale from its claws, she realized her throat was ripped open.

But she was a tough old dragon-dame. Even her neck had thickened and grown fatty with her years, and though he'd opened her windpipe enough so that she could hear air rasping and feel blood running down her throat, he hadn't managed to get to any of the great blood vessels, else her neck-hearts would already be seizing up.

Not knowing the extent of the damage to her neck, she didn't dare use her firebladder. While it probably wouldn't ignite in her throat, as the agent for turning *fuoa* into fire was generated by a gland in her jaw, she might choke on the viscous liquid.

Odd that she could assess her own chances of mortality so closely with her throat ripped open.

The one that had raked its claws on her *griff* going after her neck-hearts swooped again, trying for her eyes this time. She continued her roll and whipped her neck around. The rainlike patter of blood from her throat echoed in the tunnel, but she managed to head-butt the gruesome bird hard enough to knock it into the tunnel wall. It struck just above the beak and dropped lifelessly.

The one who'd opened her throat grabbed at the back of her neck and reached down with its plow-sized beak, ready to finish the job of severing her midneck. Everything in the tunnel was going bright and fuzzy.

Now she was down, her limbs numb and useless. The creature had to climb along her neck and shift its grip.

A hail of rocks struck it, breaking and bloodying the creature, throwing it off her. Then DharSii was at her side, panting and shielding her with outspread wings.

She vaguely heard her name shouted again and again. Why would DharSii be waking her instead of the blighters? She refused to wake, and passed into unconsciousness.

When she did wake, she was still lying in the entrance

passage. Her throat was held shut by the gripping claws of that bat—er, Larb. DharSii was at work with his snout and *sii* while Aethleethia and NaStirath looked on, fearful and anxious.

"Her eyes are shifting around," NaStirath said. "Is that good?"

"Yes, very," DharSii said. "It's when they go still and dry and staring that you have to worry."

Scabia gradually put together the idea that DharSii was sewing her together with a sharp, curved bone needle and the sort of twine they used on cooking fowl in the kitchens.

She tried to speak, but he held her still, and she fell back into unconsciousness from the effort.

When she woke again, only DharSii was nestled beside her. She'd been tucked against one wall of the passage where she'd been attacked so it was less likely that she'd roll. Odd, she'd dreamed that she had drifted on silent wings all through her home, looking for something.

On the other side of the passage was what was left of those nightmare birds. The young dragons were poking through them.

"You picked—a good time—to return," she managed.

DharSii scooped a *sii*-full of snow out of a tin tub. "Melt this in your mouth and let it go down slowly."

The snow and cold water as it melted was soothing on her throat. It gave her a brief flash of energy before she relaxed and went limp again. She gave a gentle nod.

"Don't move your head too much," DharSii advised. "How do you feel?"

"Ghastly. What vomit of the Four Spirits were those things, DharSii?"

"My guess would be *griffaran*. The proportion is about right; they're just overlarge and this skin of theirs . . ."

Larb fluttered over from the bodies, where he'd been nibbling at an eyeball. "Hisshonor's right, yer ladyship, that's exactly what they are. Griffaran of the Rock, that's what."

"Nonsense," Scabia said. "They look nothing like steadfast old Miki, colorful until his dying day."

"Griffaran of the Rock?" DharSii asked. "The *griffaran* guard the Tyr, and they certainly don't consider Imperial Rock home."

"That's all changed—sorry to counter-dict your lordship," Larb said. "That wizard, Rayg, he's been giving *griffaran* dragon-blood and breeding those that react best to it. Trying to make a better Tyr's bodyguard, he is."

Scabia took as deep a breath as she dared, holding her throat carefully still. "You returned just in time, DharSii. I'm grateful to you again. How did you knock the last one off my neck?"

"I had a mouthful of ore. I just gathered it and exhaled as hard as I could."

"More snow, please," she said, tiring.

"You have a lot of blood to make up. I'll have the blighters bring you some stew. The boiled potatoes are as soft as a cloud and far more filling."

With a massive act of will, she rose to her feet and made it back to her perch in the great hall, waving the hatchlings away.

They were piping their concern, but she was too tired to speak. Or even climb into her perch. She reared up, but her head began to swim before she could place *sii* on her rest. She slumped into the fading light in the center of the vast chamber. "Try again tomorrow," she said in a dozy voice. She was unconscious before anyone came up with a reply.

When she awoke, Larb and a couple of blighters were beside her, listening to her breathing.

DharSii hid a yawn and dropped off his temporary perch. She blinked, looked around, and asked where the rest of the dragons were. Aethleethia had taken the youths out to explore the lake, and according to DharSii, NaStirath was actually flying guard duty above.

"Sure he wasn't just fishing, now?" Scabia said, thinking DharSii must be mistaken.

"I told him that if the Lavadome could get three of those bastardized *griffaran* up here, they could probably get thirty. That shocked him into silence."

"I'm relieved something can shock him," Scabia said.

"If they come," Scabia said, "get everyone into the water-reservoir, the slow well beneath the kitchens. I've never told anyone this, but there is a tunnel down there. It comes out in the stones under the old wharf on the lake. You have to hold your breath, but it's not a long swim."

She remembered her manners. She needed to thank Larb. "It was a fortunate day for me when you arrived, Larb. To think, I've always thought of bats as vermin. Larb, why ever did you make such a long journey in a dragonelle's ear? You might easily have died at that altitude, in the cold."

"Oh, an ear's a warm little place, long as the wind's not shooting down it, yer ladyship. Truth is, I was looking for the old Tyr. We bats, we're getting exterminated right out of a home. I came to ask Tyr RuGaard to come back and set matters to right. We understand an occasional housecleaning, and sometimes a dragon rolls over in his sleep and crushes a bat or two. Most normal thing in the world. But they're hunting us down and burning us out. We! We saved 'em from the Dragonblade, not so many generations back, and this is the thanks we get."

"I'm glad you came. You'll always have a home here, and as long as blood runs through my veins."

"Oh, yer ladyship, yer too kind to me-umps and my family."

"No family! I'll not have my daughter's hatchlings slipping around on guano. Hear me, Larb, as soon as cousins and friends appear, my cooks will be asking their grandmothers for bat recipes."

NaStirath returned with Aethleethia and the hatchlings, along with a party of blighters pushing barrows.

"I thought we should dry and salt some fish," NaStirath said. "In case we get trapped in here by more of those—what were they called, Larb?"

"Ugly bas—"

"Their real name, Larb," Scabia said.

"*Griffaran*. After a manner, your ladyship."

"Good idea. DharSii, get that lot down into the kitchens. See what else we need if we are trapped in here. You might think about putting a few blighters on watch. Larb, go through all the main passages. Use your ears, listen for more of those things."

"Me stomach's—"

"Going to be filled as soon as you finish, so the sooner you begin, the sooner you eat," DharSii supplied.

"NaStirath, stay behind, would you?" she asked.

The others moved off in the direction of the kitchens, Aethleethia and the hatchlings helping to move nets full of fish.

"I should have brought more salt from the sheep-lick, I know," NaStirath said. "I'll see to it right away."

"Not, it's not that, NaStirath. I've been lying here thinking about something."

"That the great hall needs better drainage?" he said, looking at the puddles on the floor beneath the circular opening at the top.

"I won't live forever. I might not live another day; my hearts give a flutter now and then with these injuries, and I don't like—"

"Matemother, you'll outlive us all," NaStirath said. He was skilled at coming up with the right thing to say. That might be useful to a dragon in charge of a hall and its residents. She drew back from making up her mind one more time, considering.

"I certainly hope not," she said. "It's the natural order of things for me to precede you by a good many years. I wouldn't want to outlive my daughter. You—it depends on what day I'm asked. Today I would not wish to outlive you. However—"

"Let's change the subject, Matemother." NaStirath probably decided she was winding herself up into a roaring mood that would reopen her wounds.

"No. I want you to listen. If I should die, I want you to take over Vesshall and the Sadda-Vale."

"Me? Why not Aethleethia? She's your own flesh and blood. Or DharSii—he's a relation."

"It's too much for her. She needs to get those hatchlings flying. As for DharSii, he's only half here in spirit even when his body rests on his perch. I expect he'll be leaving to join Wistala anytime. You'll have to be responsible for once in your life. We are, it seems, at war with the Empire."

NaStirath looked shocked. "I don't know one end of a spear from another, and I've only ever used my fire to relight the kitchen hearth. I'm no warlord."

"The best generals rarely are."

"I'd much rather be a fool."

She found the energy to take a deep breath and slap her tail down. "You no longer have that luxury, dragon. You no longer have that luxury. It's time to remove those last bits of shell from your scale. You have no reason to be confident in yourself because you've never been challenged. Well, dragon, the challenge is coming, whether you want to play the fool or no. You can either rise to it or die as the joke you've lived."

She let that sink in a moment before continuing.

"You may not credit this, NaStirath, but I am glad you're my daughter's mate. You have brains, anyone who knows you will agree, but you just play with them rather than put them to use. You have strength and health—they've just never been tested by enemies and privation. You can be pleasing when you choose, which makes all the times you choose not to be doubly frustrating.

"For once, NaStirath—for once—prove yourself a dragon. No jokes, no tricks, no idle chatter. Your sires couldn't all have been ninnies. Reach down deep inside and find whatever drops of their blood are left in you. Let those hatchlings tell proud tales of their father to their own eggs someday."

NaStirath opened his mouth, let it hang for a moment, and shut it again.

Shut it? No quip? No jibe. Perhaps there was hope.

Chapter 11

aStirath went to work with energy that surprised everyone, save perhaps Scabia. He put the blighters through some simple trials, divided them into thirds, and took the best group and put them in modified versions of leather work-aprons that he had them set to studding with metal buttons as armor. This group became the "Black Sentinels," taken from the color of their aprons. He asked Dhar-Sii to use his experience in the outer world to select an appropriate weapon for them and see about practicing.

They could never hope to stand against dragons, of course, but they could help in another fight if more of those dreadful black *griffaran* came.

Later, he claimed that at every spare moment he reclined and thought to himself, *What would a careful and competent dragon-general do?* and then set out to do whatever came to him as best he could.

A skilled leader would set up a regular watch system and then have a method of sounding the alarm if the watchers saw something. So he rooted around in old art and artifacts, many relics of Silverhigh covered in the matted dust of generations, until he found a triumph-horn, a caramel-colored curved thing with a poured and much-tarnished brass lining. It had originally come from a hairy, four-legged titan that once wandered the steppeland marshes.

The engineering of mounting it in the highest balcony of the Vesshall defeated him, for the horn wouldn't fit on the small balcony. Then one of the blighters suggested building a watchtower out of three tree trunks leaned against each other, which would put the platform almost as high as the Vesshall dome's open peak.

So pleased was NaStirath with this solution that he gave the blighter one of the dead *griffaran*'s feathers to put in his rain-hat to mark him as an officer of engineers. The exercise of dragging tall, straight trees off the far slopes stimulated him in a way that lounging in the warm pools never had, and he suggested that his new engineer should pick a few energetic youngsters to be his construction team.

That night he ate with not a single complaint about the cooking. He was too hungry from hauling timber. DharSii's ore tasted as good as fresh blood, for once, and his mouth went thick and pasty as it was set before him. He had half a mind to go on a dwarf-raid to find some real gold, but banished the thought. Too much to do in Vesshall.

The resulting watchtower stood as stark and ugly as a gallows against the elegantly sweeping lines of the Vesshall, and according to DharSii the cording holding the trunks bound together wouldn't last more than a few years in the wet weather of the Sadda-Vale (DharSii helpfully pointed out all the construction shortcomings of the watchtower as together he and the striped dragon lifted the alarm-horn into position).

"Thank you, old friend. I couldn't face Scabia if this thing fell down and cracked. Long term, we need something else constructed. Perhaps stairs up the outside of the Vesshall dome. Could you do a study and determine the best way to mount it? Oh, the poor sentinels will get rained on, so perhaps a canopy or shelter of some kind as well."

When an iron-lunged blighter blew on the horn, it could be heard all the way down to the charcoal-shovelers in the kitchens.

The young dragons and dragonelles clamored for it to be sounded again, but NaStirath cautioned them that the alarm-horn was deadly serious business, not a toy. Their clamor silenced at once—he'd never spoken sharply to them before.

To tell the truth, he felt a little guilty. So to make amends, with youthful enthusiasm checked in one direction, he gave them something important to do. They were to do their best that night to sneak into the Vesshall past the sentinels. No fighting, not even play fighting, allowed, and as soon as they were marked and pointed out, the game was over.

They had an opportunity to test it a few days later, when the horn sounded long and loud. It rattled exercise-loosened scale.

"Dragons come!" came the shout from the Black Sentinels.

NaStirath felt his firebladder pulse. When was the last time *that* had happened? When Wistala startled him at the pools when she first arrived, all those years ago?

He found himself trembling.

Black Sentinels assembled, bearing their spiked wooden clubs. The blacksmith was at work on short curved chopping blades that would make the most of blighter musculature and Vesshall ironmongering capabilities without breaking.

He hurried up to the watchtower balcony, stood just below, and looked to the south. Blighters were running every which way, reminding him of the time a wild dog made it into the chicken coops.

He saw two dragons flying across the lake, making use of the warm air rising.

Just two? He looked across the Sadda-Vale from end to end to make sure there weren't more approaching low through the mountains. Satisfied, he turned his neck and examined the arrivals again.

A green with enormous wings and a gliding, more slender dragon approached from the south. NaStirath looked away, then looked back again, refocusing his eyes, to be sure of his identification.

"It's AuRon and Wistala," he said. It occurred to him that they might need to set up a signal for canceling the alarm.

He couldn't tell if he was relieved or disappointed that there wouldn't be a battle. His blood was well and truly aroused. Was he, against all his inclinations and attitudes, fierce?

*   *   *

Wistala landed, hard enough that a loose tile on the vast, stone-paved expanse before the entrance to Vesshall shifted noisily under her.

AuRon was a tough companion to fly alongside.

She remembered, rather grimly, that Natasatch once told her that she'd long since given up trying to keep up with her mate in the air and so she landed to rest and let AuRon's anxiety to reach his destination go off with the winds. Wistala took pride in her strength and reserves of energy. She limited her pleas to asking AuRon to slow down, lest she burst a heart struggling to keep up.

AuRon had apologized repeatedly, and he remembered for a day or so to set his speed on hers, but he liked being lead dragon—it let the follower relax a little, riding in the air that his wings broke. But his natural pace always crept back in mid-flight and she had to once again gasp for him to slow down.

The process had been repeated over the week it took them to travel north from the Sunstruck Sea back to the Sadda-Vale. They alighted in a gray dawn, with AuRon's scales almost colorless from fatigue. DharSii set the blighters to work bringing them fresh-plucked chickens with the blood still warm within.

"We came here to warn you," Wistala said, tearing into shredded chicken flesh. The blighters had left the digestive track in the birds, but she was too hungry to complain about the taint. "We've shown ourselves as enemies of the Empire."

"They moved before you," DharSii said. "Or perhaps faster than you. No way to know which."

*   *   *

They gratefully accepted food and wine hurriedly set out in Vesshall. Scabia greeted them and promised they'd talk in the morning, once they were rested. Then she slept like the dead.

Scabia ordered another overlarge breakfast. Wistala sensed that something had changed at Vesshall. Scabia was subdued— what in another dragon would be called deferential, but it was hard to apply that word to the white matriarch she'd known for so long.

Things seemed different between Aethleethia and NaStirath as well. She was less captivated by her hatchlings and more eager to settle down so that her tail rested against his.

But the greatest change was in NaStirath. He still joked, but his jokes revolved around trivial matters such as the weather or the state of the drains in the Vesshall. He talked sensibly about ways to increase the food supply should more dragons arrive, and wondered what the chances were of getting some dwarfish artisans in to set some matters straight in the kitchen and food storage. She kept expecting him to fall into his old role of Vesshall fool again and demand to know who fell for the new, masterful NaStirath and who knew it was an act.

A little blood spilled in the Sadda-Vale seemed to have created a world of change.

"We won't stay long," Wistala said, finishing her breakfast. "I go in search of my brother."

"I go along," AuRon said. "More for Wistala's sake than my brother's. I hope he knows what he's doing."

"He might say the same of you," DharSii said. "An open attack on the Empire by two dragons?"

"Sometimes all it takes is one blow to give others courage," Wistala said.

"You've been reading Ankelene sagas again," DharSii said, referring to the intellectual strain of dragons who kept records, knew strange tongues, and served as a learned caste in the Lavadome.

"We talked it over," AuRon said. "They'll be more careful in their raids on the princedoms now, worried about dragons fighting for the Sunstruck Sea. There's great discontent in the Lavadome. Some may decide to ally with us."

DharSii cleared his throat. "If no one objects, I'll come along. I know you two have never gotten along with your brother, AuRon, but I respect him. In his time as Tyr, he made enemies, not all of them fairly, but he did well in a nearly impossible job and left dragons in a better position than he found them. Skotl, Wyrr, and Ankelene found they could get along better than anyone might have believed once they no longer had to worry about which clan was carrying the title 'Tyr.' I've no idea what his vision for the Empire was, or if he even had one, but what's happened since he was overthrown has been dreadful. Shameful to hold one of a mated pair as hostage to the behavior of another. I'll oppose it with him, or I'll avenge his death and bring comfort to his mate."

"Nobly spoken, DharSii," AuRon said. "Do the same for mine, won't you?"

"Certainly."

"Can we be in less of a hurry to die and more of a hurry to fly?" Wistala asked, removing her dragonhelm. "I'm not getting anything through this."

"Let me try," Scabia said. "I used these a great deal in my youth with my mate. Hmmm. You know, Wistala, we may share but little distant blood, but I think our years together here have made us as close as though we were hatched here."

She settled it on her head and closed her eyes. After a long moment, her pinkish gaze returned to the assembly.

"Nothing. He may be dead, he may have lost it, or had it taken. He may have some injury or defect that prevents its working—how is his mindspeech?"

"I wouldn't know," Wistala said. "We never used it much."

AuRon said he'd never tried.

"Do we know he made it to the old tower of the Circle of Man?" Scabia asked.

"I believe he did," Wistala said. "I saw a tower set against the sea and clouds. Dragons, some kind of a sea-cave, or maybe it was just the ocean striking rocks at night."

"Then go to him. I have an—intuition—that the fate of our world will be decided to the east, in Hypat."

Wistala could tell AuRon was out of sorts. She flew close to him and let DharSii take the lead of the trio.

"You look unhappy, brother."

He stared grimly ahead, straight down his nose, where the point of his egg-tooth could still be marked between his nostrils. He'd kept it, believing it brought him luck, but the cartilage of his aging snout had thickened and swallowed much of it. "I've an odd feeling. Intuition, perhaps. Foreboding. I've a strange feeling that I'm on my last journey—my last corporeal journey, that is. I'm not sure what mystical paths I might tread."

"You?" She was surprised to hear this kind of statement from him; AuRon hid his emotions as his skin hid him against a cavern wall. He'd always been such a prosaic dragon. Even DharSii was more poetic.

"I'm a very frightened dragon deep down, Tala. Hiding it is survival instinct. It doesn't serve to tell others what you are thinking under the best of circumstances. Before, every flight I've taken has had purpose. On this one, I do not see how it gets me to where I wish to be."

"Where is that?" Wistala asked.

"With Natasatch by my side, in some quiet, roadless land with decent hunting."

"Our parents fulfilled that dream. It did not do them any good."

He changed course slightly to catch a shift in wind direction. "That's no reason not to try for ourselves. An ideal is no less estimable just because some fail in practice. Honesty is an ideal worth pursuing, but no one is completely honest. You, Wistala, you're one of the most honest dragons I know and I admire you for it, but you can't say you've been honest at all times with everyone."

She thought it in bad taste for AuRon to bring up her hatchlings like this, but she had to agree.

The weather warmed and dampened as they crossed the Red Mountains. Thicker forests grew on the western slopes of the Red Mountains, even the snowline held clusters of pines, clinging to each other like roped-together explorers.

Forests within forests could be found on foot. A second layer of thick, thorny shrubs with broad leaves captured what light filtered through the treetops. A third forest of lichens and fungi lived below that, more brilliantly green than either tree leaves and needles or thorny midgrowth. Fungi had turned much of the tree bark and inevitable deadfalls into a green carpet.

AuRon knew this ground—he'd hunted across it with some wolves in his youth. He found a quiet glade where they could rest and take water. Unfortunately it was poor hunting ground, unless you liked stripping bark for insects and digging up mice and shaking polecats out of fallen logs, but they could rest without fear of being disturbed by anything but jays complaining about dragon-scent from the branches.

They reached Juutfod in one long flight from the mountains. Three dragons arriving together as darkness fell struck up an alarm.

AuRon seemed to be on some sort of guardedly hostile terms with the dragons of the tower. On the one *sii*, he'd brought down the Wizard of the Isle of Ice, who'd bred and trained some of these dragons together and raised them to glory, but over on the stronger *saa* side even the most nostalgic old dragon, remembering when they'd been feared across the Inland Ocean, had to admit that every flight the wizard's dragons took was at the orders of their men, and the dragonelles had been most abominably treated, like laying hens in coops.

There were a few oaths tossed back and forth as the dragons of the tower came out on the craggy green peninsula to see what the newcomers wanted as the gannets and puffins watched and chattered.

"If it isn't NooShoahk the assassin," one of the tower dragons called, using one of the worst epithets in the dragon tongue.

"What's the matter, Blazewing, miss your nose-rings?" AuRon called back.

"Steady there, AuRon," NiVom said.

A big green dragon-dame shouldered through the males. "AuRon! Good to see you again, you old chameleon. How is Natasatch?" AuRon recognized her as one of the dragonelles who'd been chained in the dark next to his mate.

"Well enough, Hermethea. So you found a berth at the dragon tower, too?"

"I tried inland, but I missed the taste of cod and lobster. I like the air here when I wish to fly and the smell of other dragons when I sleep. I'm surprised to find you off your isle. We all thought you meant to leave your bones there."

AuRon introduced her to Wistala and DharSii. Wistala thought her nice enough, though a bit bug-eyed.

At last their brother joined the throng on the broken ground leading up to the tower. Wistala decided that the tower would be almost impossible to attack from either land or sea if it were defended by soldiers. It would take dragons in the air to destroy it.

"So here you are," the Copper said. An old woman who had been leaning on both him and a cane for support listened in. "Just in time for war."

"We came to give you news, and assistance if you need it," Wistala said. She and DharSii took turns explaining the attack on Vesshall and the ship-burning raid on the Aerial Host camp.

Wistala asked, "What happened to the dragonhelm?"

"Some locals we'd hired as guides filched it. Odd bunch— dressed poor but rich as Hypatian merchant fleeters. They hired the dragon tower to go after some dwarfs. Fortunately for me, we came to another arrangement. They've joined the tower, but we lost a few things when the humans decamped. Turned out they were professional thieves."

"They could not have traveled fast with bags of gold," DharSii said. "Did you hunt them?"

"They just took jewelry. Killed poor young Longfang, who was on watch at the gate, as they escaped. Some gems the dwarfs had, and a belt with a great crystal, and my dragon-helm, which is nothing but silver, and the Wyrmaster's old circlet of dragon-wings, which is nothing but copper wire and would hardly buy a new rowboat. I suppose they thought they might sell it south, in the Empire. We sent a couple dragons down the old north road, but no sign of them. One of the Empire dragons rose up from that town Quarryness to challenge them, and couldn't give a broken piece of scale about helping us track murdering thieves. Said it was none of our business, as if a blood debt and recovery of our own could be anyone else's. Our dragons turned around rather than start a fight."

"We'd feared you were dead," Wistala said.

The Copper snorted. "I feared it myself for a moment, down in the tunnels with the dwarfs. But it worked out in the end. They joined the tower on a temporary basis, until they build up enough wealth to reestablish themselves, perhaps on the wild coast across the Inland Ocean."

"If we're to have a council of war," the old woman said, "might we do it indoors out of the wind?"

They all agreed to continue inside the tower. They took over the lowest level, which had the most floor space between the alcoves. Wistala saw an old design in the floor tiles, a human figure with outstretched arms and legs encompassed by a circle. The circle had at one time been painted with gold, but it was heavily flaked. She suspected the dragons had been licking at it.

Men of Juutfod, so hairy they could have passed for tall dwarfs, served the inevitable mutton and honey-mead for dragons with a sweet tooth, and water with lime for those who preferred sour. Meager rations, but welcome after their days of flying from the Sadda-Vale.

Hermethea and another of the fliers attended, as well as Shadowcatch from the groundeds. It was a very informal council of war, more a series of quiet conversations among the groups of dragons.

Wistala found it touching the way Shadowcatch watched over her brother. It was hard to reconcile the lordly RuGaard from his throne in the Lavadome with the twisted, scarred, pinion-winged sulker from his years at the Sadda-Vale and the wretched hatchling who'd given his family over to slavers. She wondered if a third dragon had formed here in Juutfod, a creature of personal loyalties, just seeking the return of his mate.

DharSii was strange and remained in the background, as

though still deciding which way to jump. He had his own interests in the history of the Lavadome, its connection to Anklemere, and above all the strange crystals that all seemed connected in some fashion. She'd heard him tense briefly when they mentioned the loss of the big crystal in the dwarf's belt.

AuRon just wanted to know what he had to do to get back to his quiet life with his mate, Wistala decided.

"So they have declared war on us?" AuRon asked. "Are NiVom and Imfamnia settling old accounts?"

"I don't believe the Dragon Empire considers us worth a war," DharSii said. "To them, we're an annoying blister. A small, sharp tooth will relieve whatever pain this little pustule causes them. That's the only thing that explains so meager an effort."

The Copper thought for a moment. "Or they were trying to provoke you into rashness."

"Might we inspire others to join us?" Wistala asked. "I've been to the Lavadome recently. The few remaining dragons down there resent those on the surface. They are literally being bled dry to fund NiVom's need to fill his treasury and Rayg's experiments."

"Even were we to throw the whole strength of the dragon tower against the empire, we could be defeated by the Hypatians, with just the dragons who live there," the Copper said. "We'd be a setback, nothing more. A few sparrows can spook a horse and throw it off stride. We might trip them, briefly."

"We can't oppose them by force, then," DharSii said.

"Alone, no," the Copper said. "We need allies."

"Who would dare go against the Empire?" AuRon asked.

"What about the princedoms of the Sunstruck Sea?" Shadowcatch said. "They're already under attack."

"They're divided," AuRon said. "They don't trust dragons, for one. There are language difficulties. Though there are so many of them. City after city. It would take all the dragons of the Empire just to put one dragon in each."

"They probably will wage just enough war to force a reasonable tribute from the princes, as Ghioz did," the Copper said.

Wistala said, "I have friends in the north, among the Hypatians. They may be enough."

Gettel, who'd left another conversation and joined their group, rapped her cane on one of the old mosaic stones. "According to the tribesmen north of Juutfod, the Empire is demanding a vast levy in cattle from the barbarians. If they pay, it means there will be starvation in nearly every village. They wonder how, after giving up so many cattle, they will ever be able to pay next year's tribute if one is demanded, or the one after that. It takes a long time to replace a cattle-herd. In the meantime, no milk for the children. They and the Hypatians are old enemies. Long ago, they sacked the city and occupied it briefly. That's a story still told beside every hearth in the barbarian lands. They might be up for another try at them. I've had emissaries from the chiefs' visit, asking for help dealing with the dragons. The barbarians can handle anything but fire from the air—it terrifies them."

"One dragon, to a barbarian, is dangerous," she continued. "Two would be a calamity. Three and there would be some who'd take ship and risk the icy coast rather than stay among them."

"And six?" DharSii asked.

"I'm not sure they can count that high. It requires a second hand," AuRon said.

The dragons, save Wistala, chuckled at that. She'd seen the barbarians in their war against the dwarfs. If aroused, they were a terrible foe. She wondered if NiVom knew that, or saw only a vast expanse of villages connected by a few pack-trader trails and hunting tracks.

AuRon said the barbarians were very much like the wolves of the forest. They had no one king, but numerous chiefs. Getting the chiefs to unite in any permanent fashion was impossible. In the short term, they might unite in order to raid and plunder after a bad summer, or the loss of livestock to disease.

"Do we really want another war?" Wistala said.

"If the Empire falls in the manner of Silverhigh, that's the end of dragons," AuRon said. "I think it's inevitable. Once the Hypatians decide they are strong enough, they'll overthrow the dragons themselves."

The dragons absorbed AuRon's words. All had heard legends of the days of death at the fall of Silverhigh. For an age afterward, dragons had hidden and scattered, until the Copper had brought them back to the surface.

"That would be the end of us," the Copper said.

"They might rebuild on clan basis. Skotol and so on," DharSii said. "There are still strong affiliations, though since the civil wars and Tyr Fehazathant, clan affiliations have been discouraged and he did all he could to break up the old allegiances."

"Perhaps we could precipitate their revolt," AuRon said. "Control it, so it is directed against NiVom and Imfamnia. Turn them against the Empire. Wistala has friends high in their councils, I believe. They might rally behind reinstalling Tyr RuGaard."

"Perhaps," Wistala said, "but the librarians aren't influential. They're a bit like the Ankelenes in the Lavadome. They go to them for the answering of questions; they don't have the influence to sway a city."

"All I wish for is my mate back. I'm willing to walk alone into the Empire to demand it," the Copper said.

"RuGaard was rather clever about making the Hypatians his pets," DharSii continued. "They would lose much if the Empire falls before they've reestablished themselves all around the Inland Ocean."

"One day they will realize that *they* are the Empire, more than a handful of dragons," AuRon said. "Clever men will decide that they could do better without dragons taking the lion's share of the Empire's riches. After that, we're finished."

"If they haven't decided that already," Wistala said.

"So, we are resolved to break up the Empire," AuRon said. "And render the Hypatians impotent at the same time."

The dragons all nodded.

"A difficult task," DharSii said.

"The Empire's strong enough to resist any outside attack now, by any power I can think of," the Copper said. "Hypatian troops, Ironrider mercenaries, and slave-regiments, two fleets on the Inland Ocean and another being built on the Sunstruck Sea, both wings of the Aerial Host, Roc-rider scouts, the Griffaran Guards—any one of those could smash the barbarians if they so chose."

"I think Gettel is right," Wistala said. "If we can handle the dragons, the barbarians might humble the newly arrogant Hypatians. They only think they're strong because the dragons have won all their battles for them."

A shadow passed over the opening at the top of the tower.

"Get Gettel," a dragon voice shouted. "They are coming! The dragons of the Empire are coming!"

"It seems we weren't the only ones plotting war," the Copper said.

Chapter 12

W hy, oh why, had she ever joined the Aerial Host?
Varatheela wondered.

Of course she knew. She'd been a Firemaid and spent two years guarding an underground lake a weeks' walk from the Lavadome, halfway between Anaea and Imperial Rock. Once it had been an important artery on the *kern* trade route—the older Firemaids said that *kern* had been a vital nutrient that allowed underground dragons to remain healthy without ever getting sun.

She'd had such fun in her early years as a Firemaid, too. Parties and feasts and the sisterly affection of the First Oath. There'd been such thrilling games and contests against the young dragons, with the wingless females set against the Drakwatch and the mature dragonelles skirmishing with the young training reserves of the Aerial Host. Such colorful young males, many with wealthy parents aboveground in governorships.

One was sure to ask her to mate, and then she'd have a sad party to bid farewell to the Firemaids and a happy party with many of the same dragons to celebrate the mating.

The game of deciding on a mate was such fun. She took her time enjoying the attentions of several different males, but when the orders came for her to lead some younger drakka on a long training mission in the west tunnel she looked forward to the excursion. She would finally make up her mind while away, and alternately gladden and break hearts on her return.

So she led the dragons on the march, passing on the lessons she'd learned about tunnel fighting and finding food and water and the way to know which direction is north when you're deep underground (large patches of cave moss formed natural channels that indicated the north-south axis and glowed slightly better on the flanges facing south in the Northern Hemisphere, reversed in the Southern).

But tragedy struck. A Third-Oath Firemaid guarding the dwarf-barge crossing died of illness and as the senior Firemaid available, Varatheela had to take her place and serve with the surviving Firemaid, a dull old hypochondriac named Angalia. Strictly temporary, Angalia assured her with a wink as the trainees were sent back west under the next senior Firemaid.

So began a good many dreary years.

She sent message after message back to the Lavadome, asking when a replacement could be found for Angalia's dead partner. Every half year, she received a few brief lines from Ayafeeia that were, in essence, "I don't understand. You have replaced her?"

"But only temporarily," she would bellow out into the lake.

Angalia would chuckle. "That's what I used to say. Ohh, my poor joints. Varatheela, heat some sheepskins to throw over them, won't you, dear?"

Angalia would talk about the glory days of the *kern* trade, when they might see a new face as often as once every ten or twenty days, or the time they'd fought some demen raiders before Ayafeeia finally took the Star Tunnel. What little traffic there was these days were training marches from the Drakwatch, Firemaids, and Aerial Host. And, of course, the bloodletters, demen who showed up with the regularity of a tide.

She did learn a few words of dwarfish. The bargemen who crossed the lake brought trade-dwarfs a few times a year, on their way to sell their packs in the Lavadome. But even the luxury trade the Lavadome used to see had moved aboveground, and the dwarfs with it. The remaining traders were those unfortunates and failures who lost the better routes and made what they could off the trickle of underground dragon trade. Their beards were dark and patchy with hardly a glimmer of light.

The food was dreadful. Fish taken from the lake by the dwarfs, heavily salted, and fried in their own liver oil. Salt pork once in a great while from the Lavadome.

"There are some tunnels leading to the surface on the far end of the lake, dear," Angalia advised. "Sometimes you can find escaped thralls in them, trying to make it out. They get lost and come down to the lake to find water. Sniff around the banks, and if you smell hominid, that means some are wandering about. They usually come back. The trick is to find a good drippy spot and sit with just your nostrils up. Then when they're sucking water, you lunge up and get them by the head."

She made a halfhearted attempt to hunt thralls, but the only one she saw was hardly an adult, rail-thin, and covered in either pox or bug-bites that showed bright red against her pale skin. She didn't have the heart to take her. In fact, she silently wished her well and left her a bit of bladder-wrapped salt pork she'd brought along as provision.

After a year of listening to water drip into the lake, she applied for, and received, a week in the Lavadome.

While even the meager foodstuffs grown and livestock raised in the Lavadome seemed a banquet compared to the fare available at the crossing post, the rest of the visit was a terrible disappointment. The dragons who'd been courting her had moved on to other Firemaids, or had been promoted into the Aerial Host, or had gone on to apprenticeships. Other young dragonelles were attracting the attention of the trainees, who suddenly looked young to her. Squatting beside the lake with Angalia had left her scale dull and the dreadful food had made her lose weight. She discovered, to her horror, that her skin sagged about the wings, hips, and tail. She looked like she'd aged a decade!

At one of the dinners with the Firemaids, Ayafeeia mentioned that she was being pressed by Imfamnia, hard, to give up some more Firemaids to the Aerial Host. To Ayafeeia, the Firemaids defended the next generation of dragons: The Lavadome still had more hatchlings in it than all of the Protectorates combined. Some thought this was because dragonelles expecting eggs wanted the comforts and familiar surroundings of their home hills when about to produce a clutch, but Ayafeeia thought the dragons on the surface were too busy greedily gathering every head of livestock and ring of metal they could fit between their grasping *sii* to produce any hatchlings.

I'll go into the Host! she'd squeaked like a hatchling. She actually looked around after speaking, so strange did her voice sound to her.

Once she'd made that fateful decision, all the rest of the choices were easy. She hated the idea of carrying around a greasy, twitchy, complaining human. She'd heard from other dragons in the Host that having a rider wasn't all it was made out to be. Yes, you had someone constantly attending to your teeth, scale, and claws, but their meals came out of *your* ration, and all the clothes and boots and furs and weapons and accoutrements came out of *your* hoard.

Once you were, quite literally, saddled with a rider, you had to take care of him, yes, him, unlike with dragons, female humans almost never devoted themselves to fighting. Everyone knew that male thralls were more trouble. When they weren't fiddling about with their fronts, they were scratching at their rears. The humans of the Aerial Host—a blighter or two were sprinkled in, but elves and dwarfs didn't care to seek fortune and glory in this manner—weren't treated like other thralls. They were left reproductively intact, for one, as the warriors who excelled in their duties were encouraged to father as many offspring as possible to either take their places in the Aerial Host or serve in one of the captaincies—human garrisons led by a dragon.

And who was expected to support the mate and all the

little squalling, hungry mouths? No wonder the dragons in the Heavy Wing of the Aerial Host constantly asked for new campaigns and opportunities to pillage.

Certainly, your human—and his family—devoted hours to care of teeth and scale, but any marketplace thrall would willingly do the same, and devote himself a good deal more to filing, pulling, and arranging scale to lie in the most attractive manner possible in exchange for safety and comfort away from the mines.

But, to her mind, the humans had the better end of the bargain. The dragon had to constantly report on the human's skill at fighting from dragon-back—all that tedious tracking of missile accuracy and lance-hits on targets. And oh! if you should happen to accidentally smash him into drippy jam while attempting a tricky maneuver that results in a collision with a fellow dragon or a cavern, everyone from your winglane to the grand commander of the Aerial Host would be giving you a thorough dressing-down for carelessness. Bad for unit morale and all that. As if you intended to have an accident!

True, some dragons in the Heavies who didn't care for their rider for whatever reason tended to arrange an accident, but one shouldn't be accused of the crimes of others. That simply wasn't fair.

So she chose the Light Wing.

At first, they almost wouldn't have her. She'd been so long guarding the crossing that her wing-muscles had atrophied, and of all those tested, she came in last on endurance, last on climbing, and next-to-last in maneuverability.

One thing saved her. On her oral examination, she spoke

of her hatching on the Isle of Ice and her first years there, where under her parents' tutelage she learned to scout, hunt, find shelter, fish, crab, forage for metals—useful Upper World skills that few of the idle young dragons of the Empire could match. She had a good record with the Firemaids, too, and anyone who could spend a year with Angalia on guard duty without going mad and shrieking off into the darkness was not prone to fits of nerves or depressions. The two Light Wing veterans suddenly turned pleasant.

Welcome to the Aerial Host Lights, daughter of Natasatch, CuSarrath, the Wing Commander, said. She always thought of herself as the daughter of AuRon and Natasatch, but it would be have been impolitic of the Wing Commander to mention her father. He was in exile, after all.

Her father. She thought of him as a bit of a crank. He would have been happy living his life out on that cold little island, bathing in glacier water. As a newly winged dragonelle, she'd disliked him intensely, always trying to keep her out of the social life of the Empire, but she'd grown more sympathetic to his nature when she was in the Firemaids. She was feeling that she might like a little peace and quiet, without orders or duties or bleedings, especially if she could find a well-struck, conversational, and cultured male.

She looks stunned, the other examiner said, and she pulled herself back out of her thoughts and thanked them. They gave her directions on where to go next, and an Aerial Host identifying ring for her ear that she could show at any Empire post for garrison bedding, rations, and medicines, should she need them.

They gave her a lecture about how service in the Light Wing was very demanding but she could now consider herself among the elite of the Empire—no matter what the Heavies said about the Heavy Wing being present and key to every major victory of the Empire.

Strangely pleased with herself, she was welcomed into the main training cave for the Light Wing. It stood in the fabled dwarf halls that had once belonged to the Chartered Company traders. They'd since relocated, having taken a ridiculously small offering from a Hypatian noble for the keys to the delvings that sat picturesquely in the middle of a waterfall. Someone said he'd fallen into debt and been rescued by NoSohoth, who took possession of the halls. He offered them to the Aerial Host as patriotic duty to support the Empire—but if they'd share a small percentage of coin brought away from their pillaging expeditions, he'd see that Hypatia improved the quality of the food barged up to the delvings.

Which was its own brand of perdition. The Lights were forever being tested and judged. Speed trials. Flame accuracy trials. Observation trials. The moon never changed fully around without some kind of test where your performance was recorded, and if you were at the bottom of the class—without a certified injury or illness—twice in a year, you were booted out and given a choice of going into the Heavies, taking up garrison duty, or being allocated to dreary tunneling or thrall guard duty.

She was healthy and young, without injury or deformity,

so there was little problem with outperforming dragons who'd been injured in action or brought up on sickly diets, as seemed to be the case with some of these older dragons who'd been raised in the Lavadome. She'd known plenty of sunlight once she came aboveground on the Isle of Ice, with a diet of fresh, wiggling fish, crustaceans, and a good deal of mutton. Her only shortcoming was, perhaps, a tendency to have thinnish scale—the Isle of Ice was not rich in metals—but on Host rations of mined copper the scales were coming in thicker and faster.

So she exercised relentlessly and volunteered for everything. Like this fast-flapping flight.

Oh, Mother, how wrong you were. Perhaps Father had been right. He'd never wanted to become involved in the Empire. And now here she was, setting off to what could be a battle. She didn't have a fierce bone in her body.

They must be on an important mission. CuSarrath himself was leading it, after receiving a hasty message from NiVom, who was visiting NoSohoth in Hypatia. CuSarrath had told his six fastest fliers that they'd just volunteered for a sprint up to the northern borderlands of Hypatia, with him as the seventh flier.

He'd left orders to mobilize the rest of the Light Wing and recall all training groups. When at full strength, they were to relocate north to Quarryness.

Varatheela wondered what could possibly be going on that would need the whole strength of the Light Wing of the Aerial Host. Even training flights served a purpose for the Empire— watching roads and coastlines. Without the Lights, much of the Hypatian coast and the land between the Red Mountains and the Inland Ocean were vulnerable.

She was starved and exhausted by the time she reached the tower. She'd never been this far north since joining the Empire, not even on a reconnaissance flight.

She'd heard of this Dragon Tower of Juutfod, though. They were mercenaries, but hardly hostile. Most of the work they did was for the Hypatian Empire, helping the merchants who traded on the western coast or keeping the northern passes of the Red Mountains free of bandits, trolls, and the occasional Ironrider raid.

The fliers made one great circle over the tower, then began a slow descent, tightening each loop.

A red dragon with black stripes, riderless, flew up to meet them.

"Dragons of the Empire," he called. He spoke with a faintly clunky Skotl accent, Varatheela decided. It was halfway familiar to her. "Welcome to Juutfod. Are you in need of direction?"

Alarm bells rang faintly in the town below and Varatheela saw watercraft being hastily loaded.

CuSarrath closed with the striped dragon. "Well, DharSii, like a bit of brass in a bag of gold, you show up again."

"State your business," this DharSii—or Quick-Claw—called.

"We have learned that the criminal RuGaard has broken his parole and is making mischief against the Empire here. He is to be turned over to us. I give you the Sun King's word that he will not be harmed, but he will be rendered flightless and placed somewhere where he can be watched and attended properly."

"Broke his parole, you say? How careless. By doing what?"

"Do you admit he is here?" CuSarrath asked loudly. Cu-Sarrath was a bright enough dragon, but to his way of thinking, whoever made the most noise won an argument.

The striped red cleared his throat. "I admit to fishing with him from this tower. The sailfish are unusually large this year, CuSarrath. They must have had a rich winter in southern waters."

"Ha," CuSarrath said. "You admit it."

"He gave his word that he would not reenter the Empire, and apart from a rather shabby trick by NiVom on the Isle of Ice, he hasn't broken that word. Unless you claim Juutfod and the dragon tower, too. Shall I tell them about a change in allegiance? It might anger them—they're almost a clan unto themselves and they value their independence."

"We would, if those old saddlesore swaybacks and their gimpy hag were worth it. Bandy words all you like, but Juutfod is part of ancient Hypatia. Hypatia is part of the Dragon Empire."

"Rubbish and nonsense," DharSii said. "To listen to the Hypatians, the Eternal East is part of Hypatia, because Trader Iao of the First Directory once emptied his bladder in the sulfur pools while buying tea in Ya-ying. The nearest Hypatian hall is in Quarryness, and that's more than a day's gallop away. If you knew your Hypatian law, CuSarrath, unless a fast rider can cover the distance to a Hypatian hall in a day, any borderland is not legally part of the Empire."

Varatheela did not follow politics, but to her it seemed DharSii was getting the better of the exchange.

"I'm relieved you know where the Hypatian hall is, Dhar-Sii. Tell RuGaard that he has three days to get his affairs in order and present himself at the hall in Quarryness, or we'll come and get him and turn this tower into the legendary rubble-heap of Juutfod."

"If anyone comes to Quarryness, it will be to buy mustard," DharSii said. "It's delicious on poached sailfish. It appears you have three days left to enjoy one, should you care to spend your time in the north more profitably."

"Three days, DharSii. Tell him if he values his mate's health and the dragon tower's continued existence, he should appear."

At this, the striped dragon looked angry. He let his gaze travel up and down CuSarrath's fighting line, as if wondering how many he could cripple before being brought down. Varatheela tried to look resolute, but she couldn't help liking this fellow.

Perhaps fearing a verbal riposte, CuSarrath executed a beautiful flip and reversed direction with two hard flaps. The other six Lights fell in behind him, all trained to turn in the same direction to avoid collision. Varatheela flapped hard and regained her position as second-rearmost by seniority.

They landed in wild country, exhausted. CuSarrath took pity on his fliers and volunteered for the first watch. No telling what might be roaming the woods—Varatheela knew in a vague sort of way that her aunt Wistala had killed a troll somewhere hereabouts.

When CuSarrath's watch was over and the other dragons felt somewhat revived, there was some grousing about their empty bellies.

"Another cold, comfortless camp," the oldest of them, Au-Hazathant, said. He was a leathery old red with thick scales growing in patches.

"Wish we'd just gutted it out and made it back to Quarry-ness."

The dragon next to him groaned: "Tell that to my wings."

"Who was that DharSii fellow? I believe I've heard of him," Varatheela said. "He looked like a cross between a Skotl and a Wyrr. How often does that happen?"

"He goes back to Tyr Fehazathant's days," AuHazathant said. "I don't know his clan background. He once commanded the Aerial Host. I was told he murdered the Tyr's heir. He fled, but I don't think he was ever formally convicted of the crime. If he did do it, he's triply clever."

Varatheela decided to probe. "I was told Queen Tighlia poisoned him."

"I'd heard SiMevolant did him in."

Varatheela yawned. "I'm too tired for gossipy history. Shall we be quiet now?"

"I wouldn't mind a nice piece of sailfin this night," Au-Hazathant said. "Any of you had it, mates? It's so red you'd mistake it for beef. Mouthwatering."

Varatheela felt her mouth go wet at the thought.

"So, we're bringing in RuGaard. That's the urgency," she said.

The youngest, a silver named AgLaberarn said, "Wouldn't

you know. Politics. Politics always is triply urgent to those who give the orders. Not like a little raid by pirates or anything. No, that's hardly worth the flight."

"I don't recall anyone getting bled by demen when he was Tyr. Except in fighting them," AuHazathant said.

"That's enough of that, AuHazathant, or you'll be in my report to NiVom," CuSarrath said without opening his eyes, though his nostrils had flared in irritation. That shocked them back into silence.

Varatheela tried to ignore her empty belly and go to sleep. But it occurred to her that the Isle of Ice and the cave she'd been born in was but a long, fast flight west into the Inland Ocean. She knew every hole, the coves with the biggest crabs, and where sheep retreated in a snowstorm. It wouldn't be difficult for her to disappear, if she were determined to leave. One dragonelle more or less wouldn't make a difference to the Lights, not with so many frightened Firemaids trying to find a posting now that their leader was dead.

Chapter 13

A sunless dawn slowly revealed the landscape draped by clouds. To AuRon, the air smelled like thunder. Not surprising at this time of year—the Inland Ocean saw long, slow storms in the fall and fast-moving thunderheads in the spring.

Still, thunder made him anxious. He would rather have been underground sleeping.

Instead, he was sheltering in the lee of the dragon tower and the rocky ridge of the peninsula it sat upon, listening to the report of a scouting run, and wondering if Shadowcatch remembered him for well or ill.

The scout had made a dangerous flight. She'd flown between piney tree trunks, below the tops of the tallest green spires, to approach the dragon camp at Quarryness—a trick few dragons could manage—and returned in a single night after an Aerial Host scout had been spotted following the Old North Road and the seashore.

Also present were old Hermethea of the dragon tower, who came along because a few females could sometimes prevent quarrels from rising to violence, DharSii, and his siblings. Shadowcatch had begged to be given a one-day head start, saying he would swim all the way to Quarryness, but the Copper refused.

"I'll find you, one way or another, my Tyr, even if I have to wade across a lake of dwarfs," Shadowcatch said.

The fast-flying dragon, who suffered to bear a rider on her back to watch her tail and act as a second pair of eyes, double-checking her observations, returned and reported to the Copper.

"They rested at Roadsend. At dawn they flew back to Quarryness," the scout said.

"Where they'll wait. The question is, what they'll do when they're through with waiting," the Copper said. "Will they come north or return south?"

"Numbers?" DharSii asked. "Have other members of the Host joined them?"

"Twenty-two. Riderless dragons," the human said, consulting a bit of slate with some chalk marks on it. "One gray. Rest various."

"Red in charge, I think, many, many *laudi*," the dragonelle added. *Laudi*, or wing-legends, were given to Empire dragons who'd triumphed in battle to distinguish them. The dyes ranged from colorful to muted, depending on the dragon's taste, but whatever the color the decorations were a sign of a battle-tested dragon.

"The gray will be a messenger," DharSii said. "They're no good in battle—excuse me, AuRon—they're *thought* to be no good in battle, but their speed is unmatched."

"I wonder who this red is," the Copper said. "If it's Cu-Vallahall, he was a young dragon from my day who never liked having a rider, but he's levelheaded. One Skotl, one Wyrr parent."

"What's Roadsend?" AuRon asked. He didn't know much about the Hypatian northlands, not having roamed them since he traveled with Blackhard's pack as an unwinged drake. "The end of the Old North Road?"

"No, it goes well beyond that; it's just not kept in any real repair," Wistala said. "Roadsend is the last Imperial Post in the old system. To the south, the road is reasonably safe. It's barbarian country beyond."

"What are they doing?" the Copper asked the scout and her rider.

"Usual doings," the human said in decent Drakine. "Eat much. Drink much. Bellow much, for more eat and drink."

"I wonder if this is just a rest?" Wistala asked. "Might they go looking for AuRon at the Isle of Ice, or me at the Sadda-Vale?"

"They came to get me," the Copper said. "It's up to me to talk to them."

"If their orders are just to kill you, they'll do it," DharSii said. "They won't let you get five words out."

"They might listen to me," the Copper said. "I'll come

along. If they've been given orders to assassinate a dragon trying to parley, well—they can do it and try to live with themselves. It'll mean the Empire I grew up in truly is dead."

Wistala brought her head close to DharSii and stared levelly into his eyes. AuRon wondered what mindspeech was passing between them.

"Where my brothers go, I'll be by their side," Wistala said to the rest.

"What are your intentions?" DharSii asked.

"To join my mate," the Copper said. "That's all. This isn't politics."

"Everything is politics in the Empire," Wistala said.

"I hope they'll be satisfied with taking us back to the Tyr," AuRon said. "What would they do? Would there be a trial of some sort?"

"Countless potential rebellions have been ended with a quick set of hangings at some crossroad," DharSii said. "Let's send a rider south with a message asking for a one-to-one meeting."

"No," the Copper said. "I think we should make a show of force. NiVom needs to know if he wants to fight for control of the dragon tower, it'll cost him a hefty piece of his Aerial Host."

They took turns leading the way south, flying in a line formation. The wind was blowing strong from that direction, bringing the storm, and while the fierceness of the air made it easy to stay aloft, covering horizons in a southward lap proved exhausting in the moist, windy air.

They worked out a system, suggested by the Copper, where the front flier simply concentrated on beating the air to death. The next in the slanted line enjoyed the slipstream and made sure of navigation, and the last watched for opposing fliers, from above, below, behind—the Aerial Host trained in coming out of the sun, or using cloud banks for a stealthy approach, or "grounding" briefly to let opponents fly past before rising to the attack.

The Copper could fly in the lead only briefly before he complained of pain in his injured wing. Wistala, stalwart as always, took over for him and forged ahead into the headwinds.

No matter what his role on the flight, AuRon found his mind wandering.

He could not decide if her long association with DharSii had changed his sister. He himself admired the dragon, but DharSii always preserved an air of isolation about him, as though he were perched at the peak of a mountain, no matter what the location and company. DharSii clearly cared for Wistala, but AuRon suspected that the dragon either had an agenda of his own or had suffered so many disappointments in life that he kept a reserve against further failure.

AuRon could sympathize. His youth had been shattered in a single, brutal day when the home cave was invaded by mercenaries seeking young dragons who could be broken to the saddle. Later, he'd lost NooMoahk, the ancient black dragon who'd served as a surrogate father. He'd poured out the whole of his life into his mate and their life on the Isle of Ice, but the glitter and society of the Dragon Empire had seduced her away more easily than he could have imagined.

Still, he sensed further calamities on the horizon, much like the coming thunderstorm. It pressed on him. The massacre at the Feast was just the start of something much worse for his kind. But whom could he get to listen?

Perhaps he was cracking up. Was he committing a spectacular, public suicide and bringing his siblings along for the trip?

No, Wistala truly wanted to avoid a second Fall of Silverhigh. She feared a human/dragon war that would probably destroy both races. His brother just wanted to spend his remaining years in peace with his mate. Passions of his abdication had cooled, the Empire had grown in security, and it was reasonable to assume that NiVom and his mate would no longer see AuRon as a threat to their power.

In the Copper's mind, one of two things would happen as a result of his arriving in Quarryness.

What would *not* happen would be the dragons of the Aerial Host flying him back to NiVom and Imfamnia's palace in Ghioz for their last, triumphant audience before packing him off in chains to whichever dungeon they'd selected for him to inhabit until they found the time and reason to murder him. They couldn't force him to fly there, and if they couldn't force him to fly they couldn't force him to walk, either. If they chose to drag him, his body would fall to pieces before he arrived at the outskirts of Hypat.

What would happen? Either he would be allowed to proceed south to claim his mate, or he'd be killed.

Either might secure Nilrasha's future. With him dead, she would no longer be a threat to NiVom and Imfamnia and they would leave her alone. They might be tempted to kill her, but her position and condition were known in the Empire. For NiVom and Imfamnia to kill a flightless dragonelle, and a widow at that, would incite opinion against them. Even the worst Tyrs evoked nostalgia when they were deceased and no longer part of the Lavadome's political life.

If he was allowed to complete the march, word would pass through the Empire like flame. Those who disliked NiVom and Imfamnia would secretly support his march even as they watched and waited for a reaction. They might even work up the courage to join him. Their courtiers and lickvents in Ghioz might talk NiVom and Imfamnia into a rashness.

The chance to confront them in front of witnesses might even be worth his life. But would he spend his last breath cursing NiVom, or calling for Nilrasha?

The dragons of the Light Wing ringed the open common in front of what Wistala identified as the Hypatian hall. It wouldn't have been hard to guess which building was the Hypatian hall even without her—it was both the tallest and broadest structure in the town.

They weren't expecting him to bring other dragons, it seemed, for a ripple of activity ran through the waiting dragons. He counted twelve winged dragons—at least that he could see.

They alighted on the town common. Northerners were

clustered in every doorway and window, watching events but ready to run to safety if flame began to fly.

The Copper, used to Hypatian grandeur, had a hard time believing he had landed in Hypatia. Even Juutfod, clinging to its steep incline beneath the cliffs on its zigzag streets and heavy wharves, seemed more built-up and cosmopolitan. This was a thatch-roofed village with a few big wooden halls and a single massive stone building. Were it not for the Hypatian hall, he would have mistaken it for the seat of some barbarian warlord.

DharSii took the role of interlocutor again and opened the negotiations. Wistala and AuRon flanked him. Hermethea watched the other direction.

"Well?" CuSarrath asked. "Have you come to face justice?"

"We come to keep dragon from killing dragon," Wistala said, stepping forward and putting herself in the empty ground between the lines of dragons.

"None need die," CuSarrath said. "I'm just ordered to bring the parole-breaking dragon who was adopted under the name RuGaard back to NiVom to face the Tyr's justice. RuGaard or war against the might of the Empire, what will it be, dragons of the north?"

"I'd like to tell my side of the parole-breaking, as you call it," the Copper said.

"He will do nothing of the kind," CuSarrath said, stepping forward. "RuGaard, in the name of the Tyr and the Empire— *glaack!*"

This last was in response to Wistala leaping upon him and encircling his neck with hers. Wistala was the strongest dragonelle he'd ever known, probably stronger than most dragons, and CuSarrath had been watching DharSii as he came forward.

"We are not going to harm him," DharSii bellowed. "On my hatchlings' sheltering eggs, I will keep this oath. Hear Tyr RuGaard out and judge for yourselves."

The Copper waited to speak. He waited so long it became excruciating for him, but it only honed his audience's attention. When a hundred heartbeats had passed, he took a deep breath—

And began to speak. He kept still, moving only his head, which he held high. AuRon grudgingly credited him with a certain craftiness. Were he to turn and walk about, his limping would either disgust or evoke pity in his audience and he wanted neither.

"I've come here to surrender myself to you. Not in the manner you believe, to be put under escort, muzzled like a convict, and marched into captivity where, if I'm lucky, I'll be comfortable as I'm slowly fed poisoned meat.

"No, I'm surrendering myself to your judgment. While many of you were not yet fledged, I was presented with a dreadful choice by NiVom and Imfamnia: resign my title as Tyr and go into exile, with my mate held as hostage to my good behavior, or see her die under my gaze before having my own throat torn out.

"While my own life is just as precious to me as yours is to you, I was willing, as you are, to sacrifice it for my dragons if I thought by doing so I could gain safety and security for the next generation. It would be much tougher to condemn my mate to death through my pride and obstinacy, so I chose exile.

"Keeping my promise and hoping NiVom and Imfamnia would keep theirs—though once before the Jade Queen had betrayed dragonkind when she handed us over to the Dragon-blade and his hag-riders—I went to my brother's remote island, only to find assassins waiting. While the words of our agreement were still echoing they broke their bond. I barely escaped with my life.

"Did they expect me to come south again after that, and meet my death immediately? Perhaps."

The audience looked at each other uncomfortably, swishing their tails and shifting their feet. *Were there orders to fall on him the instant he was within reach?*

"Instead I went to the Sadda-Vale, and there waited and hoped. Hoped that a new Tyr would rise and right the wrong done to me and reunite me with my mate.

"This hasn't happened. I've recently learned that in the intervening years, matters have become much, much worse. Perhaps to you it does not seem so terrible, for their madness has crept into the Empire slowly, like lichens, which you never see growing but when conditions are right can take over a cave in a matter of days. To me, when I heard how conditions in the Empire had changed, I could only believe that I'd been exposed to rumor and exaggeration."

DharSii had helped him with his verbal presentation, teaching him to pace his speech and gradually let the speed and intensity grow.

"I intend to take my mate out, and as many dragons as I can," the Copper finished.

This started a buzz from the assembled dragons. The Copper heard the words "Heavies" and "civil war" used.

Now, to take the offensive, the Copper thought.

"I can't promise you anything, but that you won't be bled and butchered for NiVom's schemes.

"Yes, butchered. Didn't you hear? The dead from the massacre at Ghioz were loaded onto a barge, taken up the Falnges, and dumped into the Star Tunnel. You've heard the Star Tunnel is off-limits, no doubt. Would you like to know why?"

He didn't give them the chance to say no. "Someone is raising trolls in those tunnels. I don't know how many of you have ever dealt with trolls, but they are the one creature moved by the Four Spirits with both the will and the ability to hunt dragons for food. They're dreaded moonspawn, if you ask me, and now they're twice as tough.

"What purpose have they? They're very hard to command, so it's not to serve as soldiers of the Empire. Mindless yet cunning murder is all they are capable of. If NiVom and Imfamnia could plan a murder of a score of feasting dragons, what else might they attempt? I'm convinced that one day they're to be loosed into the Lavadome, when NiVom is finally done with the last of his enemies. When someone has something NiVom wants, they die. I would warn NoSohoth to keep clear of the Lavadome, for I'm sure NiVom wouldn't mind having his wealth."

"What do you want of us?" a dragon called.

"All I want is my mate. The dragonelle I pledged myself to.

The Empire has gone mad, and sooner or later NiVom and Imfamnia will decide she's an inconvenience who must be destroyed. I must protect her, whatever the risk to myself. Were I killed, she might even be allowed to go free, as there'd be no further use for her."

DharSii stifled an attempt by CuSarrath to speak. He probably wanted to mention his first mate, Halaflora, who allegedly died with fertilized eggs inside her. Lavadome rumor, based on court gossip, said they were another male's, but he knew that to be false. Lavadome rumor also said that Nilrasha, his mate, had choked her, for she'd been found standing over the body with poor Halaflora's blood on her *sii*. Halaflora had always been sickly and had difficulty eating. The Copper believed Nilrasha's story that she'd choked on a chicken bone. He had to believe it, or many difficult years in the world had been wasted.

"I intend to rescue her from the rocky tower of her captivity and take her away, on foot, as she can no longer fly any more than I can see out of this eye."

Wistala looked at the ground at that, he noticed.

The Copper walked up and down the line of the Aerial Host, as he had seen their commanders do before battle. "Then I will depart the Empire, never to return, at least while it exists in this fashion, literally bleeding dragons to death for a single powerful dragon's purpose. I will take as many dragons as wish to come with me. Whether I will be your Tyr or not in our new home, that's for you to decide. I don't particularly want the burdens—I'd much rather act as an occasional adviser to a younger, more vigorous dragon, or a veteran of many lands and many battles such as DharSii."

That perked them up. Some looked at DharSii with new interest.

"Now, who will join me on this march? I can guarantee, nothing like it has ever happened in the history of dragons. We will go south, through the heart of the Hypatian Empire, seeking neither enmity nor succor, until we stand at the base of the rocky tower that keeps my mate from me. I do not expect the rightness of my cause to shield me, but it will strengthen me to face whatever the fates have in store for us. If I find that they have murdered Nilrasha, a flightless dragon, alone in a remote fastness, held without communication or congress, I will attempt to avenge her. I will not ask any of you to join me for that.

"One final journey, into the Empire and then back out again. We will proclaim, again and again, that we seek nothing but my mate and then the freedom to leave unmolested. Which of you will come with me and DharSii?"

They're about to jump, AuRon thought to Wistala. *They'll all jump one way or another. Either with us, or on us.*

He wished his brother had given him some warning of the nature of the speech. Wistala hadn't known, either; she'd jumped when the Copper said he was accompanying him on his march.

As he listened, he was shocked to see Varatheela in the group of listeners. She looked well, strong and supple and in condition, with Wistala's wingspan and his own mother's long neck and tail.

AuRon did his best to ignore his daughter, tempted as he was to admire her. She hadn't much cared for him since she'd breathed her first fire and he knew it. If he stared at her, she would never move, or worse, would say something against the Copper's speech.

"I'll come with you, my Tyr," a thin golden dragon said.

That was the first. A malcontent, a dragon who bore a grudge against his fellows. . . . It proved nothing. It was the second that counted. If two would join the Copper, he might have the rest jumping in.

"You fools! You'll burn!" CuSarrath snarled.

"All the better," said the haggard gold dragon who was the first to join the Copper. "Trolls won't be able to eat us."

In the end, a majority of the Lights joined their old Tyr. They ended up with seven, all of whom had memories of his time as Tyr. AuRon suspected they'd been moved to sympathy. He felt them go over to his brother when his brother said that the rightness of his cause would not shield him, but it would strengthen him. He wondered just how much of that speech was DharSii and what belonged to his brother. DharSii certainly looked satisfied with the result.

Chapter 14

NiVom startled at the step of the messenger-flier. His firebladder ached as though it had been stabbed, and it took a moment for it to calm down. Anxiety always gave him a sour bladder. The messenger had been the wrong color for his mood. For just a moment, RuGaard stood in front of him. Then he realized it was a gray, serving as messenger for the Light Wing of the Aerial Host. He was standing in their expansive quarters in front of a copper sheet etched with ancient Elvish characters. Imfamnia had found it somewhere among the Red Queen's possessions years ago and saved it from being shredded and devoured. He really should make a study of Elvish someday. There was a good deal of it lying about in the Red Queen's old archives and some of it might be very interesting reading. It would be nice to know the words ringing his face every time he looked at it. For all he knew, it was the Red Queen's final curse on those who would steal her palace.

The Red Queen and Imfamnia shared a fault: vanity.

"My Tyr," the messenger said, bowing.

No briskness to the bow, no excitement to the step. It must be bad news. Messengers always crackled with energy when delivering good news, even when exhausted after a long flight.

"Refreshment? Food? Wine? Co-comfortable lounger?" he finished awkwardly, realizing he was about to offer a gray coin.

"No, my Tyr. Thank you, my Tyr," the messenger said.

"Out with it, then."

"CuSarrath found the former Tyr. He was with his brother, sister, and that renegade DharSii."

"I take it CuSarrath didn't bag the lot."

"No, my Tyr. In fact—"

"Well, he's a slippery fellow, the old Tyr. We fought together, back when a campaign in the Upper World was a rarity. With Ghioz, over a nothing dustbowl of an uphold. We won, though."

"Of course you did, my Tyr. But if you don't mind me saying, you're mistaken. He didn't get away. Not exactly. He's marching south."

"Into Hypatia? He and what army?"

"That's just it, my Tyr. Ours. Some of the Lights went over to him."

CuSarrath! Strong of wing but weak of brain! He should never have allowed the Light Wing its own headquarters; it should have remained attached to the rest of the Host. He'd have the Grand Commander's head for this—

Back to the matter at hand, NiVom. Matter at hand. He

struggled to return his face to the usual calm interest he displayed when dealing with messengers.

"Dare I ask if there's more?"

"CuSarrath asks for more dragons. All of the Aerial Host, gathered at Hypat. He sends that it is urgent, but the rebels are traveling on foot, so there is time."

On foot? Why under the stars would they do that? A dragon was ten times as fast in the air. It made no sense.

"Been in the air long, gray?"

"Three days getting here, my Tyr."

"Very well. You're relieved. Recover for a day, and report back for duty to the ready post. Before you go, send up a fresh messenger. The fastest they have available."

When the new messenger arrived, he gave orders to the Grand Commander of the Aerial Host to send as many of the Heavy Wing as he could back to Ghioz. He could suspend operations on the Sunstruck Sea for now.

Waste, waste, and more waste. If they were lucky, they'd lose only supplies. If they weren't, the supports and auxiliaries with the Aerial Host would be captured. But the political threat must be dealt with, and quickly. If he'd learned anything in his years in the Lavadome, it was that each Tyr lay atop a heap of duties and challenges, an ever-shifting mound of old bones, new enemies, traditions, and, most important, rivals.

A Tyr needed support atop such treacherous ground. He would have to consult Rayg.

*   *   *

The trip to the Lavadome was tiresome. It seemed everyone was still shocked by the massacre at the feast in Ghioz. NiVom dropped a hint or two that it may have been a very deep plot by certain interlopers who once thought they were fit to rule the Lavadome and the Upper World.

Before seeing Rayg, he paid a quick call on Regalia, the titular ruler of the Lavadome. He needed to console her on the loss of her brother. He was enormously satisfied to find her keeping to her quarters and the throne hall empty.

She refused to see him, which worried him for a moment. Maybe he should ask Rayg to fix something else . . . but best to consult with Imfamnia before making such a step. She could become so touchy, even in areas traditionally left to male dragons.

NiVom found Rayg in his workshop, fiddling with hunks of crystal again. A belt that smelled vaguely of dwarf lay discarded on the floor. It had been carefully cut out to extract the gem, not that a mere knife was likely to do a gem of that size any harm.

Someday, Rayg had confidently told him, he would puzzle out all the bits and pieces of the sun-shard and use the power that Rayg maintained was stored in the bowels of the dome to create an invincible fortress for dragons.

NiVom didn't like the idea of a thrall, no matter how long he'd been in the family or who he belonged to, wielding such a weapon. It would have to be quietly "put away" for his own safety. Surely Rayg could see that.

Rayg was a legacy of RuGaard. He had somehow fallen in among some dwarfs as a youth and been trained in their workshops. He had an astounding mind, quite out of the norm for hominids—one might almost say dragonlike.

He'd grown old in service to the Empire, lost—or forgot—his family in his search for secrets. He was something of an authority on the crystal structure of the Lavadome. He owned a few precious samples of it, keeping them around him in his laboratory.

NiVom had once calculated that it would take him a year and a half to identify every tool, piece of equipment, and obscure-language book in Rayg's laboratory.

Sadly, Rayg had designed it with his own convenience in mind, not a dragon's. It was hexagonal in shape, with five floors, each open on the one below, with gradual increases in floor height. At the top was a dome-observatory, with a painted star field that could be rolled and shifted to match the sky at any time. Delicate numbers and gears allowed one to re-create star positions at any date. It was in great demand with the few dragons who took an interest in astrology.

The six walls beneath that were his library. Thanks to the high windows looking out on the Lavadome, that level of the laboratory had the best light. For his comfort, Rayg had installed a chair, a bed, and even a rope-and-canvas hammock such as sailors use. When he wasn't working, he could usually be found sleeping on that level.

The level below held curiosities that engaged his intellectual interest. Odd skulls, unidentified teeth, freakishly thick or thin dragon-scale, cross sections of a crab—there was no telling what might be out of the shelves and cabinets and put on a table where it might be examined.

The level below that one held raw materials for his inventions. Ropes, cables, wood, bits of metal, chains of different size, and a few tools for the shaping and manufacture of some of the same. He didn't do serious blacksmithing in his lab; for that he and a few thrall assistants carried his specialized tools down to the base of Imperial Rock.

At the bottom was the workshop. This was where he spent most of his time, and constantly hovered between utter disarray and impossible chaos. There were piles of paper on the floor and plates of rotting, dust-covered food atop the cabinets. These attracted rats who'd found their way into the Lavadome—and the Imperial Rock's kitchens—but Rayg didn't mind. He set traps and took them alive for use as experimental subjects. After the experiments were over, they were reexamined.

That's what disgusted NiVom about visiting Rayg, more than his abominable personal hygiene. The bits of exploded rat scattered about the place brought the contents of his stomach up to just touching the back of his throat where he could taste it.

His First Thrall laid down the magnifying lens he'd been using on the circular crystal. "NiVom. Good to see you."

Rayg had long since given up on the formalities when addressing his dragon superiors. He guessed, correctly enough, that he was too valuable to eat, or even to punish for something as prosaic as bad manners.

"Troubles, Tyr? Are the new lower-drag saddles falling off?"

"Nothing like that. I need your opinion on a political matter."

"A *political* matter? How fascinating."

"Your old friend RuGaard is back. Not back in the Lava-dome, but he's returned to the Empire. On foot, it seems."

"Wing joint. He can't fly without it. I built him a pulley-based replacement back when he was Upholder of Anaea. It's probably broken."

"I'm not sorry to hear that an invention of yours failed, for once."

"I wouldn't call a score's worth of years of wear and tear before breaking a failure. Quite the opposite."

"That's not why I've come to see you. Do you know of . . . of any way to put a large group of dragons, outside, to sleep or something, quickly?"

"Just sleep?" Rayg said. "Suppose one or two die?"

"That's an acceptable risk."

"For how long?"

"Just a few moments would be enough. You see, some of the Host have joined him. I believe we could talk sense into them, in time. Also, I want RuGaard taken alive. I've no intention to make a martyr of him or his mate. I'd like everyone to see how wretched he is before he gets tossed into the darkest hole in the Lower World."

"Why do you hate him so? He's not a bad sort. Very decent to me, in my youth. Though he never did get around to granting me my freedom."

"I was an exile, too. Had he remained faithful to our friendship and Tyr Fehazathant, I should have become Tyr after Tighlia died. She arranged for my exile. I should have known he wanted the title for himself."

"He never gave me that impression," Rayg said. "I had the

feeling he would rather have been anything but Tyr. No ambition, you see, except perhaps for a quiet life in the country somewhere. I imagine that if you offered him his mate and that, you'd never hear from him again."

"No, I'm afraid you're wrong there, Rayg," NiVom said. "Once you get a whiff of the real power of the Lavadome, it's impossible to think about much else."

He let the toe-tapping Rayg get back to his crystal studies and left Imperial Rock, feeling vaguely dissatisfied. The coppery sorcerer was after something. NiVom had more than half a mind to order the execution of Nilrasha. The only reason they'd kept her alive this long was as a hostage to his good behavior. He'd violated that trust—never mind the little skirmish at the Isle of Ice, his orders on the matter had been greatly exceeded. He'd been punished enough for it by having to deal with Ouistrela as one of his Protectors, of an island that had contributed exactly three boatloads of salted cod the whole time it had been a part of the Empire . . .

No question, this was a setback. With a break in the action, the princedoms would have their chance to get organized. Perhaps he should have pressed them for a settlement while he had the advantage. But negotiating with the princedoms was like building a statue out of sand, as soon as you had one side formed up and began to work on the other, it all slid into the same heap you started with.

The key, of course, was completion of his plan for the Lower World. He hoped he'd live to see it: an underground system of tunnels, waterways, mines, and exits that would allow dragons to appear in any of his major provinces by surprise.

He was fortunate in finding the old Anklemere works linking so many natural passages—the wizard had expanded something the dwarfs had begun in the Red Mountains in ages past, making use of the two mighty underground rivers, one flowing north and the other south, at heights and intensities that varied with hemispheric seasons. Back then it was the center of the hominid resistance against Silverhigh and a way for rebels to get about without being observed from the air.

Once it was complete, food and coin tribute would go beneath the earth immediately in the province where it was collected and be put on dwarf-rails, not transported across a quarter of the known world, subject to weather, theft, bandit raids, and misdirection. Whole armies of dragons or demen could move in secrecy. Only dwarfs could hope to stop them, and there wasn't a dwarf army left in the world worth mentioning. Thralls of all ages were working themselves to death by the dozens each day to complete new tunnels and expand old ones under the practiced lashes of the demen.

NiVom spent a few pleasant moments imagining the paired worlds, Upper and Lower, locked in an eternal, dragon-directed embrace. His name would live forever, loom larger in draconic imagination than the greatness of Silverhigh, even if his body couldn't.

He rather hoped the name of his mate would be forgotten.

As a young dragonelle of the Imperial Family in the Lavadome, Imfamnia'd been one of the silliest young dragonelles it was ever his unpleasant duty to meet. Attractive enough and healthy, certainly, but there were plenty of healthy dragonelles to catch his eye among the hills and rock of the Lavadome, and many of them were pleasingly formed as well.

No, it wasn't until he was wandering, hiding from the Lavadome, in exile near the site of his aerial raid triumph in Bant that he met her again. She'd been hunting in an almost comic fashion, setting brush fires and then devouring whatever rushed out to escape the flames, not knowing that the nutrition lost from the fats in the firebladder would never be replaced by the lean little rodents and small birds she was snapping up.

What was attractive in the teeming Lavadome became a vision, a creation of the Four Spirits to grant him succor in the wilderness. He fell hopelessly in love with her. Her own deprivations had erased much of the callowness of her youth and taught her the value of a silent tongue. He pursued her with every elaborate courtesy he remembered from the Lavadome: presents, poetry and songs in her honor, gifts of fowl and fish, and blighter wirework that passed for jewelry in Bant.

She was very fond of jewelry. He always associated it with the change in her.

It was after he'd given her a crystalline bauble, the same one AuRon had worn into the Lavadome, bringing the Red Queen's peace offer, that she'd grown more assertive. He'd tried the jewel himself first, of course, to make sure there wasn't any danger. All it did was sharpen up the senses and clarify the thoughts. Both of which Imfamnia needed—desperately.

He found her lounging in her modest bath. It was nothing compared to the epic pools of steaming water that SiMevolant had been so fond of. This was more of a dipping pool in a tile room, where thralls could easily work you over with bristle brushes and polishing cloths, depending what the scale needed, lubricated by warm water.

He dismissed the thralls. They always did gossip.

"I suppose you've heard RuGaard is in Hypatia," NiVom said.

"I've heard little but," Imfamnia said. "What will we do about it?"

"I'm tempted to wait until he's at the base of Nilrasha's refuge and then drop her on him. She's heavy enough to kill whoever she falls upon."

"You always were direct," Imfamnia said.

She touched her snout to his. She'd scented herself with something intoxicating, probably some distillation of hominid female musk. "I'm famished," he said. "I've been flying too much lately. I think we both need to spend a few secluded days figuring out what to do about him. Dine in, two servants only, hours of undisturbed sleep—"

She brushed him gently across the neck with her wingtips.

"And a deep pool for mating purposes," he continued. "Seeing you wet and glistening gives me an appetite for you. Too bad SiMevolant's old baths are defunct."

"So what do we do about RuGaard?" Imfamnia asked, redirecting his thoughts.

"I've ordered the whole Aerial Host to Hypatia. Between them and the Hypatians, they'll make short work of him."

"That's like sending arrows to enemy archers," Imfamnia said, looking at her scale and then glaring at him as if to ask:

What, do you expect me to nibble the rough edges myself? "Why on earth would you do that?"

"He's a serious threat. I've heard his rule spoken of as *in better days*. . . . And that, after all I've done for the Lavadome and Empire."

"Well done, my love. All the scoundrels are either dead or fled, and it sounds as though RuGaard has finally gone mad and will take a number of disloyal dragons down with him. We should capture him, decorate him for helping us sniff out traitors, then remove his head."

NiVom nuzzled her. She was more for flattery than praise, so he glowed when it came. "My one fear is that he'll run back north three times as fast as he's marching south. Yes, the Host will encircle him, and that'll be the end of it. We can get on to more important matters, like acquiring prawn-farms on the Sunstruck Sea. I do enjoy a big, fat prawn in butter."

NiVom ordered a meal. Imfamnia ordered her favorite dessert, iced cream. "A double helping. No, a triple. In case NiVom wants some."

"Yes, my Queen," the old Ghiozian croaked.

They made small talk over dinner. He was worried enough about RuGaard's challenge that the taste of the food was spoiled, and subsequently his appetite. He called for more water.

His dinner wasn't sitting well. He burped, and it put a nasty, numbing stickiness in his mouth. His heartsbeats increased.

"I feel dreadful," he said.

"I shouldn't wonder," Imfamnia countered. She sniffed his breath and her eyes narrowed. "You're never very careful about what you eat. I think the cooks could put carrion in front of you and you'd have it with wine."

Breathing with difficulty, he staggered toward her.

"You've outlived your usefulness, dragon. It's time I took charge of things," she said.

"What—how?" he managed.

"It's the same poison we used on those louts at the feast. I scooped out the marrow in those bones and loaded it in."

He lost the rest of her conversation to confusion and darkness. Along with everything else.

Chapter 15

The Aerial Host's temporary riverbank camp in Dairuss was flanked by reeds and bulrushes along a sandbar where supplies were to be landed. But the supplies never appeared. Only a fishing boat or two arrived, filled with men who moved on as quickly as wind and current allowed. The dragons and men had little to do but forage, look up- and downriver in the hope of a supply barge, and attract flies.

Three days of idleness and confusion about their provision reduced AuSurath the Red's forty dragons and riders to something more like an irritated gang than like the stronger half of the Aerial Host.

He swelled with pride every time he considered that he captained these dragons and their riders, probably the most powerful fighting force under the sun. Even the Tyr's Demen Legion wouldn't stand a chance against it, aboveground or below.

Which made lounging in the summer sun, waiting for a new set of orders, all the more frustrating.

Something had rattled NiVom. That was the only explanation that made sense to AuSurath the Red. Indecision was bad for morale from top to bottom. The flight lines sensed confusion at the top and it made them nervous. The officers had the frustration of seeing plans cast aside and replaced by last-moment improvisation—then when the improvisation didn't work out, they were blamed for inadequate planning and leadership.

This sort of confusion weakened the dragons and their riders and left them vulnerable. They would have accepted delays and disorder had they only camped a horizon or two into Ironrider territory across the river. Empty bellies were expected on a campaign, almost as a planned incentive to make them edgy and in a fighting mood.

He'd been proud of them until now. The campaign against the princedoms of the Sunstruck Sea proceeded well, with only two casualties, and those were just wounds to dragons who would return to duty. This despite the fierceness of the Heavy Wing of the Aerial Host's zeal to avenge their losses from the Fallen Queen's Feast in Ghioz. They'd grown expert at tower-baiting, waiting for the southerners to launch their missiles, then dropping or bouncing boulders in to wreck the fortifications. Courier after courier returned to the Sun King's palace at Ghioz bearing the choicest of the valuables sniffed up from gardens and wells, while the rest went down hungry gullets to replace arrow-loosened scale.

Yes, he could be rightfully proud of the job they were doing on the turban-wearing humans.

Then new orders came from NiVom, bearing his seal. They were to disengage as soon as practicable with an eye toward preserving the campaign camps, or within two full days of receiving the orders, whichever came first, and fly immediately to the Iwensi Gap, where the Falnges River flowed down to Hypat through the Red Mountains. There they'd be supplied by barges while they reorganized with the remainder of the Aerial Host for a campaign in northern Hypatia.

They retreated from the campaign, covering the ground forces that had to walk and take rivercraft for as long as they could, then turning northwest for Dairuss. They flew with minimal rest and no food, and made the landing along the riverbank after three very hard days of flight. The weather was idyllic, wonderful summer weather and at just enough of an altitude to allow for pleasantly cool nights, and the dragons recovered their strength with but one day of rest, aided by baths and great draughts of river water from the clean center channel.

A second order was waiting for them at the landing, and this one caused dismay in AuSurath. It simply read: *Wait for further orders.*

Idiots! If they were going to wait, why couldn't they have ordered them to a city with garrison facilities? The City of the Golden Dome, the capital of Dairuss and Mother's Protectorate, was less than half a day's flight away. There were old halls to serve as sleeping shelter, markets full of food, an Imperial paymaster to draw funds, diversions for the men, and hunting in the mountains for the dragons. Everything his wing needed to wait for NiVom to decide where to send them.

Instead, they sat on the riverbank, supplying the mosquitoes with generous helpings of hominid blood (the dragons urinated in bits of rag and stuffed them in their ears to keep the mosquitoes away and out of the one area of their hide that was vulnerable to the tiny insect lances), but all the men could do was soothe the bites with river-mud.

AuSurath called his officers together. Nothing to do but organize some kind of games or entertainments. Perhaps the men could cook for the dragons, or the dragons could cook for the men.

They'd commandeered some of the fishermen's catch. It would be enough to feed the riders properly, anyway. An enterprising rider had found beds of wild onions beside the river, so skewered fish and onions looked to be the menu, unless one of the promised supply barges arrived. As for entertainments, there was a good deal of driftwood along the riverbank that hadn't yet been gathered for cooking fires. Perhaps they could have some kind of carving contest, with the winning dragon and rider pair being given a trip back to the palace at Ghioz to figure out just what in the glowering mood was the reason for this hungry delay.

Their meager dinner was interrupted by the arrival of the Commander of the Aerial Host.

AuSurath hated to see his dragons lined up for review showing muddy snouts, but they had been reduced to plunging their jaws in among the reeds and sucking in mouthfuls of mud and slackwater to catch frogs, fish, snakes, crayfish, worms, and water beetles. Hardly a diet that made for champion warriors, but until the barges arrived or he received orders to disperse some of his wing to hunt Ironrider lands, he had to do something to keep his dragons with the energy to fly and breathe fire.

They'd set up a command tent by stretching casualty netting between two large willow trees and weaving in reeds and willow-streamers. At night, the Dragonriders slept in it. It kept out the sun and burning fragrant wood kept some of the biting bugs down.

BaMelphistran, Grand Commander of the Aerial Host, grunted as he reviewed the Heavies. He had a newly fledged messenger with him, still wet about the wings.

"You're down how many fighting pairs?" BaMelphistran asked, nodding in recognition at AuSurath's rider, Gundar.

"Three. Two casualties, one on messenger duty."

"Ah. Well done, considering you've been on campaign since spring."

"Thank you, sir," AuSurath said.

"Still, you could polish your scale while waiting for orders."

"Red attracts enough attention in battle without adding polish, sir."

Still, he passed word for a couple of men to attend to his scale. The Grand Commander liked to see limbs in motion as soon as he gave an order.

"I've bad news for you, son," BaMelphistran went on. "Your sister's joined a mutiny."

He didn't feel any particular emotion at the news. He hadn't seen Istach in years, and never much liked her anyway. Too quiet and thoughtful. He liked lively, talkative dragonelles who enjoyed tricks and jokes and quick, flirtatious passes overhead. "Istach always was an ingrown scale. To be honest, sir, I'm not surprised."

"Not your sister in Old Uldam. It's Varatheela, in the Light Wing."

"Varatheela? She's not imaginative enough to be a mutineer. Your sources have the story wrong, I suppose."

"CuSarrath himself," BaMelphistran said. "The former Tyr RuGaard has gone mad and is committing suicide in a spectacular fashion. He's walking—walking, mind you—all the way across Hypatia to his mate's refuge to reclaim her. Several dragons of the Lights are fool enough to follow him. I'm sure when it's all over they'll claim they pretended to join him, just to see if there was a larger conspiracy at work, but it will be good fun stopping them, especially if he decides to remain on the Old North Road and on foot."

"Madness," AuSurath said.

"Yes, sounds it, doesn't it?"

"Some of the dragons won't much care for killing him. He led us in battle and promoted some of us. Including myself."

"If it comes to bloodshed, will you help Gundar take her head?"

"I'm a dragon of the Empire and Commander of the

Heavy Wing. Duty to Empire and Wing and family comes first. In that order."

"As it should be. Aaagh, I was considering flying back to the palace tonight and see if I might get NiVom out of his funk—the Queen says he's been locked up in his sleeping chamber with maps laid on every square inch for three days now—but I can't face a night-flight. Not that facing a night in the rough is all that attractive, either. Why weren't you garrisoned in the Golden Dome, for Spirits' sake?"

"Orders, sir. The Iwensi riverbank, for easy supply."

"The supplies would probably have to come from the city anyway. Who gave those orders?"

"It wasn't you, sir? Then I assume it was Tyr NiVom."

"Some courtier probably wrote his words down badly."

"Well, we'll see what we can do about making you more comfortable, my lord."

"However," BaMelphistran said. "Young wings need exercise." He turned to his freshly fledged assistant. "Fly first to the City of the Golden Dome and ask for supplies to be sent here. Then go to the Sun King's palace and ask if the Heavies might be moved to the old delvings at the falls. That's all."

The messenger repeated the orders verbally to show he understood, then launched himself eagerly into the night air.

"Should have sent you to the delvings in the first place. It's not far, and there's plenty of room and facility for the care and health of your fighting dragons. I've just come from there. Perhaps Tyr NiVom was worried that the rot had spread all the way there. I've half a mind to countermand the Tyr, but just in case there was an important reason for you to sit here, I'll leave things as they are for now."

AuSurath couldn't have agreed more with the sentiment that they should occupy the old dwarf delving, but at the moment he was racking his brain, wondering what food there was around camp fit for the Grand Commander of the Aerial Host. You couldn't tell a dragon in line of succession to the throne to just shove his snout in riverbank mud and swallow whatever he could suck up.

For the rest of his life, AuSurath never quite forgave himself for being deep asleep when the troll attack struck.

They came, as startling as a thunderclap on a clear night.

Trilling pipe-whistles the Dragonriders used to pass signals sounded first, followed by roars and cries from dragons. The *hiss-whoof* of dragon-flame bursting into life met him as he leaped from under the sheltering willow tree.

AuSurath thought he'd woken into another dream, this one a nightmare of fire and fear.

Creatures the likes of which he'd never seen danced in battle with the dragons of his precious, alarmed command. They were taller than dragons, with two massive forelimbs holding up a wedge-shaped body. A sort of gash or mouth could be seen at the base of the wedge, near two smaller limbs that seemed to be used only for stability. An orb on a kind of short tentacle stood out from somewhere between the chest and the stomach—at least that's what he would call the upper and lower half of the body. At the back, flaps of skin lifted and lowered, revealing pink tissue beneath.

They were thick-skinned and scaly. Some had huge, full sets of wings that resembled webbed spider-legs coming out of their backs; others had more rudimentary versions of a real wingspan. A few had horns and hide, crests and frills, or something that looked very much like them, running across their headless shoulders or down the back between the flapping sheets of muscular tissue.

They were silent in battle, save for a disgusting wet gulping sound and flaps of wing and back-flesh.

A headless dragon lay sprawled in front of the command tent, his dazed rider looking down at the body. He noted dully that it was his best rock-bouncer from the tower assaults.

These must be trolls. He'd heard them described in some lecture or other on exotic fauna, but he remembered being more interested in the talk about Rocs of the southern jungles.

"Rally to the tent! Defend our Commander!" he shouted.

At his shout, the tent rippled. A troll, dripping with river-water and blood, hurled a substantial piece of the Grand Commander of the Aerial Host at him. BaMelphistran's haunch bounced harmlessly off his back.

A blade flashed from the darkness. Gundar flew out of the night as though he bore wings, rather than a flashing sword. He was almost naked, having risen from sleep in just a set of riding underbreeches. The great blade chopped down on the troll's stumpy orb that was fixed on AuSurath.

Another gout of dragon-flame lit up the fierce, tooth-clamped battle grin on Gundar's face. He went into a fight wearing a smile as wide as a banner.

A dragon rolled practically under his feet, in a death grapple with a troll. The troll had those two huge limbs across his back, and judging from the way the dragon's *saa* dragged, his back was already broken. But still he fought, teeth biting and tearing at the muscular shoulders, searching for a fatal blood vessel.

When the troll rolled above the crippled dragon, AuSurath took the opportunity to leap. He came down in a manner that he'd learned long before the Aerial Host. His father had taught him to strike in a tight curl, grab *sii-* and *saa*-fuls of flesh and lash out with his powerful rear legs.

Mighty *saa*-fuls of flesh and skin ripped away from the troll and blood sprayed everywhere like a wineskin dropped from a tall tower. The troll shuddered and released the pinned dragon and AuSurath bounded toward his next opponent.

Behind, he heard a shovel-dig sound as Gundar drove his sword deep into the center of the troll.

The trolls bore dreadful deformities. Some had withered limbs, others were missing their stumpy legs and dragged themselves around upon vestigial tails by their powerful fore-limbs. No two were alike, as though each one had manifested from a unique fever-dream.

A gamboling troll came at him and he loosed his flame. He dodged the bounding, burning mass as it ran past, dripping flame and heading for water.

With the taste of fire in his mouth the battle rage was really upon him. Gundar would have to keep up without him. He had to find another troll to kill!

AuSurath picked out another troll astride a dragonelle's neck, throttling her just at the neck-hearts. Only her tail still spasmed, but it was enough to keep the troll squeezing. AuSurath bounded out of the darkness, and this time struck the troll full on the chest. He pushed one limb down with his tail and lashed out with hind legs like a snared rabbit. The troll came apart in satisfyingly large pieces.

"We're lost, we're lost, fly for the Lighthalls, dragons of the Host," he heard his lieutenant call.

A dragon or two flapped into the sky. Bounding trolls jumped out of the darkness, the clenched fingers of those huge forelimbs pounding and denting the very earth they crossed.

Gundar dug his sword into a troll's back and used it as a handle to pull himself up onto AuSurath's back, where he produced a double-edged dagger from a hidden sheath on his thigh.

"Let's fly! To stay is death."

AuSurath rose into the air but stopped with a jerk. A troll had him by the tail and one rear *saa*. He clawed with the other in a flapping panic.

"Too heavy," AuSurath grunted.

"I've got it, old friend. Avenge me!"

Gundar ran lightly down his back, drawing his sword, launched himself off his tail, and landed atop the troll. His shining dagger fell, and rose again covered in green-and-black slime. He tore through the troll's flesh like a rat digging into a corpse, using both hand and blade to tear at the thing's shoulder.

With a mighty blow, Gundar plunged his dagger deep into

the joint of the limb anchoring him. A second stab and the troll relaxed, falling as its blood pumped out into the night.

AuSurath rose, flapping hard. Two onrushing trolls jumped for him and collided with a scaly *thunk!*

He wheeled and Gundar looked up at him. His rider gave a quick salute—and was dashed into dressed meat and naked bone by the fist-swipe of the dying troll.

AuSurath watched pieces of Gundar fall, numb and cold and shocked and then his wings took over and, driven by horror, they bore him off into the night.

It took him the entire flight to the delvings to come to terms with the idea that the Heavy Wing of the Aerial Host as he'd known it was no more. The Grand Commander had fallen in battle, as had almost all of the dragons, yet the Wing Commander escaped. What would the gossips in the Lavadome say?

They didn't understand the circumstances. They hadn't seen dragons torn apart like cooked chickens on the riverbank. They would still judge him, though.

He followed the shining river to the delvings, saw the welcoming orange and yellow lights of lanterns at the sandy landing at midriver.

No. He couldn't face the enormity of it just yet. Something was nagging at him.

AuSurath was not a dragon of exemplary reason. When experience and training couldn't guide him, he had a hard time laying out arguments for and against. He was the first to admit it. But he had a way of feeling his way through to a solution in strange circumstances. At the moment, instinct told him that he needed to speak to Varatheela, perhaps more than he'd ever needed to speak to anyone.

Something was dreadfully wrong with what had happened at the riverbank. He couldn't cite the exact reason just yet, but he was sure of it, just as he would know a mammal by the general shape and fur, without going through a catechism of questions about live birth and using milk to feed its young.

Well, if they were marching up the Old North Road, they shouldn't be very hard to find.

It took him two days of steady flight without food, rest, or much more than a mouthful of water to reach them.

The way he saw it, there was little point in sleeping, anyway. His dreams, as sure as sunrise, would put him back among the trolls on the riverbank, and nothing on earth could make him return there ever again if he could help it.

They were resting in a town plaza in front of an inn, near the longest bridge on the road. The inn had, appropriately enough, a dragon on it.

The objects were wavy and unreal-looking. The world seemed to sway as he landed.

"Betrayed. NiVom wants us dead," he managed, just.

When he had his wind back he continued. "We were stationed on the riverbank so we could be attacked. We were just waiting for it. Gundar dead. BaMelphistran dead. All dead. Murder."

He tasted wine in his mouth. They were attempting to revive him. It worked just long enough for him to say:

"They don't need dragons anymore, Father. Something dreadful is driving the Tyr."

Before he finally dropped into an exhausted unconsciousness.

BOOK THREE

Outcome

"ALL TALES END IN TRAGEDY. FOLLOW THE HERO LONG ENOUGH,
YOU'LL STEP ACROSS HIS CORPSE."

—*Ballad of the Dragon Kings (Elvish origin)*

Chapter 16

The news from AuSurath left the celebration in front of the Green Dragon Inn stunned.

Wistala had been enjoying the homecoming to Mossbell and the hills and fields where she'd spent her hatchling years. The old rooflines were as familiar and comforting to her as her mother's fringe. She'd grown up at the local estate under an elf named Rainfall. He was now dead and growing in a patch of forest overlooking his beloved river valley and the four-span bridge he'd so long kept in repair.

Elves didn't die so much as transform after death. She'd read some philosophy that even dragons returned to the earth eventually, where their bodies provided nutrients for plants. The elves just removed a few steps from that chain of life and transformed directly.

She was beginning to see why RuGaard insisted on walking all the way to Nilrasha's refuge. The whole way, entire populations were turning out to see the dragons pass. To these northerners, dragons were something they saw only overhead, at a distance, or a reason for painful levies of cattle and grain. Few had seen dragons in their grandeur up close. Every little village they passed through turned into a parade, continued for a long while until the hardiest boy and girl following turned back for home.

Yes, strange and remarkable as a fox running the top rail of a fence. Strange and remarkable until you knew about the stolen chickens and the pursuing hounds. There could be no quiet little murders with a whole thane's population leaning on their shovels and berry-baskets, watching a dozen dragons file down the road.

The Green Dragon put out food for them and quickly slaughtered some pigs to be eaten in Wistala's memory of the day they'd all fought off a barbarian raid together.

"It appears the Empire had a parasite growing inside it," DharSii said. "I'm afraid that unlike a tapeworm, this one can grow large enough to kill the host and then continue on its own."

"But who or what is it?" AuRon asked.

"NiVom and Imfamnia are behind it all," RuGaard said. "I'm certain of that."

"Who's left?" Wistala asked. "Seems to me many of the aboveground dragons are dead. The fighting ones, that is. I hope the Protectors are safe, for my brothers' sakes. I don't see what NiVom and Imfamnia will gain by killing so many of their own kind."

"They're mad. It must be," AuSurath said.

"I can believe one dragon going mad," AuRon said to his son. "Two? Madnesses that feed off each other?"

"Some curse of the Red Queen. They never should have taken over her palace," the Copper said.

"It may be the Lavadome itself," DharSii said. "It's an engine of great energy. I've never been able to determine what it's gathering all that energy for. All the Tyrs grew a little—funny—toward the end. Perhaps the Lavadome was trying to take over their minds."

"Are you saying a vast mineral formation is intelligent?" AuRon asked. His *griff* rattled.

"Remember our hatching, AuRon?" the Copper asked.

"Less and less every year," AuRon said. "What about you?"

"The same. Remember the fight with our brother, the red?"

"He almost had me. Then you jumped on him and I put my egg-horn into his belly. It was over in a *griff-tchk*. I'm suggesting we repeat that. I'll keep the Empire busy on the surface. You go at them from under."

"Maybe this time we'll both end up on top of the egg shelf," the Copper said.

"You can have it. All I want is my mate."

"I could say the same thing, brother."

"Do you know a safe way into the Lower World?"

"My mate's hall, for a start."

"Tell her to abandon her post at once. I believe this is a war of eradication. Whatever power is directing those trolls, it wants to kill every rat in the barn but leave the hayloft intact."

"All the more reason for me to hurry," AuRon said, eyes wide and alarmed.

He shot into the sky like an arrow. A human toddler whooped at the sight.

They left AuSurath, exhausted, at the Green Dragon Inn, where the hosts promised to feed him until he recovered. Wistala suggested that he return to either the dragon tower or the Isle of Ice and consider his future.

He insisted that he would join them to the south as soon as he recovered. He wanted to see his mother safely out of the Empire, if the slaughter of the dragons had yet spared her.

The Copper sent the dragon tower dragons back, save for the Blind Ripper, who smelled blood and battle and refused to go. Hermethea took some convincing to go and lagged behind, even after the others had left. Wistala decided she bore more than a comradely interest in the Blind Ripper. But, at last, she was prevailed upon to return.

The rest moved south at a steady pace. Word had spread somehow that the Empire was finished and Hypatia in jeopardy.

"Our rescue of a single dragonelle is turning into a march to save Hypatia," DharSii observed to her.

"All these dragons," Wistala returned. "If this is one mass-assassination, we're making a tempting target."

For Wistala, traveling down the Old North Road was a trip through her memories—the Thanedoms, Tumbledown where she'd met Yari-Tab, and then the outskirts of Hypat, the greatest city between the Inland Ocean and the mighty East.

They met refugees on the road north, pushing barrows and carrying their children and bundles. They ran toward the dragons for protection, something Wistala had only seen a few times in her life before. They told dreadful tales of creatures pouring out of the ground, killing, burning, and enslaving before returning to mysterious tunnels concealed deep in hill and forest.

"The Blind Ripper will get his battle long before we reach Nilrasha's needle," DharSii said.

They found Hypatia a city under siege. The Copper had been cautious enough to send a scout—he picked Varatheela, as being quick and intelligent—and she returned with a tale of an army encamped outside the city wall.

The Copper decided to see for himself. They left the road and followed game trails and bridle paths to a pileup of bluffs overlooking the river Falnges and Hypat farther downstream.

Much of the lower part of the city had fallen, it seemed, or that was what the smoke indicated. A black carpet of canvas sheltering the demen from the bright sun made it look like the fields outside the city had been painted with pitch. However, the area around the directory and the Protector and other dragons' palaces were still intact. The Directory was protected by its own set of walls, towers, and redoubts, while the dragon palaces were linked together and ringed by walls to make defense against an uprising easier.

The attack on the dragons came with the speed of a swarm of enraged hornets. Suddenly, the forest at the base of the bluff was thick with black-and-red carapaced hominids. They must have been seen on the road or trails approaching the bluffs.

"Host, ring formation," DharSii called. "Backs to the Tyr!"

They looked more like insects than hominids with their red plates and thin heads with rolling, side-mounted eyes like fish. Unlike the demen she and Ayafeeia had fought in the Star Tunnel, these were a full half again as big as a tall man. Their legs gave them an odd gait thanks to the short upper leg and stiltlike lower limb.

They'd been variegated by something—dragonblood, most likely. Some had grown scythelike claws, others had sharp spikes growing out of their backs where on a regular demen there were knobby projections. Their mouths reminded Wistala of the short tongs used by blacksmiths to pick up hot metal.

"DharSii, you fly north, as fast as you can. Organize whoever you can in the dragon tower and bring as many allies as possible to Hypat. Barbarians. Dragons and blighters on the Isle of Ice. Anyone who can make it here and fight."

DharSii nodded and spread his wings. In three beats he was aloft and rising fast. He made one circling pass and emptied his firebladder across the demen front, then was gone.

The hordes of clattering attackers still mobbed the other dragons, who had wedged themselves into fallen trees or piles of rocks or just a steep cut in the hill. A carpet of bodies and pieces of bodies surrounded the remaining dragons. Patches of burning demen made the battle even more smoky and indistinct.

The dragons, even in their strength and fire, were losing.

"We have to fly," the Copper called above the roars of injured dragons and the screeching cries of the demen.

"What about the people?"

"We can't save them if we're dead," DharSii replied.

A mass threw chains around RuGaard. They swarmed over him like ants on a spider. He lifted—no, it was not RuGaard, it was the demen, carrying him as he struggled in a mesh of rope and chain.

They bore him away on their shoulders, moving like a hundred-legged insect that flowed across and through the dead, heading west out of town.

Wistala nodded, thrashed in a circle to push the demen back, and flapped into the air.

The rest of the survivors followed in a straggling line. From the air, they saw some of the town's children lying facedown in the fields or clinging flat-bellied to the roofs of barns. There were four dragons left, including Hermethea and Varatheela.

All the fates seemed to be against them. Another fall of Silverhigh seemed to be in progress. She wondered if those ancient dragons felt as helpless, seeing dragons dying all around and able only to wonder when your turn was coming.

How could the demen arrive so soon after AuSurath, who'd exhausted himself flying? Unless . . .

She followed the tracks across the pastures and fields, thick with summer growth. The land had been tramped flat by their passage.

Yes, the tracks led to the old troll cave. She hadn't explored it thoroughly enough in her youth—perhaps it had a false floor or wall or ceiling. A thousand demen had poured up from the Lower World like floodwaters rising. Who could say where the next wave would rise? How many dragons would this one kill?

She took off and flew upriver, winging over the bridge where she'd faced her first real test: the encounter with the troll that had been plaguing the local herdsmen. She'd been so small then and the bridge so high and vast—well, it still looked high to her fully grown eyes. It was still one of her prouder moments, untainted by anything but regret at the death of the old warhorse Avalanche.

She'd lost two fathers beside this river, the father of her egg and the hominid who had adopted her and helped form her thoughts and personality.

"Father," she said to the river valley, "I wish we could speak. All I've loved is soon to be lost."

"Not lost, Wistala," she thought she heard a tree say. "Never lost, as long as it's remembered."

This piece of forest she'd known all her life suddenly seemed closed in. The trunks had come impossibly close to each other, like a wall with only a crack here and there—but shielding what?

Sunlight shone between the cracks in the trunks as though this forest had its own private sun—Wistala's sky was smeared with high thin clouds coming in off the Inland Ocean, but inside that gathering of trunks different weather held sway.

An elf clothed in living ivy emerged from one trunk. A

she-elf with cheeks as bright as a polished apple dropped from a tree.

Their hair was as bright green as the first tulip leaves of spring and filled with unopened buds. These were elves, young and strong.

"Few really understand elves. We are like seeds that lie dormant waiting for the right conditions. We wait for the right need."

"We are the family Rainfall now. Mist, Sprinkle, Down-pour, Thundershower, Drops, and Cloudburst. I am Drizzle, sister and daughter. It's been too many years since we have spoken."

They looked like him, certainly, the way a group of pine trees look alike. All the same family with minor variations from specimen to specimen.

Elves continued to emerge, until the handfuls turned to dozens, and the dozens into a hundred. She knew this stand of trees to be an elf burial-ground—every elf interred here returned as a new family. She'd never heard of anything like this, beyond hatchling tales that elves "sprang from trees" when born into the world.

It made her feel young. She'd witnessed an event that was half spring sprouting and half reincarnation, according to the mystics of the Great East. How amazing to live in a world where such things were possible.

"Drizzle, you know—everything Rainfall knew?"

Drizzle nodded. "As we're much the same being, I do. Perhaps with a sense of remoteness yet authority, like words of a song learned by heart off the page but never heard live."

The elves were milling about, touching each other on the fingertips with flutters like leaves of trees meeting. They spoke in whispery trills and creaks, the language of trees bending in the wind.

"Why now?"

"Because you asked to speak to me. We've been waking up for some time and wondering when the time would be right. Is Hypatia still friendly to elvenkind, I hope? Once, they learned much from us."

"You told me a story once, about how dragons were each given a gift by the elements."

"There is another player in that game. There's no exact term for it, but you can think of it as a shadow world of aether. A mirror element. 'Aether' is another word for 'magic,' and our world is desperately short of it."

"Why?"

"I wish I knew. Perhaps if I knew why the aether was draining, we could discover a way to refill it. It is my belief that aether is a product of beauty, serenity, and grace. I've felt it in the presence of the graceful arches of my old bridge. Music might create it, or a high temple filled with worshippers before an altar. A brilliant thought sends waves through it.

"I am convinced that when enough of this energy builds up, there is some manner of transformation. A species grows in intelligence, or a society advances—as when the Hypatians got rid of the kings and began choosing who would make the decisions affecting the nation. Perhaps some great burst of magic formed the dragons.

"In any case, a wave of that energy rolled across Hypatia,

and it awakened us. Nothing like this has happened since the first dragons appeared before the rise of Anklemere."

"The demen are about to pass through wooded country," an elf said. He touched a tree branch, ran his hand down it, and straightened, tightened, and formed it into a rather gnarled spear. "They may think a wooded road much like tunnel-fighting, but we'll teach them better."

"Don't despair, Wistala. What's an end and what's a beginning depends a great deal on the observer. You said you think this is the end of dragonkind. I believe we stand on the threshold of a new beginning. Something has returned the shadow energy to the world. Now, where are we most needed?"

Chapter 17

AuRon landed atop the cool stone of the Protector's mountainside refuge in Dairuss, not caring who saw him and reported it to whom. It was the dog days of summer in Dairuss, and the afternoon sun had one more hour of beating the land like a hammer before it disappeared behind the mountains. Even at this altitude it was hot and still. Thirst closed and roughened his throat, and his head hurt. Under different circumstances, he'd have found a mountainside pool, drunk his fill, and napped in the sun until the heat loosened muscles sore from flying. But he'd not come to enjoy basking in the sun like a lizard.

The City of the Golden Dome and whatever troubles it had with the world would have to sort themselves out. He had but one goal: getting Natasatch and taking her somewhere safe. A secret hole in the Sadda-Vale, perhaps.

"Natasatch!" he called through the balcony. Nothing answered but the rustling of the plain cotton curtains. He noted, rather dully, that they were still the heavier winter ones.

He sniffed around the sleeping chamber. He smelled his mate. Also, cleaning-vinegar, oranges, and *oliban*, dried hunks of tree sap that, when burned, smelled profoundly soothing. Someone had burned a good deal of it in the dining pit fire. Had she thrown a party? To celebrate what?

In any case, the thralls were keeping busy maintaining what he still, oddly, considered "their" temporary home.

His hearts beat hard. It was too still. Especially for the middle of the day. The refuge held its breath, waiting for him to discover whatever gruesome display of death awaited within.

The eating-pit room was awash in fabrics. Colors hung on the wall, bolts of cloth were laid out and marked with chalk, and a net on the ceiling held tools and buckets and sea-fishing instruments.

Halfway across it he heard a step. Natasatch! He looked twice to make sure it was she, and alone.

"I'm—I'm so sorry, AuRon."

"I understand, and you have to forgive me as well. The dazzle of the Empire, jealousy for my brother—"

She tucked her face back, into her wing. "No, that's not what I meant. I'm sorry you came back. For this."

A net came crashing down on him. The weights and hooks made his natural thrashing only entangle him further. He heard the clattering rush of demen entering the eating room. They clamped his nose and pinched his nostrils until he relaxed enough to allow them to put chains on his legs.

"So, so, sorry, my love. I think we shall die together. Soon. It's all gone wrong."

"Don't be, my dear," Imfamnia said. She strode into the room briskly, carelessly catching scale on the fabrics that had hidden the crouching demen. "To think, I once took a mild interest in you. Your skin may change color, lizard, but your behavior is entirely predictable."

She considered AuRon. "Hmmm. It will take at least two trolls to move him."

"Where are you taking him?" Natasatch asked her.

"You'll find out the same moment he does. Now, come along, please, dear, or I'll slit your graceful little throat open one side to the other."

Chapter 18

DharSii found Gettel and the tower surrounded by corpse fires.

There's a distinctive smell to a pyre of recently living flesh. It was appetizing, at least to a dragon. He passed low over the fires—not much could be distinguished from the burning remains, but the hooked swords and twin-point spears favored by the demen were lying all around the tower.

For a dreadful moment he thought he'd arrived too late, but then he saw a dragon-neck poke out of the top of the tower and survey him.

Gettel wanted the news from the south, first. She already knew what had happened in Juutfod. When DharSii relayed the news of the Copper's abduction, she looked genuinely grieved.

"I'll miss him even more than the groundeds," she said with a sigh.

"He was carried into Hypat. He may still be there, for all we know."

"To think, he was on his way to rescue his mate. Now he needs rescuing, too."

"I'm not so sure," DharSii said. "I thought he made it awfully easy for his enemies to know exactly where he was. It might have been a tactic to bring dragons over to his side—you saw how easily he did that with the Aerial Host."

"The demen didn't know about the groundeds," Gettel said. Or the dwarfs. That was a nasty surprise for them. Turns out dwarfs hate demen more than they do blighters, humans, dragons, or elves. I think they expected a few spiritless, crippled dragons. Couple of blasts of fire and then off with their heads. Somebody told them a half-truth or a bad tale. They knew, I think, that six or seven dragons were out, some of them moving south, so they took their chance. Expecting to murder tired, landing dragons, I suppose."

There were barbarians eager to go to Hypat on what they called a "mighteous sack," if he understood the tongue correctly, but there were several problems that seemed impossible to surmount, at least in any length of time that would make a difference.

First, the barbarians fought on foot. They had very few horses and pastureland in their crags and mountains was rare and reserved for more productive sheep and cattle. The lumbercutters had a few, their warlords and merchants who could afford them rode, but the ordinary yeoman who picked up spear, sword, and axe when battle came marched and fought on foot. So to assemble even half of them at the northernmost stretches of the Old North Road would take days, and they would show up ravenous and thirsty.

Which was another difficulty. Barbarians on a raid ate as they went, barging into chicken coops, pigpens, vegetable patches, and granaries for their food. If they did that on the trip south to Hypat, he wondered if it was in the power of the local thanes to prevent violence—if the local thanes could be prevailed on to supply a horde of barbarians in the first place, especially with so much in doubt.

What he needed was some bit of magic to transport them south, like flying carpets from the old Hypatian tales of the sorcerers of Silverhigh.

Shipping was out of the question. The demen raid had wrecked everything bigger than a rowboat. Standing and running rigging had been cut, masts and spars chopped down, there were holes knocked in some of the hulls. There were some lighters left, and the small fishing boats that happened to be out among the lobster pots when the demen attacked, but not enough to float a force large enough to make a difference. Though there were probably glory-hunters who would go, just for the chance to die fighting in an important battle. A death in battle gave you some sort of special key to a hall of heroes in the afterlife, in their reckoning.

The fastest way was to fly them down, of course, but that presented greater difficulties than sailing them. A fully grown, healthy dragon could carry perhaps six men in flight, fewer if they were large, fewer still if they had heavy weapons, shields, and armor. Every barbarian went into battle with a huge shield and at least two weapons in case his favorite failed, so DharSii calculated it would be a strain to carry even four. On an all-day flight, two.

He could just see the dragons of the tower flying to Wistala's aid with twenty or thirty warriors and arriving too tired to fight.

"Why don't we swim 'em down?" Thunderwing asked.

"What's that?"

"One time I was fishing, and I got bit by one of those big black-and-white beasties. They eat seals and so on. Ever seen one?"

"No," DharSii said. "But I've never spent much time around oceans."

"Well, doesn't matter. Point is, they weigh a fair bit. This one must have been sick or blind—it thought I was food and started a terrible scrape. It tried to drag me down and drown me—that's a terrifying experience. You'd do best to avoid it, Stripes, but I dug into its side good and got some vitals out and that was the end of that. Soon as I had some air in my lungs, I grabbed it by the tail and hauled it to shore. Lost a bit to some sharks, the louts, but there was still more meat than I could eat."

DharSii reckoned himself a clever dragon, but he seemed to be missing the point. It had happened before, too. Sometimes he was so lost in mathematics and parabola that he missed the greater whole.

"You're the one they call the philosopher-king?"

"Thunderwing philosopher-king. They make it rhyme, like a hatchling taunt."

"You're saying pull them down, like rats clinging to a rope after a shipwreck? Humans don't last long in cool water, let alone cold, and the coastal water here is quite cool."

"No, I mean we load them like bales of wool into coasters and barges and such. Haul them down on rafts on our backs if we have to."

DharSii froze for a moment. "You're—you may have something. But their craft are mostly wrecked."

"All the gear and stuff for those wrecked ships, the rudders and masts and lines—they're to make the boat sail, correct."

"Those that aren't rowed or pulled, yes."

DharSii's warnings fell on deaf ears, until refugees appeared from the south.

The demen were taking slaves and carrying off anything that could be pried up and dragged out. They made a clean sweep of Quarryness, leaving behind only bodies of those who fought.

"We will go south, but not as conquerors and pillagers. We will come as friends, so that north and south face this new threat together."

"I suspect they're moving on Hypatia, too."

"They have to. The demen breed like rodents if there's adequate food. It's an elegant system: When food is plentiful, demen halls teem with life. When it runs out, they eat each other until their numbers match the current food supply. Most other creatures have their population adjusted by predators or disease. Demen self-regulate."

*   *   *

The boatwrights and shipfitters went to work with a will. The challenge and uniqueness of the task appealed. Even Seeg's dwarfs joined in. At first the locals were suspicious and hostile, refusing to share a tool or tell them where they could find more cordage. But once they saw how neatly their clinker hulls overlapped and the tight staving, they were gradually won over to the dwarfs' two-prow design.

"It's so in the underground rivers we can go either direction if there's no room to turn," Seeg explained. The men of Juutfod followed the Hypatian tradition of putting a woman on the prow—their unsleeping eyes maintained a steady vigil ahead for ice and shoal, protecting the men with maternal instinct—but the dwarfs carved dragon heads, or wings, or a *griff*-and-tail design that looked like an elaborate battle-axe, and soon there were so many requests for the art that the dwarfs were working days on the clinker hulls and nights on the figureheads.

The grounded dragons were more used to swimming than the others, so they made the best "drak-kaar" pullers, as the barbarians called the queer hybrid craft.

DharSii learned another advantage to the craft when he observed some sea trials with strong-swimming volunteers filling the hulls. With no mast and sail, the ships vanished into the Inland Ocean mists where warm southern water met cool northern air, and disappeared over the horizon more quickly than a regular sailing vessel would. They could still hug the coast for safety and travel unnoticed; without the aid of powerful—and rare—optics the whole fleet could be mistaken as whales at a distance. To aid in this they rigged weathered and gray canvas covers on the hulls, which would both keep out the rain and disguise the outline.

Among the tower's stores were old helmets from the Wyrmaster's days. His warriors had fixed dragonhorns on their heads, or high ridges in imitation of a male dragon's crest or a female dragon's fringe. The barbarians who could speak Parl well enough to take orders were given those helms to wear, so dragons could instantly recognize a man who could understand instruction. The others made fun of the outlandish headgear at first, but were soon scrounging for dragonhorn of their own.

"Learn some Parl, then, and you'll get helmets, too," DharSii advised his translators to tell them. "Even if I have to saw it off my own crest."

"There's one last thing you can do, Gettel," DharSii said. "Send out your weather-dragons. Because of the seaworthiness of our craft—or rather the lack of it—we'll have to do the last horizon or two in darkness, coming from the north. I'd rather do it in daylight so we might circle around the city and come with rain from the south. That way we could strike up the Falnges."

"Will do, DharSii."

"Don't let the aerial dragons get carried away and come in ahead of is. Just before or once we're engaged would do nicely."

"Most of them have experience in properly joining in on an

attack going back to the Wyrmaster's days," Gettle said, eyes bright and young with the prospect of action. "Don't you worry, Stripes, we'll see to it. You know, Stripes, I'm an old woman, been around dragons all my life. I've never ridden one into battle. Too late now, I suppose."

"I am relieved to hear that you concluded that. It's cold, often wet, always dangerous. Illness would probably make you unfit for riding after a day in the air. And that's before a single blow is struck in battle."

"I can't heft anything much more than my soup spoon. Even what's left of my teeth wouldn't hurt a demen."

"Best you stay here. Isn't there a rumor that Varangia had a clutch? She'll need someone keeping an eye on her food and metal supplies."

"Ahh, she can take care of her own, easy enough. You say I'd probably drop dead like a frozen sparrow before we even reached Hypat?"

"That would be where I'd bet my foreclaw," DharSii said.

"You talked me into it, DharSii. Always hated the idea of having my body rolling around in the surf till the crabs find it. Death in battle and a pyre lit by dragonflame—that's the way for—"

"I was trying to discourage you, Gettel. You'll die. Pointlessly. You have years left here."

"You'll read the will and all that. See that it's carried out according to direction. It's in that legalistic high-church tongue the Hypatians use. I only get one word in six, but the local altar-circlers vouch for the wheretofores and puffery. You'll find I've been generous to my dragons."

*　　*　　*

Wistala was on her third night flight between the remainder of the Hypat garrison and the elves.

The elves had not struck yet. They'd engaged with the monstrous demen, at a distance, with bow and spear-thrower.

The Hypatians held but a sliver of their former city, hugging the coastal cliffs and the riverbank. The Directory was filled with starving refugees improvising water-catchers and ground mist condensers. The rest of the city belonged to demen.

What was left of the resistance was concentrated at NoSohoth's vast new palace, where his private dwarfish guard still held the high walls and javelin-launcher minarets, the old walled city by the docks, and, of course, the Directory. With the fight against the Ironriders still within living memory, the Directory had established a fine outer wall with metal-sheathed gates.

Wistala had seen their whips flicker as they drove captives to the sinks that had opened beneath home and street.

So many! So many! When three were killed, thirty took their place. Against such force of numbers, even dragons were helpless.

The dragon-ships, filled to capacity with the barbarians, crept south.

To DharSii, by all rights half their company should be sunk and dead. They'd seen a burst of heavy weather coming and tried to make landfall, but the storm caught them just ahead of the surf.

Which was a tricky enough barrier. They lost one backbourn boat, and the barbarians—rather cheerfully, to Wistala's idea of dutch—switched over to another dragon's overcrowded back. Someone might have asked first; they weren't oxen with longer tails, after all. Still, they found room for a few more in the manner of rabbits in a winter den.

At DharSii's signal, the groundeds heaved themselves up and out of the water along a pleasant stretch of Hypatian riverbank park. Shadowcatch shook seaweed from his limbs. The barbarians clinging to his back returned their round shields to their arms and slipped off the cargo netting tied across his back from tail-vet to neck. Someone had cut himself on sharp dragon-scale sliding off his back. Shadowcatch risked his throat to arrows and raised his head high to bellow orders to his dragons.

The dome of the Directory and NoSohoth's palace could just be seen over the hill in the distance. Hypat was unimaginably vast—unimaginable, that is, until you tried to cross its twisty streets and muddy lanes without being assassinated.

DharSii led them up to a wide, column-flanked avenue leading to the Directory. Ignoring javelins and arrows fired from rooftop and window, the mass of dragons and barbarians followed. Sensibly, the human warriors sheltered behind the dragon's scale-wrapped bulk.

DharSii wanted room to maneuver. The demen were born tunnel-fighters, experts at lunging out of an alley or doorway and then retreating. The dragons had their flame, and could lay many enemies low with a long sweep of the tail or a plunge-and-roll. The barbarians liked to see their enemy at a distance, too. They would begin to sing and chant and shove each other as they jostled to be at the forefront of the battle. Then, when every face was red and the eyes wide and fanatic, they charged forward as a mass.

His best guess was that Wistala would be helping defend the Directory. That seemed more likely than that she would let others do the fighting while she aided DharSii. The two of them were obviously in love and neither wished to step on the other's toes.

"Tooth line," DharSii called, using the one formation they'd had time to practice. The dragons staggered themselves in two lines, so the rear dragon looked through the wingtip-to-wingtip open line of the rank in front. The front could deploy their fire, and in the confusion and destruction the rear rank would dash forward and become the front rank. They could then add further terror by loosing their flame on whatever part of the enemy was still capable of resistance.

Then and only then could the howling barbarians be released, to leap through the pools of dragon film and bring axes to the heads of their enemies.

Warfare wasn't meant to be sporting—it was meant to be won.

The dragons advanced from Falnges, looked around anxiously. One overzealous member who'd either never or not recently seen a battlefield had sprayed fire at the sudden rise of a flock of pigeons and seagulls, feasting on the pile of garbage waiting to be scraped into the bay.

"Uff tha?" one of the barbarians asked. *Off now?*

"*No!*" DharSii snarled, quieting the youth who was seeing his first real battle.

"Wait until we see them close enough to make out fingers," DharSii called to his battle line. He repeated it down the other end.

War makes strange backfellows, DharSii thought, glancing back at the barbarians on what was left of a barge. Wistala would have liked this, the challenge to carry more than any other dragon.

The demen did them no favors. They did not come out to join battle, instead retreating into the city, where they clustered in the alleys, doorways, and rooftops.

"Bad-mannered of them," DharSii said to no one in particular, but a barbarian who understood some Drakine translated it, and soon the men were shouting it up and down water-dripping vessels.

"We'll have to improvise. Form head-to-toe lines. Let's try to keep our warriors above them. We'll never fit down some of those streets, so we'll have to disembark some of the barbarians, but only once battle is joined and they're good and keyed up."

"Formation coming in from the left," Thunderwing reported.

DharSii lifted his head. He did a double take. The hominid forms wore ordinary Hypatian rain-cloaks, a cheap and oil-clothed tight weave favored by lumberers and miners. But he saw green and flowery colors about their brows. Either they were men garlanded for a summer solstice baby-counting festival, or they were . . .

Elves? Elves coming to the aid of Hypat?

In such numbers, too. By the hundreds, formed into the traditional swan-wings of the northern Hypatian coast, with two companies in front, spread in open-order carrying bows, the traditional groups of unbonded males and females, and a more tightly packed set of male spearmen behind, the battle-givers.

They flowed over the fields and pens of the outskirts of Hypatia like a wind.

The elves fired a volley of arrows into the joined wall-faces of the city proper, dropping some gathered demen trying to set up a dragon-killing lance-thrower on the main avenue. Other arrows rained down on carts, paving-stones, signs, and barrels that had been wedged together as a roadblock.

"To the Directory!" DharSii called.

"Which one is the Directory?" Thunderwing asked, having already forgotten the council of war at the tower.

"I'll go first," the Blind Ripper roared, starting a dragon-dash that threatened to spill his warriors out of the vessel on his back like a pail of water carried by a running child.

The warriors from the barges behind formed into the usual barbarian mobs, order and chaos in one. The warriors with the biggest roundshields and small axes formed the first two ranks, spear-carriers behind, and the swordsmen behind them, ready to be vaulted into action up over the backs of the shield-men when the fighting grew thick.

They swept forward into Hypat, leaving a trail of seawater that soon became mixed with blood.

Chapter 19

The long nightmare was almost over, the Copper calculated. There'd be no bargaining with demen, not NiVom's horde. They'd carried him through burning quarters of Hypatia. The slaughter on the streets was sickening; the demen had made a quick inventory of their captives and slaughtered those determined to be either too young or too old to survive the underground march to their picks and shovels.

Then they took him underground, following in the wake of a dropped and dead captive or two. They hit a small underground river that bore the tunneled look of dwarf-work on their old Ghioz canal system and threw him into a tube of wood, half filled with coconut coir. They threw him in, bound, and arranged the coir so it padded him—and, incidentally, helped keep the cage afloat—and started dragging it by what he assumed were tow ropes along the canal. He heard human-sounding coughs and cries from the drag-ropes.

It was an uncomfortable journey. Chilly water half filled the cage, and it was impossible to shift himself so that he could vary what part of his body rested in water and what didn't. At least he wasn't bound so tightly that it interfered with his circulation. He could be grateful for that.

The journey sped up and they entered a new channel after he heard the sound of locks being closed and filled.

A last trip inside the Lavadome. Funny that NiVom wasn't going to do something spectacular, like hang him from the brass dragon-snout in Ghioz, but then NiVom was always more intelligent than imaginative. He remembered the day when NiVom had come up with the idea of bouncing rocks into the Ghioz fortifications after seeing his thrall skip stones on the river.

A team of demen with four chained-together trolls opened the leaky vessel where he had expected, at the far side of the river ring, the circular underground lake encompassing the Lavadome. How fitting. This was where his life really began, crossing this engineered body of water with a *griffaran* egg. This is where it would end, beneath these old columns that harbored the Griffaran Guard. There was something satisfying about coming full circle. He'd achieved more than most, though it was hard not to count much of the labor he'd put into building the Dragon Empire as wasted. Instead of securing his species' future, he'd sealed its fate.

Under barbed whips of the demen, the trolls lifted his wet cage and carried him up the tunnel leading into the Lavadome.

It was the tunnel he'd used the first time he'd entered the Lavadome. Fitting that he should use it for his last trip.

Cramped and cold from the long, soggy journey, he accepted his fate. So be it. If NiVom expected him to beg, polish his conquerors *saa* claws with spittled tongue, call on old memories of their time together in the Drakwatch, he'd be disappointed. He would just ask that Nilrasha be spared.

He revived enough to revisit the Lavadome as they carried him through its orange-lit expanse. Where there'd been pens and laboriously built-up potato and onion patches, muddy masses that looked like cattle-wades remained. One of the signaling towers he'd had built—the one on Skotl hill, a rock column with a lantern and mirror atop so a signal could be flashed to other hills or the observation post on Imperial Rock—had collapsed into a pile of rubble with ugly, thorny dwarfhook thriving and expanding through the cracks.

The gentle rocking and the warmth of finally being out of the cold of the river overwhelmed him. Despite a firm conviction of being carried to his death by trolls, he fell soundly asleep.

He awoke in a dark chamber. A few moments of snuffling around in the dark convinced him he was in one of the cells in a rocky outcropping adjacent to Imperial Rock, where some fragments of the forming monolith fell and piled up in a broken imitation of the colossal growth towering above.

The rocks had been re-dug and rearranged into holding pens for dragons awaiting the Tyr's justice. No bars as in hominid cell doors; dragon-flame could burn wood and weaken iron. No, extremely heavy slabs were dragged over the tops of the cell-pits with a boulder or two thrown in for good measure. Air came in through the uneven seal between slab and cell-pit, and there was a cistern for drinking and washing if you wished.

His cistern was dry and smelled as though it hadn't seen water in a year.

In his time as Tyr these cells had been used only rarely. Only the worst class of dragon, or those deranged by illness or injury, were put here while their fate was considered and decided. Most dragons waited quietly at the home-cave for the Tyr's decision, if they'd committed some breach of the peace.

Nothing to do but wait. If he was very lucky, one of the Lavadome's smaller bats might find him. . . .

Odd that NiVom never came to triumph over him. He was the sort of dragon who, when he'd beaten you, offered you the courtesy of a visit as though to seal his triumph by looking down his snout at you. All very affably, of course, with intelligent conversation about where the loser had misstepped.

The trolls took him to the base of Imperial Rock and down into the old dueling pit beneath.

It was a strange sort of structure, sort of a darker lavadome-within-the-Lavadome. When Imperial Rock had been formed, something had pushed up against the bottom of the rock, leaving a domed chamber. An air channel led up from it to the main open staircase winding up through the whole length of the rock. Some time before records were kept, it had been discovered, hollowed-out further, shaped, and then filled with sand. Three rows of shelves where dragons could recline ringed the sandy pit in the center.

The Copper had done away with dueling when he became Tyr. Ever the smaller and handicapped by his injuries, he had never been treated well by duels. He preferred to use the chamber to address larger groups of dragons than could meet before the throne, but still in more privacy than in the gardens atop Imperial Rock.

The place looked dusty and there were old crates and barrels stored on the shelves where dragons once reclined and listened or spoke. Old banners, somewhat mildewed, ringed the walls—they were trophies of poorer quality from battles that weren't good enough for the throne room but still worth keeping as reminders of victories. Now the banners, like his victories, were disintegrating.

Rayg and Imfamnia stood in the old Tyr's shelf looking out over the dueling pit. Rayg, with an old human's run-wild hairiness, managed to look more vital than the emaciated dragondame. When he'd known her growing up, she was a beautiful, vital dragon, sleek and well fed, all swooping lines made for the smooth passage of wing. Now she looked thin—you could actually see hip joints and where the ribs ended, all angles and sharp edges. The overindulged, mocking gaze that held you until, embarrassed, you looked away had been replaced by brief, pointed glances at those all around and in the shadows, as if she expected an assassin's lunge from the old banners hung around the walls. The years of exile must have sharpened her, like a broken decorative sword cut down and sharpened into a stabbing dagger.

"Meet the new exemplar of your tired, fractious species," Rayg said.

The red dragon was newly fledged, though his wings drooped and dragged along behind him like a gown on a female hominid of the Directory. He was a rather dull silver, with a stupid half-smile on his face.

"Wave to the old-kind, SuSunuth," Rayg said. The red held up a *sii*. Its claws had been removed, only sawn-off-looking digits remained. They were red and raw, as though they'd been chewed at.

"Three operations," Rayg said. "Simple enough for a blighter to do. Clip two tendons at the base of each wing, take out the front and rear claws and cauterize, and then—most important—a minor operation, drilling into the skull just behind each eye along the horizontal to the base of the crest. It renders the dragon docile and cooperative. The only harm this dragon is capable of doing is by accident. I'm still working on removing the glands to ignite the firebladder oil. I haven't quite managed that yet. The roof of a dragon mouth seems prone to infection—tinker with it and it goes dry and then black rot sets in and it reaches the brain in a flash. I keep losing hatchlings that way. Perhaps I should try permanently tapping the firebladder, hmmm?"

AuRon wished he could tap Rayg's brain with a piece of bamboo. right to the base of the skull, and then see what secrets leaked out.

All my fault, AuRon, his brother thought to him. *Rayg's been too long chained in the dark. First by dwarfs, then by dragons. No wonder he cracked.*

"Are you going to let him do this, Imfamnia?" the Copper asked. "You, a fellow dragon?"

"But I'm not a dragon, blockhead. I may look like Imfamnia, and I'm ashamed to say I've been practiced into speaking like her, but she's long gone. I'm just making use of the very serviceable body. I'm the Red Queen. Didn't I once tell you, AuRon, that I was too busy to die?"

"Infamnia—when?"

"Shortly after she met up with NiVom. I've been engineering their return to power ever since. She came to me through the attentions of my society—we can be found here and there, traveling with entertainments and telling fortunes."

"Let's not waste time on speeches, Queen of Hosts," Rayg said. "The important point is that a dragon in this condition is rendered harmless, but is still thick with blood and flesh. Even thicker, as the brain operation renders it rather listless, so it tends to put on flesh rather than burn it off. One day, every palace in the east will have one, fed and bled for vitality draughts for rich princes. They'll go out rendered incapable of breeding, of course. I don't want competition. The Lavadome will be home to only the remaining dragons capable of having offspring, once we clear out a few odds and ends."

"You might find the odds and ends tougher to clear out than you think," the Copper said.

"What will you send up to deal with Scabia?" AuRon asked. "Hatchlings in the Sadda-Vale are rolling your assassins' skulls across the Vesshall to knock over wooden pins."

"Even the Sadda-Vale isn't remote enough, AuRon. The trolls will clear it out eventually."

"I think it shall be my summer palace," Imfamnia said. AuRon had trouble thinking of a hominid spirit—soul, whatever one wished to call it—in the body of a dragon. No wonder she'd lost weight—probably still had a hominid's appetite.

The sand smelled like the place had been used to store rotten potatoes. Vermin had the run of it, judging from the slightly sweet, dead-mouse smell coming from the piles of crates. Like much else in the Lavadome these days, the old dueling pit was half empty and going decrepit. He looked up and the glint of a bat eye peering at him from the darkness of a crack in the ceiling twinkled back like a star.

In his time, they'd held public debates in this space. Now the only squabbles settled were by bats looking to take a more comfortable perch.

"Whoever wins gets to have their mate live," Rayg said.

"A little battie told me you two have never much liked each other," Imfamnia added.

Trolls, answering a hooted call blatted out from a short brassy horn Rayg carried, brought in Nilrasha and Natasatch. They were muzzled and hobbled, back left *saa* to front right *sii*.

The Copper sidestepped, circling to his right to keep his injured limb away from AuRon. For an instant, AuRon's posture seemed to be the same as when he was on the egg shelf at their hatching: *Charge, charge and push him over. . . .*

His brother made no move to grapple, though his tail lashed angrily. Tail—AuRon noticed that his brother, at the longest extent of the lash, briefly pointed at the high perch where Imfamnia rested with Rayg beside her, beyond their wall of troll-flesh.

Me above, you below, came the mindspeech. *Just like on the egg shelf.*

No. The trolls will have us.

They'll have us anyway. Eventually. Rayg is the key. He directs the trolls somehow. If he can be distracted . . .

AuRon made a feint, snapped where the Copper's throat had been a moment before. That would impress the watchers in the stands—a good bite always did. The problem was, as Father pointed out all those years ago, a dragon's mouth isn't powerful enough to kill anything but smaller, hominid-sized quarry. When fighting something your own size, you let the *saa,* with their thick claws, do the ripping and killing.

The Copper charged in return, rearing up and raining blows on him. AuRon backed up, blocking with *griff* and his wings. The Copper backed up, let out a snarl to get the blood up, and sprang forward in two great bounds.

On the third he leaped for AuRon's back. AuRon had to find it in his hearts to trust his brother not to dig in and sever his spine at the neck. He braced himself.

Instead of landing with claws digging in, the Copper gathered himself for another bound off AuRon's back between his wings. AuRon threw his body up with all his might, giving what leverage he could to the Copper's leap, before turning himself.

He watched the Copper extend, striving to reach the shelf holding Rayg and Imfamnia.

The wizard and the self-proclaimed Queen of the Hosts recoiled in fear. The Copper landed just short of their shelf, his *sii* extended and holding on, keeping him from falling back into the fighting pit.

Had he only been able to spread both wings—

A troll reached up and grabbed his brother by the tail. They fell together, messily, into the sand.

AuRon rushed to his brother's aid, ignoring the shrieks of Imfamnia—something about Rayg hiding behind her, as always—and Rayg's frantic hooting amplified through a speaking tube.

He tore into a troll with frustrated fury. An elf would appreciate the irony of dying next to his brother, after all the years and all the distance they'd traveled separately. But every dragon meets his end, death being even more certain than the rising of the sun, and if this was to be his, so be it. He didn't care to live to see what sort of world Rayg and Imfamnia would fashion, full of declawed, flightless dragons.

Remarkably, he brought down the troll that he'd been fighting. It continually raised its head to hear Rayg's frantic hoots, and AuRon managed to get a *saa* up and popped it off its stalk like a grapefruit loosed from a tree.

The troll picked itself up and charged off in a frantic search for its sense-organ cluster.

His brother was beneath another troll. Both were bloody, but his brother seemed to be getting the worst of it.

He moved to help, but one of the trolls from the balcony bounded down and landed squarely on his back. He heard a bone in his wing snap.

We tried. Proud to be teamed up with you, brother. We should have tried this sooner, the Copper thought to him.

AuRon heard the reed-cutting sound of cartilage snapping in the troll's grip, and his brother's head dropped. The troll released its grip when the Copper's eyes ceased whirling and bulging and went glassy-still. A mechanical death rattle escaped his brother and no breath followed.

The troll placed his hand on the Copper's chest, felt around, then turned away, kicking sand upon the corpse with those ridiculous back limbs.

"It appears you win again, AuRon," Rayg said. "Though by default. Your amazing string of luck in single combat—"

With a screech Nilrasha ran forward.

"Wait, you won't be harmed!" Rayg called. "That was just—"

She threw herself upon the huge troll, back legs tight against her side after the leap. She pedaled frantically with them, removing the troll's scaly skin in bloody strips. The troll let out a gibbering hoot and then the blood quit spraying as it collapsed.

"You may depart, Natasatch," Imfamnia said. "I think you'll find it an easy glide to the surface."

"No. Whatever fate my beloved and the father of my hatchlings faces, I share it with him."

"As for the loser's mate, you may go, too." Rayg let out a corkscrew call and the trolls pawed back from Nilrasha. "We'll see that the former Tyr's body is properly—"

"No," she snarled at the trolls, covering her mate's body with her own.

Nilrasha, bleeding, wormed beneath her mate and with a heave of her back legs, lifted him across her back.

"Kill her!" Imfamnia shouted. "Rayg, you fool, have the trolls take her head."

"They're not going anywhere," Rayg said.

Leaving a bright trail of commingled blood, Nilrasha pulled the limp body of her mate toward the exit, clutching it across the back with her stumps of wings.

"Are you mad?" Imfamnia asked.

Rayg shrugged. "He was good to me. What I am now is because of him, more than anything. I'd hoped he'd triumph over his brother."

"I'll deal with them myself, then," she said, gathering herself for a leap.

Nilrasha raised her bloodied head. "You do that, Jade Queen. Oh, for that chance. If my last grapple is with you, I die exalted." She spat out the stump of a broken tooth, leaving a trail of bloody slime hanging from her maw. She set her *sii* atop her mate's body, ready to leave a ring of blood around it. "Well?"

Imfamnia paused. "Perhaps . . . not. Oh, crawl into a hole and die together. The world spins on and we shall ride it."

She continued her crawl, made it past AuRon.

Was he imagining things, or did his brother's good eye give a tiny wink?

Wistala thought it would be a battle for the history books, just because NoSohoth fought in it.

The ungainly old dragon panted through the air but must have been in some kind of training, because he managed to fly down the spine of the Red Mountains without collapsing or lagging behind.

It appeared he was capable of fury after all. "Betray me, will you? You pup!" This and much more issued forth from him, even in his exhausted slumbers between flights.

On the journey, DharSii did what he could to get them ready for battle. He divided his younger and more fit fliers from the older, lumbering dragons. Then each of those groups was divided into pairs. The front dragon would fly toward the destination, the one behind his wing keeping up and keeping watch on the lead. It was an old system dating back to Dhar-Sii's days in the Lavadome as a very young dragon. How it would fare against the fancier evolutions of the Aerial Host—if much was left of it—these days remained to be seen.

They avoided Ghioz on the way, and stopped at Nilrasha's needle to free her, but she'd been removed, along with her *griffaran* guard. Some local eagles said that before the last quarter moon—three weeks or so by a dwarfish calendar—a party of dragons and big, broad-shouldered beasts the eagles didn't recognize came and took her away, the whole team of them carrying her off through the air in a net the way loads were swung up into a big ship.

Wistala quizzed them closely. It sounded as though the flying trolls had left the Star Tunnel and were ready to do NiVom and Imfamnia's bidding.

Their enemy rose out of mountain to meet them. NiVom must have had word of their coming.

"A fight in the open air will be better," DharSii said. "Room to maneuver against those trolls. They don't look fast."

"That's a swarm of *griffaran*," Wistala said. "Black as the pit. I prefer the old sort."

"Don't judge yet," DharSii said. Wistala waited for him to elaborate, but he gave orders for the fast dragons to gain altitude and the slower ones to make for the Lavadome.

All at once the fight was upon them. The trolls and *griffaran* grew from distant dots to sets of claws and wings swooping through the air in an instant, it seemed. A *griffaran* raked a dragon—one of the Hypat contingent—across the flank and a red mist appeared and fell, spreading into nothingness. The crippled dragon plunged.

Another went down, one of the dragon tower contingent who'd flown south for the glory of battle. His flame gouted up in frustration. A troll smashed another dragon across the back with a massive fist and it folded horribly backward under the blow. Wistala plunged toward the troll, determined to destroy it. She loosed her fire but too soon, as the troll closed a wing and fell off fast to its left, avoiding the flame's path. She managed to catch part of its wing with her tail nevertheless.

There were other black smears of dying dragon-flame in the sky. They'd done no damage to the enemy that she could see. Even the Aerial Host dragons hadn't caused blood to rain down. Was this the death-flight of dragonkind?

Finally a troll fell, but it took a dragon with it. They went down together, both trailing wing skin and bone in a fluttering mass as they fell.

"We're done for," a dragon called.

"Hunting them is one thing, but this!"

Wistala watched one of the *griffaran* turn in pursuit of a

dragon. The graceful female dragon turned tight, her wings, body, neck, and tail working together, and even her spinal fringe doing its duty to stabilize her in the air. The *griffaran* tried to match it, and like a runner losing his balance, the air went out from under it and it fluttered and fell in a confused manner for a moment before righting itself.

They're body-heavy and underwinged, Wistala thought.

NiVom and Imfamnia had made a mistake, tinkering with the *griffaran*. Nature is capable of perfection and adding dragon-blood means a subtraction somewhere else. They took a supremely deadly flier and made it tough and frightful, resistant to arrow and fire, but it had lost the lethal speed and maneuverability that made it such a threat to dragons. Flying against the *griffaran* was a contest between an osprey and a buzzard.

"Sloppy fliers. Like bumblebees! Don't engage, hit light and dodge the counterstrike."

"Pair off," DharSii bellowed. "Pass word: Pair off! Just nip them at the wingtips!"

For the more experienced former warriors of the Aerial Host, the tactical advice wasn't necessary. They'd already sniffed out these mutated *griffaran*'s weakness and were improvising methods for taking advantage of it.

One of the Lights—AuRon's daughter Varatheela, by the look of it—flapped hard, her wingmate trying to keep up. She went straight at one of the glistening, reptilian *griffaran*. It raised its claws to meet her snout, but at the last moment she turned on her belly—a very dangerous move—and grabbed a *sii*-ful of feathers out of the edge of its wing as she passed.

Ungainly before, the dreadful *griffaran* plummeted like a duck with an arrow through its wing.

"Those edges are everything with a bird-wing," DharSii said. He executed a dive and two *griffaran* swooped to follow. Extending legs, wings, tail, and even *griff* to their maximum, he slowed his pace in the air and they passed overhead, claws out and grasping at air. Both were marking DharSii's course rather than each other and collided. A loose feather flew up and the two *griffaran*, senseless or dead, fell limp from the sky.

"I watched your brother making that move once," DharSii said, watching with satisfaction as the *griffaran* struck the mountainside. "He slows himself more easily than I."

NiVom must not have had much time to evaluate his new *griffaran* against live dragons. Of course, keeping secrets meant no one could tell you when you've gone wrong.

The trolls were another matter.

Don't think of it as a battle. Think of it as a big hunt.

"Same thing as our hunts, only in the air," Wistala said. "One of us draws its attention, the other one strikes!"

"I'm first," DharSii said.

He plunged into the path of a troll and spat whatever remnants of his firebladder he could—more to get the troll's attention than in expectation of setting it alight. He made a convincing show attack, lashing out with quick flips of his wingtips and tail in a series of blows aimed at its stalked sense-organ cluster.

The troll rolled—an unexpected move—and its arms windmilled, striking DharSii hard in the side. DharSii sagged under the blow and a wing went folded, the sign of a bad injury to the back muscles or ribs.

Wistala, silently asking the sun and spirits to have it be a clever ruse, folded her wings and dove. She didn't open them again, even when she struck the troll a hard body blow. She ripped with *sii* and *saa*, tearing the roots of the troll's butterfly-like wings to shreds, felt it pounding her back, but she kept her wings closed tight as they fell like bloodily mating dragons.

The troll panicked and released her and she turned as she fell away, dodged a *griffaran*, and opened her wings again. DharSii fell in a tight series of spirals on his good wing, heading for the unforgiving mountainside beneath the Lavadome's crest.

Chapter 20

With Rayg and Imfamnia leading the way up, they climbed Imperial Rock.

"You're welcome to the throne room, if you want to eat and rest for a bit. Regalia certainly has no use for it anymore. It's cleaner than most quarters. Some of the lower levels are still a bit—damp," Rayg said.

A troll led each of them. It held a thick piece of chain wrapped around their necks. One hard pull from the trolls just under the jaw and their vertebrae would snap.

"Each of you will do anything to keep the other alive," Rayg said. "You won't risk fighting us, because the trolls will throttle you. If you try to escape, I'll get one. Which means I'll get both of you."

"Weakness indeed," Imfamnia said.

"Yes, it's better to partner with someone you despise," Au-Ron said. "Perhaps you two will set the new social standard."

Imfamnia laughed. "I'm remembering why she used to admire you."

"What are you going to do with us?" AuRon asked.

"In memory of your kindly brother," Rayg said, "we'll keep you alive, but imprisoned. I need a few couples for breeding stock, after all. Someone has to produce my perfected dragons."

Can we find the strength to die together, AuRon? Natasatch asked. *I won't be chained in the dark again.*

I won't have my offspring declawed and desensitized.

They led them up onto the gardens atop Imperial Rock and toward Rayg's lab.

"I'm just going to do one minor operation," Rayg said. "I'll sever the muscles around your firebladder. Better safe than spontaneously combusted."

"You gave us a scare, there, dragon," the wizard continued "We weren't really ready to move for a few years yet. I would have liked some more time to gather the rest of the sun-shard, but I have enough to control the Lavadome and see through the various veils of space and time."

"Time? You can tell the future?"

"I'll keep a few dragons alive, for distilling youth draughts. They won't keep me going forever, of course, but a thousand-year lifespan should be enough for me to design an even more perfect vessel."

I'd rather be back in the hands of the Wyrmaster, Natasatch thought.

Or the Dragonblade. He was an honest enemy, AuRon thought back

Rayg opened the door to his tower. The trolls pulled them in. AuRon saw rows of sharp, gleaming instruments on the wall. "And I'll work on my ideal strain. The perfect amalgamation of dragon and hominid. The demen are close to the shape I have in mind. I think if I form a dragon-man and cross the two—"

"You and your breeding!" Imfamnia said. Or rather not Imfamnia but the Red Queen, speaking through Imfamnia's body, AuRon had to remind himself. "Men are good enough for me—they learn for themselves and increase naturally."

"They can be a little recalcitrant," Rayg said. "Not quite as stiff-necked as dwarfs, or as dangerous as dragons."

A gargolyle and a *griffaran*, both a little bloody about the wings and claws, waddled over and whispered, alternately, in Rayg's ear.

"Well, we'll have to do something else a little early," Rayg said, reaching for a long crystal staff. He tapped it three times and it lit up, a brilliant, room-filling white light that seemed to clean AuRon's skin of the troll-stink and blood from the dueling pit. The light was answered from a mini-sun above. The huge piece of the sun-shard that AuRon had once encountered in NooMoahk's library that was resting at the top of his observation dome, warmed them like a flame.

"I do so hate uninvited guests," Rayg said. "Best relocate the house."

* * *

DharSii had made a hard landing on the mountainside. Far above, they could just see the rim of the crystal at the apex of the Lavadome.

"In one piece?" she asked.

"My head hurts too much to count," he said. "Check for me, won't you?"

She nuzzled him, *griff* to *griff.*

"Who won?" he asked, looking up.

"I think both sides retreated," Wistala said. "We might want to think about getting off this mountain. They might come after stragglers."

The earth heaved beneath their feet. "What's this?" Wistala cried.

The mountain bulged, for just a moment. Then, a thunder that shook the ground beneath their feet broke out. Cracks and fissures raced down the side of the mountain. Brown clouds shot into the sky. The air shimmered with released heat.

The Lavadome rose into the air, shedding boulders and mountainside the way a rising cormorant sheds water. Pieces of mountain slid off the faceted surface and fell in ruin into the crater below.

It was not a perfect circle, as she had thought when inside the upper half. The shape, if anything, reminded her of a jellyfish with an inverted forest of streamers beneath. The projections at the bottom followed no plan; some were longer, some shorter, thicker in some parts and thinner in others, with the irregularity of tree roots, save that all grew straight down and narrowed like fangs.

Yes, perhaps that was the way to describe it. A skull, vast

beyond comprehension, hanging in the air, missing the lower mandible, so downward-growing teeth formed its base.

Wistala felt stupefied by the sight. She feared that if she tried to talk, nothing but gibberish would erupt.

"AuRon is in there!" she said.

"Go, Wistala," DharSii said. "Go to him, if you must. But I fear Rayg has won. He's learned how to use the sun-shard to channel the power of the Lavadome. Or perhaps not. It's still here."

"Where would it go?"

"Another time and place. I believe Anklemere came here from it. It might have been a vessel for traveling across time and space, the way humans cross the ocean in a ship, or it might have been a prison. I don't believe Anklemere existed as you and I do—he was part of the Lavadome and the sun-shard."

The interior of the Lavadome was suddenly, brilliantly lit. The rational side of AuRon's brain knew what must have happened in all the trembling, lurching, falling dust and sudden wash of light outside the tower, but his gut refused to believe that anything as vast as the Lavadome could just lift itself up out of the crater it rested in.

Rayg put down the staff and went back to work with his surgical tools, selecting them and laying them out on a tray.

"The partnership will never work," AuRon said, looking at Imfamnia. "While you had enemies, it made sense to work together. But you've defeated them and secured your refuge.

From now on, every gain by one is a loss to the other. You're competitors now, not teammates."

"That's not—," Imfamnia said.

"One of you is bound to kill the other," AuRon continued. "I wonder which it will be. And who will move first. I imagine historians will be debating the subject for centuries. The Red Queen has the advantage, in that if Rayg kills one, another can take its place. Perhaps a new tree is growing somewhere, so she has a supply of copies. Unless Rayg has figured out where the new tree is. In the Lavadome, somewhere, I expect. Down below in the crystalline caverns?

"Now, from the Red Queen's point of view, the job is much easier. She has the physical advantage, being in a dragon. Rayg is just one wizard, and right now he's passing orders to his bodyguard."

"Blather and rot," Rayg said. "Sing another pleasant little ditty, AuRon, while I carve up your mate's breast." Rayg stepped across the room with a long, razor-edged knife.

AuRon could feel the tension in the air, like the energy stored in the Lavadome's crystals.

"Imfamnia, ware!" AuRon shouted.

Rayg had done nothing, of course, but Imfamnia didn't know that. She crouched and spat fire in Rayg's direction.

He cartwheeled out of the way, showing the agility of an elvish dancer. He reached into his voluminous overcoat and hurled a handful of glittering, starlike spiked shapes at Imfamnia. They passed through her scale like arrows shot through a gauze curtain, leaving black rings at the holes.

Imfamnia howled in rage and pain. Smoke from her flame

filled the room. The trolls hauled on the chains and dragged AuRon and Natasatch to the ground.

But he could still see the action. And, more important, breathe. Maddened, Imfamnia threw herself at Rayg, who jumped out of the way again, perhaps not quite so quickly as the last time. Instead of an elvish dancer, he was a supremely agile human warrior.

Imfamnia crashed into the hard stone of his tower, cracking it and opening a wide fissure in a window. Scale and bits of masonry flew. AuRon wondered who'd built the tower. Certainly not dwarfs if the base cracked from just the force of a dragon striking it.

"I think, Rayg, you overbuilt. I'm no dwarf, but it looks like you built your tower on a poor foundation," Natasatch said.

The tower swayed but did not give way.

AuRon heard the trolls' lung-flaps working harder in the smoke.

"Get them out!" he shouted at the trolls. They just stood there. He took out his horn and started blasting.

Imfamnia charged out of the smoke, blood smearing down her forehead, and AuRon saw her hindquarters lash around as the trolls dragged them outside.

He saw Imfamnia with the crystal staff in her hand. She hurled it like a spear at Rayg, an unnatural motion for a dragon but a perfectly sound one for a hominid. The staff broke and the Lavadome lurched in the air, tilted.

Suddenly everything was groaning and cracking in the tower. AuRon scrambled to push Natasatch out, dragging a troll.

"Rayg, when you built that tower, I imagine you thought it would always sit on a level surface."

The Lavadome shifted back level again. The tower didn't cease groaning, however, and pieces of masonry and jets of dust shot from the bottom two levels.

He heard a pained cry from Imfamnia.

The air above was full of whirling bats, disturbed by the change in the light in the Lavadome, AuRon guessed. Flocks like clouds circled about the gardens. The vermin had multiplied in the years of the Lavadome's neglect.

Rayg staggered out and into the bats.

"Revenges! Revenges for our Tyr and our dark!" they squeaked, covering him in flapping wing and fur. Just like his brother, AuRon thought, to inspire such loyalty in vermin.

A cloud of bats whirled overhead like a living tornado. The funnel reached down . . .

AuRon lashed out sideways with a *saa*. Now that he knew where to hit a troll, it was easy to detach the sense-orb.

The remaining troll, waving those oversized, overmuscled, dragon-killing arms, staggered through the cloud of bats, its sense organ covered in a bag of brown balls of hair and leathery wings. The bats in the air around it dodged its blows as easily as they circumnavigated stalactites. It plunged off the edge of Imperial Rock with a last surprised hoot.

The tower gave a final shudder and fell in on itself *blam blam blam blam!* as each floor collapsed into the other. Metallic shrieks and the sound of glass breaking added to the noise.

The tower's collapse shocked Rayg and Imfamnia out of their duel. "Hurry, before the Firemaids find us!" Rayg said.

Infamnia came to her senses, picked up Rayg, and threw herself into the air, out over the edge of the Imperial Rock. But there are disadvantages to not being born a dragon but living within one. She forgot to check her wings before trying to fly. A cut tendon left a third of one wing flapping. They both followed the troll off the edge.

"How did the bats know?" Natasatch asked.

"I imagine Nilrasha or my brother told them."

The Lavadome belonged to the dragons again. And the bats, of course.

Epilogue

Years later—not too many, at least not in the reckoning of a long life of a dragon—Wistala and DharSii established themselves in the old Queen's Eyrie; Nilrasha's Needle, a few roving hunters called it.

A new Dragon-Hominid alliance, the Chartered Trust—drawn up by dwarfs and based on legalistic elven political philosophy—had replaced the Empire. No one much liked the compromises, for the dragons had to hand over much of the precious metal they'd accumulated and the hominids agreed that the dragons would keep their Upper World estates and vast hunting preserves.

The Lavadome had come to rest back in the crater it rose from, though not quite as deep. With so much sun coming in, it was a cheerier place, but a great deal of work had to be done to even restore an exit where you could just walk up a path rather than do a twisting, turning scramble thorough rock and slag.

Neither her Copper brother nor Nilrasha was ever found. They certainly never came to claim their remote refuge. Dhar-Sii assumed she was still dragging him toward the last place they'd been seen heading, the river ring, when the cataclysm struck. Their bodies might be buried under the better part of what had been the Lavadome's mountain, or they might have been burned in molten rock, or even scalded and swept away by the steaming waters.

Still, rumors persisted that they'd survived. A story gained currency among Hypatian dragon-fanciers and historians that some blighters in Bant had helped a mated pair open an old, forgotten exit to the Lavadome for a pair of crippled and grounded dragons, and showed copper and green scale to prove it. But the blighters of the savannah were notorious for creating juicy and mysterious tales to tell travelers by the fireside, in the hope of hiring more scouts to lead them to elephant graveyards, lost diamond mines, or even a former Tyr of Dragons and his family in their spacious cave overlooking the crashing sea.

Yes, as if rumor of survival wasn't enough, the notoriously barren Nilrasha had supposedly had a clutch. Of course, Aeth-leethia had spent a lifetime being thought eggless, and she and NaStirath had produced two clutches and thought they might have one more in them.

Wistala liked the solitude. Only a dragon could easily cross the rocky, thickly wooded hills, cut deep by a tangle of rushing streams and rivers. The altitude made for a comfortable climate, just cool enough in the evenings to be invigorating and make a cozy bed welcome, but Wistala and DharSii weren't so high that frost often touched them. The sunsets were spectacular. There was desert country far off on the other side of the Inland Ocean, DharSii told her, and the blowing winds threw up sand, coloring the sky to the west. Leave it to DharSii to explain away beauty and joy with talk of types of sand and prevailing local winds.

They were happy, busy years for those of the Trust. Wistala and DharSii were minor figures in this new Age of Foundations, as some were calling it. DharSii had attempted to name it an Age of Reason, but that never caught on with people trying to build homes by picking through rubble, or reclaiming fields from quick-growing pines and birches.

A colony of elves had gathered at their old seaside home not too far away. One of Rainfall's "daughters" was training dolphins to herd schools of fish, much as human shepherds used dogs.

On what felt like the other side of the world, in the Sadda-Vale, old Scabia finally had a court. The dragons of the Empire who weren't interested in mixing with hominids in the bubbling cauldron of activity that was the Age of Salvage had sought respite there. Art, memorials to old glories, and long-but-sparing meals gave her a chance to exercise her manners. Wistala had no doubt that NaStirath's jokes found a receptive audience and Aethleethia could speak of the doings of hatchlings to her hearts' content.

The dwarfs had reclaimed the old river roads deep underground, and claimed they could move cargo from south to north and back again faster than a dragon could travel. Of course their formula used a weight favorable to the tunnel ships rather than one that might be carried in the air or borne on the ground, but then dwarfs always did shape and color the truth much as their shaded glass might shape or color light.

Her old friends in the north were enjoying their new position at the crossroads of the world. The great river going to the Red Mountains now rivaled the Falnges in river traffic, with elves and dwarfs at both the headwaters and the mouth of the river and humans in between. The trolls' old cave was the midpoint in a long stair that brought goods up from a new wharf. From there, commerce moved north and south on Rainfall's old road. Rainfall's old estate was now a lodge, village, and temple. From his hall, Thane Ragwrist bought and sold vast herds of horses and larger beasts for pulling loads.

As for the dragons, the great halls they'd built in Hypatia were still standing, but thanks to losses in the Second Civil War only a few were still occupied. "Free Wings" of mercenary dragons had a few, with a dozen or so fighting dragons and dragon-dames and their mates. Others were now temples of the Hypatian gods, or cavernous "exchanges" where goods or contracts for future products were bought or sold. NoSohoth's colossal palace, with its deep holes for his wealth, was now Hypatia's major financial concern, and the mild-mannered but avaricious old majordomo of the royal family was trying to re-establish a trade in spices and silks with the Great East so he might own the other half of the world as well, but rumor had it that some canny old eastern dragon was beating him at his game.

"I think dragons will do better in Hypatia than anywhere else, for all that I'm sympathetic to the 'reclusives,'" DharSii said. "The Hypatian concept of citizenship could work to their advantage. They would get the protection of Hypatian law, and even if the duties of money prove onerous to a family with gold-hungry hatchlings to feed, by their size and power they could choose service."

As for AuRon's old blighters, they had expanded into the Ironrider lands and broken up into quarreling factions. Many had become nomads in the fashion of the old Ironriders, and a few tribal leaders were building tall chariots to draw them. To DharSii's mind, they might one day prove a threat to the more civilized worlds east, west, and south. AuRon and Natasatch were back with their surviving family in Old Uldam, trying to build an alliance with the princedoms with the help of Hieba. Wistala wished them luck.

"But that's long in the future," DharSii said. "We may not live to see it, and we certainly won't take any important part in it, even if we still can fly at that age. I think we're done with great wars, for now. It's been three generations of men since there's been any real peace, and I believe the world's ready for a respite."

DharSii was not a dragon given to wishful thinking, and rarely gave an opinion unless he'd thought it through. In this specimen of thinking, Wistala was inclined to agree with him. Especially in his use of "we" and "us." It elicited a *prrum* from her.

"Everyone blames the Lavadome—a fallen star, an engine of evil. If a dwarf miscounts, it's because the black star is whispering in his ear."

"We both know that's not true. There's blame enough to go around. The Lavadome was just a tool, and like any tool, it could be used for good or ill. That tool was just spectacularly powerful."

"We'll never know what happened in the end, will we?"

"I did get one quick flash as it vanished. I saw green lands and a clear blue sky. I didn't recognize any landmarks, but the impression came and went as quickly as thinking. Impossible to say if that's where it was going, or if that was some last picture in Rayg's head—a wish or a dream."

"You think it's some kind of vessel for traveling," Wistala said. "Perhaps we've been mistaken—perhaps it doesn't go from place to place, but from time to time. Maybe they're back before Silverhigh, even. The Age of Wheels, when the blighters ruled."

"Your brothers have it in them to tame the blighters, I suppose."

"There are so few dragons left. Some philosophers think that below a certain point, a population just can't make a comeback. Natural decrease and all that."

"Fates forbid," Wistala said. "I intend to put up a fight."

"How will you do that?" DharSii asked.

"I'm sure now, so I'll tell you. There are more eggs on the way. Quite a few, judging from my appetite. I'm twice as ravenous as I was with the set from the Sadda-Vale."

"You wish to have them up here?"

"I like the view. They'll have to be tough little drakes and drakkas to make the climb down when the time comes for them to go into the world."

"I suppose I'd better arrange for a few herds of sheep and goats. They'd do well in these hills. Dwarfs, you think, as herdsmen? It's remote enough for them. There's a lot of good limestone about, so they could establish an impressive delving. Who knows if these streams have been prospected for gold?"

"I'll leave that to you. I wonder what sort of world they'll grow up in."

"That's rather up to all of us, isn't it?" DharSii said.

The moon was coming up, swollen and greenish, as it always seemed when near the horizon. Wistala felt a kinship with it; they were both in their full and heavy phase. But rising toward a future zenith. In the clear air each splash and mottle on its chalky surface stood out.

DharSii yawned and stretched, a sign that he was putting his thoughts away for the evening. He settled into a comfortable repose and placed his neck across hers.

"Remarkable," he mused. "I can't remember when I've seen such a moon."

Together, they watched it rise.

Drakine Glossary

FOUA: A product of the firebladder. When mixed with the liquid fats stored within and then exposed to oxygen, it ignites into oily flame.

GRIFF: The armored fans descending from the forehead and jaw that cover sensitive ear-holes and throat pulse-points in battle.

GRIFF-TCHK: An instant, an immeasurably short amount of time.

LAUDI: Brave and glorious deeds in a dragon's life that make it into the lifesong.

PRRUM: The low thrumming sound a dragon makes when it is pleased or particularly content.

OLIBAN: A valuable resin that, when burned, has a calming effect on male dragons.

SAA: The rear legs of a dragon. The three rear true-toes are able to grip, but the fighting spur is little more than decoration.

SII: The front legs of a dragon. The claws are shorter and the fighting spur on the rear leg is closer to the other digits and opposable. The digits are more elegantly formed for manipulation.

TORF: A small gob from the firebladder, used to provide a few moments of illumination.

Draconic Personae

AETHLEETHIA—Daughter of Scabia, mate of NaStirath

AGLABERARN—Silver, member of the Light Wing

AYAFEEIA—Leader of the Firemaids

AUSURATH—Red, AuRon and Natasatch's son, Commander of the Heavy Wing of the Aerial Host

AURON—Gray, brother to RuGaard the Copper and Wistala

BAMELPHISTRAN—Commander of the Aerial Host

CUSARRATH—Wing Commander of the Aerial Host

DHARSII—Red striped, formerly of the Lavadome, dragon of the Sadda-Vale

HERMETHEA—A dragonelle of the Juutfod tower, formerly prisoner on the Isle of Ice

ISTACH—Daughter of AuRon and Natasatch, the former Protector and "Recluse" of Old Uldam

NASTIRATH—Gold, Aethleethia's mate, dragon of the Sadda-Vale

NATASATCH—Protector of Dairuss, AuRon's mate

NoSohoth—Formerly RuGaard's adviser, now the wealthiest dragon in the Empire

NiVom—White, Tyr of the Upper World

OuThroth—Silver, Protector of Wallander

RuGaard—Copper, brother to AuRon and Wistala, former Tyr of the Lavadome

Scabia—White female (rare), ruler of the Sadda-Vale

Seeg, of the Deep Alliance—A free dwarf

Varatheela—Daughter of AuRon and Natasatch, member of the Aerial Host

Wistala—Sister to RuGaard the Copper and AuRon

Yefkoa—Fastest-flying dragonelle in the Firemaids, Aya-feeia's personal messenger

E. E. Knight graduated from Northern Illinois University with a double major in history and political science, then made his way through a number of jobs that had nothing to do with history or political science. He resides in Chicago. For more information on the author and his worlds, E. E. Knight invites you to visit his Web site at eeknight.com.